And even as the thought crossed her mind, he was lowering his head, claiming her lips with his. It never occurred to her to resist.

She went up on her tiptoes, her arms twining around his neck, her eyelids fluttering down as one of her favorite teenage fantasies came to life. Unlike so many other things she had wished for, the reality was ever so much better than the dream. His mouth was warm and firm on hers; his arms held her body close to his. A distant part of her mind, the part that was still functioning, took note of the fact that they fit well together despite the difference in their height.

One of them moaned, a soft cry of need and longing . . .

His Dark Embrace

AMANDA ASHLEY

ZEBRA BOOKS
KENSINGTON PUBLISHING CORP.
http://www.kensingtonbooks.com

ZEBRA BOOKS are published by

Kensington Publishing Corp.
119 West 40th Street
New York, NY 10018

All Kensington titles, imprints, and distributed lines are available at special quantity discounts for bulk purchases for sales
promotion, premiums, fund-raising, educational, or institu-
tional use.

Special book excerpts or customized printings can also be
created to fit specific needs. For details, write or phone the
office of the Kensington Special Sales Manager: Attn. Special
Sales Department. Kensington Publishing Corp., 119 West
40th Street, New York, NY 10018. Phone: 1-800-221-2647.

Zebra and the Z logo Reg. U.S. Pat. & TM Off.

ISBN-13: 978-1-4201-2133-9
ISBN-10: 1-4201-2133-2

First Printing: June 2012

10 9 8 7 6 5 4 3 2 1

Printed in the United States of America

For Vicki Crum,
who introduced me to her friend,
Glenna Capece

and

for Glenna.
She knows why.

"My Dark Visitor"

A dark exquisite dream we share,
This mystic Hallow's Eve.
The fog and mist come creeping in,
They brush across my sleeve

My breath comes quick, amid the drift
My heart begins to flutter
One beat, then two, within I feel
The presence of another.

I leap, I fly to cross the space,
For something draws me in.
His touch, his kiss, his strong embrace,
Dark magic from within.

No common thought can touch my mind,
For secrets are his cover.
How sleek, how dark, the spell he weaves
The promise of a lover.

My sigh, my plea, my beckoned call,
I seek eternal bliss.
My heart, my soul he does not take
I give him even this.

Our spirits dance among the stars
Complete without restraint
A love so pure it conquers all
And never hears complaint

Dare I look inside to see
The mystery of this night
One dark embrace forever his
It started with a bite.

~MICHELLE DONALD

Prologue

When Skylynn McNamara O'Brien came home to bury her grandfather and settle his estate, she was surprised to see that the house across the street was still vacant. The big, old, three-story house, surrounded by a high wrought-iron fence, sat on a half-acre lot. A covered porch spanned the front of the house. The place put her in mind of a giant among midgets, surrounded as it was by newer, smaller, more modern homes. Granda had once told her that Kaiden Thorne's grandfather had refused to sell the place to real estate developers, and so they had built around him.

Kaiden Thorne had moved away shortly after Skylynn left for college. She thought it odd that he hadn't sold the house when he moved. As far as she knew, the house had been vacant ever since.

He had been a strange one, Mr. Thorne. For years, he had collected his mail and his newspaper after dark and always mowed his front yard after the sun went down. He had gone to the high school football games, but only the ones held at night.

Sky had been five or six the first time she had seen Kaiden Thorne. She remembered it as if it had happened yesterday. She had been sitting on the front porch that summer evening, playing with her favorite Barbie dolls, when a moving van pulled into the driveway of the house across the street. Curious, she had watched two men in gray overalls jump out of the cab and begin unloading the truck. There hadn't been much in the way of furniture, just a black leather sofa and a matching chair, a couple of glass-topped end tables, a dresser and chest of drawers, an antique sideboard, and a big-screen TV. The last thing the movers had unloaded had been a large oblong box.

Skylynn had frowned when she saw it. What on earth was in there? Her interest in the new neighbor soon waned when she realized there would be no playmates her age moving into the house, only a tall man with thick black hair. At five, she had thought of Kaiden Thorne as an old man. Looking back, she realized he had probably been no more than in his thirties.

Her second distinct memory of Kaiden Thorne occurred on Halloween, Sky's favorite holiday, except for Christmas, of course. Back then, everyone in the neighborhood decorated their houses, each family trying to outdo the other, but none of them could hold a candle to Mr. Thorne. His yard looked like something out of a Hammer horror movie. There had been a coffin that looked as if it was a hundred years old, a skeleton that looked so real, it had given Sky the creeps. Ancient torture devices had lined his driveway. A scary-looking clock that would have looked at home in a Vincent Price movie chimed the hours as assorted ghouls and monsters popped up out of old pirate chests and from behind weathered headstones.

Sky had been seven when her brother, Sam, took her trick-or-treating at the Thorne house. Sam had been ten at the time, and even though her brother could be a major pain, she had idolized him. He had told her, straight-faced, that Mr. Thorne was a vampire, but Skylynn hadn't believed him because Granda had told her there were no such things as vampires, witches, ghosts, ghouls, or skeletons that walked and talked. But when Mr. Thorne opened the door, Sky had taken one look at his bloodred eyes, his gleaming fangs and long black cape, and screamed bloody murder. Her brother had teased her for months about the way she had turned tail and run back home just as fast as her legs would carry her. She'd had nightmares for weeks afterward, even though her grandfather had persuaded Mr. Thorne to come over and explain that he had been wearing an elaborate costume.

As time passed, Granda and Mr. Thorne spent more and more time together. They made an odd couple—her short, gray-haired grandfather and the tall, dark-haired Mr. Thorne. As far as Sky could tell, they'd had nothing in common. Granda was a retired doctor who dabbled in chemistry in his lab down in the basement. He had often kidded her that he was looking for the secret of eternal life. As for Mr. Thorne, she didn't know what he did for a living. For all she knew, he, too, had been retired. The two men had spent many a night locked up in Granda's lab.

More than once, she had snuck down to the basement. With her ear pressed to the door, she had caught snatches of conversation, but Granda's talk of plasma and platelets and transfusions meant nothing to her.

Occasionally, a strange man came to visit Granda. Sky never saw his face, never heard his name, but there was something about him that, even back then, had made her skin crawl.

The summer Sky turned twelve, she started spying on Mr. Thorne. She wasn't sure why. Curiosity? Boredom? Who could say? She bought a notebook and made copious notes about his habits, the cars he drove, the clothes he wore. He rarely had visitors, but when he did, she wrote down the color and make of the car and the license plate number and descriptions of the people who came and went so infrequently. Sam thought he was a drug dealer or a hit man.

Sky had always had a flare for art and she drew numerous pictures and portraits of the elusive Mr. Thorne. A faint white scar bisected his right cheek. He had another scar on his back near his left shoulder blade. She had seen it one night during a scavenger hunt. The last item on her list had been to find an old newspaper and she had gone knocking on Mr. Thorne's door in the hope that he could help. He had answered the door wearing a pair of swim trunks and nothing else. He had invited her to step inside while he went to fetch the paper, and she had glimpsed the scar when he turned away. As she grew older, she began to wonder how he had gotten those scars.

By the time she was thirteen, she had a full-blown crush on the mysterious Mr. Thorne. And then, when she was fifteen or sixteen, an odd thing happened. For no apparent reason, he stopped staying inside during the day.

She would never forget the Friday afternoon she had come home from school and seen him outside, mowing his lawn. Wearing only a pair of cut-off blue jeans and sunglasses, he looked sexier than any man his age had a right to.

But that had been eight years ago, and she was no longer the wide-eyed innocent child she had once been.

Chapter 1

Skylynn sat on the front porch swing, staring blankly into the distance. Yesterday, she had buried her grandfather in the family plot, alongside her grandmother and her parents. Now, sitting in Granda's creaky old two-seater swing and listening to the clock inside strike midnight, she wondered if she carried some kind of curse. How else to explain that everyone she cared for left her? Her parents had been killed in a traffic accident when she was only three. Her grandmother had passed on a few years later, leaving Granda to raise Sky and her brother, Sam.

Sam had been sent to Iraq nine months ago, shortly before her divorce. For the last four months, he had been missing in action, presumed dead. When he had first gone missing, she hadn't slept for days. She had written to several of the men in his unit, asking for information, but they had all said the same thing. Their unit had been in a firefight. Sam had been with them one minute and gone the next. They had searched for him until enemy fire had driven them out of the area. Since then, there had been no word of Sam's whereabouts. Not a day went by that she didn't think of him, worry about him. Knowing there was little else she could do to help him, she sent fervent prayers to heaven each night, praying for his safe return home.

And now she was back in Vista Verde, California, with a failed marriage to her credit, a brother who was missing, and no family to lean on.

In an effort to shake off her melancholy mood, she studied the three-story monstrosity across the street. They didn't build houses like that anymore. Heck, they hadn't built houses like that in over a hundred years. She had always wanted to see the inside, but she had never been invited past the entry hall. As far as she knew, no one else in the neighborhood had ever even gotten that far. The owner, Mr. Thorne, had been willing to let the kids on the block swim in his pool during the day, but neither the kids nor their parents had been welcome on the property after dark, and none had ever been allowed inside the house. She had often wondered what he was hiding in there. Maybe Sam had been right. Maybe Mr. Thorne really had been a drug dealer. That seemed far more probable than his being a Mafia hit man.

Thunder rumbled across the darkening sky, promising rain before morning. She shivered as a cold breeze rustled the leaves of the trees alongside the house. She should go inside, she thought, make a cup of hot chocolate while she tried to decide what to do with Granda's house, what to do about Harry, what to do about the rest of her life.

Harry wanted to marry her, but after one failed marriage, Sky just wasn't ready to try again, nor was she certain she loved Harry Poteet the way he deserved. He had wanted to come to Vista Verde with her, but she had told him she needed some time alone. He hadn't argued, just told her he loved her and would be waiting for her when she returned to Chicago.

Sitting on the porch, wrapped in layers of nostalgia, Sky wasn't sure she would ever be ready to return to Illinois.

Like it or not, Vista Verde would always be home. Stay or go back to Chicago? That was the question. But she didn't have to decide tonight. She had three weeks vacation from work to make up her mind.

Wrapping her arms around her middle for warmth, she gazed at the house across the way again, blinked in surprise when the front door opened, and a tall man stepped out onto the covered veranda.

Sky leaned forward, squinting into the darkness. Could it be . . . ? A shiver ran down her spine as the man descended the stairs and crossed the street toward her. Dressed in black from head to foot, he almost disappeared into the night that surrounded him.

"Mr. Thorne." His name whispered past her lips as he approached her.

He inclined his head. "Good evening, Miss McNamara."

"You used to call me Sky Blue."

"You were much younger then," he murmured with a faint smile.

Skylynn studied him in the glow of the porch light. She hadn't seen him in eight years and he hadn't changed a bit. He had appeared to be in his early to mid-thirties when she went away to college, and he still looked that way. His face remained unlined, his eyes were the same shade of dark, dark brown, his hair was still shaggy and black, his body long and lean and muscular. The faint scar on his right cheek, which should have detracted from his devastating good looks, only served to make him appear more mysterious. Standing there, with his arms folded across his chest, he exuded an aura of raw sensuality and masculine confidence.

"I was sorry to hear about your grandfather," he said quietly.

"His passing came as a shock," Sky murmured. "Or as much of a shock as it can be, I guess, considering his age."

Still, Granda had been in good health when she had seen him at Christmas only last year.

"I'm sorry I didn't get here in time for the funeral."

Sky nodded. "Please, sit down."

She had expected him to take the chair across from her. Instead, he sat beside her on the swing, his thigh scant inches from her own. His nearness prickled along her spine.

"Are you planning to stay in Vista Verde?" he asked.

"I don't know. I don't think I can. I have a good job in Chicago. Friends." And Harry was there. She blew out a sigh. "I hate to sell the old house, though." Realistically, she knew she didn't have much choice. She couldn't afford to live in Chicago and pay the taxes and the upkeep on this place, too.

"Too many memories," Thorne remarked. It wasn't a question, but a statement of fact.

"Yes." She laughed softly. "And too many goldfish and hamsters and birds buried under the palm tree in the backyard."

His laughter, rich and deep and decidedly masculine, joined hers.

It felt good to laugh. "I guess you think it's silly."

"No." He draped his arm over the back of the swing. "I keep that old house across the street for the same reason."

"Don't tell me your backyard is a burial ground for deceased pets, too."

"In a way." He gazed into the distance for a moment. "Did your grandfather leave anything for me?"

"Not that I know of. There was nothing mentioned in the will. Were you expecting something?"

"No, not exactly."

She looked at him askance. "What, exactly?"

"Paddy had developed a rather unique vitamin drink for me that I found most beneficial. I'm very nearly out of it and I was hoping he'd left the recipe for me."

"A vitamin drink?" she asked, frowning.

"More like a tonic," he replied smoothly. "Something to thicken the blood."

"Really?" Was that why Thorne and her grandfather had spent so much time in the basement? "I'm sorry, Granda never said anything about that."

"Perhaps you'd be good enough to look around in his lab when you have a chance?"

"Sure. Granda told me you moved away shortly after I left for college."

Thorne nodded.

"Quite a coincidence, your coming back here at the same time I did," she remarked, though, in truth, she didn't believe in coincidence.

"Sometimes life is funny that way."

Sky nodded, although there was nothing funny about the way he was looking at her, or the way her whole body vibrated at his nearness. It was an oddly sensual experience, as if every cell in her body had suddenly awakened from a deep sleep.

Unsettled by the intensity of his gaze, she looked away. What wasn't he telling her? She thought it odd that Granda had never mentioned the mysterious tonic. And odder still that Kaiden Thorne, who looked as fit and healthy as a young stud horse, needed a tonic in the first place.

"I should let you go," Thorne remarked, glancing at the dark clouds overhead. "It's going to rain. And you're cold."

"What? Oh, yes, it's a little chilly," she said, and then frowned. She had stopped shivering as soon as he sat beside her. "Are you here to stay?" she asked, and held her breath, waiting for his answer.

"I'm not sure." His gaze moved over her, as warm as a summer day. "Good night, Skylynn."

"Good night." She stared after him as he descended the

stairs and crossed the street to his house. She felt oddly bereft when he disappeared inside.

It started raining as soon as he closed the door.

After turning off the inside lights, Thorne stood at the front window, his gaze focused on the woman across the street. In spite of the distance and the darkness, he was able to see her clearly. She had always been a pretty girl but now, in her early twenties, she was exquisite. Her hair was a deep reddish-brown; her eyes, beneath delicately arched brows, were the rich warm blue of a midsummer sky. She wore a long-sleeved, square-necked lavender sweater that emphasized the swell of her breasts. A pair of white jeans hugged her legs. He was sure he could span her narrow waist with his hands.

Thorne had felt protective of Skylynn ever since she had been a little girl. Having no children of his own, he had enjoyed watching her grow up. She had been a sweet, chubby-cheeked child, a leggy adolescent, a truly beautiful teen. By the time she was seventeen, he started to feel like a dirty old man lusting after an innocent young girl, although it hadn't been her body he lusted for. And even though he was still old, she was no longer young. Or innocent. She had been married and divorced and was now dating an investment banker in Chicago who would never be good enough for her.

It had been coincidence that brought Thorne back to Vista Verde shortly after Paddy McNamara passed away. Paddy had asked Thorne to keep an eye on Skylynn while she was away from home. Thorne never knew why. Skylynn had always been a level-headed girl, able to take care of herself. Perhaps Paddy's concern had merely been worry for a granddaughter about to be away from home and on her own for the first time in her life. At any rate, Thorne would have looked after Sky without being asked. And he had done so, without her being the wiser, until the day she married Nick O'Brien.

Of course, Paddy's granddaughter hadn't been the only reason he had stayed in touch with the old man. Thanks to Paddy McNamara's remarkable potion, Thorne had been able to live a relatively normal life for the last eight years. But the sun would soon be lost to him again if Skylynn couldn't find her grandfather's notes.

In the morning, shortly after breakfast, Sky went downstairs to the basement that housed Granda's lab. The basement was divided into three rooms. There was also a half-bath to the left of the staircase.

The largest room was Granda's workroom. It held every conceivable medical book known to man, as well as metal shelves crammed with beakers and test tubes and a plethora of other instruments. A small wooden table and chair were shoved into one corner.

A door connected his workroom to his office. A state-of-the-art computer, a twenty-four-inch monitor, and a printer took up space on an oversized desk. A small TV was mounted in one corner. A bank of gray metal file cabinets lined one wall.

The last room was the smallest. Located to the right of the staircase, it held a number of wire cages in a variety of sizes. All were empty now. One of the first things Skylynn had done after she got home was drive out to the country where she had released half a dozen mice and a handful of baby rats. In retrospect, she wondered if that had been a smart thing to do, but it was too late to worry about it now.

Sky stood at the foot of the stairs for a moment, Granda's keys in hand; then, heaving a sigh, she unlocked the door to the room that held the filing cabinets and stepped inside. The basement had always been off-limits to Sky and she had never been down here except with Granda. It seemed wrong, somehow, to be there now, without him.

The drawers to the filing cabinets were all color-coded, labeled, and locked. The first cabinet held folders labeled INVOICES, CURRENT FILES, OLD FILES, RESEARCH NOTES, and TAX RECORDS. The next three filing cabinets contained Granda's journals, with the first drawer labeled 1957–1962, the next 1963–1968, and so on.

The top drawer in the last filing cabinet was labeled EXPERIMENTS. Did that cabinet hold the mysterious recipe Kaiden Thorne was hoping to find?

Sky glanced at the keys in her hand. Each key was color-coded to match a particular filing cabinet.

She was about to unlock the drawer marked EXPERIMENTS when the doorbell rang. Wondering who would possibly be calling so early, she pocketed the keys and ran up the stairs, her slippers flapping.

"Mr. Thorne!" she exclaimed when she opened the door. She felt a flush heat her cheeks. Had she known he was going to show up so early, she would have changed out of her pj's.

"I know it's early," he said, somewhat sheepishly. "I just wondered if you'd had a chance to look around for that formula."

"Not really." She slipped a hand into her pocket, her fingers curling around the keys. "It must be important."

"Only to me."

She tilted her head to one side. "It must work. You look great."

His gaze moved over her with undisguised admiration. "Thanks, so do you." He rocked back on his heels. "I should go."

"Would you like to come over later for lunch?"

"I'd like that."

"Around one?"

He nodded. "I'll be here."

Sky watched him cross the street, admiring the way his jeans hugged his taut backside, his easy, long-legged stride, the way the sun cast silver highlights in his black hair.

Murmuring, "Oh, my," she made her way back down to Granda's lab.

She spent the next three hours going through his filing cabinets, sorting out old receipts and purchase orders for a variety of medical supplies, perusing copious memos written in her grandfather's spidery hand, most of which she couldn't decipher. The drawer labeled EXPERIMENTS held a number of spiral-bound journals, the pages covered with notes, diagrams, and scientific jargon that made no sense to her.

Sitting cross-legged on the floor, she thumbed through his most recent entries, but found nothing that looked like a recipe for a vitamin drink.

At twelve-thirty, she stood and stretched her aching back and shoulders. If there was a formula hiding in any of Granda's notes, it would have to wait until tomorrow. She was going cross-eyed, trying to decipher his handwriting.

After locking the basement door, she went upstairs, found her cell phone, and ordered two large pizzas—one pepperoni, one sausage—two orders of spicy chicken wings, and breadsticks. While waiting for the pizzas, she made a fruit salad and a pitcher of iced tea, then set two plates, two glasses, two cloth napkins, and a pair of forks on a tray.

She kept glancing at the clock, her stomach fluttering with anticipation at the thought of having lunch with a handsome man. A man who hadn't changed at all in eight years.

How was that possible?

* * *

Thorne prowled through the big old house, his thoughts chaotic. He shouldn't have waited so long to come back to visit Paddy McNamara. It had been coincidence that brought him back to Vista Verde after such a long absence. Had he kept closer tabs on the old man, he would have known McNamara didn't have long to live.

Thorne raked his fingers through his hair. Dammit! If he had come back sooner, he would have had time to speak to the old man and obtain the formula that had so drastically changed his life.

Striding down to the wine cellar, he bypassed the coffin that rested in the center of the floor and moved to the wall safe on the far side of the room. After unlocking the safe, he withdrew a round cobalt blue bottle that was about five inches tall. It held the last of Paddy McNamara's unique tonic.

Thorne rubbed the bottle against his cheek. The glass felt cold against his skin. He had attempted to get his hands on the formula before, but McNamara had refused to part with it. Thorne had tried coaxing the formula out of the stubborn old man, but that, too, had failed. One night Thorne had offered to bring Paddy across in exchange for the formula, but despite Paddy's research into aging and longevity, he had no interest in living forever.

"'Tis against nature, what you're offering," Paddy had said. "And though I've no wish to leave me darlin' Skylynn, me wife and son are waiting for me on the other side."

As a last resort, Thorne had tried reading Paddy's mind, but the wily old fox had blocked him at every turn. And now it was too late. Eternally too late. Dammit.

After returning the bottle to the safe, Thorne went back upstairs. Maybe it was time to leave Vista Verde for a few decades. If he stayed for any length of time, people were going to start noticing that he hadn't aged.

He glanced out the front window, his gaze lingering on

the house across the street. No need to leave right away, he thought. At least not until he learned if Sky was going to stay here. Seeing her again made him realize how much he had missed her.

His inner clock told him it was almost time to join Skylynn for lunch. For a moment, he closed his eyes, dreading the thought of going back to his old diet, his old lifestyle. Right now, he had the best of both worlds. Dammit! Sky had to find that formula. After all the trial and error it had taken for the old man to get it just right, he must have written it down somewhere.

His thoughts turned to Skylynn as he left the house. Being near her and not touching her would be a real test of his self-control.

Sky was a bundle of nerves when the doorbell rang. It was like one of her teenage daydreams come true, having Kaiden Thorne over for lunch. She just hoped the reality lived up to her girlish dreams.

Too late to worry about that now. She blew a wisp of hair from her forehead. So many of the things she had looked forward to when she was growing up had been disappointments. Her first real date. Her first kiss. Her first marriage. None of them had lived up to the hype.

Sky took a deep breath before she opened the door. And he was there.

"Hi," she said brightly. "Come on in." She pressed a hand to her heart as Kaiden moved past her. Lordy, the man was tall. And incredibly handsome. Well-worn jeans hugged his long legs, a shirt the color of red wine clung to his broad shoulders. "I thought we'd eat out on the patio."

"Okay by me." Lifting his head, Thorne sniffed the air. "Pizza?"

"I didn't know what kind you liked, so I ordered one sausage and one pepperoni."

"Either one works for me."

"Great."

He followed her into the kitchen. It hadn't changed much since he had last seen it just over eight years ago. The walls were the same pale green, the curtains still white with pink and yellow daisies, the square table and ladder-back chairs were well-used oak.

Sky opened the fridge and took out the bowl of fruit salad and the pitcher of iced tea and added them to the tray.

"Here, let me take that," Kaiden offered.

"Thanks." Picking up the boxes of pizza, chicken wings, and breadsticks, she headed for the back door, acutely aware of Kaiden walking behind her.

"Just put the tray there, on the table." She put the pizzas next to the tray, then poured a glass of tea for Kaiden and one for herself. "Please, sit down." She handed Kaiden a plate and a napkin, and took the chair across from his. "Help yourself."

Thorne drew in a deep breath as he lifted the lids on both pizza boxes, the scents of sausage, pepperoni, cheese, and tomatoes tickling his nostrils. "Smells great." He took a slice of each, a couple of chicken wings, and a generous serving of fruit salad. For a moment, he was oblivious to everything but the food on his plate.

"How is it?" Sky asked.

Thorne looked up, a wry smile curving his lips. "Sometimes I forget how good food can be."

"Save room for dessert."

"Not to worry," he said with a wink. He was surprised he hadn't gained a hundred pounds, the way he had been eating lately. But everything tasted so good. Fresh fruit and cheese, cake and ice cream. And was there anything better in all the world than a good, thick steak with the rich, red juices still flowing? Just thinking about it made his mouth water.

They made small talk while they ate, commenting on the weather, which had been unseasonably cold, the way the neighborhood had become run-down in the last few years, the number of foreclosures that were cropping up all over the town.

Sky served warm apple pie and vanilla ice cream for dessert.

"Did you make this?" Thorne asked, gesturing at the pie with his fork.

"No, I never learned how to make a decent crust. It's really good, isn't it?"

He nodded as he lifted another forkful to his mouth. Apple pie had quickly become one of his favorites.

A last bite and he pushed his plate away.

"Are you sure I can't tempt you with another slice?" Sky asked with a grin.

"I think I'd better say no." Leaning back in his chair, he regarded her through hooded eyes. "I was sorry to hear about your divorce."

"It was inevitable." She shrugged, as if it was of no importance. "I married the wrong man at the wrong time for all the wrong reasons."

"If you'd rather not talk about it . . ."

"No, it's okay. I met Nick in a dance club several months after Sam was sent to Iraq. I was feeling lonely and stressed out when Nicky showed up. He was all smiles and good-natured fun and I told myself I loved him." She shrugged. "But I didn't. And once the excitement wore off, I realized we had nothing in common and that when he was sober, I didn't like him very much. We were divorced before the ink dried on our marriage license." She hadn't wanted anything to remind her of her disastrous marriage; as soon as the divorce was final, she had resumed her maiden name.

"I'm sorry, Sky Blue," he said quietly, but it was a lie. The thought of her with another man was like acid in his gut.

She blew out a sigh, then smiled wistfully. "I guess I'll just have to keep looking for Mr. Right." She laughed softly. "A nightclub probably isn't the best place to go looking for a man who's interested in a serious relationship."

"Is that what you're looking for?"

"I don't know. I guess so. I'm not getting any younger."

"None of us are," he murmured.

"What about you? You weren't married when you lived here before. Has that changed?"

"No."

"You've never married?"

"I never found a woman who could put up with me."

"Oh, come on. You don't seem that hard to get along with, although you did scare me half to death one Halloween night."

"I remember. I'm sorry about that."

"You should be. I had nightmares for weeks."

Thorne chuckled softly. He recalled that night all too well. He hadn't meant to frighten her; he had, in fact, thought it was a couple of teenage boys who had been harassing him earlier in the evening. He would never forget the look of horror on Sky's face when he opened the door, his eyes red, his fangs bared.

"Even after Granda assured me that vampires didn't exist, and even after you came over and showed me those fake plastic fangs and red contacts, I still woke up screaming."

"I'm sorry," he said again.

"It's all right," she said, laughing. "But you sure know how to make an impression on a girl."

"Hardly the kind I want to make when the girl is as lovely as you."

His soft-spoken words, the smoldering heat in his dark eyes, stilled Sky's laughter. A sudden rush of warmth crept up her neck and into her cheeks as a giddy wave of pleasure swept through her.

"Forgive me," he murmured. "I didn't mean to make you uncomfortable."

"No, I'm flattered."

He arched one brow. "But?"

"It just seems odd for us to be on an equal footing, that's all. I always thought of you as being so much older than I am, but . . ." She tilted her head to the side. "How old are you, anyway?"

"Thirty-nine."

Her eyes widened in surprise. "Really? You haven't aged a day since I saw you last."

"Comes of living a good clean life and having excellent genes, I suppose."

"Hmm, I guess that would explain it," she replied thoughtfully. "Some people never seem to look any older."

"You don't sound convinced."

"Well, Granda said he wanted to find the secret to eternal life. . . ."

Thorne laughed softly. "And you think he found it and gave it to me?"

She laughed, too. "It sounds ridiculous when you say it out loud, doesn't it?"

"Well, you can't blame him for trying. Most people would give anything to be immortal, or at least young forever."

"Maybe. I don't know," she said, her brow furrowed. "Would you want to live forever?"

"Definitely," he replied. "If I could spend eternity with you."

His words pleased her as much as they surprised her. Sure, she'd had a teenage crush on him, and there was no denying that he was still drop-dead handsome, but she had never seriously considered him in a romantic way. At least, not until now.

Her cheeks grew warm as his gaze moved over her. There was no mistaking the look in his eyes.

He wanted her.

There was no mistaking the excited flutter in the pit of her stomach, either.

The one that meant she wanted him.

Chapter 2

Afraid his self-control was weakening, Thorne pushed his chair away from the table. "Perhaps I should go."

Sky stared at him, her thoughts scattering like leaves in a high wind. She didn't want him to go, but she wasn't sure she wanted him to stay. Maybe she had misread the heat in the depths of his dark eyes. Maybe she was imagining things that weren't there.

He stood, his gaze meeting hers. "Thank you for lunch."

"Please, stay." The words spilled out before she could stop them. "I looked around in Granda's lab today."

Thorne dropped back into his chair. He couldn't leave now, not until he heard what she had to say. "And?"

"I didn't find anything that looked like a recipe or a formula for a drink. Do you have any of it left?"

"A small amount."

"Why don't you just have it analyzed?"

"I tried that. It contains a number of herbs and roots in varying amounts." He'd had the potion analyzed by several different scientists. Each time, the report had been the same.

"Like what, for instance?"

"Fennel, sage, lavender, absinthe, rosemary, yarrow, bloodroot, henbane—"

"Henbane!" Sky shook her head. "You must be mistaken. That's poisonous."

Thorne shrugged. "Perhaps one of the other ingredients counteracts it."

"So, if you know what's in it, why do you need the formula? Can't they just duplicate it?"

"No. There's another ingredient in it, something none of them have been able to identify."

"That's odd."

"Perhaps I could help you go through Paddy's files. I might be able to find something you've missed."

"Sure, if you want. Just let me clear the dishes."

Minutes later, Thorne followed Skylynn down the basement stairs to Paddy McNamara's lab. Thorne had been there before on numerous occasions, had sat in a chair, hands and feet bound with silver, while Paddy experimented with one concoction after another until, miraculously, the old man had found one that worked.

Thorne raked a hand through his hair. Paddy must have written the formula down somewhere. Dammit, he must have!

While Sky went through her grandfather's journals, Thorne sat at the old man's computer and went through the files. As Thorne had feared, it was a waste of time. None of the files were password protected. None of them contained the information he was looking for.

Thorne glanced over his shoulder at Skylynn. "Did Paddy have an external hard drive or a jump drive?"

"Not that I know of. He only used his computer for research and correspondence. He never kept any of his important stuff on it. He said it was too easy to hack into computer files."

"Well, he was right about that." Taking a place on the floor beside Skylynn, Thorne lifted a journal from the stack and began reading through it, no easy task, given Paddy's abominable handwriting. What was it about doctors?

Thorne wondered as he turned a page. He had seen six-year-olds with better penmanship.

He picked up another journal. Like the last one, this contained nothing other than routine notes about routine operations, and questions and comments about an occasional experiment gone awry.

After three hours, Skylynn closed the book she had been reading and stood up to stretch the kinks out of her back and shoulders. "I'm afraid this is a lost cause."

"So it would seem."

"I guess you'll just have to find another tonic."

He looked up at her, mute, the muscles in his jaw clenching as he stood.

"You can, can't you?" she asked. "I mean, it isn't keeping you alive or anything, is it?"

"No, it's not keeping me alive."

"Well, then," she said, smiling. "That's a relief."

"Indeed," he muttered. But time was running out. "Would you like to have dinner with me this evening?"

She blinked up at him. "You mean, like a date?"

He laughed softly. "Yes, if that's all right. I was thinking we could go to The Manor."

"Oh, I'd like that." The Manor, which was built along the lines of an old English castle, complete with a bridge and a moat, was nestled high in the hills overlooking the city. "What time?"

"Seven-thirty?"

"All right."

His gaze moved over her, as soft as a caress, as hot as a forest fire. "See you then," he said, and went up the stairs.

Sky stared after him, her thoughts reeling. She had just agreed to have dinner with the mysterious Mr. Thorne. Mysterious, indeed, she thought, and then frowned. Earlier, he had told her he was thirty-nine, but that was impossible. Kaiden had been living in the house across the street ever since she was five or six. Even if Kaiden had been in his twenties at the time, he would now be in his mid-forties.

Talk about dating an older man, she thought with a grin.

Apparently women weren't the only ones who lied about their age. Either that, or Granda really had found the secret to eternal life.

Sky dressed with care that night. After donning her favorite navy blue dress and matching heels, she brushed her hair until it shone, then applied a bit of makeup. She slipped a silver bracelet on her wrist, dabbed a bit of perfume behind her ears, and then, after a last look in the mirror, she went downstairs to wait.

Kaiden arrived at the stroke of seven-thirty. Clad in black slacks, a white shirt open at the throat, and a long black leather coat, he was easily the sexiest thing she had ever seen on two legs.

He whistled softly when he saw her.

"Right back at ya," she said, grinning.

"Better get a coat," he advised. "It's chilly out, although it's a shame to cover that dress, or what's in it."

"Flatterer."

"You look exquisite."

His breath fanned her cheek, but it was his words that made her insides curl with pleasure as he helped her into her coat.

His car, a low-slung, silver-gray sport's model, was parked at the curb.

"Nice," she murmured as he opened her door.

"I just bought it today." Rounding the front of the car, he opened the door and slid behind the wheel. "Buckle up and let's see if she's as fast as the dealer said."

It was in Sky's mind to protest. She had never been crazy about fast cars, but she couldn't resist the twinkle in

Kaiden's eyes. "Try not to wrap it around a telephone pole," she muttered as she fastened her seat belt.

"Don't worry, Sky Blue. Nothing bad will happen to you while you're with me."

Oddly enough, she believed him.

She had to admit, going down the freeway at over ninety miles an hour was thrilling, exciting, and scary as hell. She had leased a Honda in Chicago and never driven it over sixty. These days, she drove Granda's old Lincoln.

Kaiden looked over at her and smiled, and Sky couldn't help smiling back. He looked like a little boy who had just gotten everything he ever wanted for Christmas.

A scarce ten minutes later, Thorne pulled up in front of the restaurant's valet parking area. He looked over at Sky, his hand caressing the leather-covered steering wheel. "So, what do you think?"

"It's very nice."

"Nice?" he exclaimed, looking offended. "Nice? Is that all you've got to say?"

Sky grinned at him. "What do you want me to say?"

He laughed as he exited the car and came around to open her door. "A summer day is nice. Good music is nice. This car . . ." He shook his head. "This car is the bomb."

"Well, just don't blow it up on the way home," Sky said, putting her hand in his.

"Not to worry, fair lady."

The interior of the restaurant was reminiscent of a castle, with shields and banners and a coat-of-arms depicting a knight on a black charger. An enormous chandelier hung from the ceiling; a life-size mannequin wearing what looked like an authentic suit of armor stood beside the front door. Sky noted that the booths were curved and high-backed for privacy. The tablecloths were dark red. Flickering candlelight added a touch of romance and mystery.

A hostess wearing a period costume seated them immediately. A waitress dressed as a medieval serving girl brought menus, then asked if they would care for a glass of wine or an appetizer.

At Sky's request, Thorne ordered a bottle of Kendall-Jackson Merlot and a plate of pâté de fois gras.

"I've never been here before," Sky said, admiring the decor. "It's lovely."

"I'm glad you like it." Thorne picked up his menu. "So, what are you in the mood for? Chicken? Fish? Steak? Lobster?"

"I don't know." She glanced at the bill of fare. The prices were outrageous. She would have loved to order the lobster, but it was over forty dollars.

"Don't worry about the price," Thorne said, noting her hesitation. "Order anything you like."

"Are you sure?"

"I can afford it, Sky Blue. Why not have the lobster? It's excellent."

"You must have been reading my mind."

He didn't say anything, just looked at her and smiled when she ordered the lobster.

Kaiden Thorne proved to be a fantastic dinner companion. He was knowledgeable on a wide range of subjects, everything from the life and times of Abraham Lincoln to the latest James Bond movie. They discussed books and movies and the current world situation, but wisely avoided politics and religion.

By the time they ordered dessert, Sky's schoolgirl crush had reasserted itself. She loved the way Kaiden smiled, the hypnotic sound of his voice, the fact that, unlike most men, he loved chocolate almost as much as she did.

Sky leaned back in her chair, stuffed to the brim with lobster and chocolate fudge cake. "I could die happy right now," she murmured with a smile.

He grinned at her, his eyes crinkling at the corners.

"Could you wait a few hours? I thought maybe we could go dancing, or take in a late movie."

"Dancing! I haven't been dancing in, gosh, I don't remember the last time."

"Then we should remedy that right away."

"It's not a disease."

"No," he agreed, reaching for the check. "But it will give me the perfect excuse to hold you in my arms."

He took her to a high-class nightclub located on a moonlit lake. Sky had never been there before, since membership was required, and only the elite could afford the dues.

She couldn't help feeling like one of the ugly stepsisters as Kaiden escorted her into the club. The women inside wore designer gowns accented by glittering diamonds and rubies. The men wore Armani. The room itself was exquisite, with parquet floors, crystal chandeliers, and tables covered in rich, cream-colored damask. Floor-to-ceiling mirrors adorned two of the walls opposite each other, making it appear as if the dancers went on and on, into infinity.

A tall, slender woman in an elegant black dress welcomed Thorne by name, then escorted them to a booth. Thorne slid in beside Sky. His thigh brushed hers, sending a tingle of awareness through her from head to heel.

After ordering a good bottle of Chardonnay, he looked at her and asked if she wanted to dance.

"Isn't that why we're here?" she replied with a saucy grin.

"Indeed." Rising, he offered Sky his hand and led her onto the dance floor.

Excitement thrummed through every fiber of her being when Kaiden drew her into his arms. She had always loved to dance. At seventeen, she had fantasized about dancing with Kaiden at the junior prom, but she wasn't a teenager any longer and the reality of being this close to him was far more exhilarating than any daydream she'd ever had.

Kaiden's breath fanned her ear as he whispered, "Relax."

Relax? Was he kidding? How could she relax with his big body pressed so intimately against hers? When he was looking at her like that, as if he was a starving man and she was the last meal on the planet? When he smelled so good? When all she could think about was pressing her mouth to his to see if he tasted as good as he looked?

Taking a deep breath, she forced herself to concentrate on the music, and as she did so, some of her tension melted away.

Kaiden smiled at her. "That's better."

"I love this song," she murmured.

He nodded as he twirled her around the floor. "'Unchained Melody' just became one of my favorites."

His words warmed her heart. It was a magical night, she thought as she lost herself in his embrace. The music was soft and romantic, the man was handsome and danced divinely. When the song ended, another began, and as they moved across the floor, it seemed they had danced together forever. She loved the confident way he held her, the way he looked at her, as if she was the most beguiling female he had ever known, the way his hand dwarfed hers. He was so blatantly male. Everything that was female within her responded to him. She took a deep breath and her nostrils filled with his unique scent. Try as she might, she couldn't place it.

When the song ended, they returned to the table to sample the wine, and then they danced again. Once, when he twirled her around the floor, she caught sight of the two of them in the mirror. She smiled inwardly, thinking how good they looked together.

Sky hated to see the night end, but when she yawned behind her hand for the third time, Kaiden suggested it might be time to go home.

He drove much more slowly on the return trip. Sky smiled inwardly. Dared she hope it was because he wanted to spend more time with her? She certainly wanted to spend more time with him.

He parked the car in his driveway and after opening her door, he took Sky's hand in his and walked her across the street.

Sky's heart was beating triple time when they reached the porch. Butterflies fluttered in Sky's stomach as she delved in her handbag for her keys. Would he kiss her good night?

"I'd like to do this again real soon," he said as she slid the key into the lock.

"Me, too." After opening the front door, she reached inside and switched on the hall light.

"Is tomorrow too soon?"

Turning to face him, she murmured, "Not for me."

"Pick you up at four?"

"All right. Where are we going?"

"I'm not sure yet. Dress casual."

She nodded, wishing the night would never end. Being with him was exhilarating. Riding in his car, dancing, sharing a meal . . . They were all mundane things, yet sharing them with Thorne was like experiencing each one for the first time. Why didn't he kiss her? What if she kissed him?

Thorne gazed into Skylynn's eyes, eyes as blue and clear as sapphires, and before he had time to talk himself out of it, he drew her into his arms and kissed her. He was prepared for outrage, maybe a well-deserved slap. He wasn't prepared for the way she melted into his embrace, or the way her eyelids fluttered down as she locked her hands behind his neck, went up on her tiptoes, and kissed him back.

His tongue plundered her mouth. She tasted of melted butter and wild rice, of red wine and warm, willing woman and he wondered what she would do if he swung her into his arms and carried her up the stairs to her bedroom.

It took every ounce of willpower he possessed to break the kiss, to loosen his hold on her, to put a respectable distance between them.

She blinked up at him, her lips parted, her eyes wide. "Wow."

"I'll take that as a compliment," he remarked with a grin.

"Please do."

He rocked back on his heels. "I might be able to do better."

"I doubt it," she murmured.

Muttering, "I could never resist a challenge," he folded his hands over her shoulders, drew her body against his, and claimed her lips once more.

His tongue dueled with hers, tasting, teasing, until, with a startled cry, she pulled away. "Ouch!"

He released her instantly. "I'm sorry."

"That's okay." She lifted a finger to her tongue, frowned when it came away bloody. "Grandma, what sharp teeth you have."

He laughed softly. She had no idea how sharp they really were, or how that tiny taste of her life's essence stirred a hunger in him that had been dormant for years.

Drawing her into his arms yet again, he gave her a chaste kiss on the forehead. "Sweet dreams, Sky Blue."

"Thank you. I had a wonderful time."

"As did I."

"Good night, Kaiden."

He waited until she went inside before crossing the street to his own house.

Inside, he locked and bolted the door, then stood with his back pressed against the heavy oak, his eyes closed as he savored the memory of holding Skylynn in his arms. The taste of her kisses lingered on his tongue, the scent of her perfume, of the woman herself, clung to his clothing.

He blew out a sigh as he headed for his lair.

For her sake, they had better find that formula, and soon.

Chapter 3

Skylynn woke filled with anticipation. She had another date with Kaiden Thorne! She glanced at the clock, surprised that she had slept so late. It was almost ten.

With the words to "Unchained Melody" playing in her head, she quickly washed her face and brushed her teeth, then skipped downstairs to fix breakfast, only to find she was too excited to eat. Six hours until four o'clock. What was she going to do until then?

She tapped her fingertips on the kitchen table. Perhaps now would be a good time to go through Granda's things and decide what to keep and what to give to the local homeless shelter.

With that thought in mind, she went upstairs. After pulling on a pair of old sweatpants and a T-shirt, she drove to the supermarket for some empty boxes. Returning home, she put on a pot of coffee, then carried the boxes upstairs.

Sky took a deep breath when she reached the landing; then, squaring her shoulders, she opened the door to her grandfather's room and stepped inside. And was instantly transported back to her childhood. How many times had she crept into this room in the middle of the night after her parents died? How many hours of sleep had Granda lost while he dried her tears, or held her on his lap and told her fairy tales until she fell asleep in his arms?

The room looked the same as always. A quilt her grandmother had made covered the double bed. Her grandparents' wedding picture sat on the dresser alongside a family photo that had been taken only weeks before her parents were killed. The scent of her grandfather's pipe tobacco lingered in the air.

Heaving a sigh of resignation, she began sorting through her grandfather's things, placing his clothing in one pile, his personal effects in another.

A third pile held Granda's silver-backed pocket watch, the jackknife he had always carried, his lucky silver dollar, his favorite paisley tie, and his money clip. She would keep those things for Sam until he came home.

After a good long cry and a late lunch, she carried the boxes out to the garage to await pickup.

Returning to the house, she paused on the front porch and glanced across the street. The place looked deserted, she thought, and then frowned, wondering what had made her think that.

With a shake of her head, she went inside. It was three o'clock. Time to get ready for her date. Kaiden had told her to dress casual. How casual? She debated a few minutes, then decided on a pair of black jeans, a pink sweater with a shawl collar, and a pair of comfortable shoes.

Kaiden arrived at her door at three-fifty-five. Dressed in faded blue jeans, a black jacket over a blue T-shirt, and black boots, he looked ready for anything.

"I thought we'd go to the county fair," he said as he opened the car door for her. "Are you game?"

"Sure. Sounds like fun." Heaven knew she could use some laughs after spending the day sorting through her grandfather's belongings.

Minutes later, Thorne pulled onto the freeway and stomped on the gas.

"You really are a speed demon, aren't you? Don't you ever worry about accidents or blowouts? Or tickets?"

He slid a glance in her direction. "Not really," he admitted with a grin.

"Hmm. So, how was your day?"

"Pretty boring, until now." Truth was, he had slept through most of it. Not a good sign. "How was yours?"

"Kind of depressing, actually. I spent a good part of it going through my grandfather's things, trying to decide what to keep and what to give away."

"I'm sorry, Sky Blue. That must have been painful."

She nodded. "It was hard, packing his things. I know it sounds silly, but it made me feel like I was throwing him away."

"You can't hang on to the past, Skylynn," Thorne said quietly. "Life is for the living. Have you decided what to do with the house?"

"I'm . . . I'm going to keep it," she said, only then realizing that she intended to stay in Vista Verde. "I can't sell it anyway, not until Sam comes home." She refused to admit that might never happen. "It's half his, after all."

"What about your job back East?"

"I'll have to quit, of course. I'll call my boss in a day or two." Quitting would be the easy part. Finding a way to tell Harry she was staying in California would be a little more difficult.

They reached the fair in record time, no surprise with Kaiden behind the wheel. The man was definitely a speed freak.

"So, what do you want to try first?" Thorne asked as they made their way toward the rides.

"Anything and everything. I love them all!" Granda had taken her and Sam to the fair every year from the time Sky was three. She didn't like Halloween masks, she was nervous about driving too fast on the freeway, but she loved carnival rides—the scarier, the faster, the better.

"Great! Let's go!"

The next hour passed in a whirlwind of wild rides from the Tilt-a-Whirl to the giant roller coaster, from the Ferris wheel to the fun house.

From there, they went to the game zone.

While Kaiden looked on, Sky tried her hand at knocking over milk bottles with a baseball. She missed every time. She tried her hand at breaking balloons with darts, and tossing Ping-Pong balls into a goldfish bowl, with no success. Next, she tested her skill at the shooting gallery. Again, with no luck.

Throwing up her hands in exasperation, she muttered, "I give up. There's no way to win. I think the games are rigged."

"Is that so?" he asked, laughing. "Well, let's see about that."

She watched in amazement as he picked up the rifle she had just used, sighted down the barrel, and hit the target every time. Twenty minutes later, she had an armful of stuffed animals and Kaiden had been asked, none too politely, to go try his luck somewhere else.

"What am I supposed to do with all these?" Sky asked, juggling an armful of colorful teddy bears, alligators, bunnies, and penguins. "If they all move in with me, I'll have to move out."

"An easy fix," Thorne said, and while she was pondering what he meant, he handed a pink bunny to a little girl in pigtails, a yellow alligator to a little boy missing his two front teeth, a purple teddy bear to a preteen sporting a Minnie Mouse T-shirt. "See?"

"Wait," she protested when he reached for a small blue dragon. "I want to keep that one."

Minutes later, the dragon was the only animal left. Sky tucked it inside her tote bag.

"I'm hungry," Thorne remarked as they neared the food area. "How about you?"

"I'd love a corn dog and a Coke," Sky said. "And a churro. And a snow cone."

"I love a junk food junkie," Thorne said, taking her by the hand. "Come on."

A short time later, their arms filled with boxes of food, they found a bench and sat down. Sky watched in amazement as Thorne put away four corn dogs, two churros, a snow cone, and a large Coke.

"I don't know why you're not as fat as that prize-winning hog we saw," Sky muttered. She had forced down a second hot dog and felt as stuffed as one of the teddy bears Kaiden had given away.

"High metabolism?" he suggested with a shrug.

"I guess. Here." She thrust the last corn dog at him. "I can't eat another one." He had bought her three, even though she had assured him that one was more than enough.

"Best not to let it go to waste." Four bites, and there was nothing left but the stick. He held it up, turning it this way and that, thinking it looked very much like a miniature stake.

Sky glanced from Kaiden to the stick and back again. "You seem fascinated by that little piece of wood," she said. "Am I missing something?"

"Not really. I was just thinking . . . never mind."

"Tell me!"

"Does it remind you of anything?"

"I don't think so. Should it?"

"Not really."

"Honestly, you can be the most infuriating man!"

"Sorry, Sky Blue."

"Come on, tell me what it reminds you of."

"I was thinking it looked like a wooden stake for miniature vampires."

She blinked at him. "A stake? For miniature vampires?"

She shook her head. "I think it was a mistake to go on that Tilt-a-Whirl so many times. It's scrambled your brains."

He laughed softly. "I think you're right." Gathering their trash, he tossed it into a nearby receptacle, then reached for her hand. "You ready to go?"

"If you are."

Once they were in the car, he turned to face her. "How about a walk on the beach?"

"Are you kidding? It's after eleven and it's miles to the beach."

"Have you got something better to do?"

She pretended to think about it a minute before saying, "Not really."

"Let's go then."

With Kaiden behind the wheel, it took hardly any time at all to reach their destination. Before leaving the car, they both removed their shoes and socks, then ran barefooted across the sand toward the ocean.

Moonlight sparkled on the water. A million stars twinkled in the heavens. The quiet shushing of the waves serenaded them as they walked hand in hand along the shore.

"This was a wonderful idea," Skylynn remarked, glancing out at the ocean. "I haven't been down here for a long time."

"It's one of my favorite places," Thorne said.

"Mine, too. Granda used to bring me and Sam here when we were younger. He liked to fish off of the rocks over there . . ." She turned away, her voice trailing off as tears stung her eyes and clogged her throat. It suddenly seemed wrong to be here, enjoying Kaiden's company, enjoying life, when her grandfather was dead and her brother was missing somewhere in Iraq.

"You don't have to hide your tears from me," Thorne said, drawing her into his arms. "Go ahead and cry."

She buried her face in the hollow of his shoulder and let

her tears flow. "You probably shouldn't be with me," she said, hiccoughing.

"Why is that?"

"Everyone I love dies."

"I promise not to die," Thorne said solemnly.

"You can't keep a promise like that," she said, sniffling.

He brushed his lips across the top of her head. "No?"

She looked up at him, her eyes shining with tears, her lips slightly parted. Before she could ask him a question he wasn't ready to answer, he lowered his head and kissed her. He had intended only to distract her, but one touch and he was the one who was distracted. She tasted of salty air and salty tears, of mustard and hot dogs and snow cone syrup. But mostly, she tasted of woman. A beautiful, desirable, woman.

With his mouth still on hers, he sank onto the sand, carrying her with him, then stretched out beside her, aligning her body with his.

For a time, he was oblivious to everything but the sweetness of her kisses, the warmth of her breasts pressed against his chest, the silkiness of her hair beneath his hand, the softness of her skin. He had thought of her, dreamed of her, yearned for her, ever since she became an adult, but timing and circumstances had always been against them. First she had been too young. Then she had gone away to college, and even though he had kept an eye on her, the difference in their ages had still been too great. And then she had married that idiot Nick.

But she was here now, wrapped in his arms, the soft curves of her body pressed intimately against the hardness of his.

She moaned softly, a small, needy whimper that fanned his desire and his need.

And brought his hellacious hunger roaring to life, reminding him that his unholy thirst for Sky's blood and his lust for her flesh were putting her life in grave danger.

He kissed her again, long and hard, and then, fighting the urge to take what he so desperately wanted, he sat up. "We should go."

"Go?" She looked up at him, her gaze slightly unfocused. "You want to go? Now?"

"It's late, and . . ."

"No, you're right. It's late." She sat up, wondering what had just happened. One minute he had been kissing her as if he wanted to devour her body and soul, and the next, he wanted to go home. Had she missed something?

He leaned forward to lightly brush a stray wisp of hair from her cheek. "You're beautiful, Sky, more beautiful than any woman I've ever known."

She stared at him, confused by the mixed signals he was sending. He had kissed her, almost desperately, then said it was time to go. Now he was telling her she was beautiful. One of them was slightly crazy and she didn't think it was her. "Thank you."

"But you're young, so young."

"I'm not that young," she protested.

"And you're still grieving for your grandfather." Thorne skimmed his knuckles over her cheek, tracing the tracks of her tears. "I don't want to take advantage of you when you're vulnerable. Do you understand?"

She nodded, but she couldn't help wishing that, just for tonight, he would have been a little less noble.

"Come on, Sky Blue." Taking her hands in his, he stood and pulled her to her feet. "Let's go home."

Chapter 4

Sky was fixing breakfast the next morning when Kaiden knocked on her front door.

"Hi," he said. "I hope I'm not too early."

"No, I was just fixing breakfast."

"I was hoping we could go through Paddy's files again. There must be something there that we missed." There had to be. Time was running out.

"Sure, if you want. Come on in. Have you eaten?"

"No." As much as he enjoyed eating, he didn't care for cooking. Most of the time, he ate in restaurants or ordered take-out.

"Well, I've got enough for two if you like waffles and sausage."

"I do, indeed."

He followed her into the kitchen, then stood in the doorway.

Sky gestured at the table. "Please, sit down." Moving to the counter, she removed the waffle she had fixed for herself from the waffle iron, put it on a plate, added some sausage links, and set it before him. "What would you like to drink? I've got coffee, tea, milk, orange juice . . ."

"Orange juice, thanks."

"Eat it while it's hot," she said, smiling. She poured batter onto the waffle iron, dumped the rest of the sausages into the frying pan, then filled a glass with juice.

He finished the waffle and sausage before hers had cooked.

"Do you want this one, too?" she asked, amused.

"No, thanks. But now a cup of coffee would hit the spot."

She poured him a cup, served up her own breakfast, and sat down at the table across from him. "Are you sure I can't fix you another waffle?"

He thought about it a minute, then shook his head. "I'm good." He added milk and a generous amount of sugar to his coffee. "Home cooking is a rare treat for me."

"I take it you're not one of those bachelors who's handy in the kitchen," she remarked as she spread blueberry jam on her waffle.

"You got that right. Anything more than a bowl of cereal is beyond me," he replied. "Although I grill a mean steak."

"Well, at least you're not totally helpless." She finished her waffle and set her fork aside. "What will you do if we can't find the formula?"

"I don't know. Did Paddy have many visitors?"

"Sure, lots of people. A lot of the folks in town didn't care for the new doctor, so even after Granda retired, some of his old patients came to him with their complaints."

"Was there anybody who acted suspicious?"

"Suspicious? I don't think so." She frowned. "You know, now that you mention it, there was this one guy. I remember seeing him several times when I came home on vacation last year. I don't think he was a patient, but I don't think he was a friend, either."

"What was his name?"

"I don't know. I never heard it." She took a drink of her orange juice, her brow furrowed. "I never saw his face, either. He always wore a long gray cloak with a hood, kind of like monks wear."

A muscle throbbed in Thorne's jaw. "Like a monk, you say. Was he tall?"

"Yes, very." She leaned forward, her eyes alight with interest. "Do you know him?"

"No." It couldn't be Desmarais. The man had died years ago. Or so everyone thought.

Sky leaned forward, her arms folded on the table. "Then how do you know he was tall?"

"I didn't. It was just a question."

"Hmm. Why don't I believe you?"

He offered her his most winning smile. "I don't know."

With a little huff of annoyance, Sky rose and began to clear the table. Drat the man! He knew something, all right, but what? And how was she going to find out?

After Sky finished cleaning up the kitchen, Thorne followed her down to the basement. He paused in front of the door to the lab. "We haven't looked in there."

"I don't think Granda kept any of his notes in the lab. He always recorded them in one of his journals and then locked them in one of the file cabinets."

"Have you been inside the room since he passed away?"

"No." As a little girl, Sky had never liked going into the lab because her grandfather had sometimes done experiments on animals, and even though he had claimed he never hurt any of them, she couldn't stand to think about the cute little black-and-white mice and rats or guinea pigs getting shots, or worse.

"Couldn't hurt to have a look around," Thorne remarked.

"I guess not." Sky unlocked the door and switched on the overhead light. And blinked in astonishment at the utter disarray that met her eyes. Tables lay on their sides, broken vials, tubes, and beakers were strewn around the floor. The large glass-fronted cabinet that had held a number of jars and bottles had been ransacked. Broken glass crunched beneath her feet as she moved farther into the room. The door on the right side of the cabinet was open, the contents scattered. Someone had picked the locks on the three draw-ers on the left side and rummaged through them before tossing the drawers and their contents aside.

Thorne took a deep breath, his nostrils filling with a fa-miliar scent. So, Desmarais wasn't dead after all.

Sky looked up at him, her expression troubled. "I don't know who could have done this. Or when," she added, and then frowned. The "when" was obvious. It had to have been last night, while she was at the fair with Thorne. She knew a moment of relief that it had happened while she was away. Anyone desperate enough to break into the house might also be desperate enough to silence whoever got in their way.

Thorne glanced around. Sky might not know who had done this, but he did. Eyes narrowed, he perused the room, only then noticing the edge of an old spiral notebook stick-ing out from underneath one of the overturned drawers.

Moving quickly across the room, he pulled the notebook free. Someone had drawn the outline of a large red heart surrounded by a dozen little hearts on the cover. His name and Skylynn's were written inside the large heart.

Skylynn felt a rush of heat flood her cheeks when she saw her old high school notebook in his hand. What on earth was that doing in the lab?

Thorne glanced at her over his shoulder, one brow raised. "Yours?"

She nodded. "I was only sixteen," she muttered, her em-barrassment growing with every passing moment. "And you were . . ." She cleared her throat. "You were older and mysterious and . . ." She folded her arms. "I had a crush on you back then, that's all."

He bit back a grin as he opened the notebook. More hearts, large and small, had been drawn on the inside cover, along with the words *Mr. and Mrs. Thorne, Sky and Kaiden*, and *Mrs. Skylynn Thorne*.

"I must admit, I'm flattered," he said, unable to hold back his grin any longer.

Sky held up her hand. "Please, just forget it."

"Poetry, too?" he mused.

"What? Oh, no! I'd forgotten about that."

The words were neatly written inside another heart.

As the rising sun
Chases the night from the sky
So the memory of your smile
Fills my heart
Chasing the darkness
From my soul

"It was a long time ago," Sky said, not meeting his gaze. "Is there anything else in there? Anything useful?"

"Just a spiral notebook." He thumbed through the pages. Paddy's familiar scrawl covered line after line with notations on experiments apparently made on animals. Toward the back of the book, he could see where several pages had been torn out. Another page had been torn in half. Thorne's name was scribbled across the bottom of the half that remained. "Dammit!"

"What's wrong?"

"I think the ingredients and the instructions for mixing the formula might have been in here."

Sky looked up at him, her eyes wide. "And now the thief has it!"

Thorne nodded. "Yeah," he murmured. Dammit! Of all the bad luck.

"I need to call the police and report this," Sky said, suddenly all business. "Maybe they can determine who the vandal is."

"You don't need the police. I know who did it."

"You do?" Sky exclaimed. "How can you possibly know that?"

"It doesn't matter."

"What are you going to do now?"

"Go after him, of course."

"Do you know where he is?"

"No, but find him I will," Thorne said, his voice laced with determination.

"I hope so." She took another look around, her gaze settling on her grandfather's favorite cup which lay near the cabinet, miraculously unbroken. Kneeling, she reached for the cup, let out a small cry as a tiny sliver of broken glass pierced her knee.

Thorne sucked in a ragged breath as the scent of fresh blood filled his nostrils. He whirled around, his gaze zeroing in on the single drop of blood oozing from Sky's knee.

"You're not squeamish, are you?" Sky asked, wiping the blood away with her fingertips.

"No." He swallowed hard. They had to get that formula, and it had to be soon. He could feel himself reverting. With every breath, he was growing increasingly aware of Skylynn, not as a woman, but as prey. The steady beat of her heart echoed like thunder in his ears; the rich, coppery scent of her blood made his fangs ache with need.

He clenched his hands into tight fists. He dared not put it off any longer.

He would have to drink the last of the potion, and soon.

Thorne had offered to help Sky put Paddy's lab back to rights, but she had refused his help, saying that she wanted to go through the rest of the house and make sure nothing else was missing before she called the police.

He had taken his leave shortly thereafter. Being near Sky, listening to the beat of her heart, the whisper of the blood flowing through her veins, was a temptation he wasn't sure he could resist much longer. Better to put some distance between them than risk doing something he would have a hard time explaining to her.

At home, he prowled through the house he had occupied, on and off, for the last 150 years. It was a grand place, more like a mansion than a home. Originally built as a summer retreat by an Italian count, the house boasted vaulted ceilings, paneled walls, and hardwood floors. The front parlor had a large stone fireplace, as did the back parlor, the spacious dining room, the servants' quarters downstairs, and all five bedrooms upstairs.

From time to time, he had done some remodeling. What had once been a water closet had been made over into the master bathroom, with the latest fixtures and plumbing. He had replaced all the original windows, added screens, and heavy-duty locks on all the doors and windows. Only three of the rooms were furnished—the front parlor, the master bedroom, and the kitchen.

The kitchen was located in a separate part of the house, connected to the dining room by a narrow hallway. When he'd bought the house, the kitchen had contained no modern appliances. The stove had burned wood, there had been no running water, no electricity.

Nine years ago, he'd had the kitchen remodeled. He had replaced the old floor, built new cabinets, and installed a black granite sink top. Although he didn't do much cooking, he liked to eat, and so he had purchased a refrigerator, a stove, and a microwave.

The servants' quarters, located on the third floor, had been accessible from the kitchen and also by a separate outside entrance. He had plastered over the outside entrance.

He paused at the front window and stared at the house across the street. The police had been there earlier. He doubted they would find anything helpful. Desmarais was a past master at obliterating any and all evidence of his presence.

Thorne drummed his fingertips on the sill. What was Sky doing now? Was she curled up in a chair, reading? It had been a pastime she had loved as a child. Watching TV, perhaps? Working in Paddy's garden? Preparing lunch?

Frustration rose within him as a hunger he had not felt in years—a hunger aroused by a single drop of Sky's blood—stirred deep within him. He slammed his palm against the wall. He had to find that damn formula!

Turning away from the window, he began to pace the floor. Desmarais had been in Paddy's office, so Thorne had to assume that Desmarais had stolen the formula for the potion, but why? What effect did the concoction have on humans, if any?

At one time, Girard Desmarais had been a hunter without equal. Fearless, merciless, tenacious, he claimed to have taken more than two hundred heads before he had quit hunting and taken refuge in a monastery after the death of his wife.

It was rumored that Desmarais was a descendent of Abraham Van Helsing, the most famous slayer of them all. Generations of Van Helsings considered vampire hunting a sacred calling, sacrificing home, family, and livelihood to rid the world of the Undead. The monastery where Desmarais had taken refuge was believed to be a sanctuary for slayers who had grown too old to hunt, or who had lost their nerve.

Thorne had tangled with Desmarais in France some thirty-odd years ago and considered himself lucky to be alive today. He had not heard anything of Desmarais in more than twenty years. Desmarais had been old when Thorne knew him. Like everyone else, he had assumed Desmarais had passed away years ago.

One thing about Desmarais, old or young, the man knew how to carry a grudge. Desmarais held Thorne responsible for the death of his wife. It was true Thorne had killed Marie Desmarais, but hell, the woman hadn't given him any other choice. She had been a hunter every bit as determined and ruthless as her husband. In the end, it had been her life or Thorne's.

"So, Desmarais, my old friend," he muttered, "where the hell are you now?"

He was still pondering that question later that night as he made his way down to the wine cellar.

Unlocking the safe, he withdrew the blue bottle with its priceless contents. For a moment, he simply held it in his hands, reluctant to drink the last of the precious liquid. How long would this dose last? There was no telling. Even though he always drank the same amount, the results varied. Some doses lasted several months, some only a few weeks. Paddy had been at a loss to explain the variation in the doses and, try as he might, the old man hadn't been able to stabilize the formula. It hadn't been a problem as long as Paddy was alive, but now . . .

Swearing under his breath, Thorne lifted the bottle to his lips, grimacing as the foul-tasting liquid burned a path down his throat.

And then, drowning in despair, he hurled the bottle against the far wall, watching in anguish as it shattered into a million sparkling blue pieces and with it, the life he had come to know.

Chapter 5

Skylynn stood at the sink, staring out the window as she rinsed off the plate and glass she had used at lunch. She had called the police soon after Kaiden left. Two uniformed officers had arrived within the hour, taken a report, dusted for fingerprints, and said they would keep in touch.

She glanced at the clock, dismayed that it was barely four. Never had a day passed so slowly. She had tried all afternoon to come up with a good excuse to go across the street and see Kaiden, but every reason she came up with sounded more contrived than the one before.

After putting the dishes in the dishwasher, she turned the machine on, then went into the front room. Sitting in Granda's squeaky rocker, she drummed her fingertips on the arms. What was Kaiden doing? What if she made a batch of chocolate chip cookies and took a dozen or so across the street? That would be a nice, neighborly gesture.

Lordy, she had it bad. Ever since coming home and seeing Kaiden again, she hadn't been able to get him out of her mind. At fourteen, she had known he was a handsome man, but, like all teenagers, she had viewed anyone over thirty as having one foot in the grave.

At fifteen, she hadn't fully realized how amazingly sexy he was, although just looking at him had made her feel warm all over. At the time, she had thought she was just embarrassed, but now she realized she had been unwittingly responding to his innate sexuality.

She was still responding to that air of sensuality, but now she recognized it for what it was. Just being near him caused all her hormones to sing a happy song. Those dark eyes, that incredibly sexy smile, that deep, whiskey-smooth voice that could coax the birds out of the trees. She could hardly wait to see him again. Just the thought of being close to him, hearing his voice say her name, made her stomach curl with anticipation and brought a smile to her face.

"Oh, for crying out loud, Skylynn, stop it! You're practically engaged to another man."

Ah, yes, Harry. She hadn't thought about him more than once or twice since Kaiden arrived on the scene. She suddenly realized why she kept putting Harry off. Without consciously being aware of it, she had been comparing Harry to Kaiden. And there was just no contest, no way Harry could possibly win.

She rocked back and forth for a few minutes, then frowned as a horrible thought occurred to her. Had her marriage failed because Nick hadn't measured up to Kaiden Thorne? Of course, to be fair, what man could? There was something about Kaiden that was lacking in other men, though, try as she might, she couldn't quite put her finger on just what it was. It was more than his stunning good looks. After all, there were a lot of handsome men running around. Maybe it was the intensity of his gaze when he looked at her, as if she were the only woman on the planet. Maybe it was the husky, sexy quality in his voice when he spoke her name. Maybe it was the incredible attraction that sizzled between them whenever his gaze met hers. Whatever it was, she found him completely irresistible.

What was he doing now?

He seemed obsessed with finding the formula to Granda's potion. Was it more than just a tonic? Some kind of medication, perhaps? What if Kaiden was sick and he needed Granda's tonic to survive? That would explain why Kaiden was so desperate to find the missing ingredient.

She frowned as she thought about the man in the gray cloak. Did he have the same illness as Kaiden? Was that why he had stolen the formula? If the formula didn't include the missing ingredient, would the man in the gray cloak come looking for it again? Mercy, that was a scary thought!

She needed to see Kaiden, needed to make sure he was all right. Once again, she searched her mind for some excuse to visit him and then smacked her forehead with her palm. She had the perfect excuse. He had offered to help her clean up the mess in Granda's lab.

Smiling, she went into the kitchen, whipped up a devil's food cake, and put it in the oven. She brushed her hair and her teeth, slipped on a clean sweater and a pair of jeans, and hurried across the street.

Thorne knew it was Skylynn even before she knocked on the door. He would have known she was nearby if he was deaf, dumb, and blind by the way his whole body yearned toward her.

"Hi," she said breathlessly. "Is your offer to help me clean up Granda's lab still good?"

"Sure. Just tell me when."

"I was thinking about tonight, if you're not too busy."

His gaze met hers. "Never too busy for you."

Her stomach did a quick somersault as his voice caressed her. Was that throaty, sensual purr something he practiced, or did it just come naturally? It slid over her skin like velvet warmed by the sun.

"Sky?"

"What? I mean, that's great! I made a cake."

"What kind?"

"Devil's food. I hope you like fudge frosting."

"Women and chocolate," he muttered with a good-natured grin. "Is there a reason why you want to wait until tonight?"

"Not really."

"Then let's go. I'm not doing anything, and the sooner we get started, the sooner we can have that dessert."

"Works for me," Sky said, grinning. "I might even throw in a scoop of ice cream."

"All the better." After closing the door, he followed her across the street.

A patrol car pulled up as they reached the opposite curb and a ruddy-faced cop leaned out the window. "Everything okay here, Miss McNamara?"

"Yes, fine, Officer."

"We'll be keeping an eye on your place for the next few days. Be sure to call if you see anyone suspicious in the area."

"I will. Thank you."

With a nod, the cop put the car in gear and continued on down the street.

"Did anything else come up missing?" Thorne asked as they climbed the porch stairs.

"No. Apparently all the thief wanted was the formula, if that's what he got. We really don't have any way of knowing for sure what he took."

"True, but my gut tells me it was the formula."

In the kitchen, Skylynn filled a bucket with hot, soapy water. After pulling on a pair of rubber gloves, she grabbed a roll of paper towels, located a couple of old dishrags in a drawer, picked up the bucket, and headed for the basement.

"Here, let me carry that," Thorne said, reaching for the pail.

"I'm not helpless."

He inclined his head in her direction. "I know that. You're a liberated female, but I'm still a gentleman. In my day, we looked after our women."

She looked up at him, head canted to one side. "Your day? You couldn't have been more than a baby when the women's lib movement started."

"Humor me," he said with a wry grin.

With a shrug, she relinquished the bucket, then opened the door to the basement.

Thorne followed her down the stairs. Being a healthy male, he couldn't help but admire the subtle sway of her hips, or the delightful curve of her derriere, nor could he ignore the flowery fragrance that clung to her skin. Or the way the front of his jeans suddenly felt very, very tight.

When they reached the bottom of the stairs, he reined in his lust. Drawing his gaze from her delectable backside, he focused his attention on Paddy's lab. It looked as he had seen it last, except now every visible surface was covered with fingerprint powder.

Thorne quickly put the furniture to rights while Skylynn attacked the fingerprint powder. His was by far the easier task.

Sky muttered under her breath as she washed the black powder off the top of one of the filing cabinets. She had heard stories of how difficult the stuff was to remove, but it was even worse than she had expected. Fortunately, the dust was only in the lab and the floor was linoleum and not carpet. When the Cunninghams down the street had been robbed, the crime lab technicians hadn't been too careful about dusting for prints. The sticky stuff had gotten into the

Cunninghams' carpet and ruined it. Mr. Cunningham, who
was a lawyer, had filed a claim against the police department and the city had replaced the Cunninghams' carpet.

Sky was in the middle of washing down the doorjamb
when Kaiden sniffed the air. "Something's burning."

"What? Oh, no! My cake!" Sky exclaimed. Dropping the
rag on the floor, she ran out of the lab and up the stairs.
"Darn it!" Grabbing a hot pad, she opened the oven door
and pulled the pan from the oven.

"Looks a little singed," Thorne remarked, coming up
behind her.

Muttering, "It's ruined," she dropped the pan in the sink.
"That darn thief! It's all his fault," she said, and burst into
tears.

Kaiden reached around her to turn off the oven; then,
blowing out a sigh, he drew her into his arms. "It's only a
cake, Sky Blue. It's not the end of the world."

"It's not the cake," she wailed. "It's just . . . everything."

Drawing Sky with him, Kaiden braced his back against
the counter. Unless he was mistaken, the floodgates were
about to open.

"It's okay, darlin'," he murmured, "let it all out."

And she did. She shed tears for her failed marriage and
for her grandfather's death. She wept because a good man
wanted to marry her and she didn't love him, and because
she was afraid Sam was dead. She cried for the mess in the
lab, for the cremated cake stinking up the kitchen, and because she didn't know what to do about her future, her job,
or the feasibility of keeping Granda's house.

As her tears subsided, she grew increasingly aware of the
man who was holding her close. One large hand lightly
stroked her back. His breath ruffled her hair.

Sniffling, she looked up at him. "I'm sorry. I'm getting
you all wet."

"I'll dry." With the pads of his thumbs, he wiped the tears from her cheeks. "Feel better?"

She nodded, suddenly self-conscious. She must look a fright, with her eyes and nose all red and swollen. When she would have moved away, his arms curled around her waist again.

He's going to kiss me.

And even as the thought crossed her mind, he was lowering his head, claiming her lips with his. It never occurred to her to resist.

She went up on her tiptoes, her arms twining around his neck, her eyelids fluttering down as one of her favorite teenage fantasies came to life. Unlike so many other things she had wished for, the reality was ever so much better than the dream. His mouth was warm and firm on hers; his arms held her body close to his. A distant part of her mind, the part that was still functioning, took note of the fact that they fit well together despite the difference in their height.

One of them moaned, a soft cry of need and longing.

Just when she realized that that needy purr had come from her own throat, Kaiden put her away from him, then turned his back toward her.

Sky stared at him. He was breathing hard, his hands clenched at his sides. She placed a tentative hand on his shoulder and realized he was trembling. "Kaiden?"

He blew out a shaky breath. "Just give me a minute."

Her hand fell away and she bit down on the corner of her lip, confused by his behavior. She wasn't an untouched innocent. She knew when a man wanted her. And she for sure wanted him, so why had he pulled away? She hadn't been with a man since her divorce. Was she so desperate for a man's touch that she had imagined the sensual spark that had ignited between them like a match striking tinder?

No, that had been real. Butterflies danced in her stomach when he turned to face her again.

"I'm sorry," he said, his voice gruff. "I didn't mean for things to get so out of hand."

She blinked up at him, uncertain of how to respond.

Thorne took a deep breath, held it, then blew it out in an impatient sigh. He didn't want to take advantage of her. She was recently divorced. Her brother was missing in action. She had buried her grandfather only days ago. She was grieving and, oh, so vulnerable. Not to mention the fact that she had a boyfriend waiting for her in Chicago.

Sky folded her arms and took a step backward. Apparently, she had imagined that spark, after all.

"I appreciate all your help," she said, her voice cool, "but I think I can manage the rest on my own."

He regarded her through narrowed eyes, then shoved his hands into his pants pockets. "Okay, Sky Blue," he said quietly. "If you need help with anything else, you know where I live."

Lips tightly pressed together, she nodded. Right now, she only wanted one thing.

It wasn't until she heard the front door close behind him that the tears came again.

Thorne muttered every curse word he knew, in every language he knew, as he stormed across the street and into his own house. Dammit! He hadn't meant to hurt her feelings or start something he knew he shouldn't finish, but how the hell was he supposed to have known that one innocent kiss would so quickly turn into something far more provocative? Still, he shouldn't have been surprised, not when she smelled so good and felt so right in his arms. Not when he had spent every day since he had come back to town thinking of her, dreaming of her. Wanting her in the most primal way.

He stood in front of the big stone hearth in the living room, his hands braced against the mantel. Dammit! He had known scores of women in the course of his existence. Beautiful or plain, rich or poor, young or old, none of them had ever stirred his desire or touched his heart quite the way Sky did. He had seduced them, used them, forgotten them. But there would be no forgetting Skylynn, not in this lifetime or any other.

The best thing he could do for Sky McNamara was keep out of her way and out of her life. In a week or two, a month at best, it wouldn't be safe for her, or any other mortal female, to be near him.

Chapter 6

Skylynn woke feeling grumpy after a restless night. Her dreams had been oddly disjointed, more like remembered scenes from her past than the kind of dreams she usually had. The images had changed quickly from one to the other, with no rhyme or reason.

She had been at her parents' funeral, crying in Granda's arms when, suddenly, she was in Iraq with Sam, making mud pies out of sand while bullets and grenades whistled over their heads. She was inside Kaiden's house on Halloween night and it was full of trick-or-treaters—ghouls and ghosts, talking scarecrows, witches on broomsticks, vampires, and werewolves. And then, abruptly, she was out on the sidewalk in front of Granda's house, playing hopscotch with a tall man in a gray cloak. And always, in the background, someone was watching her, someone who wore a long black leather coat with the collar turned up. Someone whose eyes burned as red as the fires of hell.

Going into the bathroom, Sky threw off her pj's and stepped into the shower. She closed her eyes while the warm water sprayed over her, washing away the last of the troubling images, but nothing could wash away her concern for Sam. It had been four months since he had disappeared.

It was horrible, not knowing where he was, not knowing if he was dead or alive.

She murmured, "Please be alive," as she dressed and went downstairs to fix breakfast. She refused to believe Sam was dead. He had been her hero, the one she confided in, the one who had made her laugh when no one else could. He couldn't be gone. Without him, her last anchor would be lost and she would truly be alone in the world.

Going into the kitchen, she pulled back the curtains, revealing a day as gray as her mood. With a sigh, she plugged in the coffeemaker, then sat at the table, trying to decide what she wanted for breakfast, only to realize she was too depressed to eat.

When the coffee was ready, she poured herself a cup, added a little milk and sugar, then went into the living room.

She was sitting on the sofa, staring at the far wall, when her cell phone rang.

"Tara!" she exclaimed. "How are you?" Sky had met Tara Reed in Chicago and they had quickly become best friends. They worked together at McGraw, Strait & Dunne.

"I'm fine," Tara said, a smile in her voice. "I just called to see how you are."

"I'm doing all right," Sky murmured, leaning back against the cushions.

"Now, why don't I believe that?"

"Probably because I'm lying. But I'll be all right. It's just hard, you know? I wish I'd called home more often."

"Sky, you called him every week."

"I know." But she still felt guilty for not calling Granda more often. With Sam missing, she had been the only family her grandfather had left. "So, how's everything at MS & D?"

"Miserable without you. Leena from Accounting eloped with CJ. Everybody's talking about it. I mean, really, he's old enough to be her father."

"No kidding!" CJ McGraw was the CEO of MS & D, and Tara's boss. "Boy, I didn't see that one coming."

"Neither did anybody else, including me! Oh, guess what? I saw Harry at Gene & Georgetti's the night before last."

"Oh?" Gene & Georgetti's was Harry's favorite restaurant. She told herself she didn't really care, but curiosity made her ask, "Was he alone?"

"No, he was with Ron and his wife."

Ron was Harry's older brother.

"Is everything all right with you and Harry?" Tara asked. "He seemed a little down."

"I should probably call him." Sky felt a twinge of guilt. She had hardly thought of Harry since she had come home. "We didn't part on the best of terms."

"You didn't have a fight, did you?"

"Not exactly. He wanted to come to California with me, and I told him I wanted to be alone."

"Ah. Well, you know how men are. They try to be so macho, but inside, they're cream puffs."

"Right," Sky said, laughing. "So, what else is going on?"

"I have news," Tara said. "I'm just not sure this is the right time to share it."

"So, we've finally come to the real reason you called."

"I think I'll save it until you get back here."

"Oh, no, you don't. Come on, Tara Louise Reed, spit it out."

"Well . . . Lance asked me to marry him!"

"He did? When?"

"Last night. It was so romantic. We went to dinner and then he surprised me with tickets to *Wicked*. You know I've been dying to see it." She blew out an exaggerated sigh. "He proposed during intermission."

"That's wonderful! When's the big day?"

"Not until you get back here where you belong. After all,

I can't very well get married without my maid of honor, can I?"

"Are you asking me?"

"Of course. Who else would I ask? Anyway, we haven't set a date yet, but it probably won't be for at least a couple of months. I have to buy a dress, find a church and a caterer, pick out invitations, and get them in the mail. Bridesmaid dresses. I was thinking about lavender for the bridesmaids and maybe a darker shade for you. What do you think?"

"Whatever you want is fine with me. As long as it's not yellow!"

Tara laughed. "No yellow, I promise. Anyway, all that takes time. And money. And planning."

"Everything will work out. You'll be a beautiful bride."

"I know," Tara said, and then giggled. "Oh, but that sounds vain, doesn't it? But you know, all brides are beautiful. Listen, I've gotta go. CJ is calling me. I'll talk to you soon, okay?"

"Sure. And Tara? It was great hearing from you. Thanks for calling."

"Hang in there, girlfriend."

"Will do. Bye."

Sky felt better after disconnecting the call. She wasn't really alone in the world. She had Tara and a few other friends at work. She had Harry, if she wanted him. But did she want him? Maybe she should have invited him to come home with her . . .

She shook her head. The fact that she didn't want Harry there, didn't need him there, spoke volumes about their relationship.

Going into the kitchen, she refilled her coffee cup, then went back into the living room and sank down on the sofa, one leg tucked beneath her. Picking up the newspaper, she read the headlines and the funnies, checked the want ads, then curled up on the sofa and closed her eyes.

When she woke, it was late afternoon. She lay there for a few minutes, listening to the gentle patter of the rain on the roof, remembering how Granda had always made hot chocolate with lots of mini marshmallows for her and Sam whenever the weather turned cold or wet.

Smiling with the memory, she stood and stretched her arms over her head. After fixing herself a cup of hot chocolate, she added a generous helping of marshmallows, then sat at the kitchen table and wrote a letter to Sam. She wrote him every week. She didn't mail the letters, of course, since no one knew where he was. Instead, she kept the correspondence in a shoe box. She would give it to him when he got home so he would know what had happened while he was gone, and that she had been thinking of him.

After finishing the letter, she returned to the living room. She switched on a light, then moved to the front window to watch the rain.

"What on earth?" Leaning forward, she blinked and blinked again. Kaiden Thorne was mad, she thought, completely mad. Clad in a pair of leopard-print swim trunks and nothing else, he was sitting on the grass in his front yard, pulling the weeds that grew along the edge of the driveway.

As though feeling her gaze, he looked up and glanced across the street. Then he lifted his arm and waved her over.

"Is he kidding?" she muttered when he repeated the gesture. "Well, why not? It's only water, and I don't have anything else to do."

Feeling suddenly lighthearted, she slipped on a jacket and a pair of fur-lined boots and ran across the street. Too late, she realized she should have worn a raincoat, or at least brought an umbrella. The rain was coming down harder than she'd thought.

"Are you crazy?" she asked as she slogged across the wet grass. "It's raining cats and dogs out here."

He shrugged. "I was bored. The weeds needed pulling, and it's easier when the ground is damp."

"Damp!" she exclaimed, glancing at the thick black clouds overhead. "I think there's a monsoon coming."

He laughed at that, a big masculine laugh that had her joining in as she hunkered down beside him.

"So, what have you been doing this blustery day?" he asked as he pulled another weed and dropped it into a bucket.

"Moping. Feeling sorry for myself. Wishing I knew where Sam was. Missing Granda." She shrugged. "Just generally having a pity party, I guess."

"Well, you picked a good day for it." He glanced up. "The angels are crying, too."

"My grandmother used to say that whenever it rained."

"You really are down, aren't you?" Rising, he took her by the hand and pulled her to her feet. "Come on, let's see if we can change that."

Startled, she let him lead her up the steps to the porch and into the house.

"First, we need to get you into some dry clothes before you catch your death."

Shivering, she wrapped her arms around her waist. "I can go home and change, you know. It isn't that far."

"Nope, I'm not letting you out of my sight. Besides, the rain's coming down in buckets." Moving toward the fireplace, he plucked a match from a container on the mantel and started a fire. Taking her by the hand, he led her closer to the hearth. "Stay here," he said sternly, and left the room.

Sky glanced around. It was the first time she had been past the entry hall. The living room had high ceilings, paneled walls, and beautiful hardwood floors. Although it was a big room, it was sparsely furnished with only a black leather sofa, a matching chair, and a couple of end tables. The same furniture she had seen when he'd moved in years ago. A beautiful Oriental carpet was spread before the fireplace. An enormous crystal chandelier hung from a thick black chain.

The walls were bare save for a large painting of a green-and-gold dragon breathing fire at a sword-wielding knight in silver armor while a raven-haired maiden clad in a red dress looked on.

Kaiden returned moments later wearing a pair of gray sweatpants and a long-sleeved, V-necked T-shirt.

"There's a small bathroom down the hall," he said, pointing. "Go get out of those wet things." He thrust a black velour bathrobe into her hands. "I'll make you a cup of coffee while you change. Or would you rather have tea?"

"Coffee's fine." Sky hesitated a moment; then, with a shrug, she went into the bathroom. After kicking off her boots, she peeled off her jacket, jeans, and sweater. Her underwear wasn't wet so she left it on. After towel-drying her hair, she slipped into the robe. It had to be his, she thought, belting it tightly. It smelled just like him.

He was waiting for her on the sofa when she returned to the living room. A round wooden tray bearing two coffee mugs, a sugar bowl, and cream pitcher waited on an end table.

"I'm afraid I can't offer you any cake, burnt or otherwise," he said with a wry grin.

"You're not going to let me forget that, are you?" she muttered, taking a place beside him on the sofa.

"Sorry," he said, stifling a grin.

"No, you're not."

He shrugged. "Are you warm enough?"

"Yes, the fire is wonderful."

He handed her one of the cups. "Milk? Sugar?"

"Thanks." She took a sip, her eyes widening. "What's in this?"

"A bit of brandy to take away the chill."

"Oh."

He added a generous amount of sugar to his cup, then sat back, one arm draped over the sofa.

Sky noticed he was barefooted. It seemed oddly intimate, the two of them both sitting there in their bare feet, as if they had just made love and were relaxing in front of the fire. . . .

Sky felt her cheeks grow hot. Lordy, where had *that* thought come from?

"You look flushed," Thorne remarked. "Is the fire too hot?"

"What? Oh, no, it's . . . I . . . no."

He nodded, a faint smile tugging at the corners of his mouth.

Sky stared into her coffee cup to avoid his gaze. Good grief, did he know what she was thinking? But that was impossible. Wasn't it?

Thorne pretended to watch the fire, but he was aware of the woman beside him with every fiber of his being. Less than twenty-four hours ago, he had acknowledged that the best thing he could do for Skylynn was to stay away from her, yet here she was, in his house, at his invitation, within arm's reach. What the hell was he thinking?

The answer was, he wasn't thinking. His lust and his hunger had combined to override his common sense and now all he could think about was Skylynn, sitting quietly beside him, ripe for the taking.

She jumped when the cup shattered in his hand, raining bits of crockery and spraying drops of coffee onto her lap and the floor.

"What happened?" she asked. "Are you all right?"

"Fine."

"Your hand's bleeding."

"Leave it." He clenched his fist, heedless of the shards

that cut into his skin, or the blood dripping between his fingers.

Sky looked at him, her brow furrowed. "Kaiden, are you ill?" She leaned forward. "Your eyes . . ."

Rising quickly to his feet, he turned his back to her and took a deep breath. "I think you'd better go."

"Should I call someone?" she asked anxiously. "A doctor? I think you might need stitches. And your eyes . . ."

"I'm fine," he said gruffly. "Please, just go."

She stared at his back, at his hands, tightly clenched at his sides. Blood trickled through the fingers of his right hand. She couldn't just leave him, not when he was bleeding, not when he might be sick. She took a step toward him. "At least let me bandage that cut."

"Dammit, Skylynn, just get out of here! Now!"

She wasn't about to argue, not with that tone of voice. Lifting the hem of the robe, she ran out of the room and didn't stop running until she was inside her own house, with the door closed and locked behind her.

Breathing heavily, one hand pressed to her chest, she leaned back against the door.

What had just happened?

The sound of Sky's front door slamming shut behind her echoed in Thorne's ears like a death knell. And indeed, that was what it was, he thought bitterly.

The death of his humanity.

He could feel his dark nature returning, the constricting of his veins as the thirst for blood surged up within him. He grimaced at the near-forgotten ache in his jaw as his fangs ran out. The potion was quickly wearing off, but why?

Blood. He could think of nothing else. It was a remarkable fluid, warm and red and smooth. It was 90 percent plasma and of that 90 percent, 55 percent was water. The other 45 percent was made up of antibodies, hormones, proteins, glucose, and amino acids. The remaining 10 percent of blood consisted of red and white blood cells. Whatever it was made of, humans couldn't survive without it.

And now, neither could he.

Agitated, he paced the floor in front of the hearth. True, the last dose he had taken had been smaller than usual, but it should have been good for a few weeks. Had waiting so long to take the last of it weakened its effectiveness?

Dammit!

Feeling as though the walls were closing in on him, he went out into the backyard, oblivious to the thunder and the lightning, to the rain that pummeled his head and shoulders like wet, angry fists.

Standing there with his eyes closed, Thorne was aware of the dark wrapping around him, the mist caressing him like a woman's loving arms while the night whispered in Kaiden's ears, welcoming him home.

When her breathing returned to normal, Sky went into the kitchen. After pouring herself a glass of ice water, she stood at the sink, staring out the window at the rain.

What had just happened? One minute she had been on the sofa next to Kaiden, thinking how cozy it was, just the two of them sitting side by side, and the next the coffee cup in his hand had shattered and he had ordered her out of the house.

She frowned. Maybe he was ill and didn't want her to know. Maybe Granda's tonic really was keeping him alive.

After putting the glass in the dishwasher, she went into the front room and looked out the casement window. The lights were still on in his house. She clutched the collar of her robe—his robe. Should she go over and make sure he was all right? He hadn't looked very well when she'd left.

Maybe that's why he had been so abrupt. She could get dressed and run over on the pretext of returning his robe and retrieving her clothes, she thought, and then dismissed the idea. He wasn't likely to fall for a ruse like that. Maybe she should just wait until tomorrow.

But what if he was really sick?

What if he needed help?

Maybe she hadn't imagined that eerie red glow in his eyes. Maybe it was a symptom of his illness.

And maybe she should just mind her own business.

She jumped as a brilliant flash of lightning lit up the sky and the lights went out.

Chapter 7

Thorne lifted his face to the heavens. The storm reminded him of the night he had been turned so many centuries ago. It had happened in the heart of London in the middle of winter. He had been a bit of a scoundrel back then, much to his mother's shame and his father's disgust. He had spent most of his time in the pubs, drinking, gambling, and wenching, and had gone through his grandfather's inheritance in less than a year.

Not surprisingly, his father had disowned him, declaring he was a wastrel and a disgrace to the family name. His mother had taken to her bed whenever her youngest son's name was mentioned.

Being young and full of the juices of life, Thorne had turned his back on his family and taken to being a highwayman, a role that he had embraced with a great deal of enthusiasm. He had slept by day, ridden the highways and the byways by night, and generally had a rip-roaring good time stealing from the rich to line his own pockets. His companions had been no better than they ought to have been, all young and carefree, eager to wench and wine until the wee small hours of the morning.

Thorne had been in the middle of a rousing game of

euchre when a woman sidled up to him. He had never seen her before, but one look, and he knew he would never forget her. Waist-length brown hair tumbled in riotous waves around her bare shoulders. Her skin was like fine alabaster, her eyes as green as the meadows of Scotland. One look into those eyes and he had followed her out of the pub and into the teeth of the storm.

She paused under an overhanging balcony. "What a handsome fellow you are. Have you a name?" She spoke softly, yet he heard her clearly.

"Thorne." He couldn't stop staring at her—the red of her lips, the swell of her breasts.

She had run one delicate finger down his cheek. "Are you happy, Sir Thorne?"

"My thanks for the title," he replied, grinning foolishly, "but it's just Thorne." His gaze moved over her from head to heel. The rain had plastered her gown to her form, revealing a slender but voluptuous figure. "As for being happy," he said, lifting his gaze to hers. "I didn't know what happiness was until you walked into the pub."

She laughed softly. "Sweet words," she murmured, her voice laced with amusement. "I wonder, do you taste as sweet?"

"Taste me and see," he invited her.

"Indeed, I shall. But not out here."

"You must be cold." He started to remove his coat, but she waved it away, then linked her arm with his.

Like a lamb to the slaughter, he followed her down a muddy street, into a respectable inn, and up the stairs. He was staggering a little now, the night's drinking finally catching up with him.

She laughed as she steadied him. "Careful, now. No need to rush. We have all night."

It was dark inside the room. "Shouldn't we have a light?" he asked.

"No need."

The moon broke through the clouds, shining across the open window along with a few raindrops. Had he been sober, he might have realized he was in danger, but he was well in his cups and she was exquisitely beautiful.

"No light?" He rocked back on his heels. "Don't tell me you're shy."

"Hardly that." Taking him by the hand, she led him to her bed and pushed him down on the mattress.

He fell back, surprised and a little unsettled by her strength.

In an instant, she was sitting astride his hips, a dark shape barely discernable in the dusky room.

He grinned up at her. "Like to be on top, do you?"

"Always."

"Not this time." He took hold of her waist with both hands, intending to roll over and tuck her beneath him, only to find that, without seeming to move, she now had him pinned to the bed, both of his large hands caught in one of her much smaller ones.

The first thread of fear skittered down Thorne's spine when he tried to break her grip. And failed.

The second came when she leaned down toward him. Moonlight shone on her face now, and in that pale light he saw that her eyes were no longer green, but red. And glowing.

"Who are you?" he asked. "What are you?"

"I am the daughter of Nyx." She lifted one brow. "Have you never heard of me?"

He shook his head, suddenly incapable of speech.

"My name is Death. My sisters are Sleep, Strife, and Pain."

Of course, he thought, his mind racing to make sense of her words. According to Greek mythology, Nyx was a goddess, daughter of Chaos, who had, without benefit of a husband, given birth to Death, Strife, Sleep, and Pain.

Thorne stared into her eyes. She was mad, he thought, quite mad.

And then her lips peeled back in an evil grin, revealing a pair of very white, very sharply pointed teeth.

"I am Death," she whispered, and buried her fangs in the side of his neck.

His first reaction was horror. He struggled against her hold on him, but to no avail. And then a strange thing happened. When he stopped struggling, his fear melted away and he was awash in sensual pleasure, more intense than anything he had ever known. He grew weak, light-headed, knew he was dying, and he didn't care.

When he awoke the following night, he was a vampire, with a new vampire's raging thirst and no compunction about how he quenched it.

For all that he hated the beautiful vampire who had turned him, he was grateful that she had stayed with him long enough to teach him how to hunt, how to handle the sensory overload that pummeled him, to tune out the barrage of sights, sounds, and smells that poured in from every side, how to cloak himself in the deep shadows of the night, and later, how to dissolve into mist or assume another shape.

She had warned him that the sun would destroy him and silver would burn him. She admonished him to be wary of strangers with wooden stakes, and to maintain a secure lair. As an afterthought, she told him that most animals would recognize him as a predator and avoid his presence.

She had explained that he didn't have to kill his prey to survive, but he had been young and angry then, and killing came naturally to his kind.

Lady Death, Thorne mused, staring at the fast-moving clouds, *where are you now?*

He was heading back to the house when he heard a knock at the front door. A single indrawn breath told him who it was.

Driven by an overwhelming need to make sure Kaiden was all right, Sky had changed into a pair of jeans and a bulky sweater, slipped on her raincoat and boots, and run across the street, Kaiden's robe folded over her arm.

She had no sooner knocked on his door when she was overcome by doubts and second thoughts. What was she doing here? He obviously didn't want her around, and if he was sick, he could call a doctor.

Muttering, "This was a bad idea," she turned away from the door. She was halfway down the porch steps when the front door swung open.

"Sky, is something wrong?"

"The lights are out," she said, pausing to look over her shoulder.

He stepped out onto the porch and glanced up and down the street. "So they are. Are you afraid of the dark?"

Sky shook her head. She hadn't come here to tell him the lights were out. "No, I just . . . I mean, you seemed so upset earlier . . . I just wanted to make sure you were all right. And return your robe."

He laughed softly. No one had worried about him or his health since he'd left home so many years ago. "I'm fine. Would you like to come in?"

His invitation confused her almost as much as his abrupt change of mood. He had practically thrown her out less than thirty minutes ago.

"I promise not to bite."

"Oh, well, in that case." Grinning faintly, she ascended the steps and followed him into the living room, stood there fidgeting with the collar of her jacket while he threw another log on the fire in the hearth. "You're all wet," she murmured, frowning.

"I was outside."

"You do know it's still raining, don't you?"

He glanced at her over his shoulder. "A little water never hurt anyone."

"Tell that to Noah."

"You're a little damp yourself," he remarked, grinning. "Come, sit by the fire."

Feeling suddenly nervous, Sky dropped his robe over the back of the sofa, then took a seat in the overstuffed chair near the hearth. So, what now? She had accomplished her mission. She had returned his robe and ascertained that he was all right.

"I'm sorry for the way I behaved earlier," he said quietly.

She shrugged. "I'm just glad you're okay."

"Would you care for something to drink? I've a good bottle of wine just waiting to be sampled."

"Sounds lovely."

A carved wooden tray holding a bottle of Madeira and several crystal wineglasses sat on an ancient sideboard. After pouring two glasses, he handed her one, then sat on the edge of the sofa.

"What shall we drink to?" Sky asked.

"How about sunny skies and smiling blue eyes?"

She laughed, remembering the first time he had said that. It had been New Year's Eve. Granda had invited Kaiden over to toast in the New Year. Granda had poured wine for himself and Kaiden, and a glass of sparkling apple cider for Sky. Sam hadn't been home that night, having gone to a party at a friend's house.

Granda had lifted his glass. "Will you give us a toast, Mr. Thorne?"

"I'd be honored," he had replied. "May you have a prosperous New Year, Paddy, and may your fair granddaughter be blessed with sunny skies and smiling blue eyes."

Thorne touched his glass to hers. "You're thinking of Paddy, aren't you?"

Blinking rapidly to keep from crying, Sky nodded.

"He was a good man, gone too soon."

"Yes." Sipping her drink, she gazed at the dancing flames, wondering if Kaiden was still going after the man who had broken into Granda's lab, but reluctant to bring the subject up because it might mean leaving Vista Verde, and she didn't want him to go.

Thorne drained his glass and put it aside. The wine warmed him, but it was as nothing compared to the heat Sky's nearness aroused in him. How exquisite she looked, with the fire's glow pinking her cheeks and gilding her hair. The steady beat of her heart was like music to his ears, the flowery scent of her perfume, the scent of the woman herself, sweetly alluring.

She was beautiful.

She was desirable.

She was here.

Alone.

In his house.

And she had what he so desperately craved.

Sky's hand tightened around her glass as the atmosphere in the room, which had been cozy and relaxed, suddenly hummed with tension. The hair on her arms stood at attention when she met Kaiden's gaze. Men had looked at her before, some with interest, some with lust, some with admiration, but never had a man looked at her like this, as if he were on the verge of certain destruction and only she could save him. With a hand that shook, she lifted her glass and took a long swallow.

"Skylynn . . ."

There was no mistaking the undercurrent of need in his voice, or the blatant hunger in his eyes that sent a warning shiver down her spine. That was odd, she thought, because she wasn't really afraid of him.

Was she?

She watched, suddenly wary, as he leaned toward her.

A low rumble of thunder made her jump. Wine sloshed out of her glass onto her jeans. The perfect excuse to make a hasty exit, she thought, and putting the goblet down, she quickly gained her feet.

"I should go wash this out right away," she said, and without waiting for a reply, she hurried out of the room toward the front door.

A squeak, like that of a mouse caught by a cat, erupted from her throat when she felt his hand on her arm.

"Sky, don't go."

His voice trapped her as surely as a net.

He turned her around to face him, his dark eyes gazing deep into her own. "Relax, Skylynn, I'm not going to hurt you."

She stared up at him, her insides churning with terror. "What are you going to do?"

"Nothing for you to worry about." He stroked her cheek; then, pushing her hair behind her ear, he caressed her neck with his fingertips. He swallowed hard as he heard the whisper of her blood flowing through her veins. "You have something I need."

She shook her head. "I don't have the formula. You know that."

"I know." His voice was low, his gaze hypnotic. "There's something else."

"Just tell me what it is, and I'll find it. I give you my word."

"Close your eyes, Sky Blue. That's right." He slipped his arms around her and drew her close. "This won't hurt, I promise." And so saying, he bent her back over his arm and took what he needed.

And even as he lost himself in the pleasure of it, he hated himself for what he was doing, for lacking the will, the strength, to resist.

He only hoped she would forgive him for breaking his promise.

Sky felt herself falling, falling, into nothingness. This was death, she thought, and wondered why she wasn't more afraid, and why the world seemed to be clothed in ribbons of shimmering red. She had never thought that dying would feel so wonderfully soft and sensuous.

Awareness returned gradually. She tried to cling to the hazy, sensual scarlet world, but it slipped away and she was thrust into a realm of darkness, a thick blackness that was more than just the absence of light. Lost and alone, she wandered through an alien landscape, blindly searching for something that was familiar.

And then, in the distance, she saw a large black box, the same black box she had seen as a child the night Kaiden Thorne moved into the house across the street. Odd, that she could see so clearly in the darkness.

Drawn with Pandora-like curiosity, she moved slowly toward the box. Only when she drew near did she realize it wasn't a box at all, but an old-fashioned casket.

She tried to turn back, but her feet seemed to have a mind of their own and she drew closer, ever closer. As if it belonged to someone else, she watched her hand lift the lid.

Kaiden Thorne lay inside.

She woke screaming in her own bed with no memory of how she had gotten there.

Sitting up, she clutched her pillow to her chest until her heart stopped beating double time and her breathing returned to normal.

"It was just a nightmare." She brushed a lock of hair from her cheek. "Just a nightmare," she repeated.

And yet it had seemed so real.

Throwing the covers aside, she got out of bed, then sat on the edge of the mattress when the room began to spin out of focus. Why did she feel so dizzy? Was she coming down with the flu? She lifted a hand to her forehead. She didn't have a fever. Maybe she had just gotten up too fast.

She sat there for several moments, taking slow, deep breaths, and then tried again. When nothing happened, she went into the bathroom, where she washed her face and brushed her teeth.

After dressing in a pair of old comfy sweats, she went downstairs. Coffee, she needed coffee—and lots of it.

Minutes later, steaming cup in hand, she went out to sit on the front porch swing. The storm had passed and the morning was bright and clear and beautiful. She stared at the house across the way, wondering if Kaiden was awake.

She frowned. She had a vague recollection of going over there last night. Or had she only dreamed it? Her thoughts seemed fuzzy this morning. Odd. She didn't feel hung over. She didn't remember drinking anything stronger than a single glass of wine.

In fact, she didn't remember much of anything at all. So, what had happened and why was it so hard to remember? She frowned, concentrating. She had gone over to Kaiden's house when the lights went out. They had talked about Granda. She remembered Kaiden telling her she had something he needed . . . but he had never told her what it was. She didn't remember anything after that.

After finishing her coffee, she put her cup aside, then sat there, staring at Kaiden's house. She couldn't remember what had happened last night, but she remembered something from a rainy night years ago. How old had she been back then? Ten, eleven? She recalled being awakened by a nightmare and going into Granda's room, only he hadn't been there. Frightened, she had gone downstairs, but he hadn't been there, either. Noticing that the door leading to the basement was open, she had tiptoed to the top of the stairs, then hesitated. She wasn't supposed to go down there, but a rumble of thunder sent her scurrying down the stairs in search of her grandfather. Light shone under the door of Granda's lab. Curious, she had pressed her ear to the door, and heard Kaiden's voice.

"Dammit, old man, that hurts like hell!"

"Do you want to give up?" Granda's voice.

"Of course not! But do you have to use silver? You know it burns like acid."

"It's the only thing that will hold you."

"I gave you my word!"

"That you did," Granda said. "But better safe than sorry where you're concerned."

Sky recoiled as an angry growl rattled the door. Was there a wild animal in there?

Taking a tight rein on her courage, her nightmare forgotten, she pressed her ear to the door again.

"Relax," Granda said. "I'm just taking a little blood."

A harsh bark of laughter and then Kaiden said, "I could use a little of that myself."

"If this works, you won't have to worry about that anymore."

Sky didn't remember making any noise, but suddenly Kaiden said, "We've got company."

A moment later, the door opened and Granda stood there, blocking her view of the lab. "What are you doing here?" he asked sharply. "You should be in bed."

"I had a nightmare." She moved to the left as a groan that sounded as if it had been ripped from Kaiden Thorne's throat reached her ears.

Granda moved with her, blocking her view. "Go back to bed, Skylynn."

Sky had stood her ground, her curiosity growing with every passing second. Why were Granda and Mr. Thorne working so late? Why was Mr. Thorne groaning? Was he in pain? Why wouldn't Granda let her look inside the lab?

"What are you and Mr. Thorne doing down here?" she asked.

But Granda had never answered her question.

Thinking of it now, she realized Granda must have been experimenting with the formula, but what on earth did blood and silver have to do with it? Surely they weren't ingredients in Kaiden's tonic. And what had Granda been doing to Kaiden that had caused him so much distress? He could have been drawing some blood, she supposed, but from the pain in Kaiden's voice, that seemed unlikely.

Rising, Sky strolled to the other end of the front porch, then sat on the rail. What had really been going on in the lab that night? If she marched across the street and asked Kaiden, would he tell her?

Did she really want to know?

Moving back to the swing, she found herself watching Kaiden's house again. Nothing seemed to be stirring over there. Maybe he wasn't even home.

Eventually, hunger drove her inside. She fixed a big breakfast, thinking how much more pleasant it was when shared with Kaiden.

After breakfast, she called her boss and told him she had decided to stay in California. He grumbled about it, complained that she was leaving him shorthanded, but in the end, he wished her well and even offered to pack up the things in her office and send them to her.

"Thank you, Mr. Laskey, but would you please just send them to my apartment? I'll be coming back to Chicago to get the rest of my clothes and things." When he agreed, she murmured, "Thank you so much," and disconnected the call.

There was no hurry to return to Chicago. Her rent was paid until the end of the year. She just hoped her landlord would consider giving her a refund.

* * *

Thorne came awake as the sun slid below the horizon. He remained in bed, staring up at the ceiling for several minutes. Sleeping through the day was the final sign that the effects of Paddy's miraculous potion had completely worn off. Even more damning was the voracious thirst that had awakened with him, a hunger the likes of which he hadn't known since the night he had first risen as a new vampire. It coursed through his veins like hot lead, searing nerves and cells. His jaw ached as his fangs ran out. Dammit! He had known it was only a matter of time before he reverted completely, but he had hoped he would have a few more weeks with Skylynn, a few more days to pretend he was no different from any other man.

He sat up and as he did so, his surroundings took on a faint red glow. But it wasn't the room that was changing. Had he been able to see his reflection, he knew his eyes would be hell-red, his skin stretched taut over cheekbones gaunt with hunger.

He didn't waste time showering. Didn't bother to change out of the faded gray sweats he had worn to bed. A thought took him out of the house, away from the temptation that was Skylynn, to a neighboring town.

Death stalked the streets as Thorne searched for prey. There had been a time, before Paddy's potion, when he had been selective, even picky, about those he preyed upon. But not tonight, with his veins burning and his body cramping, on fire with need. Tonight anything—man or beast—was fair game.

He took the first lone male he encountered. It didn't matter that the man was old and drunk, or that he smelled of cheap wine and rotten teeth. Nothing mattered but the blood flowing in the man's veins, the hot coppery elixir that would put an end to Thorne's torment.

He didn't care that the blood tasted old and sour. All that mattered was that it eased his hunger and took the edge off his thirst.

Another swallow and he turned away. He didn't bother to make the man forget what had happened. No one would believe anything the drunken old derelict said.

In control again, Thorne sought another victim, a young woman with white-blond hair and brown eyes. He mesmerized her with a look, took what he needed, and after erasing the incident from her mind, he sent the woman on her way.

Standing in the shadows, all his preternatural instincts stirring to life, he bid a sad farewell to the man he had been for the last eight years.

Kaiden Thorne, the man, had died tonight.

Kaiden Thorne, the vampire, had been reborn.

For the tenth time that day, Sky peeked out the curtains in the living room. It had been a week since she had last seen Kaiden—seven days—with each day seeming longer, lonelier, than the last.

Where was he?

Had he left town—left her—without so much as a fare-thee-well?

The thought hurt more than it should have. True, they had shared a few heated kisses, but, in reality, they were little more than friends.

She had gone knocking on his door twice, but there had been no answer. The house had seemed oddly deserted, as if no one lived there anymore.

With a sigh, she let the curtains fall back into place. It surprised her how quickly Kaiden had become an integral part of her life. She felt as if something vital was missing, as if someone had taken an old rusty saw and carved out a piece of her heart, leaving a gaping wound in its place.

Turning away from the window, Sky wandered through the house. It wasn't a big place by today's standards. Just a living room, den, kitchen, and half-bath on the first floor, with a master suite, two smaller bedrooms, and a bathroom upstairs. And Granda's lab in the basement. Sky had considered moving into the master bedroom, mainly because it had its own bathroom and a large closet, but she just couldn't bring herself to do it. Not yet, anyway.

Returning to the living room, she straightened the pillows on the sofa, rearranged the pictures on the mantel. She ran her fingertips over the head of the little blue dragon Kaiden had won at the fair. Picking it up, she rubbed it against her cheek. The soft plush reminded her of the fun they'd had at the fair, of Kaiden's kisses.

With a shake of her head, she set the dragon back on the mantel and then, as if drawn by an invisible string, she found herself at the front window again.

Where was he?

Thorne prowled the dark shadows along the waterfront, hands clenched as he sorted through the myriad smells that assaulted his nostrils—sand and salt and sea, the stink of diesel oil and rotting fish, the stench of a dead seal somewhere on the beach. Noise battered his ears—music from a nearby nightclub, traffic from the freeway, an angry couple fighting about money in an apartment two streets over.

Ten days had passed since he'd drunk the last of the potion and he was still coming to terms with the return of his vampiric senses. When he had first been turned, it had taken months to learn how to shut out the multitude of sounds and smells that had assailed him from every side, to adjust to the changes in his vision, his acute sense of touch, his increased strength.

While taking Paddy's potion, his preternatural powers had gradually diminished. His senses had still been sharper than those of an ordinary mortal, but far less keen than he was accustomed to. It had taken some getting used to but, in the long run, the weakening of his vampiric abilities had seemed a fair trade for the chance to walk in the sun again, to enjoy all the pleasures of mortality that had been stolen from him one rainy night.

Now, it was like being a fledgling again, learning how to tune out the constant barrage of voices and city chaos, to control the strength and power that had lain dormant, to subdue his hunger, to rein in the ever-present urge to kill.

He had hunted every evening, always fighting the innate instinct to take it all. He had hoped it would get easier to resist the blood-lust, and perhaps it would again, given enough time. But for now . . .

He paused in the shadows as the scent of prey drifted on the wind.

Like a lion on the trail of fresh blood, he turned toward the scent, his fangs lengthening in response to the steady beat of a living heart, the irresistible smell of fresh, hot blood.

Chapter 8

Girard Desmarais paced the basement floor of the monastery, his long gray cloak billowing behind him like the shadow of death. He muttered under his breath, his frustration growing, as he read the blasted formula again and again. He had followed McNamara's instructions to the letter. Every herb and spice had been picked at the peak of freshness and properly dried; each ingredient, both liquid and dry, had been painstakingly measured to make sure they were exact. And still the blasted concoction did not ferment as it should.

Even as he stood there, Girard could feel the aging process begin again, feel the vitality leaving his body, his eyesight growing dim, his muscles weakening, his thoughts harder to focus.

A row of wire cages, both large and small, ran on either side of a long wooden workbench. All the animals he had tested the potion on were either dead or dying. Those remaining stared at him through liquid, mournful eyes, as if they knew their own days were numbered.

Girard smacked his fist against the door frame. It was obvious that some vital active ingredient was missing from the formula, but what the hell was it? Now that McNamara had passed away, there was no way of knowing.

Muttering an oath, Girard swept his arm across the countertop, sending beakers and bottles flying in every direction.

"Damn you, Patrick McNamara! Could you not have survived until I got there?" He stared at the notebook pages scattered across the floor. What if the formula he had stolen wasn't the correct one? What if this batch of the potion had failed, and the formula for the potion that worked was still in the old man's lab?

Girard frowned as he considered his options, although there was really only one.

He would have to go back to McNamara's and search the house again.

Chapter 9

Sky dumped a load of clean laundry on the sofa. Two weeks had passed since she had last seen Kaiden and she had finally come to terms with the fact that he had left town. Had he gone after the man who'd broken into Granda's laboratory? Had he been called away on an emergency—a death in the family, perhaps, although he had never mentioned having brothers or sisters or any other relatives. He didn't have a job, so a crisis at work was out of the question. If he had decided to take a vacation, he certainly could have found the time to tell her.

She paused in the act of folding a bath towel. Maybe he had just grown tired of her and didn't want to hurt her feelings by saying so. She could understand that. After all, she wasn't anybody special. Her looks were average. She hadn't been blessed with a fantastic sense of humor. She couldn't sing or play the piano.

Kaiden, on the other hand, was an amazingly handsome man who had been born with an astonishing amount of charisma, not to mention being blessed with a voice that could melt steel and a smile that should come with a warning label. Just being around him had made her feel good. And she missed him terribly.

Putting the towel aside, she sank down in the chair beside the fireplace, suddenly overcome with a keen sense of loss. Granda was gone. She'd had no word about Sam in months, making it harder and harder to cling to the hope that he was still alive. And now Kaiden was gone.

She glanced at the mantel, at the cute little stuffed blue dragon sitting there beside a photograph of her parents, and felt the sharp sting of tears behind her eyes. She wouldn't cry. Crying never solved anything. It hadn't brought her parents back. It hadn't brought Granda back. Sam was still missing in action. And Kaiden . . . Thinking of him only made her tears come harder and faster, until it was easier to just give in and have a good cry.

Sky woke curled up in the chair, her shoulders and back aching, her eyes feeling gritty and swollen.

She rose with a groan, surprised to see that it was almost dark outside. Unable to resist, she went to the front window and peered at the house across the street. Was that a light on downstairs? She rubbed her eyes and looked again. The light was still there.

He was back.

Ignoring the inner voice that warned her to stay home and let him come to her if he was of a mind to, she finger-combed her hair and hurried across the street.

The door opened before she had a chance to knock and Kaiden stood silhouetted in the doorway. She couldn't see his face in the shadows, but he loomed before her, tall and broad. Had he been a stranger, she would have been intimidated by his size alone.

"Skylynn." There was no emotion in his voice, no hint of welcome.

"I've been so worried. I didn't know where you were . . . I . . . I . . ." She bit down on her lower lip, the flood of words drying up. It was obvious that he wasn't glad to see her. "I'm . . . I'm sorry," she stammered. "I was afraid . . . that is . . . I mean . . ." She paused to take a breath. "I'm sorry, I shouldn't have come."

She was turning to go when his hand closed over her forearm. "Slow down, Sky, and tell me what's wrong."

"Nothing." She was too embarrassed to meet his gaze. Why hadn't she stayed home where she belonged?

He tugged lightly on her arm. "Come in."

Still not meeting his eyes, she shook her head. "I don't want to intrude."

"Then why are you here?" he asked, a note of amusement in his voice.

She glared at him. "I was worried about you, you big jerk. Good-bye."

"Get in here. You look like hell. Have you been sick?"

She tried to twist out of his grip, but it was like trying to break iron. Resigned, she let him pull her into the house.

He shut the door, then turned to face her, his arms folded across his chest. "Okay, Sky Blue, spit it out. What's wrong?"

Her gaze slid away from his. "You left."

Thorne frowned, waiting for her to go on, but she remained mute, her head bowed so he couldn't see her expression. After a moment, he slipped inside her mind. And everything became perfectly clear.

Expelling a deep breath, he drew her gently into his arms. "I'm sorry, Skylynn," he said quietly. "I shouldn't have left without telling you." Not that he had actually gone anywhere, but what else could he say? *Your grandfather's potion wore off and, oh, yeah, I'm a full-fledged vampire again and it wasn't safe for you to be around me.*

She shuddered in his arms. A moment later, her tears dampened his shirtfront.

"Sky . . ." Dammit, why did she smell so good? All he

could think about was burying his fangs in the tender skin beneath her ear. He should have left town. That would have been the smart thing to do. So, why the hell hadn't he taken off? Stupid question. The answer was currently sobbing in his arms as if her heart would break.

She sniffed, the sound muffled against his shoulder.

Cursing softly, he guided her to the sofa, sat down, and cradled her against his chest. She deserved a good cry. She had been through a lot in the last few years. A nasty divorce. Her brother missing in action. The loss of her grandfather.

Thorne cursed softly. And then he had come along. He had spent every day and night with her, and then he had left her just like everyone else.

He brushed a kiss across the top of her head. "I'm sorry, Sky. I won't leave you like that again, I promise."

"You don't owe me anything," she said, sniffling.

"We're friends, and friends shouldn't treat each other that way."

Friends, she thought dully. *Was that all they were?* It wasn't enough, not for her. She wanted their relationship to be more. Much more. "Where were you?"

"I had to go out of town," he said, and hoped she would leave it at that. He should have known better.

"Oh?"

There were a wealth of unspoken questions in that single word. He decided to go with a version of the truth. "Paddy's potion wore off. I told you it wasn't a matter of life and death, but I needed to find something to replace it."

"Another tonic?"

"You could call it that."

She looked up at him, her gaze searching his face. "Did you find one? Are you all right now?"

"I'm doing better all the time."

Her smile was brilliant, like the sun breaking through the clouds. "I'm glad, Kaiden."

He murmured his thanks, wondering how he would explain his sudden aversion to sunlight and why he could no longer visit with her during the day.

"Well," Sky said reluctantly, "I guess I should go . . ."

It was for the best, Thorne mused, so why in hell was he tempted to ask her to stay?

He clenched his hands to keep from holding on to her as she slid off his lap and gained her feet.

"Well," she murmured, straightening her sweater, "good night."

She sounded as lonely and unhappy as he felt, and in spite of all his good intentions, he heard himself saying, "Don't go."

She looked up at him, her bright blue eyes alight with hope.

He lifted one shoulder and let it fall. "Stay and have a glass of wine. It's going to rain."

"It is?" She glanced at the window. "How do you know?"

"I can smell it. Will you stay?"

"All right."

She wiped the last of her tears away with her fingertips, then sat on the sofa while he opened a bottle of burgundy and filled two delicate crystal glasses.

"What shall we drink to?" she asked as he handed her one of the goblets.

Thorne swirled the wine in his glass, absently observing the play of the firelight on the wine. The way the dark red liquid lingered on the inner wall reminded him of blood.

His gaze moved to Sky's throat, to the pulse steadily beating there. The scent of her blood was far more intoxicating than any wine could ever be.

Her heart began to beat faster under his intense regard.

With an effort, he drew his gaze from her throat. "To better days," he murmured.

Sky nodded. "To better days," she repeated.

Lifting his glass, Thorne sipped his wine, only it wasn't the burgundy he tasted on his tongue, it was the warm, coppery flavor of Skylynn's blood. He should leave town, he thought, now, tonight, before it was too late. Because if he stayed, he knew without a doubt that he would have to taste her again.

Sky was online late the next afternoon, looking for available jobs in Vista Verde, when the doorbell rang. Hoping it might be Kaiden, she ran a hand over her hair as she hurried to answer it.

But it wasn't Kaiden. "Harry!"

"Hello, Skylynn."

She stared at him, stunned. She had never known Harry Poteet to go anywhere, including visiting his parents, without first making an appointment.

Sky glanced past Harry to the house across the street. Was Kaiden home? Maybe looking out the window?

Harry cleared his throat. "May I come in?"

Sky gave herself a mental shake, wondering why she felt guilty for seeing another man. "Of course."

She stepped back, her thoughts chaotic as Harry entered the house. What was he doing here? He looked fit and trim in a pair of brown slacks, a white button-down shirt, power tie, and brown loafers. His light brown hair had been cut recently, his cheeks were clean-shaven.

She led the way into the living room and gestured toward the sofa. "Please, sit down." She took a seat on the chair across from him and folded her hands in her lap. "What brings you here?"

"You, of course. I know you're upset about your grand-father's death, but is that any reason to quit your job?"

"How'd you hear about that?"

"I saw Don Laskey at the club day before yesterday. He told me you had tendered your resignation."

How could she have forgotten that her boss and Harry occasionally played golf together?

"I can't believe you've decided to stay here," he said, glancing around.

Sky followed his gaze, seeing the room the way he would. The furniture was well-worn and outdated, the carpet near the front window had faded. But a home wasn't made up of material things, it was built on memories. And all of her best memories were tied to this house. "I like it here."

He made a dismissive gesture with his hand. "How can you give up Chicago for this nothing town?"

"This is my home, Harry. I'll thank you to remember that."

"Skylynn, I thought we had a future together. We've always gotten along. We like the same things, the same people. I want you to come home with me."

She stared at him, at his perfectly creased trousers, his carefully styled hair, and wondered why she had ever thought herself in love with him. "I'm sorry, Harry, I can't."

He sat up a little straighter. "Is there someone else?"

"Would that make it easier?"

His eyes narrowed. "Who is it?"

"There's no one else. Coming back here made me real-ize I've never been happy in Chicago, never really happy with my job."

The words *never really happy with you,* lingered unspo-ken in the air between them.

"I guess I wasted my time coming here."

"I'm sorry, Harry."

With a nod, he rose smoothly to his feet. "I won't bother you again, Skylynn. I hope you don't regret your decision."

"I won't." Rising, she accompanied him to the front door. "Good-bye, Harry."

With a curt "Good-bye, Skylynn," he swept past her.

She watched him climb into the baby blue Cadillac convertible that was parked at the curb. Leave it to Harry to rent a high-end automobile.

She stared down the street long after he had driven away. Someone had gone out of her life again, but this time the decision had been hers, and she had no regrets.

Chapter 10

From his vantage point at the corner across from the McNamara house, Girard Desmarais watched the well-dressed young man get into his car and drive away. Girard had been keeping an eye on the McNamara house for the last two days and in that time, McNamara's granddaughter had seen only two people—this young man, and the vampire, Kaiden Thorne.

The young man was of no consequence. But the vampire . . . Girard braced his hand against the side of a brick wall. He had no doubt the bloodsucker was searching for the same information he was. He lifted a hand to his cheek, his fingertips tracing the ugly scar that ran from his right cheekbone to his jaw and continued down the side of his neck, a souvenir from his encounter with Kaiden Thorne some thirty years ago.

Girard grimaced at the memory. He had been past his prime back then, but still a hunter without equal. He had pursued Thorne for almost three years before he finally tracked him down. The vampire had been living in Strasbourg, France, at the time. It had been midafternoon of a warm, sunny day when Girard slipped into the vampire's lair. He had discovered the bloodsucker's coffin in the basement of a two-story apartment. Jubilant to have found his quarry after such a long time, Girard had moved soundlessly across the floor, a hawthorn stake in one hand, his favorite mallet in the other. To this day, he still didn't know what had roused the vampire. One minute, his prey had been as still and silent as death, the next, the creature had leaped out of the casket, his eyes blazing red, his lips peeled back to reveal his fangs.

Man and vampire had come together in a rush. To Girard's astonishment, the stake, which had served him well for decades, had proved to be a feeble weapon against the ancient vampire's fangs and wickedly sharp nails.

Girard stroked his cheek again. They had fought for what seemed like hours. Finally, Girard had managed to drive the stake into the vampire's chest. He had known a brief moment of victory as Thorne reeled backward, then sank to the ground. Girard's triumph had been short-lived when he realized that he had missed the vampire's heart.

Covered with deep bites and scratches, Girard had decided retreat was the better part of valor and escaped into the sunlight.

Turning away from the house, he walked back to where he had left his car. Sliding behind the wheel, he turned the key in the ignition and pulled away from the curb.

He had met Paddy McNamara many years after his ill-fated encounter with Kaiden Thorne. Paddy had been experimenting with a longevity potion and had been looking for a few men willing to test it. Girard had been in his late fifties at the time. The potion had failed, but Girard had kept in touch with McNamara. Several years later, Paddy had asked Girard if he would be willing to test another potion. When Girard asked what the potion was for, Paddy had mumbled something about a tonic similar to the first one and explained he was creating it specifically for a client who had an aversion to the sun.

After months of experimentation, a few careful questions, and some subtle snooping in Paddy's lab, Girard had come to the conclusion that the intended recipient of the potion was a vampire; a slip of the lip by McNamara revealed that the vampire was Kaiden Thorne. The second thing, and perhaps the most important, was the realization that the new potion restored Girard's health and vigor until he was as strong and fit as he had been at twenty-five.

He had spent the last two years trying to find Thorne again, but to no avail. On his last visit to McNamara, Girard had learned that the potion he had come to rely on had originally been concocted for Thorne. When Girard had demanded a copy of the formula, Paddy had refused.

And now Paddy was dead and gone, and the formula's secret ingredient with him.

Girard loosed a string of profanity as he pulled into the hotel parking lot. Killing the engine, he stared into the distance. He couldn't go after Thorne now, not in his present, weakened condition.

Girard rubbed his scarred cheek thoughtfully. He needed that missing component, and he needed it now, before he got any older, any weaker.

Before the bloodsucker moved on.

Chapter 11

Thorne woke with the setting of the sun. After showering and dressing, he glanced out the front window, debating the wisdom of going to see Skylynn before he fed, only then noticing that the grass in his front yard needed cutting badly.

He blew out a sigh of regret as he realized his experience working in the yard during the day was over. He had enjoyed being able to mow the lawn in the afternoon. He had enjoyed the smell of fresh cut grass, the feel of it beneath his bare feet, the heat of the sun on his back and shoulders. Mowing the yard at night was just a chore. Still, it needed to be done and he had nothing better to do.

Going into the backyard, he got the lawn mower out of the shed. He quickly mowed the backyard, then went out to the front.

He was about to start the mower again when a familiar odor drifted his way. Desmarais! Striding to the sidewalk, Thorne lifted his head to scent the wind. Desmarais, here?

The lawn forgotten, Thorne hurried across the street and

knocked on Sky's door, softly at first, and then with more urgency.

His tension eased when he heard her voice calling, "All right, all right, I'm coming!"

She opened the door a moment later. "Kaiden! You don't have to break down the door, you know . . ." she said, a smile teasing her lips. And then, seeing the worried expression on his face, she sobered. "Is something wrong?"

A deep breath told him Desmarais hadn't been in the house. With a shake of his head, he murmured, "Sorry."

She looked up at him curiously. "So, what's going on?"

He glanced past her into the entryway. "Has anyone come by to see you today?"

"Are you checking up on me?"

"Yes. No." He swore under his breath. "Just answer me."

"My old boyfriend was here a little while ago," she replied, and wondered again why seeing Harry made her feel guilty. After all, she was free to see anyone she liked.

"Is that right?" He crossed his arms over his chest. "Did you kiss and make up?"

"Of course not. What's this all about?"

"Nothing."

"Nothing?" Exasperated, she planted her fists on her hips and glared up at him. "Nothing? You practically break down my door over nothing?" She poked him in the chest with her forefinger. "I. Don't. Think. So."

"All right, it's like this. You remember that monk I told you about? I think he's here, in town."

She stared up at him, her eyes wide, and then she stepped out onto the porch and glanced up and down the street. "Are you talking about the man who broke into the lab? Did you see him?"

"Not exactly, but I know he was here, and not long ago."

"If you didn't see him . . . ?"

"He was here." Girard Desmarais' scent wasn't something Thorne was likely to forget or mistake for anyone else's.

"But . . . why would he come here again? He's got the formula."

"I don't know," Thorne remarked thoughtfully. But he had a pretty good idea. Maybe he wasn't the only one searching for that elusive missing ingredient. Maybe Desmarais needed it, too. But why? What possible use could a mortal have for McNamara's potion?

And where was Desmarais now?

Girard cursed softly as he closed and locked the door to his hotel room. A short walk from the elevator to his room had him panting as if he had just run a marathon. It was hell to get old.

Shivering, he pulled a blanket from the bed and wrapped it around his shoulders, then slumped in the chair by the window. He was always cold now, his bones aching. Since using the last of the potion, he seemed to be aging faster than normal. True, he wasn't a young man anymore. Now in his seventies, he was well past the age when most men retired and settled down, but these last few days he had felt far older than his years. As for retiring, that was something he couldn't do until he had put a stake through Kaiden Thorne's black heart and taken his head.

Thorne. The vampire was over four hundred years old and still as strong as an ox.

Girard bolted upright. Of course! Why hadn't he thought of it before? Mortals grew weaker as they aged but not vampires. They grew stronger with every passing year.

Girard snorted in disgust. Why was he wasting time worrying about McNamara's potion? Even if he found the missing ingredient and managed to recreate the potion, it wouldn't keep him alive forever. Sure, it might extend his life and restore his vigor for another ten or twenty years, but he was bound to die eventually. But vampires . . . ah, vampires didn't grow old and weak. And if they were careful, they never died.

What if he became a vampire?

Girard shook his head, stunned by the direction his thoughts were taking. Vampires were loathsome creatures, yet he couldn't help envying them their vigor and longevity. What he was thinking was tantamount to treason. He was a slayer, descended from a long line of hunters. And yet the hunters grew old and died while the vampires remained.

Of course, the answer was so clear, he was amazed he hadn't thought of it sooner. If he became one of the Undead, he could hunt vampires forever.

He laughed out loud as inspiration washed over him.

He didn't need the damn formula.

He needed a vampire.

Chapter 12

Sky pulled a chair up to the front room window, then sat down, her elbows braced on the sill, and watched Kaiden mow the lawn. Maybe she was crazy, but she loved watching him. There had been a time, years ago, when he had always mowed his yard at night. She had never figured out why, and then, for no reason she could discern, he stopped cutting the grass in the dark and did it during the day, like everyone else. And now he was mowing the lawn in the dark again. Why?

Earlier, she had been upset when Thorne told her the man in the gray cloak—Desmarais—had been nearby. Of course, enigmatic creature that he was, Thorne hadn't explained how he had come by that information. He had, however, assured her that the monk was gone and that she had nothing to worry about. As much as she wanted to believe him, it hadn't kept her from making sure all the doors and windows were locked and all the curtains fully drawn save for the one she was now peeking through.

It was soothing, somehow, sitting there watching Kaiden cut the grass. Bathed in silver moonlight, he looked like some kind of otherworldly creature and she imagined that he was a humanoid version of E.T., a tall, dark, sexy alien being from some distant planet who had inadvertently been left behind and had had to learn to adapt to life on Earth.

She laughed softly, amused by the whimsical turn of her thoughts. Otherworldly, indeed. And yet, there was something inherently mysterious about Kaiden that didn't make her fantastical thoughts seem all that far-fetched.

Feeling the need to look into his eyes, to hear her name on his lips, she decided he needed a cup of coffee to warm him up. It would give her the perfect excuse to go over there. After all, it was cold outside.

Hurrying into the kitchen, she quickly poured him a cup of hot coffee, added milk and a heaping teaspoon of sugar, and carried it across the street.

He looked up, surprised, when she approached him. "Sky! What are you doing here?"

"It's cold. You're working hard." She shrugged as she offered him the cup. "I thought you could use this."

"Thanks." Thorne kept his features carefully impassive. Only days ago, he had loved the strong smell of freshly brewed coffee. Now, it was all he could do not to grimace with distaste. Drinking it was out of the question. "I think I'll finish the yard first, if you don't mind."

"No, of course not." She smiled up at him. "Maybe I'll drink this cup and bring you a fresh one later."

"Good idea." He returned the mug, wondering how he could refuse the next cup without hurting her feelings.

"Mind if I stay and watch?"

"Not at all," he said with a teasing grin, "but I'd have to charge admission." He had sensed her watching him before he had looked across the street and glimpsed her in the window. "You might be more comfortable watching from the window. Like you said, it's cold out here." For her, anyway. The cold no longer bothered him.

Sky felt a rush of heat climb up her neck to her cheeks. How had he known? She had done her best to stay out of sight.

A faint smile tugged at the corners of his mouth. "Next

time turn the lights off behind you," he suggested, and her humiliation was complete.

"I'll just go crawl in a hole now," she said, her gaze sliding away from his.

"Don't go," Thorne said, chuckling. "I'm about through here anyway. Instead of coffee, why don't you come in for a glass of wine?"

"Sounds wonderful," she said, thinking that her eager acceptance was just one more sign of how badly smitten she was with Kaiden.

While he parked the mower alongside the garage, she poured the coffee into the gutter, then followed Kaiden into the house and took a seat on the sofa while he filled two glasses with wine. It was becoming a habit, she thought, sharing a glass of port with Kaiden, a habit she thoroughly enjoyed.

Sky placed her empty cup on the end table, smiled when Kaiden handed her a glass, then joined her on the sofa. She glanced at him, then looked away. Something was different about him. She studied him surreptitiously for a few moments, and then frowned. He looked as handsome and virile as always, and yet, more so. His hair looked thicker, blacker, his voice seemed deeper, more resonant. How was that possible?

"Something wrong?" he asked.

"No," she said quickly, hating the quaver in her voice. "Why should anything be wrong?"

He cocked his head to the side, his eyes narrowing.

Unable to think of anything to say, Sky sipped her wine, wondering why she suddenly felt on edge, like a rabbit who had stumbled into a lion's den.

Thorne leaned back against the sofa, his mind brushing hers. It took only a moment to realize what was bothering her. His preternatural powers had returned in full. Without realizing it, her subconscious had sensed the change in him, the subtle alterations in his appearance, the inherent glamour that was part of being a vampire. She was also wondering why he had started mowing the yard after dark again. In the summer, he could have used the heat as an excuse, but it was late fall now and the days and nights were cool.

"More wine?" he asked.

"Yes, please." Sky worried her lower lip with her teeth as he refilled her glass. Maybe she was imagining things.

Thorne resumed his seat. Her nearness tempted him, her blood sang to him. The fact that she had once had a crush on him was flattering. Knowing that she wanted him now was more exhilarating than the wine.

"Skylynn."

When she looked up at him, he caught and held her gaze with his. Taking the glass from her hand, he set it on the end table beside his own.

Holding out his hand, he murmured, "Come to me, Sky."

She scooted closer to him without question, her gaze slightly unfocused.

He kissed her, his lips gentle on hers, and then kissed her again. The taste of the wine that lingered on her sweet lips was a potent combination. He stroked her back with one hand while the other slid up into her hair.

"Ah, Sky, what am I to do with you?"

Trapped in the web of his gaze, she remained pliant in his embrace. At his command, she closed her eyes and slept.

Leaning forward, he pressed his lips to the pulse beating slow and steady in the hollow of her throat and then, unable to resist, he ran his tongue along the side of her neck, just below her ear.

Filled with soul-deep regret for what he was about to do, he murmured, "Forgive me," and then he took that which he so desperately craved.

Sweet. Warm. Ambrosia for a starving man.

It required every ounce of willpower he possessed to

draw back. He brushed a wisp of hair from her cheek, wondering if he dared risk taking one more taste.

He was still debating when her eyelids fluttered open. She stared up at him, her expression confused. "What happened?"

Thorne frowned. No one had ever roused before he'd awakened them. "You fell asleep."

"I did?" Easing out of his arms, she blinked several times. "That wine must be stronger than I thought. What time is it?"

"A little after ten."

"I should go home." She levered herself off the sofa, then swayed unsteadily.

Thorne rose quickly, one arm snaking around her waist to steady her.

After easing her onto the sofa again, he thrust one of the wineglasses into her hand. "Drink this."

"Hair of the dog?" she murmured with a wry grin.

"Something like that. Just drink it."

She took several sips, her gaze fixed on his face, her brow furrowed.

"Is something wrong?" he asked.

"I don't know. I had the weirdest dream."

"Oh?" He lifted one brow. "Care to share it?"

She shook her head. "I don't think so. It was silly."

"I could use a good laugh," he muttered, sitting on the arm of the sofa.

She blinked several times, then lifted her shoulders and let them fall. "I dreamed you were a vampire."

She had expected him to laugh; instead, he looked at her sharply. "Go on."

"It was such a strange dream." She ran her hand along the side of her neck. "Do you remember that Halloween when I came trick-or-treating at your house after Sam told me you were a vampire? I must have been thinking about that before I fell asleep."

He nodded. "That would explain it."

"I guess so," she agreed, and then frowned. "It seemed so real when you bit me. Things like that aren't supposed to hurt in a dream."

"And it hurt when your dream vampire bit you?"

"Not exactly." She stared at him, a faint smile playing over her lips. "You're beautiful, you know." She laughed softly, her gaze sliding away from his as she set the glass aside. "I know the preferred word is *handsome,* but . . ." She shrugged. "I had such a crush on you when I was a teenager."

He grinned inwardly, remembering the notebook covered with red hearts.

"While my girlfriends were fantasizing about Orlando Bloom and Johnny Depp, I daydreamed about making love to you." She gazed into his eyes, deep dark eyes, while she ran her fingertips along the line of his jaw.

"If you keep looking at me like that, we're going to make love for real," he said, his voice tight. "Right here, right now."

"I'd like that."

He stared at her, wondering if it was the wine making her so bold. He could think of a hundred reasons why making love to Skylynn would be a bad idea, but none of them seemed to matter, not when she was so close, so willing. He had waited such a long time for this moment.

He slid down onto the sofa beside her, his arm wrapping around her shoulders. She leaned into him and then, cupping his face in her hands, she pressed her lips to his, ever so gently. Her lips were warm, her tongue sweet with the taste of the wine. The scent of musk rose from her heated skin. Her hair carried the lingering fragrance of sunshine and strawberry shampoo.

With a low growl, he swept her into his arms and carried her swiftly up the winding staircase and down the carpeted hallway to the master bedroom. A thought lit a fire in the hearth. Cradling her to his chest with one arm, he used his free hand to pull down the covers on the bed, then lowered her onto the mattress.

His gaze met hers, one brow arched as he gave her one last chance to change her mind. When she didn't say anything, he stripped down to his briefs, then waited to see if her wine-induced courage would desert her.

Sky's gaze moved over him. Mercy, but he was gorgeous. She had seen him without his shirt before, seen him in nothing but a pair of trunks, but this was different. Never before had she realized how broad his shoulders were, or how muscular he was. He gave new meaning to the words *six-pack abs*. The black briefs he wore did nothing to disguise his burgeoning desire.

Thorne watched as Sky rose to her knees and began to undress, her cheeks growing pinker by the minute. He thought it odd that she was embarrassed. After all, she had been married once, however briefly. He wondered if her husband had been her first lover and felt an unmistakable rush of jealousy at the thought of another man holding her, touching her.

She was beautiful, more beautiful than any woman he had ever known. His yearning grew stronger, hotter, with each newly revealed expanse of satiny skin.

When she finished undressing, she quickly slid under the covers. "Are you going to stand there all night? It's lonely in this big old bed."

She didn't have to ask him twice. Removing his briefs, he joined her under the covers and drew her into his arms.

"I've waited a long time for this," she murmured, snuggling against him.

"Not as long as I have."

She smiled up at him. "I never thought this would happen." Her hands slid over his skin, measuring the width of his shoulders before sliding down his arms. She smiled when he flexed his biceps.

Thorne drew her closer, molding her body to his. She was soft, supple, her skin smooth, warm against the coolness of his own. He stroked her lightly from shoulder to thigh, caressing each curve, lingering on the swell of her breasts, the smooth contours of her hips. Every stroke, every caress, aroused his desire and his hunger. He told himself to go slow. He wasn't yet in full control of his vampire nature; if he wasn't careful, he was liable to go too far, take too much, but with each kiss, his self-control grew weaker, his insatiable hunger stronger.

With a low growl, he rose over her, his only thought to satisfy his desire, to quench his raging thirst.

Caught up in the sheer ecstasy of Kaiden's caresses, Sky writhed beneath him, wanting to be closer, closer. She basked in the touch of his hands, reveled in his kisses, which were sometimes sweet and tender and sometimes more ardent.

She had been a virgin when she'd married Nick. With no one to compare him to, she had assumed that all men made love the way her husband did. He had rarely satisfied her, but, being inexperienced, she had blamed herself for the lack of fire in their relationship. And so had Nick. There had been no one in her bed since her divorce.

She closed her eyes, moaning softly as Kaiden rained butterfly kisses along the side of her neck. She had never known lovemaking could be so wonderful, never dreamed she was capable of such passion. With Nick, she had been shy, inhibited, and unfulfilled.

With Kaiden, she felt free, alive. Desirable. There was no need to be afraid or embarrassed to tell him that she needed him, that she wanted him more than her next breath. Love, she thought, this was what love felt like. Warm and safe with nothing held back. She ran her hands over his arms, his back, his chest, reveling in the feel of his skin beneath her fingertips, the way his muscles flexed at her touch, his low groan of pleasure as she caressed him.

She whispered his name, and then, wanting to see his face as his body melded with hers, she opened her eyes.

For a moment, she could only stare at him, too stunned to move, too dumbfounded to believe what she was seeing.

"Your eyes," she gasped. "They're . . . they're red!" She blinked, certain she must be seeing things. "Red," she repeated. "And glowing!"

"Skylynn . . ."

She might have dismissed the strange glow in his eyes as a trick of the light from the flames, but his fangs . . . yes, real fangs . . . couldn't be explained away. With sudden clarity, she realized that the fangs she had seen on that long-ago Halloween night hadn't been plastic.

"Skylynn, listen. I can explain . . ."

She shook her head in disbelief. There was no need for an explanation, not with the truth staring her in the face. Sam had been right all the time!

With a shriek, she brought her knee up, hard and fast, catching Kaiden square in the groin.

He let out a harsh groan and rolled onto his side.

Scrambling out of the bed, Sky ran out of the bedroom as if all the hounds of hell were snapping at her heels. She descended the stairs two at a time and hit the first floor running. She paused in the entry only long enough to grab Kaiden's long black coat and wrap it around her nakedness before she bolted out the door and ran across the street.

Safely inside her own house, Sky shut the door and turned the lock, then stood there, her heart pounding, her breath coming in painful gasps, while the word *vampire* screamed in her mind, over and over again.

* * *

Grimacing, Thorne sat up. Well, the cat was out of the bag now, he thought bleakly. And all because he couldn't control his lust or his hellish thirst. He groaned as he swung his legs over the side of the bed. Damn! She sure knew where and how to cool a man's ardor. If he had been a normal man, he would probably never get an erection again.

Grunting softly, he eased off the mattress and limped into the bathroom. In the shower, he turned on the taps and let the hot water sluice over his back and shoulders while he considered his options. He could pack up and leave town and never see her again. He could get dressed and go across the street and try to explain. Or he could simply wipe everything that had happened between them from her mind.

Leaving town held no appeal.

Explaining the last eight years might take a lot of . . . explaining.

As for erasing everything that had happened between them since he'd returned to town, he decided to keep that option open until he had tried door number two.

Stepping out of the shower, he went to the bedroom window and glanced at the house across the street.

It looked like every light in the place was on. All the curtains in the front of the house were closed. He was pretty sure all the doors and windows were locked up tight, too. Well, he couldn't blame her for being scared. She was only human, after all, reacting the way any mortal would when confronted with a monster.

Not much point in going over there tonight, he thought with a rueful grin. She would never invite him in. Of course, since she had invited him in once, he didn't have to ask for her permission. Or go through the door. But it was unlikely she was aware of that.

Thorne raked his fingers through his hair. He could just imagine Sky's reaction if he suddenly appeared in her living room. Especially in his current state of undress!

Dammit! He had known better than to take her to bed, known it would be dangerous when he wasn't fully in control of his restored vampiric powers, his thirst, or much of anything else. But it was hard to think straight when the beat of her heart sang to him, when the scent of her blood enflamed him, when a single kiss went through him like chain lightning.

How was he ever going to repair the damage he'd done?

Sky went through the house a second time, making sure all the doors and windows were locked, then paced the living room floor, trying to remember everything she had ever heard about vampires, but all she could recall was that they drank blood and slept in coffins.

Only one place to find the answers, she thought. Thank goodness for Google! Sitting at her computer, she quickly typed "vampire" into the search engine, then sat back, stunned by the number of hits that came up. Good grief, there were hundreds, maybe thousands, of vampire Web sites.

She picked one at random, clicked on vampire traits, and quickly scanned the list. Vampires could transform themselves into mist, bats, and wolves. They couldn't cross running water, were repelled by garlic and crosses, were burned by silver and holy water, and didn't cast a reflection in a mirror.

She frowned. That couldn't be true. She had seen Kaiden's reflection when they danced together.

Another site noted that the Undead couldn't enter a dwelling without an invitation. A footnote at the bottom of the page explained that such an invitation could be revoked by merely saying the words.

"Could it be that easy?" Sky muttered. Feeling a little foolish, she took a deep breath, then murmured, "Kaiden

Thorne, I hereby revoke any and all invitations, past and present, whether extended by myself or my grandfather . . ."

Her grandfather? Had he known about Kaiden? Of course he did. She remembered the night she had crept down to the lab and heard the two of them talking. Granda had been experimenting on Kaiden, she was certain. It explained so much.

"By myself or my grandfather," she repeated, And then, as an afterthought, she added, "Or Sam." She nodded once. "That should cover it," she said, and resumed her research.

Every country in the world had legends about vampires. In the old days, unexplained sickness and death were often attributed to the work of the Undead. A plague in the village? Must be a vampire on the loose. Did your cow suddenly dry up? Could be a vampire in the neighborhood.

Sunlight would destroy a vampire. Which explained why Kaiden mowed his yard in the dark. But didn't explain how he had been able to do it during the day only weeks ago.

Other ways to destroy a vampire included lopping off its head or driving a wooden stake into its heart. The best way was to employ both methods, then burn the body and scatter the ashes.

Sky shuddered as she imagined chopping off Kaiden's head. Had people really done that? Her stomach clenched just thinking about it.

If you couldn't bring yourself to chop off the creature's head, it was believed that driving a stake through its heart and into the ground would keep the thing from rising again. Burying it facedown was also recommended to keep the Undead in the ground where they belonged, the belief being that if they tried to dig their way out, they would only dig themselves deeper into the earth.

She skimmed several other Web sites, but most of them said basically the same thing. Vampires were evil, soulless creatures, parasites who survived on the blood of humans. Until Bram Stoker published his now-famous book, vampires had been pretty much off the radar. The story of Dracula had revived people's interest in the paranormal and the occult. Then Bela Lugosi came along and portrayed the infamous count in a movie. Anne Rice wrote a bestseller. Frank Langella played Dracula. His sexy portrayal on the Broadway stage had women swooning in their seats. Sky had seen the movie version. It took very little imagination to picture Kaiden Thorne in the role. No acting required.

Kaiden was a vampire. He had been a vampire when she went trick-or-treating at his house. He had been a vampire when she drew all those silly hearts on the cover of her notebook. He had been a vampire when he kissed her . . . and when she kissed him back.

Pushing away from the desk, she went into the living room and peeked out the front window. There were no lights showing in the house across the street. What was he doing? What was he going to do with her?

The thought made her shiver. She was pretty sure that he didn't go around telling people what he was. She hadn't seen any mobs with pitchforks lately, but if there were vampires, there might still be vampire hunters. Did vampires dispose of mortals who inadvertently discovered their secret? Or did they turn them into monsters like themselves? She supposed it was wishful thinking to hope he would just go away.

Lordy, what should she do? Call the police? She shook her head. What could the cops do? What to do, what to do? Search the phone book for Vampire Hunters R Us? Stock up on holy water? Carry a wooden stake and a hammer in her back pocket?

She crossed her arms over her breasts and took several deep breaths.

"Calm down, Sky, you're getting hysterical." But she couldn't help it. It all seemed so Stephen King-ish. Ordinary girl meets monster in small town.

It was late, she thought, yawning. She should go to bed. "Yeah, like that's gonna happen tonight," she muttered.

Smothering another yawn, she went into the living room, then settled down on the sofa and snuggled under a soft, furry blanket.

She would watch TV tonight.

She could sleep in the morning.

Like the vampire across the street.

Chapter 13

Girard sat on the sofa in his hotel room, a cup of coffee cooling on the table beside him while he thumbed through the battered notebook he had compiled over the years. It held the names of all known existing vampires, vampire slayers, and vampire hangouts.

As might be expected, big cities had the highest concentration of vampires and vampire clubs. It was easier for the monsters to hide in towns with large populations, easier to hunt in big cities. There were more transients in big towns, which meant fewer people who would be missed. Another draw was that in cities like L.A. and New York, people tended to ignore those who were a trifle bizarre in their behavior or appearance.

Girard grunted with satisfaction when he found a Goth club only a few miles away. He knew he was taking a chance, approaching a vampire and asking for the Dark Gift, but what the hell, life was a crap shoot. If his father had been a doctor instead of a slayer, Girard had no doubt that he would have learned how to wield a scalpel instead of a wooden stake and a mallet.

Going into the bedroom, he changed into a pair of black slacks and a long-sleeved black sweater. He slicked back his hair, swearing softly as he caught sight of his reflection in the mirror. He had been a handsome man in his youth, his skin smooth, his hair thick and black, his shoulders broad and unbowed. Now, his hair was thin and gray, his skin as wrinkled as the hide of an elephant, his shoulders stooped, his eyes pale and sunken. McNamara's potion hadn't restored his youth, but it had restored his vigor, taken the gray from his hair, smoothed his skin, put the starch back in his posture.

Dammit! Becoming a vampire wouldn't restore his youth, either, but it would give him immortality and the strength of twenty men.

A last glance in the mirror and he went to the minibar. He poured himself a good stiff drink, downed it in a single swallow before grabbing his keys and heading out the door.

The Scarlet Cabaret was exactly what it looked like—a hangout for Goths and vampires, real or make-believe. Girard thought of all the alternative lifestyles of the last fifty years—the rockers of the fifties, the long-haired, anti-war, peace-loving hippies of the late sixties, the punk movement in the seventies. None had lasted as long as the Goths. The Goth crowd loved all things dark and Victorian.

Girard paused at the club's entrance, weighing the wisdom of what he was about to do. Chances were good that there was at least one dyed-in-the-wool vampire inside. He hoped it was a young one who had never heard of Girard Desmarais.

Wiping the sweat from his brow, he paced away from the door. There was no discounting the danger of what he was contemplating. A young vampire could inadvertently kill him while attempting to turn him. An old one who suspected who he was would likely kill him out of hand. There was, after all, no love lost between vampires and slayers.

Putting his fears behind him, Girard walked quickly

back to the entrance, pushed the door open, and stepped inside. It took a moment for his eyes to adjust to the dim interior. Lit only by candles, the large room was very nearly dark. The air reeked of perfume, perspiration, and weed. As was to be expected, black was the dominant color of choice for décor, clothing, and makeup.

Girard was aware of several covert glances as he moved toward the long, narrow bar and ordered a shot of whiskey, neat. Men and women at the bar edged away from him as if he were a leper. He wasn't offended. He was new here and these people were suspicious of strangers, and rightly so.

He remained at the bar, quietly observing the patrons. As far as he could tell, only mortals were present. He ordered another drink, and then another.

Girard was about to call it a night when the atmosphere in the room changed. He noticed it first as a sort of tingle that skittered over his skin, raising the hair along the back of his neck. It was evident that the others in the club felt it, too. There was an instant when all movement came to an abrupt halt, when everyone's attention swung toward the entrance.

The vampire was female. Even in the subdued lighting, Girard could see that her hair was dark brown, her eyes a brilliant green against the alabaster of her skin. She drifted into the room, her steps so light he had to look twice to see if her feet were touching the floor. She wore black, of course, the silky stretch pants clinging to her lower body like a second skin, the black shirt a whisper of silk covering just enough for modesty's sake.

Girard was an old man, but not so old he couldn't appreciate a beautiful woman. Or imagine taking her to bed, which was certainly what every other male in the room was fantasizing about.

He was startled when she moved purposefully to his side. His heart seemed to skip a beat as she gazed at him through the veil of her lashes. A faint smile played over her crimson lips.

Girard had never considered himself to be a coward, but the intensity of her regard brought a cold sweat to his brow. "What do you want?" he asked brusquely.

"You were looking for a vampire, were you not?" she asked in a deep, velvety voice.

"How . . ." He cleared his throat. "How did you know that?"

She shrugged, as if the answer should be obvious. "I can give you what you want." Her eyes flashed red as she placed the tip of one well-manicured fingernail over the rapidly beating pulse in the hollow of his throat. "Are you ready?"

He swallowed hard. Was he ready? He closed his eyes while his mind reviewed his options: grow weaker, older, and die, or live forever with a vampire's strength and pre-ternatural power? There really was no choice.

He opened his eyes, his gaze meeting hers. "I'm ready."

A smile that could only be called wicked played across her lips as she took his hand in hers and led him out of the club.

Before he could ask where they were going, they were there.

Girard shook his head. "What happened? Where are we?"

"My place, of course. Do you like it?"

"What's not to like?" he muttered as he glanced around. The room could only be described as opulent. The walls were white, the furniture deep red velvet, the tables black lacquer. A big-screen TV hung from the wall over a low, white marble fireplace. Black and red candles of every shape and size adorned the mantel, the tables, a bookshelf. His feet made no sound in the plush deep gray carpet as she led him out of the room and down a narrow hallway into a large bedroom that was just as sumptuous as the living room.

The round bed in the middle of the floor was topped by

a thick black quilt and six or seven pink and white throw pillows in varying shapes and sizes. Candles were plentiful in this room, too, their yellow flames casting the room in a soft, golden glow. A chaise lounge covered in black velvet occupied one corner.

She dropped onto it, then patted the place beside her. "Come, Girard."

His feet felt weighted with lead as he crossed the thick burgundy carpet toward her. This was it. The end of one life and the beginning of another. Unless . . . He shook the thought from his mind. Surely, if she was going to kill him, she wouldn't have brought him to her home. Would she?

He was trembling uncontrollably when he sat beside her.

"There's nothing to be afraid of," she murmured, stroking his cheek. "When you rise tomorrow night, you will be strong again, virile, vital. Isn't that what you want?"

He nodded, suddenly incapable of speech as her eyes went red.

She smiled, revealing a hint of fang and then, with the speed of a striking cobra, she wrapped her arms around him and buried her fangs in his throat.

He cried out once, the instinct to survive overwhelming all other thoughts until, suddenly, it didn't seem to matter anymore. The world faded away as he grew weaker, weightless. His eyelids closed, seemingly of their own accord, and he imagined he was swimming in a tranquil sea of bright crimson.

And then everything went black.

Chapter 14

Sky woke abruptly. Jackknifing into a sitting position, she glanced around the living room, relieved to see that it was morning. She had survived the night. She was safe until sundown.

Safe from Kaiden Thorne.

Scrambling to her feet, she grabbed her cell phone, called the airport, and booked a flight to Chicago. When that was done, she hurried up the stairs, threw a few things into a suitcase, changed her clothes, and drove to the airport.

Two hours later, she was airborne.

With a sigh, she closed her eyes and forced herself to relax. She had never cared for flying, but right now she was grateful for anything that would put a lot of miles between herself and Kaiden as quickly as possible.

She came awake to the sound of the flight attendant announcing that the weather in Chicago was a chilly forty-two degrees.

Feeling as though she was in a fog, Sky collected her luggage, stowed it in the trunk of her rental car, and left the airport.

And all the while, the words *Kaiden is a vampire* played through the corridors of her mind, over and over again.

It felt strange, climbing the stairs to her apartment. So much had changed in such a short time. Her view of the world and her place in it had shifted radically. If there were vampires, she shuddered to think of what else might be out there.

She nodded to old Mrs. Cranston as they passed each other on the stairs. Mrs. Cranston was an odd duck if ever there was one. Summer or winter, she wore men's tennis shoes, broomstick skirts, brightly colored blouses, a long brown coat, and a floppy-brimmed straw hat adorned with a big purple flower.

Sky took a deep breath when she reached the landing. Hers was the only apartment on the third floor. She unlocked the door and stepped inside. The living room looked just as she had left it. Her blue jacket lay on the floor beside her snow boots, the heavy coat she had decided to leave behind was folded over the back of a chair. Her plants had withered; the furniture was covered with a fine layer of dust.

She dropped her suitcase beside the sofa and went into the kitchen. The words *Kaiden is a vampire* echoed through her mind while she watered the plants, dusted the furniture, vacuumed the rugs.

Moving like a zombie, she went into the bedroom and began taking her clothes from the closet and laying them out on the bed.

Kaiden is a vampire.

The words continued to circle through her mind like a vulture over a fresh kill while she folded her clothes. She stuffed the essentials in a suitcase and put the rest of her things aside to be packed into boxes later. She cleaned out the bathroom shelves and drawers.

In the living room, she dropped onto the sofa and stared blankly at the floor. Maybe she shouldn't go back to California. Maybe she should sell Granda's house and stay here. She was pretty sure Mr. Laskey would let her have her old job back.

Kaiden is a vampire.

What, exactly, did that mean as far as she was concerned? And how did she really feel about it, deep down
inside? The only word that came to mind was *scared*: totally, completely freaked out. It was her Halloween nightmare come true. Vampires existed. And if they existed,
what about all the other monsters that Sam and Granda had
assured her were just in fables and old wives' tales? An odd
question for a woman her age and yet, learning that Kaiden
was a vampire had turned her world upside down. Maybe
the sky wasn't blue. Maybe the world wasn't round. Maybe
good didn't always triumph over evil.

Maybe she was going out of her mind.

She sat there for a long time, trying to decide what to
do. She had a good job in Chicago, assuming Mr. Laskey
would take her back. She had recently bought new drapes
for her apartment. Her best friend was here. Harry was here,
although that wasn't necessarily a reason to stay.

She blew out a sigh of exasperation. Maybe she should
just go back to California. You couldn't beat the weather
there. She loved that you could go to the beach and the
mountains in the same day, that you could wear shorts all
year long. If she stayed in Chicago, she would have to sell
Granda's house and that just seemed wrong. All of her best
memories were there.

And Kaiden was there. She told herself that was a bad
thing, but the truth was, she missed him. Even knowing
what he was didn't change that. Worse, she thought she
might be seriously in love with him. Definitely a reason to
stay in Chicago because, try as she might, she couldn't
see any way for her and Kaiden to have a life together.

Frustrated because she couldn't decide what to do, she
picked up her phone and ordered a pizza, a Caesar salad,
and a soft drink for dinner, then went into the bathroom and
took a nice, long shower, hoping it would clear her mind.

She was standing there, eyes closed, hot water flowing

over her shoulders and down her back, when she heard
Kaiden's voice, softly entreating her to come home.

Expecting to see him standing behind her, she whirled
around, her feet slipping on the wet tile as she tried to cover
her nakedness with her hands.

Heart pounding with apprehension, she glanced around
the room. It took her a moment to realize he wasn't actually there, that the voice she had heard had come from
inside her head. And how scary was that?

Skylynn, come home, he had said. *Let's talk about it.*

Talk about it? Yeah, right. What was there to say? *Hi,
Kaiden, what's your favorite blood type? Tasted anybody
good lately?*

She lifted a hand to her throat as a horrible thought occurred to her. What if he had taken her blood?

Hands trembling, she turned off the taps, stepped out of
the shower, and reached for her robe. In the bedroom, she
sank down on the edge of the bed. Had Kaiden taken her
blood? Was that why she'd had that awful dream about
dying? Why she had dreamed that Kaiden was a vampire?
Had she known, subconsciously, that he was feeding on her?

The very idea made her grimace with revulsion. How
could he drink blood? What happened to the people he
drank from? Did he kill them? Why hadn't he killed her?

She cradled her head in her hands. If she didn't think of
something else soon, she was certain to have nightmares
tonight.

It took her several minutes to realize someone was ringing the doorbell. Rising, she hurried into the living room.
Kaiden had her so upset, she had forgotten all about the
pizza she'd ordered earlier.

Calling, "Hold on, I'm coming!" she pulled a twenty
from her wallet, opened the door, and felt all the blood drain
from her face.

Kaiden stood in the hallway, balancing the pizza and

salad boxes in one hand and holding a large Coke in the other.

"What are you doing here?" she exclaimed, hating the tremor in her voice.

"We need to talk."

"No, we don't." She shook her head. "Not now. I'm not ready. I don't know if I'll ever be ready."

"Dammit, Skylynn, stop looking at me as if I was the big bad wolf. I'm not going to eat you."

"But you have, haven't you? You don't have to answer. I can see the truth in your eyes." Eyes that were thankfully a dark brown instead of red and glowing.

"Here." He thrust the food at her. "Your pizza's getting cold."

Muttering "Thank you," she kicked the door shut with her foot. Feeling light-headed, she carried everything into the kitchen and set it on the counter, then dropped into one of the kitchen chairs, her head spinning. Fat lot of good running away did, she thought bleakly. How had he found her? Foolish question. Where else would she have gone but back to Chicago?

He had taken her blood. According to vampire lore, he would now be able to find her no matter where she went. Did it also give him access to her thoughts? Was that how she had heard his voice in her head?

She propped her elbows on the table, her chin resting on her hands. Like a nightmare that wouldn't end, it just got worse and worse.

Thorne stared at the closed door for several moments before he turned away. Well, what had he expected? That she would welcome him into her apartment with open arms? Intellectually, he had known that wouldn't happen, but he had hoped she would at least let him explain. Of course, now that he thought about it, there really wasn't much to say. He was a vampire and nothing could change that. Even McNamara's miraculous potion hadn't been able to accomplish it, though it had come close. So damn close.

Outside, Thorne glanced up and down the street and then, with no destination in mind, he began to walk. There had to be some way to reestablish communication with Skylynn, some way to get her to trust him again. Some way to get her back into his life.

Sky would never have discovered what he was if he could only have persuaded Paddy to give him the formula. If . . . if . . . if.

After a time, he found himself in the business district. Most of the places were closed for the night, but piano music drifted from the open door of a small neighborhood bar. He paused in the doorway a moment and then went inside. Other than the bartender, there were only two people in the place—a gray-haired man sipping a glass of beer and a frowsy, red-headed woman who appeared to be dozing in one of the booths.

Thorne ordered a glass of wine, which he carried to a booth in the rear. He stared at the burgundy, his mind going back in time, back to the night he had saved Paddy Mc-Namara's life . . .

It had been a cold night in January, a year or two after Thorne had returned to Vista Verde. He had been on the hunt when he heard a scuffle behind the old hospital on Mill Creek Road. Curious, he had gone to investigate and found two street toughs going through McNamara's pockets. Never one to pass up a meal, Thorne had quickly hypnotized the two thugs and drank from both. And then, for a lark, he had ordered them to go to the police station and turn themselves in. Thorne had been about to leave when Paddy muttered a word that glued Thorne's feet to the spot.

"Vampire."

Thorne had whirled around, his only thought to wipe the incident from his neighbor's mind.

Paddy held up one hand. "Before you kill me, Mr. Thorne, I think I can help you."

"Help me? Help me what?"

"Do you like being a monster?" Paddy asked boldly.

"What do you know about it?"

The old man gained his feet and dusted himself off. He was bleeding from his nose and mouth, one eye was already swollen shut. "I've been doing some experimentation with an elixir to prolong life. . . ."

Thorne snorted. "That's not something I need."

Paddy shrugged. "I think, with a few modifications, I can restore your humanity."

"You can make me human again?"

"Not exactly, but I think my formula might inhibit vampire tendencies. Wouldn't you like to walk in the sun again? Enjoy a glass of cold beer on a hot day? Eat mortal food?"

Thorne rocked back on his heels, intrigued by the man's offer. He hadn't seen the sun or eaten solid food in centuries.

"So, what do you say?" Paddy asked. "Are you game to give it a try?"

Thorne shook his head. "I don't think so." He didn't know what the old man was up to, but being a vampire wasn't an illness that could be treated. Once a vampire, always a vampire. "You'd better go get those cuts stitched up."

Paddy shrugged off Thorne's concern. "I'll be all right, thanks to you."

"Suit yourself. If you want to stay healthy, you won't tell anyone about me."

"Don't worry, Mr. Thorne. I can keep a secret. If you change your mind, you know where I live."

Thorne had thought about what McNamara said for several days. In the end, curiosity had sent him across the street and down to Paddy's lab where he had endured numerous excruciating tests. The worst part had been letting

Paddy secure him to a chair with thick silver chains while the old man conducted his experiments.

Thorne rubbed his wrists, remembering how the silver had burned through his clothing to his skin. It had taken years of tests, of trial and error, before Paddy came up with the right formula, but in the end, it had been worth it.

But that was all in the past. His problem now was how to restore Skylynn's trust in him. And that, he thought, would take an even bigger miracle than the one McNamara's potion had wrought.

Chapter 15

The last thing Girard Desmarais had seen before the world went black was the first thing he saw when his senses returned the next night—a pair of hell-red eyes.

"Am I dead?" He hadn't realized he had spoken aloud until she laughed.

"Undead," she purred. She ran her hand over his shoulder and up the side of his neck. "How do you feel?"

"I don't know." Sitting up, he scrubbed his hands over his face. His skin felt different, smoother, firmer.

Cassandra smiled a knowing smile but didn't say anything.

Girard lifted his hands. They were still spotted with age, but the tremor was gone.

He took a deep breath and felt the preternatural power rise up within him like the fountain of youth. "Is this how you feel? As if you could tear the world apart with your teeth?"

Her laughter filled the room. "I have, from time to time."

Springing to his feet, Girard paced the floor. He felt as strong and invincible as he had in his prime, as if the juices of youth were flowing through him again. "I should have done this years ago."

"Why didn't you tell me who you were last night?" The laughter was gone from her voice now and she was watching him like a cat at a mouse hole.

Fear skittered down Girard's spine. "What do you mean?"

"I know who you are, Girard Desmarais," she said, her voice as cold as the grave. "What you are."

"What am I?" His renewed vigor made him insolent.

"A hunter." Venom dripped from the words.

He didn't deny it. What was the point? As soon as she had taken his blood, all his secrets had been revealed. "Now what?"

She rose in a single fluid movement and in the blink of an eye, she stood before him. Even though he was a good six inches taller, there was no doubt in his mind who was stronger.

Her power pushed against him, forcing him to take a step backward. "I should destroy you, if for no other reason than to avenge those of my kind that you have destroyed."

Girard had known fear before, many times, but never anything like the gut-wrenching terror that trapped the breath in his lungs and turned his blood to ice. He had no doubt that she could destroy him with no effort at all.

"Nothing to say?" She raked her nail across his cheek, hard enough to draw blood. "Have you seen Kaiden lately?"

He hadn't thought his fear could get any worse. He had been wrong.

She leaned forward, licking the blood from his cheek. "Did you know I'm the one who brought him across?"

Incapable of speech, Girard shook his head.

"Still hunting him, are you?"

There was little to be gained by denying it.

She laughed softly. "You were no match for him as a mortal, even when you were in your prime. And you're no match for him now. If you want to enjoy your new life, I suggest you forget about avenging yourself on him." She circled him like a shark closing in on a wounded fish, her hand trailing over his back, his chest, coming to rest on his throat. "I was going to destroy you, but I've changed my mind. I'm curious to see how you adjust to your new life. But be warned. If you hurt Kaiden Thorne, you will answer to me."

The heat of her gaze seared him, hotter than a thousand suns.

Girard staggered backward, then tumbled onto the bed. Suddenly, becoming a vampire didn't seem like such a smart idea after all.

Her gaze burned into him a moment longer and then the red faded from her eyes.

"You must be hungry."

He nodded.

"Well, what are you waiting for?"

Gathering what dignity he could, he regained his feet and made a big production of straightening his clothing. "I was waiting to see if *I* was going to be *your* dinner."

She laughed, a remarkably youthful, sexy sound. "Let's go."

Chapter 16

Skylynn had spent a restless night after Kaiden's visit. She had gone to bed early, only to lie awake for hours sorting through her feelings.

The next morning, she awoke feeling as though she hadn't slept at all. Reluctant to face the day, she pulled the covers back over her head and went back to sleep.

It was midafternoon when she dragged herself into the kitchen. Two cups of strong coffee had her feeling a little better.

When she could think coherently, she dialed Tara's number.

"Hey," Tara said. "I was just going to call you. How are you?"

"I don't know."

"Uh-oh, what's wrong? Is it . . . you didn't . . . oh, Lord, it's not Sam, is it?"

"No, I still haven't heard anything."

"Thank goodness. Well, what is it then?"

"I'm so confused, I just don't know what to do."

"Sounds like man trouble to me. Come on, tell me all about it."

"You remember I told you about the guy across the street?"

"The odd one who mowed his yard in the dark? That guy?"

"Yeah."

"Don't tell me he's mowing the yard in the nude now."

"No, silly, nothing like that." Sky tucked her legs under her as she tried to decide what to say. "I've been seeing a lot of him, or I was."

"Really? I remember you said you had a crush on him when you were younger, but . . . well, isn't he a lot older than you are?"

"You have no idea," Sky muttered. "The thing is, I'm afraid that crush has turned into something much stronger."

"How strong?"

"I might be in love with him." *Admit it,* she thought. *There's no might about it.*

"Sky, that's great!"

"No, not so great. I found out something about him. Something I don't think I can live with."

"Oh, no, what is it? He's not already married, is he?"

"No, it's nothing like that. I can't tell you what it is. I'm not sure why I even called except I had to talk to someone."

"You can tell me. You know I won't tell anyone else."

"I wish I could, believe me, but I just can't."

"Is this one of those 'I could tell you but I'd have to kill you' kind of things?" Tara asked dryly.

"Sort of. The thing is, I just don't know what to do. He wants us to talk it over, but the thing is, talking won't help. It's part of him, something that can't be changed."

Tara made a soft sound of sympathy. "He's not impotent, is he?"

"No, silly."

"And you know that because . . . ?"

"Never mind."

"Well, I'd love to be able to give you some advice, but

without knowing what the problem is, all I can say is, if you really love him . . . well, I guess you just have to accept it if you can, and if you can't . . ."

"I know. Enough about me," Sky said, suddenly eager to change the subject. "How's the wedding coming along? Have you set the date yet?"

There was a long silence before Tara said, "No. My dad had a heart attack. He's scheduled for a triple bypass as soon as he's strong enough for the operation, so the wedding's on hold."

"Oh, Tara, I'm so sorry. Is there anything I can do?"

"Just pray for him."

"I will. Listen, I'm in town for a few days. Maybe we can get together. . . ."

"I wish I could, but I'm not home. My mom isn't handling this very well, so I took a leave of absence to stay with her."

"Of course, she needs you." Tara's parents lived in Vermont. "Keep in touch."

"I will. And let me know how things work out between you and . . . what's his name, anyway?"

"Kaiden."

"Oh, girl, you've got it bad, don't you? I can hear it in your voice."

"Yeah, I'm afraid so. Talk to you soon."

Skylynn sighed as she disconnected the call. You just never knew what twists and turns waited for you down the road.

She needed some fresh air. Grabbing her handbag, she hurried outside, got into her rental car, and drove to her favorite restaurant.

Lingering over a piece of blueberry pie, she contemplated going to a movie, but, mindful that Kaiden might still be in town, she hurried home, determined to be inside before dark.

After returning to her apartment, she went from room to

room to make sure she hadn't missed anything. With Tara out of town, there was no point in staying any longer.

Once everything was packed, she curled up on the sofa with an old photograph album that had belonged to her parents. As soon as she flipped to the first page, she was swept into the past. She smiled as she turned the pages. There were photos of her parents, of Granda and Grams, of herself and Sam, of numerous cats, rabbits, guinea pigs, and chickens. A photo of the dog that had eaten one of the chickens.

She leaned forward, her gaze narrowing as she studied an old photo of Kaiden's house. It had been taken on Halloween. She squinted at the image of the little girl in the fairy costume on the front porch. She remembered that night. It was the first time she had gone trick-or-treating at Kaiden's. Granda must have taken it before she turned and ran for home, screaming bloody murder. The next photo showed someone wearing a skeleton costume, doubled over laughing. Sam.

She thumbed through the pages, stopping when she came to a photo of Sam in his uniform. He looked so young, she thought, so proud. Where was he now? Would she ever see him again? As always, whenever she thought of her brother, she sent a silent prayer to heaven begging for his safe return.

Thorne stood on the sidewalk in front of Sky's apartment, considering and rejecting ways to get back into her good graces, or at least convince her to talk to him.

He could always force her to listen. It would be all too easy to overpower her will with his, to make her listen. If he was so inclined, he could mess with her mind. He could make her think she was in love with him, make her forget he was a vampire. He had to admit the idea was tempting except for one thing. He didn't want a robot.

He was still considering and rejecting ideas when a

subtle ripple in the air warned him he was no longer alone. He turned as the other vampire materialized beside him.

She was still the most beautiful creature he had ever known. Her hair fell in a long brown braid down her back, her eyes were still the greenest he had ever seen. Her skin was still like alabaster, clear and perfect.

"Death." Her name slipped past his lips, soft as a sigh.

She laughed softly. "I haven't gone by that name in centuries."

He wasn't surprised. Living as long as they did, vampires often changed their names, sometimes because of necessity, sometimes out of boredom.

"It was so old-fashioned," she explained airily. "No one believes in the old gods anymore. I go by Cassandra now. But enough about me. How have you been, Kaiden?"

"The same as always." He saw no reason to tell her of his brief stint as a near mortal. "What brings you here?"

"I thought you should know that I brought a friend of yours across."

That gave him pause. A friend? He didn't have any mortal friends, and damn few immortal ones. "Really? Who might that be?"

"Desmarais."

Thorne stared at her, unable to believe what he was hearing. "Why the hell would you do that?"

"I didn't know who he was until the deed was done." She held up her hand, silencing him. "I know, I should have been more careful, but"—she shrugged—"he was looking for a vampire, and I was hungry."

"Well, that's just great," Thorne muttered.

"I know he's been hunting you, but don't worry. I warned him that if he hurt you, he would answer to me."

"Hurt me? He wants my head."

"If he takes it, he'll lose his own."

"I'm sure that'll be a great comfort when the time comes."

"Very funny."

"As for Desmarais, I'm a big boy. I can fight my own battles."

"You know how mothers are," she said, grinning. "No matter how old our sons get, they're still our little boys."

Thorne snorted. "What the devil would you know about being a mother?"

Eyes narrowed, she scowled at him, and then shrugged. "What are you doing out here?" she asked, glancing up at the building.

"Nothing you need to know."

Her husky laugh rose in the air with the deep-throated resonance of a cathedral bell. "There must be a woman involved. I wonder, is she prey? Or lay?"

"Neither," he retorted, his voice little more than a growl.

"This one must be special," she said with a pout. "I was hoping you and I could spend some time together."

"Not right now."

"I can wait," she replied with ill-disguised arrogance.

She was gone before he could reply.

Thorne glanced up at Sky's apartment. Desmarais was a problem that could also wait. The feud between the two of them had been going on for decades, and whether the hunter was human or vampire was immaterial. For now, the only thing that mattered was reestablishing communications with Skylynn. Once that was done, he would find Desmarais and, hopefully, the missing ingredient in Paddy's formula.

She was dreaming. She had to be dreaming; there was no other explanation. One minute she was relaxing on a warm, sunny beach, laughing with Sam, and the next, she was wandering through a haunted house, her heart pounding loudly in her ears as she ran from room to room, looking for the only man who could save her.

And that was how she knew it was a dream. The only man indeed.

Wake up. She had to wake up. And even as she tried to escape sleep's hold, he appeared. Tall and dark, he loomed over her. A long black cape fell from his shoulders, making him seem even larger and more forbidding.

She stared into his eyes. "Go away. I'm dreaming."

"You must want me here," he said, his voice a husky purr. She shook her head. "No. That's impossible."

"Is it?" He held out his arms and she went to him willingly, her face lifting for his kiss, her eyelids fluttering down as his mouth closed over hers. Heat ignited in the deepest part of her being and ran through her veins like liquid fire. She clung to him, afraid to let go, as his tongue stroked her lower lip.

Her moan was part protest, part pleasure. In a distant part of her mind, she knew it had to be a dream because he was a vampire and she would never willingly have kissed him. Would she?

In the way of dreams, there was no sense of time passing. His lips moved over hers in a seemingly endless dance of seduction.

He continued to kiss her as he swept her into his arms and carried her up a long winding staircase that seemed to go on forever until, finally, he kicked open a door at the top of the stairs and stepped into a room as black as pitch. It was disorienting, being held in the dark by a man she couldn't see.

"A light," she murmured. "I want a light."

Wriggling out of his hold, she stumbled forward, searching for a window. Miraculously, her fingers slid over what felt like a velvet curtain and she drew it back, smiling as a shaft of bright golden sunlight illuminated the room.

Sunlight! No, she thought frantically, sunlight was bad. Clumsy in her haste, she tried to close the curtain, but it was too late.

There was a horrible cry, a hiss, the stink of burning flesh.
   She screamed, "No! No!" as Kaiden disintegrated before
her eyes, screamed again as an errant breeze whispered
through the room, scattering the ashes that had been left
behind.

   Sky bolted upright, her body bathed in perspiration.
"Kaiden!" She switched on the bedside light, her gaze
moving frantically around the room. Relieved to find
herself alone in her own apartment, she slumped back on
the pillows. That was by far the worst nightmare she had
ever had.

   She mopped her brow with a corner of the sheet, then
closed her eyes, waiting for her heart to stop pounding, her
breathing to return to normal.

   Lying there, recalling her dream and how horrified she
had been when Kaiden had been destroyed, she admitted
what she had feared all along.

   Human or vampire, she was in love with him.

Chapter 17

Girard sat up, instantly awake and alert. No aches and pains, no disorientation. He felt young, vigorous, and hungry.

"Ready to hunt?"

Vampire or not, having Cassandra materialize in front of him made him jump. "Dammit, woman, if I wasn't a vampire, you'd have given me a heart attack."

"Come along," she said with a toss of her head. "You still have a lot to learn about hunting."

Leaving his hotel room, they walked down the street side by side.

"Tonight we'll work on your technique. For one thing, it isn't necessary to terrorize your prey, or rip their throat to shreds," Cassandra remarked with a knowing grin. "Unless you enjoy it."

If he could, he would have flushed with shame. He hadn't meant to behave like the monsters he had once destroyed, but the smell of the woman's blood, the rapid beating of her heart, the scent of fear on her skin . . . he had been like an addict who was unable to control his addiction. He'd had no thought save one—to take what he so desperately craved as fast as he could.

"Nor is it necessary to kill them," Cassandra added.

"No?"

She shook her head in exasperation. "I thought you were a hunter. Don't you know anything about us?"

"Of course I do!" he exclaimed. "And one thing I know is that vampires kill! I watched Thorne kill my wife!"

"That was over thirty years ago."

"What difference does that make?" he demanded angrily.

"I also heard it was self-defense."

"Self-defense or not, my Marie is just as dead." Squaring his shoulders, Girard looked her in the eye. "Are you going to tell me you've never killed anyone?"

"No, but as I have always said, do as I say, not as I do. So, tonight, let's try a little restraint, shall we? I'll teach you how to hunt without killing. If you want to kill in the future, don't do it in any city where another vampire makes his lair, or your new life will be over before it's really begun. Most of us are very tidy. We don't like to leave bodies where they might be found. It's much easier to drink from a few and leave them alive, their memories wiped clean, than to dispose of a body drained of blood without arousing suspicion. Do you understand?"

He nodded curtly.

"Good. I'm assuming you know what will destroy you, and that you need to find a secure lair?"

"Of course I do," he muttered. "I'm not an idiot."

"To my knowledge, Kaiden is the only vampire who resides in Vista Verde. You would be wise to leave here as soon as possible. If you plan to stay in a town inhabited by a vampire older than you are, which will be every vampire you meet for a while, it is customary to make your presence known and ask permission to stay. Our numbers are not as large as they once were, but most big cities have their share of the Undead. If there are more than one or two, the oldest is usually designated as the Master of the City, and you would do well to stay in his or her good graces. Places like Vegas and Rio are popular with our kind as they attract a lot of tourists and transients."

She paused, her nostrils flaring. "Just ahead, a man and a woman. Do you smell them?"

Girard nodded, his whole body throbbing with anticipation.

"Remember, we're not going to kill them."

"Are you through lecturing me?" he asked impatiently.

"I don't like your tone."

"And I don't like being treated like a child."

She smiled in spite of herself. "Thus endeth the lecture. For the time being."

"About time! So, what are we waiting for?"

Chapter 18

Sky dropped her suitcases on the floor, then stretched her arms over her head. It was good to be home. She had arranged to have whatever she couldn't carry on the plane sent overland. Her apartment in Chicago had come furnished, so there hadn't been much to ship other than her winter wardrobe, about twenty pairs of shoes, her book collection, a few photo albums, a hope chest that had belonged to her grandmother, and a large box of odds and ends that she didn't need but couldn't part with.

She kicked off her shoes and ran a hand through her hair. Granda's house had always been home, and now it belonged to her. And Sam. How she wished her brother was here now.

Curious, she went to the front window and pulled back the curtain. Was Kaiden still in Chicago? Or had he returned to Vista Verde, as well? And if he had, what then?

Turning away from the window, she carried her suitcases upstairs. Why couldn't she have fallen in love with Harry? He was a nice enough guy, he made good money, had a promising future, and he loved her. But no, like Bella Swan, she had to fall in love with a vampire.

She grinned as she tossed her underwear into the top drawer of her dresser. Edward Cullen was pretty sexy, but her vampire was sexier.

Her vampire. Sky closed the drawer with a bang and began hanging her jeans in the closet.

Logically, she knew she should have nothing more to do with Kaiden Thorne. After all, she had seen a number of horror movies, and things rarely ended happily for the foolish female who fell in love with the sexy vampire or werewolf or mummy.

But all the logic in the world couldn't change how she felt about Kaiden. Right or wrong, vampire or not, she loved him and there was nothing she could do about it.

After putting everything away, she looked out the window. A single light burned in the front window of the house across the street.

Was it for her?

Was she crazy to be thinking about going over there, alone, at night? Maybe so, but if he'd wanted to hurt her or drain her dry or turn her into a monster, he'd had plenty of chances over the years.

But was giving him another chance now, when she knew what he was, a good idea? Or the stupidest thing she had ever done? She bit down on her lower lip. He had gone to Chicago to see her, claiming he wanted to talk. So, she would go over there and listen to what he had to say.

Before she could talk herself out of it, she took a quick shower, put on her favorite blue sweater and a pair of jeans, carefully applied lipstick and eye shadow, dabbed a little perfume behind her ears, and she was ready to go.

Humming softly to keep her courage up, she hurried down the stairs and ran across the street before she could change her mind.

The door opened before she rang the bell.

She wished she had a camera to capture the look of surprise on Kaiden's face, then wondered if vampires could be photographed.

"Sky." The tone of his voice mirrored the surprise in his eyes.

"Hi. Are you busy?"

"No." He frowned, a deep V forming between his brows. "Is something wrong?"

She shook her head. "You said we needed to talk." She bit down on her lip, suddenly uncertain. "So, talk."

"The front porch is hardly the place," he said, taking a step back. "Maybe you should come inside."

"Said the spider to the fly," she murmured as she crossed the threshold.

"We can go over to your place if that will make you feel safer," he said. "Or we can go to one of the clubs."

"No, here is fine." She stifled the urge to laugh at the look of bewilderment on his face.

Moving into the front room, she perched on the edge of the sofa. "I'm listening."

He looked down at her, his arms folded over his chest. "What do you want to know?"

"What do you think?" She looked at him as if he wasn't too bright. "This was your idea, remember?"

Thorne nodded. Why had he thought talking about this would be a good thing? What could he say? What should he say? Curious to know what she was thinking, he let his mind brush hers. He wasn't sure what he expected to find—confusion, fear, curiosity. Certainly not love and acceptance.

"You're not talking," she remarked, a faint smile playing over her lips.

"There's really not a lot to say. I was turned a long time ago. I've been around the world. I've seen some things, done some things I'm not proud of." He paused, wondering how honest to be.

"What kinds of things?"

"What do *you* think?"

"Oh." She chewed on the edge of her thumbnail, trying to find a tactful way to ask the question uppermost in her mind. In the end, she just blurted it out. "Do you still kill people?"

"No, not for a long time."

"Do you like being a vampire?" Even though she knew that's what he was, it was still a shock saying the word out loud, knowing it was true.

"What choice do I have? It's what I am."

"You weren't acting like one until just recently. Did Granda's potion have anything to do with that?"

"Everything." He sat in the chair beside the sofa, then leaned forward, his elbows braced on his knees. "Whatever was in it kept my vampire tendencies at bay and allowed me to live like a mortal. I tried like hell to recreate it, but like I told you, something's missing and no one knows what it is."

"Why did that man, Desmarais, want it? He's not a vampire."

"He is now."

"When did that happen?" she exclaimed.

"A few days ago. Apparently he went looking for a vampire to turn him."

Her eyes grew wide with disbelief. "Why would anybody do that?"

"I don't know for sure, of course. I don't know what effect Paddy's potion had on Desmarais, but I'm guessing it increased his vigor, made him stronger, maybe slowed the aging process. Without the potion . . ." He shrugged. "If you want to stop aging, becoming Nosferatu is the best way to do it."

Sky shuddered. "I hope you won't take offense at this, but I can't imagine why anyone would ever want to become a vampire," she said, and then frowned. "Did you want to be one?"

"No. The same vampire who turned Desmarais seduced me a few hundred years ago."

She blinked at him. "A few *hundred* years ago? How old are you, anyway?"

After a moment's hesitation, he said, "I've been a vampire for 432 years."

She stared at him, unable to think of anything to say. Four hundred and thirty-two years. It was impossible, incomprehensible. And even as she tried to wrap her mind around the idea of living for such a long, long time, she wondered what it would be like to stay forever young. She had watched Granda grow old, noticed as the lines and wrinkles multiplied year by year, watched his dark brown hair turn gray. She had listened to his complaints as his steps grew slow, his eyesight dimmed, his hearing faded. It was the price you paid for living a long life. Unless you were a vampire.

She studied Kaiden's face. His skin was unlined, his jaw line firm. There were no age spots on his hands, no gray in his hair. His dark eyes were vibrant.

Maybe being a vampire wasn't so bad, after all, she thought. Until she remembered the blood part.

Kaiden sat back, his gaze narrowing as he watched the play of emotions on Skylynn's face. He didn't have to read her mind to know what she was thinking.

"You're wondering about the blood," he said quietly.

"How can you . . . I mean . . ." She grimaced. "How can you bite people and drink their blood? It sounds so repulsive."

"It is, to a mortal. But you have to understand that when

you're a vampire, it's entirely different. You're different. The scent of mortal food, the taste, becomes repugnant."

"And all that changed, with Granda's potion?"

He nodded. "It was like being human again."

"Do you miss it?"

"Yes." He missed the sunlight, the food, the quiet that came with the lessening of his powers. He missed dreaming. With the potion, he'd even been able to avoid the Dark Sleep, that awful sense of falling into nothingness.

Leaning back on the sofa, Skylynn heaved a sigh. "It's all so . . . so . . ."

"Unbelievable? Incredible?"

"Exactly." She cocked her head to the side. "Do you sleep in a coffin?"

"No."

"What was in that big black box you brought with you when you first moved in?"

"I wasn't moving in," he said, grinning. "I was moving back."

"Back?"

"I've lived here, off and on, for the last 150 years."

She digested that a moment. Then, like a dog worrying over a bone, she said, "The box. What was in the box?"

"A coffin."

"But you don't sleep in it?"

"Not anymore."

"But you used to?"

He shrugged. "It felt right, when I was a new vampire."

"Do you still have it?"

"Yeah." He kept it in the basement. He wasn't sure why. It wasn't as if he needed a reminder of what he was, although, with Paddy's potion, he had been able to forget it for long periods of time.

"You've been a vampire for centuries," she remarked thoughtfully. "There must have been women in your life."

"Of course. I'm a vampire, not a eunuch, but those relationships never turned out well."

"What do you mean?"

He considered lying but decided she deserved to know the truth. "I never trusted most of them enough to tell them what I was. When they started to care too much, or I did, I left." He thought briefly of Mariana. She had fallen in love with him, had begged him to marry her, and when he refused, when he told her the truth in hopes of cooling her ardor, she had killed herself. Her death still weighed heavily on his conscience.

"Four hundred years is a long time to be alone," Sky mused thoughtfully. "Is it because of what you are that you never married? That you never let yourself care too deeply for anyone?"

"Not entirely." His gaze met hers, honest and direct. "It wasn't easy, watching you grow up. Even saying it out loud sounds twisted, like I was some dirty old lecher lusting after a young girl. But it wasn't like that. I wasn't lusting after you, but I'm a healthy male and I couldn't help noticing how pretty you were, couldn't help wishing that I was a teenage boy so I could take you to a football game, or out for a Coke, or steal a kiss at the movies."

"I had no idea."

"It's a good thing. Paddy would have had me arrested."

"You already knew I had a crush on you."

"Yeah. I sort of figured that out."

"How? I never said or did anything about it."

"Come on, Sky, I saw the way you watched me when I was out working in the yard. I heard you giggling with your girlfriends. . . ."

Sky stared at him, her cheeks burning with embarrassment as she recalled the afternoons she and Sally, who had been her best friend back then, used to sit on the porch and talk about him. "You heard that?"

Kaiden tapped his ear with his finger. "Preternatural hearing, remember?"

Mortified, she pressed her hands to her cheeks, then shook her head. "I don't know what to say."

He grinned at her. "Do you still think I'm as sexy as Rick Springfield?"

"I don't know. Can you sing 'Jessie's Girl'?"

"Only in the shower," Kaiden replied, and burst out laughing.

"Well, I think I'll just be going now," Sky muttered.

His hand closed over her wrist when she started to rise. "Come on, it was a long time ago. Besides, I was flattered." His gaze moved over her, all laughter gone from his expression. "Why did you really come here today?"

"Don't you know?"

"I guess I'm just an old romantic, but I want to hear you say it."

"I'm in love with you. And it's not a teenage crush this time. I love you and I don't know what to do about it, about what you are. I don't know how you feel about me. . . ."

He lifted one brow. "Come on, Sky Blue, you must know how I feel."

"Is there any chance for us?"

"That's up to you. I don't want to hurt you. If you want to give us a try, I'm willing. If not, I'll leave. Just tell me what you want."

"You," she said, her voice little more than a whisper. "I want you to make love to me. Here. Now."

"Sky!" Rising, he swept her into his arms and carried her swiftly up the stairs.

They undressed each other with fevered hands, then fell onto the bed, locked in each other's arms.

Thorne brushed his lips across her cheek. "Do you have any idea how beautiful you are?"

"You are."

Laughing softly, he rained kisses over her cheeks, the tip of her nose, along her collarbone, up the side of her neck. He ran his tongue ever so lightly over her shoulder. Her skin was soft, smooth, warm. He closed his eyes, fighting the urge to taste the warm red elixir he could smell flowing just beneath the surface of her skin.

He hadn't yet fed.

It wasn't safe for her to be here, in his bed, in his arms. Not now.

She wriggled against him, her body undulating against his groin.

He closed his eyes and prayed for patience. Things were moving too fast. For her sake, he needed to feed before this went any further. "Skylynn . . . wait."

"No." She kissed him, her tongue sliding over his lips, dipping inside. "I've waited too long already."

"You don't understand. It isn't . . ."

She pressed her fingertips to his lips. "Stop talking. You're not taking advantage of me. I'm not some innocent child. I know what I'm doing. I know what I want."

He groaned softly, unable to resist the yearning in her voice, the taste of her lips, the touch of her breasts and belly against his skin as she rubbed herself against him in blatant invitation.

With a low growl, he rose over her. There would be no turning back now.

"Kaiden . . ."

He heard the sudden doubt in her voice, knew his eyes had gone red.

"Too late," he said, his voice gruff with desire. He caught both of her hands in his, holding them over her head as his mouth ravaged hers. "Too late," he lamented again, and with a hoarse cry of regret, he cocooned her in his embrace.

Her nearness enflamed his hunger, the touch of her satin-smooth flesh ignited his desire. He kissed her again, and yet again, his only thought to satisfy his hunger, his raging need to take everything she had to offer—her love, her life.

"Kaiden! Stop! You're hurting me."

Her voice, filled with soft entreaty and edged with fear, splashed over him like ice water, bringing him back to his senses.

Overcome with self-disgust, he released her immediately. When he started to rise, she wrapped her arms around him, holding him close. "Don't go."

"Sky, I don't want to hurt you."

She gazed up at him, her eyes shiny with unshed tears.

He brushed a few damp strands of hair away from her cheek. "It's better this way."

Sky shook her head, knowing if he left her now, she might lose him forever. "I'm not afraid of you."

"No?"

"No."

"You should be."

Cupping his face in her palms, she kissed him, pouring all her love and affection into that one lingering kiss.

He surrendered with a groan, damning himself for his weakness even as he slowly aroused her. She smelled so good, tasted so sweet, it took every bit of his considerable self-control to keep from hurting her as he claimed her for his own.

Skylynn woke slowly, reluctantly. She'd had the most amazing dream and she hated to see it end. Stretching her arms over her head, she drew in a deep breath, held it a moment before exhaling. If only reality was as wonderful as the erotic night she had imagined. In her dreams, Kaiden had made slow, sweet love to her, satisfying her every desire, fulfilling every fantasy she'd ever had. She smiled, thinking that if ordinary men knew what being a vampire could do for their libido, men all over the world would be lining up to join the ranks of the Undead.

Uttering a little sigh of contentment, she rolled onto her side and opened her eyes. The room was dark save for a fat white candle burning on the nightstand.

Two things became clear very quickly. She wasn't in her own bed. And fantasy and reality lay sleeping beside her.

With the realization that it hadn't been a dream came another memory. While making love, Kaiden had asked if he could taste her. Caught up in the throes of passion, she had acquiesced. Now, she lifted a hand to her neck, to the tender place just beneath her left ear. She didn't feel any bite marks, but the skin felt warm to her touch. Just a taste, he had said, but how much was a taste?

Thinking about it, she wondered why his drinking from her no longer seemed repulsive. Had he worked some sort of vampire mind meld to make her so agreeable? As much as she'd like to think he had forced her, she knew it wasn't true. She had wanted to please him, to ease his pain, and if she was going to be totally honest, to satisfy her own curiosity. She didn't know what it had been like for him, but, to her great surprise, she was eager to have him bite her again. It had been a remarkably sensual experience and had, to her astonishment, only made their lovemaking even more satisfying.

Propping herself up on her elbow, she studied the face of the man she loved. Funny, she had never noticed how long and thick his lashes were before. What was it like when he slept during the day? Was it like death? She glanced at his chest, startled to see that he wasn't breathing. Was that natural for vampires? Did he breathe during the day? He must, she thought. Surely she would have noticed if he didn't.

Curious, she touched his shoulder. His skin felt hard and cool. It hadn't felt that way last night. Quite the opposite, she mused with a grin. There had been so much heat between them, she was surprised the mattress hadn't gone up in flames.

If she called his name, would he hear her?

"Kaiden?"

Nothing.

She tried again, louder. "Kaiden?"

Still nothing.

She stared at him for several moments, then shouted, "Kaiden, help!"

The covers fell away from his chest as he jackknifed into a sitting position, his movement little more than a blur.

"Skylynn?" He frowned when he realized there was no danger. "What the hell?"

"I'm sorry. I was just, you know, curious to know . . ." Feeling suddenly foolish, she looked away.

Cupping her jaw in his hand, he gently forced her to look at him. "To know what?"

"If you could hear me while you're sleeping."

"Ah."

"Are you mad at me?"

"Of course not. I don't hear ordinary sounds, but after so many years, I have a keen sense of self-preservation. It's not easy for anyone intent on destroying me to sneak up on me."

She glanced at his chest, relieved to see that he was breathing.

He followed her gaze. There was no need to ask what she was thinking. "Anything else you want to know?" He smothered a yawn with his hand.

She shook her head.

Slowly, he sank back down on the mattress. "See you tonight," he murmured.

His eyes closed and he went still.

Deathly still.

Skylynn chewed on her thumbnail. So, she was head-over-heels, crazy in love with a vampire. If she stayed with him, she would spend all her days alone. She ran her fingertips across his lips, over his broad chest, down his belly, then leaned forward and kissed his cheek, thinking that spending her nights in his arms would more than make up for the daylight hours she spent without him.

Chapter 19

Cassandra stood in the shadows, watching Girard as he called a young woman to him. The girl was extremely pretty and unblemished for a prostitute, leading Cassandra to believe that she hadn't been out on the streets very long. Women who worked the streets tended to age rapidly. Their eyes took on a hard, world-weary look, their expressions were often wary. Most carried scars, souvenirs of repeated beatings by angry pimps, or from customers who liked it rough.

Girard fed quickly, erased the incident from the whore's mind, and after giving her a pat on the rump, sent her on her way.

"You should have come to me years ago," Cassandra remarked with a shake of her head. "You were born to be a vampire."

Girard licked a drop of blood from his lips and then grinned at her. "I think you're right."

Cassandra linked an arm with his and they left the alley. To her surprise, she had become rather fond of Desmarais. He had quickly become a skilled hunter. He possessed a wicked sense of humor, and, like most vampires, he felt no remorse for what he did to survive. In her long existence, she had found that right and wrong most often depended on which side of the fence you were on.

"I'm still thirsty," Girard confessed as they emerged from the alley and headed down the street.

Cassandra grinned wryly. "There's just no filling you up, is there?"

He lifted one shoulder in a negligent shrug. "It tastes so good. And makes me feel invincible. I think I could feed from sundown to sunrise."

"I think you must have done that last night," she muttered, but there was no derision in her tone. Truth be told, she was proud of how quickly her most recent fledgling had adapted to his new lifestyle, and a little sorrowful that he no longer needed her guidance. "I'll be leaving Vista Verde in a few days."

"Leaving?" He looked up at her, startled by her announcement. "Why?"

"It's a small town. Three vampires are two too many. Why don't you come with me?"

"I don't know."

She came to an abrupt halt, her hand falling away from his arm. "You're not still thinking of going after Kaiden, are you?"

"No, of course not," he said quickly.

"Don't lie to me, Girard."

He stared at her, mute, damning her ability to read his thoughts, cursing the fact that he had not yet learned how to keep her out of his head, although he wasn't sure that was possible, since she had sired him.

"You haven't forgotten what I said, have you?"

"No," he replied sullenly. "I haven't forgotten."

"I'll know if anything happens to him. And I'll know who to blame."

"All right! You've made your point."

With a nod, she linked her arm with his again. "Just so we understand each other," she said. "Now, let's go see if we can find someone to help satisfy that appetite of yours."

Chapter 20

Nightmares, nothing but nightmares. He thrashed on the blankets that served as his bed. He had to go home. He had to get out of here. But where was here? Lonely and afraid, he wandered through the darkness, ever aware of the eyes that followed him. Red eyes that glowed in the dark. A voice in the back of his mind whispered that he must keep the secret, but he couldn't remember what the secret was, or why he had to keep it.

Exhausted, he paused in the shadows to rest, and the eyes were there, staring at him. Into him. Through him. Unable to run any longer, tired of fighting an enemy he couldn't see, he threw back his head and screamed and screamed . . .

He came awake with a jerk, his body bathed in a cold sweat. The girl who brought him food and water twice a day sat beside him, her dark brown eyes wide.

When she saw that he was awake, she left the tent.

He stared after her. What lay outside? Who were the men in long brown robes who came and went so silently? They spoke in a harsh guttural language he didn't understand. They were all armed with rifles and knives. Sometimes they stood on either side of him, shouting and gesturing at one another. Several times, he had been certain they were going to kill him. They had taken his clothes, his boots, his watch, everything he owned, and given him a long brown robe in return.

He lifted a hand to his left ear and snapped his fingers. Nothing. He'd definitely lost the hearing in that ear.

If only he could remember who he was, where he was.

He needed a haircut and a shave and a bath. He needed to brush his teeth.

He needed a doctor. Probably a shrink, since he had no memory of his past, no recollection of how he happened to come here, wherever the hell here was. Maybe it really was hell.

The woman returned a short time later, offering him soup, a chunk of hard bread, a tin cup of water. Because they kept his hands bound behind his back, the woman had to feed him.

It was humiliating.

He wasn't sure, but judging by the thickness of his beard, he guessed he had been unconscious for more than a few days; whether from an injury or from being drugged, he didn't know.

He had tried several times to speak to the woman, but she only shook her head, leaving him to wonder whether she didn't answer because she didn't speak English, or if it was because she had been forbidden to speak to him.

Pain throbbed in his skull and he closed his eyes.

Would this nightmare never end?

Chapter 21

Thorne came awake with the setting of the sun. As always, he awoke instantly aware of his surroundings. He was in his own bed, a bed he had shared with Skylynn only hours ago. Where was she now?

Sitting up, he opened his senses and knew within seconds that she wasn't in the house. No doubt she had gone home. Well, he couldn't blame her for that. There was no food in his house, nothing for her to do here while he slept.

Throwing back the covers, he padded into the bathroom and somewhat reluctantly washed Skylynn's scent from his skin. Being a healthy male, he wondered how soon he could get her back into his bed. But not until he had fed. And that was something he needed to do as soon as he dressed. Last night, it had taken all the willpower he possessed to stop before it was too late. It was a risk he couldn't take again.

After drying off, he pulled on a pair of jeans and a long-sleeved T-shirt, stepped into a pair of scuffed leather boots, and left the house.

He paused on the porch a moment, gazing at the house across the street. He took a deep breath, remembering the softness of Sky's skin beneath his hands, the velvet touch of her hands running over him. He was mightily tempted to go see her for a few minutes, but, knowing it was for her own good, he resisted the urge.

He drove to the Scarlet Cabaret, a club located just outside the town limits. It was a favorite haunt of his when he was in a hurry and didn't want to waste time hunting. The place was usually crawling with foolish mortals. Most came hoping to see a real vampire. A few were addicted to the vampire's bite, which granted ordinary humans a high like no other.

Walking into the club was like slipping on a pair of comfortable old shoes. The dimly lit interior, the heady fragrance of blood of all types, the melody of so many beating hearts all blending together, the unmistakable scent of musk that filled the air, the low, sensual music coming from the jukebox.

Thorne moved through the crowd toward the bar. He was aware of the glances sent his way, the quickening of female hearts. He nodded at the bartender. Few were aware that the owner was a werewolf.

A tall redhead broke away from a group of women clustered at the end of the bar. Her smile was confident as she approached him. "I'm Miya," she said, her voice a throaty purr.

Thorne inclined his head. "Kaiden."

She brushed the hair away from her neck with a slender hand. "I have what you're looking for."

"Oh? And what might that be?"

"Blood, of course. Isn't that why the vampires come here?"

Interesting, he thought, that she knew what he was. Few mortals were able to discern the Undead at a glance.

"Am I wrong?" she asked boldly.

"What makes you think you're right?"

"You have the look. You know, that arrogant, just a little too perfect to be human look that we mere mortals never attain. And your eyes. They're deeper, darker, and they see right through us. But mostly it's the innate allure that we can't resist."

Interesting, Thorne thought again. "Sounds like you've made a thorough study of the Undead."

"You could say that."

"Anything else?"

She shrugged. "You smell like death."

Damn, she *was* good. "Who the hell are you?"

"I told you. I'm Miya. Van Helsing."

"Van Helsing?" He snorted. "Are you kidding me?"

She laughed. "What do you think?"

"I think you're lying." She didn't smell like a vampire, but she didn't smell human, either. Try as he might, Kaiden couldn't figure out what she was, or what she was up to.

"Believe what you like. Why should I lie?"

"Because if you were a true descendent of Abraham Van Helsing, you'd be hunting vampires, not offering to feed them."

"No way." She shuddered delicately. "Taking heads or hearts is far too messy, and not nearly as satisfying." She moved closer, her hand sliding seductively across his chest. "So, what do you say?"

"I think I'd be a fool to trust you."

She ran her hands down the front of her dress. "Do I look like I'm hiding a weapon anywhere?"

He laughed softly. Her clingy black dress fit like a second skin, defining every luscious curve. The only thing under that dress was Miya herself, and that, in itself, was a dangerous weapon.

"I'd be the best you ever had."

"Honey, the best I ever had is waiting for me at home."

"I can't believe you're turning me down!" she exclaimed. "No one has ever told me no."

"I believe you."

"But you don't want me?" She was angry now.

He was about to tell her he was sorry when he caught the

scent of a newly made vampire. He glanced over Miya's head, muttered a vile oath when he saw Desmarais enter the club.

Being a vampire certainly agreed with the former hunter. Dressed in an expertly tailored black suit that would have done Valentino proud, Girard Desmarais strolled into the club as if he owned it. There was no sign of age in his stride or his posture. His gray hair appeared thicker, his skin, though still lined with age, looked distinguished instead of merely old.

Desmarais came to an abrupt halt when he saw Thorne.

Murmuring, "Excuse me," Thorne moved past Miya to confront his old enemy.

"I'm not looking for any trouble in here," Desmarais said, his voice pitched low so that only Thorne could hear.

"I trust Cassandra told you everything you need to know about your new lifestyle."

"She told me I need to ask your permission to stay in Vista Verde. Any point in my doing that?"

"You know what they say, keep your friends close and your enemies closer."

"Is that a yes?"

"Do whatever you want, old man. But if you come after me again, I'll destroy you."

Desmarais snorted. "You can try."

Thorne grinned. "If I don't get you, Cassandra will." He jerked his thumb in Miya's direction. "She's looking for a bite. Of course, I don't know how she feels about old men or old blood." He laughed softly. "You might be a good match at that. She claims to come from a long line of hunters."

Before Desmarais could reply, Thorne murmured, "Have fun," and went in search of more suitable prey.

It didn't take long. His choice for the evening was a woman he had sought out on other occasions. Olivia was an attractive brunette in her early fifties. She had been a member of the Goth scene ever since her husband passed away fifteen years ago. Thorne liked her because she knew when to talk and when to be quiet, because she was willing to satisfy his thirst for blood as well as slake his physical desire when he was in the mood.

She smiled at his approach. No words were necessary between them. Taking her by the hand, he led her into one of the cribs in the back. The rooms were small, bare of all but the simplest furnishings, and reserved for vampire use only.

She required no foreplay, no words of seduction. Sitting on the edge of the bed, she tilted her head to one side in silent invitation.

With a sigh, Thorne sat down and drew Olivia into his embrace, his fangs extending as the scent of her blood called to him. She was sweet, her blood satisfying on many levels, yet even as he drank, he couldn't help wishing it was Skylynn he held in his arms, Skylynn's soft moans of pleasure that whispered through the room.

"Miss Van Helsing?"

"Yes?"

"It's a pleasure to meet you," Girard said sincerely. "I'm a great fan of Abraham's. He's one of the reasons I got into vampire hunting." It was partly true, Girard mused, along with the fact his father and grandfather had been slayers.

"You're a hunter?" she asked, her expression skeptical.

"Yes."

"I don't think so."

"Don't doubt it for a minute, lady," he said, his voice like ice. "I'm the best slayer still living."

"Except you aren't living."

"How the hell would you know?"

"It's a gift. You're a vampire, recently turned, unless I miss my guess. And I never miss."

Girard studied her, his eyes narrowed. "You're a hunter, too." It wasn't a question.

She laughed softly. "I'm many things."

Girard stared at her, completely baffled. Who the hell was she? What was she? He had been around a long time and he had never heard of a mortal who could discern vampire from human, nor had he ever seen a vampire hunter who possessed the voluptuous body of a siren and the angelic face of a saint.

She held out a hand in invitation. "Shall we go?"

"Go?"

She pressed her fingertips to the pulse in the hollow of her throat. "Didn't you come here to feed?"

He nodded.

"Well? What are you waiting for?"

Girard stared at her, his mind reeling. He knew there were people who got off on having vampires feed on them, but there was something about Miya that didn't ring true. Why was she so eager? Just what was she up to, really?

He took a step backward. He hadn't survived as a slayer as long as he had by ignoring his instincts, and every instinct he possessed was screaming a warning.

And yet . . . his fangs extended as he imagined holding that curvy young body in his arms and taking what she was so blatantly offering.

"You'll hurt my feelings if you say no," she said, pouting. "It's bad enough that Kaiden turned me down."

"He did?"

Miya nodded. "Some men are afraid of a woman who knows what she wants and isn't afraid to ask for it." She ran one dark red nail across his cheek. "Are you afraid?"

Girard shook his head. What did he have to be afraid of? He was a vampire. Sure, he was newly turned, but he had been sired by an ancient vampire, which made him stronger than an ordinary fledgling. As for Miya, hell, she couldn't weigh more than a hundred pounds soaking wet.

Miya smiled as she reached forward, took him by the hand, and led him toward the rooms in the back.

And even as Girard followed her, the words *like a lamb to the slaughter* played in the back of his mind.

Olivia straightened the collar of her dress. "Will you stay the night?"

Thorne winced inwardly. He should have seen this coming. "Olivia . . ."

"Please, Kaiden."

How could he say yes? How could he say no? She had given herself to him for years and never asked for anything in return other than to spend an occasional night in his arms. But, because of Skylynn, things were different now. True, they hadn't made any commitments to each other, but how could he take Olivia to bed when it was Sky he loved? Doing so would be a betrayal of the worst kind.

He took a deep breath. "Olivia, listen to me," he began, then stopped.

"What . . . ?"

"Shh." Rising, he cocked his head to the side, his brow furrowed. There it was again. A muted cry for help. Muttering, "Stay here," he was out the door before she realized he was gone.

The muffled cry came from the last room at the end of the hall. Thorne didn't bother with the door, but simply dissolved into mist and slipped through the crack.

Desmarais was on the other side, fighting Miya for his life.

Only, she didn't look like Miya now. With her supernatural glamour gone, she was no longer a beautiful woman but a skeletal black-haired demon with wrinkled gray skin and blazing yellow eyes. She sat astride Desmarais' hips, one gnarled hand circling his throat.

She hissed as Thorne materialized inside the room. "Go!" She pointed at the door with a long, skinny finger. "Go, or I'll kill him."

Damn. What kind of demon was she? Not a succubus. They came to men, especially monks, by night and seduced them. This creature wasn't looking for sex.

A mutant, then? Some kind of vampire succubus who drained men, not only of their blood, but of their life's essence, as well. What better place for such a one to hunt than a Goth club?

"Go!" The demon's voice was shrill now, her agitation growing.

Thorne shrugged. "Kill him if you wish. He's no friend of mine."

Desmarais stared at him, his eyes bulging with fear.

The demon studied Thorne curiously, and then she smiled, displaying yellowed teeth and fangs. "Come, join me."

With a nod, Thorne moved toward the bed. With the demon watching him intently, he bent toward Desmarais' neck, his own fangs running out at the scent of fresh blood on the hunter's neck.

A cackle rose in the demon's throat as she again bent her head to Desmarais' neck.

A choked cry issued from Desmarais' lips as the demon's teeth sank into his flesh.

Thorne was moving, too. With all the speed at his command, he grabbed a handful of the demon's hair and hurled her against the wall. She hit it with a loud thud and a snarl and then simply disappeared.

Thorne stepped away from the bed. In all his 432 years as a vampire, he had never seen another supernatural creature disappear like that.

Desmarais sat up, one hand massaging his throat. "What the hell? Why'd you save . . . ?"

"If anyone's going to destroy you, I want it to be me."

Desmarais stood. With a visible effort of will, he gathered his dignity around him. "This doesn't change anything between us."

"I didn't think it would," Thorne replied. "But if you're

still determined to take my head, you might want to be a little more circumspect in your choice of prey in the future."

Desmarais glared at him.

With a wave of his hand, Thorne left the room.

The sound of Desmarais grinding his teeth in anger followed him out the door.

"A demon?" Skylynn exclaimed after inviting Kaiden into the house. "You saw a demon?" Good Lord, first vampires and now demons. Suddenly chilled, she sat on the sofa and drew her feet underneath her. "Why didn't you kill it?"

"I didn't have the time or the proper incantation." Thorne sat on the other end of the sofa, his legs stretched out in front of him. "It isn't easy, you know. You need to use the proper words for an exorcism. Besides, she wasn't your ordinary, run-of-the-mill succubus. I've never known one to drink blood."

"A blood-drinking succubus," Sky muttered. "What next? Flying monkeys? Giant ants? Aliens from outer space? Werewolves?" She was babbling, but she couldn't seem to stop, couldn't wrap her mind around the possibility that there might be worse things than vampires lurking in the dark.

Suddenly chilled, she rubbed her hands up and down her arms, then took a deep breath. "What are you going to do about Desmarais?"

"Wait and see what his next move will be, I guess."

"I can't believe you saved his life," she muttered, and then clapped her hand over her mouth as she realized how bloodthirsty that sounded. She had never wished anyone ill before. She believed it was a sin to take a human life. There were exceptions, of course, like self-defense or to protect one's home and family but, by and large, murder was morally wrong. Where did that leave Thorne? How many lives had he taken in his long existence? And why did she have to think about that now?

"I'm supposed to be the bloodthirsty one in our two-some," Thorne remarked dryly.

"I can't believe I said that. I've never wished anyone was dead before."

"You're probably right. I should have destroyed him." He rubbed a hand over his jaw. "He's made no secret of the fact that he intends to kill me."

"What?"

"I can't really blame him. I killed his wife years ago. He's never forgiven me for that."

"His wife?" She couldn't disguise the horror in her voice. "Why did you do that?"

"I did what I had to do to survive."

"But . . . a woman. How could you?"

"Marie Desmarais was a vampire hunter and a damn good one. It was her life or mine."

"He had a wife? I thought he was a monk."

"Apparently her death hit him hard. For a time, he sought refuge in a monastery rumored to welcome retired hunters. I'm not sure if any of the other slayers who reside there are avowed monks or not. As for Desmarais, whether he's priest or vampire, he'll always be a slayer at heart. Nothing will change that."

"Let me get this straight. Desmarais was a hunter, then a monk, and now he's a vampire?"

"Yeah. And no matter what hat he's wearing, he wants me dead."

Skylynn shook her head, more amazed than ever that Kaiden had saved the man's life.

"Are there other vampires living in Vista Verde?"

Thorne's brow went up in silent mockery at her use of the word *living.* And then he shook his head. "No, I'm the only one who maintains a permanent residence in the town at the moment." There were vampires in surrounding cities, but he thought Sky would rest easier without that knowledge.

Sky closed her eyes and took a deep breath. Not long ago, she had been blissfully unaware that there were unearthly creatures in the world. Her life, though plagued by sorrow, had been rather mundane. Now, in a matter of weeks, all that had changed.

She had learned that Kaiden was a vampire, and before she had fully come to terms with that inconceivable reality, he had informed her that not only were there vampires, but demons, as well. What other monsters lurked out there in the shadows?

Thorne didn't have to read her mind to know what she was thinking. It was clearly written on her face—the shock, the disbelief. Life was easier when you didn't know that the scary creatures of myth and legend were real. No doubt she was wishing she could turn the clock back to a time when she believed monsters were make-believe.

As one of those monsters, there were times when Thorne wished he, too, could return to that state of blissful ignorance.

Chapter 22

Thorne draped his arm across the back of the sofa, his gaze on Skylynn's face. She was staring at the fireplace, her expression troubled. Life was easier when you didn't know the monsters were real. He resisted the urge to read her mind. If she was going to tell him good-bye, he didn't want to know about it any sooner than he had to. The thought of losing her, of never seeing her smile or hearing her laugh, never touching her again, was beyond bearing.

He had endured a lot of misery in the last four hundred years. Even though his parents had disowned him, he had mourned their passing. Love them or hate them, they had given him life. As a vampire, he had never let himself fall in love, but he had watched many men and women he had grown fond of leave this world. It wasn't easy, watching people you cared about wither and die, and after a while he had refused to care too deeply.

He had kept to himself, doing what he had to do to survive, occasionally mingling with others of his kind. For decades, he had lived a self-imposed solitary existence. Until he moved back to Vista Verde and became acquainted with Paddy and his grandchildren. He had watched Sam and Skylynn grow up and taken pride in their accomplishments.

If he lost Skylynn now, after sharing his life with her, after making love to her, he wasn't sure he would be strong enough to survive the loss.

"Sky Blue, talk to me."

With a sigh, she turned to face him. "I don't know what to say. It all sounds so far-fetched. I'm not sure how to feel or what to think."

"That's understandable," he said, careful to keep his voice impassive. "Nobody likes to think there are flesh-and-blood monsters in the world."

She stared at him, and then frowned. "You're not a monster, Kaiden."

"No? I've done some pretty monstrous things in my day."

"So, that's how you think of yourself?"

"Not when I'm with you." Gaining his feet, he moved toward the hearth. He stood with his back toward her, one hand braced against the mantel. "If you knew some of the things I've done . . ."

"It doesn't matter," she said quickly, and then, when he didn't answer right away, she added, "It's all in the past. Isn't it?"

He nodded, but didn't turn to face her.

"Kaiden?"

"I know what I've done. I know what I'm capable of. When I started reverting, after Paddy's potion wore off . . . you don't know how hard it was to control the urge to kill. You don't know"—his voice fell to a whisper—"how badly I wanted to drink from you and never stop." He shook his head. "I've been kidding myself, thinking I can control what I am and keep you safe."

"I'm not afraid. I know you won't hurt me."

"I wish I could be as sure." Earlier, he had considered what it would be like to live without her now that he'd come to know her so well. Now that he loved her. And loving her, he realized that every moment she spent with him put her life in danger.

"What are you trying to say?" Her voice broke on the last word because it sounded like he was working on good-bye. How could that be? After all they had been through, after the wonderful night they had spent in each other's arms, surely he wasn't planning to leave?

"I just want what's best for you, Sky Blue, and I'm not sure it's me."

"You promised!" she cried, hating the note of desperation in her voice. "Look at me! You promised you wouldn't leave me."

He turned. Gazing down at her, he said, "Not exactly. I promised I wouldn't leave without telling you good-bye."

"Is that what you're doing?" She blinked back her tears. "Is it?"

"Dammit, Sky . . ." He scrubbed his hands over his face. How could he leave her when he wanted her so damn bad? When he loved her more than his own life?

How could he stay when he knew leaving was the best thing he could do for her?

How could he leave when she was looking at him like that, as if her heart was breaking?

"Ah, Sky. What the hell am I going to do with you?"

"Anything you want."

He was across the floor in an instant, bending down, drawing her into his arms. This would have all been so much easier, so much safer for her, if he hadn't run out of McNamara's potion.

Skylynn pressed herself against him. It felt so good to be in his arms. He made her feel safe, secure. No matter what he said, she knew in her heart that he would never hurt her. It wouldn't be easy, having a relationship with a vampire, but then, no relationship was easy. There were always differences that had to be ironed out, compromises that had to be made.

"Differences?" Thorne muttered. "Compromises? Sky, I'm a vampire, and you're prey. We can't negotiate the differences between us. I can't conform my existence to yours. Any compromises that have to be made will have to be made by you. You realize that, don't you?"

She nodded.

"Can you live with that? We'll never be a normal couple. I can support you, but if we stay together, I think you should find a job. If you don't want to work nine to five, then you should volunteer at a school or a hospital, someplace where you'll be with other people. You need to get out and make friends. I don't want you to spend your days sitting at home, waiting for me to rise."

He put his forefinger under her chin, tilting her head up so he could see her face more clearly. "What are you thinking?"

"Don't you know?"

"Actually, I do. That's another thing you'll have to live with. You won't be able to have any secrets from me. I'll always know what you're thinking."

"Even if I ask you not to read my mind?"

"It's hard not to." He caressed her cheek. "Sometimes it isn't even necessary. What you're thinking, feeling . . ." He shrugged. "I can usually read it in your eyes. Like now." His gaze moved over her face. "I hope you won't regret your decision," he said, and swept her into his arms.

"I can walk, you know," Skylynn murmured.

"I know, but I like holding you. Have you got a problem with that?"

"No." With a sigh, she wrapped her arms around his neck and rested her head on his shoulder.

He carried her swiftly up the stairs, then paused on the landing. There were four doors. Three were closed.

Sky pointed at the open doorway.

Thorne carried her inside, then sat on the edge of the bed, cradling her to his chest. "If staying with me ever gets to be more than you can handle, if you ever regret your decision, I want you to promise to tell me."

"I won't . . ."

His hand stilled her words. "Promise me, Skylynn."

"Won't you just read it in my mind?"

"I'm going to try not to do that anymore. Promise me, Sky."

"All right, I promise. But it will never happen."

"I love you, Sky Blue," he said quietly. "I just hope you won't hate me if things don't work out."

"I won't. I do have one question, though?"

"What's that?"

"Are you through trying to talk me out of this? Because I'm dying to make love to you."

"Dying?" he repeated with a wry grin. "That's a poor choice of words, don't you think?"

"Kaiden, stop talking and kiss me."

"Sky . . ."

"Do you love me?"

"You know I do."

"How much?"

"How much do you need?"

She laughed softly as she slid her hands under his shirt. "How much do you have?"

"I'd be happy to show you," he said, and cupping her face in his hands, he kissed her as he slowly fell back on the bed, carrying her with him.

She liked being on top. Straddling his hips, she ran her hands over him, exploring the hard planes of his chest, the width of his shoulders, the corded muscles in his arms.

She ran her fingertips over his lips, then covered his mouth with her own.

Holding her gaze with his, he murmured, "It's my turn now," as he rolled over, carrying her with him, so that she lay beneath him.

He made love to her all through the night, every kiss, every caress, an unspoken declaration of his love for her.

And even as he made love to her, a little voice in the back of his mind warned him that he was putting her life in jeopardy.

Chapter 23

Girard Desmarais whistled softly as he sent his third victim on her way. He had spent most of his adult life relentlessly hunting and destroying vampires. He had hated them unconditionally, decrying their lifestyle, their wickedness in preying on innocent humans, condemning the Undead as soulless, heartless, monsters.

How could he have spent so much of his time around vampires and never understood a thing about them? Knowing what he knew now, he was amazed that people weren't lining up by the thousands to become vampires. If he had known how fantastic their powers were, how amazing it was to have the strength of twenty men, to never be sick or tired, he would have sought the Dark Gift decades ago.

He thought of Marie, dead before her time because of Kaiden Thorne. His dreams of having a son to carry on the family name had died with her. He had loved once. He would never love again. So be it. He was the last of his line, and that, too, was the fault of Kaiden Thorne. Just one more reason to destroy the man who had taken Marie's life. And yet, for all that Girard felt strong and invulnerable, he wasn't ready to face off against Cassandra. He didn't doubt for a minute that she would come after him if he killed Thorne. She would always be older, stronger.

His steps slowed. Maybe there was another way to avenge himself on his enemy. True, it would be folly on his part to defy Cassandra and destroy Thorne, but what about Thorne's woman? She was fair game as far as he was concerned.

The Good Book said an eye for an eye, Girard mused.

But he was thinking about a life for a life.

Chapter 24

Skylynn woke with a smile on her face. For a moment, she simply lay there, her eyes closed as she relived the wonder of the night past. Kaiden loved her. The thought made her giggle like a schoolgirl with her first crush. And that thought made her laugh out loud. He had been her first crush. She had daydreamed about him for years and now, at last, he was hers. And she was his. Totally and completely his.

And he was a dyed-in-the-wool, blood-drinking vampire.

She turned her face toward the window, basking in the sun's light. And then she bolted upright. Sunlight! Her gaze darted to the other side of the bed, terrified that she might find a pile of ashes. To her relief, that side of the bed was empty.

Where was Kaiden?

Swinging her legs over the edge of the mattress, she stepped into her slippers, pulled on her robe, and hurried downstairs, frowning as the scent of coffee tickled her nostrils.

"Kaiden?" She called his name as she went into the kitchen. He wasn't there, of course, but she smiled when she saw he had turned on the coffeemaker. A note rested beside it.

Morning, Sky Blue. Enjoy your day. I'll see you tonight. Don't forget, I love you forever. Kaiden.

Smiling, she hugged the note to her breast, then slipped it into the pocket of her robe. Kaiden loved her. God was in His heaven, and all was right with the world.

After pouring herself a cup of coffee, she sat at the table, her whole being glowing with the blush of first love. She wanted to sing, to shout it to the world. For the first time in her life, she was hopelessly, deeply in love.

Gradually, her sense of euphoria faded and reality stepped in. So, he loved her and she loved him. If they were a normal couple, they would get married, have a couple of kids, and live happily ever after. But they weren't a normal couple. And they never would be. Kaiden had been right about that.

She bit down on the inside corner of her lip. So, they weren't a normal couple. What was so great about being normal?

She sipped her coffee, her thoughts wandering. Would he expect them to move in together? Should she suggest it? If they decided to move in together, it would probably have to be in his house. He would undoubtedly feel more secure taking his rest there.

Well, she could live with that. And she could always go home during the day. Kaiden had suggested she find something to do with her time, and that was probably a smart idea. He had told her she didn't have to work, but she wasn't sure she felt comfortable with the idea of having him support her when they weren't married. So, she needed to find a job. Vista Verde was a small town and there weren't a lot of high-paying jobs available. But she didn't need a lot of money. Just enough to pay the utility bills and the taxes on the house. She didn't eat much. Granda's car wasn't new, but it was paid for. And if it broke down, Sam's VW was in the garage. She drove it once a week or so to keep the battery charged.

She poured herself a second cup of coffee. She had always wanted to work at a pet store. The last time she had gone looking for work, she had taken what was profitable, not what she really wanted.

But times had changed.

"Oh, yes," she murmured, smiling. "Times have changed."

A quick breakfast, a change of clothes, and she was off to seek gainful employment.

Skylynn returned home three hours later, weary and discouraged. She had tried every store in town and met with rejection at all of them.

"We're cutting back."

"We can't afford to take on any new help."

"Maybe next month."

"You're overqualified."

Thoroughly discouraged, she kicked off her shoes and tossed her handbag on the sofa. Padding to the front window, she pulled back the curtain and stared at Kaiden's house. It was still three hours until sunset.

Pulling a chair up to the window, she sat down, her arms folded on the sill, her chin resting on her arm. What was it like, to sleep without dreaming? To be drawn into nothingness with the rising of the sun whether you wanted to be or not? To live forever and never be sick or tired? To have the strength of twenty men? To be able to move faster than the human eye could follow?

To drink blood? Kaiden didn't seem to mind. Apparently when you were turned, drinking blood stopped being repulsive. Or maybe you just got used to it. She could think of a lot of things she hadn't liked the first time. Coffee had been an acquired taste. So had beer and wine and champagne. She hadn't liked any of them the first time she tried them.

She glanced at her watch, willing the hands to move faster. Why did time pass so quickly when she was with Kaiden and so slowly when she was home alone?

Rising, she went into the den. It had been Granda's room. His medical diplomas and awards lined one wall. A small mahogany table held his pipes and a box of cigars. An old footlocker sat in one corner. It held the trophies Granda had won in high school, along with an old letterman's sweater, his high school yearbooks, and a football from the last game he had played in college.

She moved toward the bookcase. It was crammed with paperbacks, most of them written by Louis L'Amour, Max Brand, and Zane Grey. Scattered among the dog-eared westerns were the books Sky had loved as a child. Among them were *Lad: A Dog*, *Little Women*, *Black Beauty,* and the *Black Stallion* books.

Sky pulled one of the *Black Stallion* books from the shelf and thumbed through it, remembering how she had imagined herself lost on a desert island with a beautiful black horse. Like many preteen girls, she had longed to own a horse of her own, but Granda had told her it just wasn't practical in a subdivision.

With a sigh, she returned the book to the shelf. For a moment, she stood there, wondering what to do. She felt a rush of guilt when she realized it had been a while since she had written to Sam.

Booting up the computer, she sat down, and began to write.

Dear Sam~

You're not going to believe this, but I'm in love with a vampire.

Stop laughing. It's true, and he's a real vampire and you know him. Are you ready for this? It's Kaiden

*Thorne! Okay, you can laugh now. I have to wonder,
though. All those years ago when we went trick-or-
treating at his house, did you really know what he was?
And if you knew, how did you have the nerve to go
there in the first place?*

*I don't know where our relationship is headed, or
how long it will last. I tell myself it doesn't matter, that
I love him, fangs and all (ha-ha). Of course, we're
going to have problems. All couples do. I guess the
biggest one is that I'll get old and he won't. I don't
know what to do about that one.*

Or children. I don't know if he even wants them . . .

Her fingers stilled on the keys. They hadn't used any
precautions. She could be pregnant even now. Lordy, if she
had a baby, would it be half vampire? Would she have to
feed it blood and keep it out of the sun? Would it be born
with fangs? Ouch!

Her letter forgotten, she went to look out the window
again.

Kaiden rose with the setting of the sun. In spite of his ea-
gerness to see Skylynn, he took time to shower and wash
his hair. The luxury of hot running water was something
that he never took for granted, not even after 471 years. He
knew a lot of vampires lived in the past, lamenting the loss
of the eras they had known, but Thorne wasn't one of them.
There was little of his old life that he missed. Given the
choice, he much preferred the conveniences of the twenty-
first century—fast cars, hot water whenever he wanted it,
flush toilets. He remembered all too well the stink of bed-
pans and water closets, of people who rarely bathed. But
the humans of today, ah, most of them smelled sweet
indeed.

And Skylynn was the sweetest of them all.

Drying off, he pulled on a pair of jeans and a black sweatshirt. The clothes of today suited him far better than the garments of four hundred years ago. They were more comfortable and certainly easier to care for.

And easier to get women out of.

Grinning, he pulled on his boots and left the house, wondering how long it would take to get Sky Blue undressed and into bed.

Chapter 25

He fought down his terror as one of his captors dropped a thick black hood over his head. With his hands lashed behind his back, there was no way to defend himself. In any case, he had no hope of defeating four men armed with enough weapons to start a small war.

Someone poked him in the back and he stumbled forward. Where were they taking him? Fear coiled in the pit of his stomach like a snake ready to strike. He had seen news coverage of Americans being beheaded. Was that to be his fate?

He swallowed hard as unseen hands lifted him into the back of what he thought was a truck. He heard the sounds of shuffling feet, had the sense that he wasn't the only prisoner there. When he started to speak, someone—one of the guards?—punched him in the stomach. The low rumble of an engine and the vehicle lurched forward, bouncing over the rough terrain.

Bowing his head, he tried to pray, but he didn't remember any prayers. He didn't know if he had ever been a praying man, didn't know what, if anything, he believed. Didn't know if there was anyone, other than himself, he should pray for.

It was stifling under the hood. The truck wasn't enclosed and the desert sun beat down on his head, shoulders, and back. Sweat beaded across his brow and dripped down his neck. How long had they been traveling? How long before they stopped? What would happen when his captors reached their destination?

Questions pounded in his head as the miles slipped by and his fear and frustration grew. Where the hell was he? How had he gotten there? Where were they going?

And why couldn't he remember who he was?

Chapter 26

Skylynn was putting the last of her dinner dishes in the dishwasher when the doorbell rang. She closed the appliance's door with a bang, then hurried into the front room. At last, the sun was down and Kaiden was here!

Butterflies were going crazy in her stomach as she unlocked the door. "Kaiden, why are you ringing the . . . You!" She stared at Desmarais in horror. Momentarily stunned, she seemed to have lost the power to think or act and then, too late, she tried to shut the door in his face.

When his foot kept it from closing all the way, she took a deep breath. He was a vampire. He couldn't come inside without an invitation, something he had apparently forgotten. She almost laughed at his look of surprise when he tried to cross the threshold and couldn't. It was one of the most amazing things Sky had ever seen. Try as he might, he couldn't get in. Each time he tried, she felt a tremor in the air, like an invisible electric current.

He stared at her, his eyes filled with malevolence. She was sure it was her imagination, but it was almost as if he was trying to hypnotize her.

Let me in.

She heard his voice in her mind, growing stronger, more

insistent. Some instinct she didn't even know she possessed warned her not to look into his eyes.

Crying, "No!" she tore her gaze from his.

Swearing vociferously, Desmarais turned on his heel and vanished from sight.

Skylynn sagged against the doorjamb. Waiting for her heartbeat to return to normal, she thought about the strange tremor she'd felt when Desmarais tried to enter the house. It was the same vibration she had experienced last night when Kaiden tried to enter the house. He had looked at her askance.

"What's wrong?" she had asked, wondering why he didn't come in.

"I can't."

"Can't?" She had stared at him in confusion. "Why not?"

"You tell me."

It had taken her a moment to realize what he meant, and then she remembered she had revoked her invitation. "You really can't come in?"

He shook his head.

"How does that work? What keeps you out?"

"Thresholds have mystical power."

"But all buildings have thresholds."

"It's only effective in homes, to protect the inhabitants. It doesn't work in places of business, only where people live."

"So, it's like some invisible force field?"

"That's as good an explanation as any."

"Amazing."

"So?"

She had grinned up at him. "Mr. Thorne, won't you please come inside?"

* * *

Sky was still standing in the open doorway, bemused by the whole can't-cross-the-threshold-without-an-invitation thing, when Kaiden walked up the porch steps.

"Waiting for me?" he asked with a wicked grin.

"No. Desmarais was just here."

"What?" Lifting his head, Thorne took a deep breath. He had been so eager to see Sky, he hadn't paid much attention to anything else.

"He couldn't get in," Sky said. "It was almost funny, watching him try."

"Well, if he'd had a gun, you wouldn't be laughing."

That sobered her mighty quick. "I never thought of that," Sky said, stepping aside so he could enter. "But why would he come here? I mean . . ." She shivered. "If he'd gotten inside . . ." She swallowed hard. She had no doubt he would have killed her on the spot.

"Exactly," Thorne said. "You need to make sure who's outside before you open the door."

"Shouldn't he have known he couldn't get in without an invitation? I mean, you said he used to be a hunter."

Thorne shrugged. "Sometimes fledglings, especially cocky ones, forget the rules. And sometimes they have to test the laws just to see if they really work."

Like children always pushing the envelope, she thought, eager to see what they could get away with. Girard Desmarais was an old man in mortal years, but he was just a baby as a vampire.

Thorne followed Skylynn into the living room, the lingering odors of fried chicken and mashed potatoes tickling his nostrils. He was already forgetting how much he had enjoyed the taste of mortal food, how pleasurable it had been to savor the many tastes and textures, to drink something besides blood.

Skylynn sat on the sofa, her hands folded in her lap to stop their trembling. She couldn't stop thinking about what might have happened if she had hollered "come in" instead of going to open the door. She pushed the troubling thought aside. It hadn't happened and there was no point in dwelling on it.

She took a deep breath. There was something she needed to know, the sooner the better.

Thorne sat beside Skylynn, his thigh brushing hers. One look at her face and he knew something was bothering her, something besides the close call with Desmarais. For a moment, he was tempted to read her mind, but he had promised not to, and so he waited.

"Kaiden . . ." Pausing, she licked her lips. "What if . . ." She took a deep breath, and said it all in a rush. "What if I'm pregnant? Will the baby be a vampire?"

He should have seen this coming, he thought, but it had been so long since he'd had to worry about fathering a child, it had never occurred to him to mention it.

She looked at him, her beautiful blue eyes filled with worry. "Would it have to have blood to survive? Would I have to keep it indoors during the day?"

"Skylynn . . ." He scrubbed his palms up and down his thighs. "I can't father a child."

She stared at him, the worry in her eyes turning to pity. "Maybe a fertility clinic . . . ?"

"It isn't that." Might as well get it out in the open, say it so she'd understand. Give her a chance to back out. "Vampires can't reproduce," he said flatly. "The dead can't create life."

The dead can't create life.

She reeled back as though he had slapped her. Did he have to put it quite so bluntly? Was he deliberately trying to drive her away? Her gaze searched his and she realized what he was doing. He was giving her an out, a valid reason to change her mind before things went any further between them.

"I'm sorry," she murmured. "I didn't know. . . . Did you have children, before?"

"No. I was too busy being a rakehell to think about getting married, let alone having children." It was something he regretted, now that it was eternally too late to do anything about it. "If you want children, I'll understand," he said quietly. "I only want what's best for you."

"You're what's best for me. Don't you know that?" She wrapped her arms around his neck. "I don't need anyone but you. Just you. Only you."

"Sky." Humbled by her love, he laid his cheek against her breast. What kind of selfish monster was he, to expect her to give up one of life's greatest blessings just to be with him? And yet, after so many centuries alone, didn't he deserve a few years of happiness? She was young. She would soon tire of sharing his bizarre lifestyle and when that happened, he would let her go. It would destroy him, but she would still be young enough to marry and have children, to watch those children grow up and have children of their own.

And perhaps, on quiet moonlit nights when she lay safe in her future husband's arms, she would think back and fondly remember the monster who had loved her.

Chapter 27

As the miles slid past, the fever took over. He drifted in and out of consciousness, his fevered dreams filled with disjointed images of planes and tanks and roadside bombs, of buddies being blown to bits, of women sobbing and frightened children, of being afraid to close his eyes. Sometimes a woman was there, her hair and face covered, her bright blue eyes wide with terror as she ran and ran from a nameless, faceless enemy. And sometimes a tall, dark-haired man was there sporting realistic plastic fangs and red contacts that blazed like twin coals plucked from the bowels of an unforgiving hell.

He saw those eyes now, boring into him, penetrating his heart, piercing his very soul, heard a voice whispering in his ear.

"Wake up, soldier. You're safe now. Wake up."

He came awake with a harsh cry, the sound of his own heartbeat echoing like thunder in his ears.

"It's all right, son."

He blinked at the man bending over him. "Who are you? Where am I?"

"You're in a hospital, here in the States."

"I'm American?" He glanced around. The room was

filled with beds. He saw several nurses moving from one patient to another, checking blood pressure here, taking a temperature there.

The man nodded. "I'm Dr. Wharton." The doctor picked up a clipboard and pulled a pen from his coat pocket. "How are you feeling, Sam?"

"Sam?"

The doctor paused in the act of looking over the chart on his clipboard. "Your dog tags were missing when they found you, but according to the fingerprints on file, you're Samuel Patrick McNamara."

"If you say so." He repeated the name in his mind but it had no meaning.

"You listed your sister, Skylynn O'Brien, as your next of kin. We tried to notify her, but the number listed in Chicago has been disconnected and there's no new listing."

Sam shrugged. So, they couldn't find the sister he couldn't remember. Big deal.

The doctor made a notation on his clipboard. "Do you remember anything that happened before you got here?"

Sam stared at him, then shook his head. "No." His fingers curled around the blanket that covered him.

"It's all right." The doctor made another notation. "Just try to relax. Let the memories come back on their own. Don't try to force them."

"What if my memory doesn't come back?"

"Let's not worry about that now," the doctor said briskly. "From the looks of you, you've had it pretty rough. A little downtime will be good for you."

"How did I get here?"

"I'm not sure of the details," the doctor replied. "It's all hush-hush, but from what I gather, the Iraqis traded you and several other men for one of their own. You were burning up with fever and suffering from severe head trauma by the time you got here."

"Sam! Hey, Sam! Is that you?"

Sam looked past the doctor to see a tall, lanky, redhead grinning from ear to ear.

"Do I know you?" Sam asked.

"Are you kidding me? Hell, we trained together at Hood. Roger Boyle. Don't you remember?" He held up his hand, two fingers crossed. "We were tight, man."

Sam shook his head. "Sorry."

Boyle hobbled closer to the bed. Only then did Sam notice that Boyle's left pant leg was empty from the knee down.

"What's his story, Doc?" Boyle asked, leaning on his crutch.

"I'd say retrograde amnesia, most likely caused by a severe blow to the head. But, all things considered, I'd say his odds of a full recovery are good."

"When can I get out of here?" Sam asked.

"Soon. You've been discharged, due to your injuries. The paperwork should be here any day now," the doctor said, "but I need to run a few more tests before you can go home. In the meantime, you take it easy, and I'll see you in the morning." With a nod, the doctor moved on to his next patient.

"That's rough," Boyle said, "not being able to remember who you are."

"You said we were tight. Do you know anything about me?"

"Just that you lived with your grandfather in Vista Verde, California, and you have a married sister, Skylynn, who lives in Chicago. You drive a restored '66 VW Bug and you're hoping to be a mechanic when your tour's up. You took a few college courses, worked at the local market before you enlisted. Does any of this ring a bell?"

Sam shook his head.

"Well, like the doc said, it might take some time."

"Yeah," Sam muttered. "Time."

"Hang in there, buddy. I need to get off my feet." Boyle grinned ruefully. "Foot."

Sam nodded as he watched Boyle carefully make his way back to his own bunk at the other end of the room. All things considered, he guessed he'd rather have lost his memory than his leg.

Sam folded his arms beneath his head and stared up at the ceiling. Sam. His name was Sam and he had a married sister, Skylynn. Was she older or younger? Did she have kids? Dammit, why couldn't he remember?

Chapter 28

Thorne lay on his side, one elbow bent, his cheek resting on his hand as his gaze moved over Skylynn's face. He had made love to her off and on all through the night. He ran his fingertips along the side of her neck. He needed to stop being so greedy, to remember that she didn't have his strength or stamina. But making love to her was like an addiction he couldn't shake. The more he held her, the more he kissed her, the more he wanted her.

He wasn't sure how it had happened, but about a week ago, he'd fallen into the habit of spending the night at her house. It was the closest he'd come to having a normal life in centuries. He found himself liking the arrangement far more than was probably good for either of them.

She smiled in her sleep. Was she dreaming of him? It didn't matter. Waking or sleeping, she was the most beautiful creature he had ever seen. It amazed him that, even knowing what he was, she loved him enough to give herself to him completely. He deserved neither her love nor her trust, not now, when the monster within him was fighting so hard to get out, when it was a struggle to keep his hellish thirst under control. When all he really wanted was to gather

her into his embrace and drink and drink until there was nothing left.

With a growl, he sprang off the bed, his hands clenched at his sides as he turned his back to her. What madness had made him agree to stay with her when just being near him put her life in danger? And yet, how could he leave when Desmarais was sniffing around like a wolf on the scent of fresh blood? An apt description for all their kind, Thorne mused. Predators all, whether they killed or not. And those who spared the lives of their prey were rare indeed because the urge to kill, to take it all and leave nothing behind, was always there.

Why had Desmarais approached Skylynn? Was he still hoping to find the missing ingredient for the formula? Now that he was a vampire, that hardly seemed likely. Unless Desmarais knew it would allow him to walk in the daylight. Would Paddy have shared that information with Desmarais? And if not, then what was Desmarais after?

The answer came with such clarity, Kaiden was surprised it hadn't occurred to him sooner. Desmarais was seeking revenge for his wife's death. Cassandra had warned Desmarais of dire consequences if he destroyed Thorne. And if the monk couldn't destroy him, what better way to avenge himself than by killing someone Thorne held dear?

The logic was inescapable.

Closing his eyes, Thorne forced himself to take several long, slow breaths. He would have to remain calm and clear-headed if he hoped to best Girard Desmarais. The man was nothing if not sly and resourceful. Add to that Desmarais' fifty years of experience as a slayer and Desmarais was not a threat to be taken lightly.

Expelling a deep breath, Thorne slid back under the covers beside Skylynn and put his arm around her. She made a soft sleepy sound as she snuggled against him. He drew her closer, basking in the warmth of her body, the softness of her skin against his.

He ran his fingers lightly through her hair. Making love to Skylynn was the most incredible high he had ever known. It made him feel young again, truly alive again, and for that, he would forever be grateful.

"Kaiden?"

"I'm here."

"You're not going home, are you? I . . ."

"What is it, love?"

"I don't want to wake up alone."

"Then I'll be here."

She snuggled against him and then she smiled. "Good. The curtains are closed, and I promise not to disturb you."

He laughed softly as he hugged her tight. "You can do whatever you like, darlin'."

"I love you," she murmured. And then her eyelids fluttered down as sleep claimed her once again.

Lying there, with the scent of their heated lovemaking all around him, he vowed he would forfeit his existence and everything he possessed before he let anyone or anything hurt a hair of her head.

Skylynn woke slowly, reluctantly. She had been having such a delicious dream, she hated to see it end. In her dream, Kaiden had made love to her all night long. Never before had she felt so cherished, so loved. He had made her feel as if anything was possible, and maybe it was. He had tasted her during their lovemaking and in some way that she would never understand, he had given her access to his thoughts and feelings. It had magnified every touch they shared, enhanced every caress. It had been amazing, their minds and hearts and bodies merging so that they really had become one flesh.

With a sigh, she rolled over and opened her eyes. And he was there, the man who made her feel like the most desirable woman in the world. Remembering the night she had spent in his arms caused her stomach to curl with pleasure. He was so gorgeous, his body hard and sculpted with muscle, his face serene at rest. A male sleeping beauty. If only she could wake him with a kiss, she thought with a sigh, and then smiled. It was probably just as well that she couldn't. She ached in places that had never ached before, but it was a wonderful kind of pain, a reminder of how thoroughly, how exquisitely, he had loved her. It was a night she would never forget, one she couldn't wait to repeat.

Whispering, "I love you," she kissed his cheek even though he couldn't feel it. And then, with a low groan, she slid her legs over the side of the bed. She sat there a moment; then, taking a deep breath, she headed into the bathroom for a hot shower.

Sky had just poured herself a cup of coffee when there was a knock at the door.

She froze a moment, remembering last night when Desmarais had come calling, and then laughed with a giddy sense of relief. The sun was up. It couldn't be the vampire.

Still, Kaiden had warned her about opening the door without knowing who was on the other side. And he was right. Better to err on the side of caution.

Wishing she had a weapon, she went to the door. She peered through the peephole and then, with a cry, she turned the lock and opened the door.

For a minute, she just stood there, too stunned to speak, and then she threw her arms around him.

"Sam! Oh, Sam! I've been so worried about you." She released him a moment and stood back so she could get a good look at him. He needed a shave, his hair was long and unkempt. He looked thinner, far older than his years.

Blinking back tears of joy, she wrapped her arms around him again. "I'm so glad you're all right." She hugged him tightly, then grabbed his hand, afraid if she let go, he might disappear again. "Come on in. We've got so much to talk about! I want to hear everything, where you've been, why I never heard from you."

When he seemed reluctant to follow her, she tugged on his hand. Once inside, she shut the door, then headed for the kitchen, pulling Sam along behind her. "I just made a fresh pot of coffee."

"Slow down, lady," he said, jerking his hand from hers. "Who are you?"

Sky turned to face him. "What?"

"Who are you?"

Skylynn blinked at him. "Are you kidding?" she asked, frowning. "It's me, Sky"

"Skylynn, right. You're my sister?"

"Yes, of course." How could he not know her?

"And I'm Sam?"

"Yes. Samuel Patrick McNamara." Fear coiled in Skylynn's belly as she saw the confusion in her brother's eyes. Had he lost his mind?

He ran his hands through his hair. "I don't remember who I am."

"Then how did you get here?" This had to be a joke. Sam had always liked to tease her, like the time he had told her that her face would turn blue if she chewed blueberry bubble gum.

"Some guy at the hospital . . ."

"Hospital?" Her gaze moved over him again. "What hospital? Were you wounded in action?"

"I had a high fever for a while." Sam lifted one hand to the back of his head. "I got shot. They said I hit my head pretty hard, probably when I fell."

"Go on."

"Anyway, some guy at the hospital recognized me. He told me my grandfather lived in Vista Verde. I looked up the address in the phone book. Is he here?"

Sky folded her arms over her chest, wishing she didn't

have to tell him bad news when he'd just returned home. But putting it off wouldn't make it any easier. "Granda passed away while you were gone."

"Were we close?"

"Very. He raised the two of us after our parents died." Sky bit down on her lower lip. How could he not remember?

"Boyle said you were living in Chicago."

"I was, but I moved back here after Granda passed away." She reached for his hand again. "Come on, let's have a cup of coffee. We have a lot to talk about."

Skylynn sat by the front window, staring out at the rain. Sam was home, wounded in mind and body. They had talked for almost three hours, with Sam asking her one question after another about their parents, their grandparents, events of the past.

Sky had dug out an old family album, hoping that photographs of people he had known and places they had visited might help him remember. She had waited, hoping that seeing their old house, his old friends, might trigger a memory, but so far it wasn't happening. Sometimes she thought she saw a spark of recognition in his eyes, but then it would fade.

"Who's this?" he had asked, pointing at a photograph of Nick taken shortly before the wedding.

Sky had stared at the picture. How had she missed that one? After the divorce, she had thrown away everything that reminded her of her ex-husband. She told Sam about her disastrous marriage and quick divorce in as few words as possible and then pointed at a photo of Sam and a small black and tan puppy.

"Do you remember Nellie?" she asked. "We found her in an alley. She'd been hit by a car and you nursed her back to health."

Sam stared at the photo for a long time, his brow furrowed, and then he shook his head.

"Maybe seeing your room will help," Sky suggested, and Sam followed her up the stairs.

She had stood in the doorway, watching as he walked around the room. It was still decorated as it had been when Sam was in high school, with posters of rock stars and baseball pennants on the walls. A number of CDs and DVDs lined the shelf over his bed, an old footlocker held his favorite baseball glove, a bat, a football, a pair of inline skates, and other odds and ends from his teen years.

When he was finished, he looked at her and shrugged.

Skylynn hid her disappointment behind a smile as they returned to the living room. Telling Sam to rest, she escaped into the kitchen. For a moment, she stood at the sink fighting back her tears. She had to stay positive for Sam's sake. Remembering that she had read somewhere that familiar scents could awaken old memories, she made a batch of chocolate chip cookies.

As soon as the cookies were done, she put a dozen or so on a plate, poured two glasses of milk, and carried everything out into the living room.

Sam looked up, smiling for the first time since he had come home. "Smells good."

"They're your favorite. Remember how we always liked to eat the raw dough and how Grams used to pretend to get mad whenever we snitched some?"

Sam's face scrunched up as he tried to remember, and then he shook his head. "No. Sorry."

"It's okay. Don't try to force it. I know it'll all come back to you."

Sam raked his hand through his hair. "What if it doesn't?"

"Then we'll just have to make new memories."

* * *

That had been two hours ago. Now, she found herself wondering why the army had released Sam when he was still suffering from amnesia. She didn't know anything about the illness other than that it was usually caused by a sharp blow to the head, which was apparently what had happened to Sam.

She paused as a horrible thought occurred to her. What if the army hadn't released Sam? What if he was AWOL? Lordy, didn't she have enough on her plate without worrying that the army would come and arrest her brother?

She glanced upstairs. Sam had gone up to take a nap. Kaiden was asleep in her room. That was going to require some explaining, she thought. What would Sam think when he found out Kaiden had been spending the night here? Then again, maybe seeing Kaiden would be the key that would unlock Sam's memory. Lord, she hoped so.

Thorne woke with the setting of the sun. A single breath, and he knew Sky wasn't alone in the house. A second breath told him the visitor was her brother, Sam. So, the boy was alive.

Rising, Thorne dissolved into mist. Moments later, he reappeared in his own house, where he took a quick shower, then pulled on a pair of clean jeans, a long-sleeved gray T-shirt, and a pair of running shoes. Whistling softly, he walked across the street and knocked on Sky's door.

He had to laugh at the expression on her face when she saw him standing on the porch.

"What are you doing out there? I thought you were upstairs."

"I was, but I needed a shower and a change of clothes."

"You could have showered here," she said, smiling up at him. "I could have washed your back."

"Sounds nice, but I wasn't sure how your brother would feel about that."

"How'd you know he was here?"

He tapped the side of his nose. "Vampire, remember?"

"Oh, right." She kept forgetting about his preternatural senses. "Well, get on in here."

Thorne followed her into the front room and sat beside her on the sofa. "So, how is he?"

"Not good. He's got amnesia."

Thorne rubbed a hand over his jaw. "I'm surprised they let him come home."

"Me, too. I'm worried about him. He looks . . . haunted."

"Well, I'd say that was normal, considering what he's been doing and where he's been."

"I know, but . . . he's so thin and pale. He doesn't remember how he got wounded or what caused him to lose his memory. Of course, he doesn't remember me, either."

Thorne slipped his arm around her shoulders and gave her a squeeze. "I'm sure he'll be fine, in time. He's young and resilient. And he's in good hands."

"Thanks." Sky leaned into him, grateful for his nearness. She wasn't afraid of anything, not when Kaiden was beside her. "Maybe you could read his mind and find out what happened?"

"Maybe. It depends on what caused his amnesia."

"What do you mean?"

"If it's a physical problem, then there's not much I can do. If he's burying something unpleasant, something he doesn't want to remember, then I might be able to help, depending on how deeply he's buried it. I can try, if you want."

"I don't know. Let me think about it."

"Sure."

"I'm so glad he's home, but I really think he needs to go back to the hospital where they can treat his amnesia."

"I guess that's something the two of you will have to decide."

She looked up at him, her eyes filled with worry. "What

if he starts having flashbacks or he decides to, oh, I don't know, just take off without telling me?"

"Calm down, Sky Blue. Letting your imagination run away with you won't help."

"I know. You're right. I just can't help worrying about him." She smiled wistfully. "That's funny, isn't it? Sam was always the one who looked after me."

"I guess that's what families are for. You take turns looking after each other."

"Was your family like that?"

"Not hardly. My parents were all about appearances."

"What do you mean?"

"My father was landed gentry."

"I'm not sure what that means, exactly."

"Back in the sixteenth century it meant a landowner who was untitled. Land equaled wealth in those days. My father lived off the rents he collected from tenant farmers. Class was all important at the time. My parents were somewhere between the aristocracy and the middle class. My mother was very conscious of her place in society, always worried about making a good impression on her betters. I didn't care about any of that. I was more interested in . . ." He paused as he reconsidered his next words.

"In what?"

"Mostly wenching and gambling."

"Wenching? Why doesn't that surprise me?"

"I seem to be down to just one wench at the moment."

"That's right, mister!" She punched him in the arm. "And you'd better keep it that way."

"Yes, ma'am, that's my plan."

"Good." She snuggled into his arms again, and that was how Sam found them a few minutes later.

Feeling suddenly self-conscious, Skylynn sat up and put some space between herself and Kaiden. "Sam, come on in."

He entered the room warily, as if he expected to be attacked. She noticed he had showered and shaved and changed into a shirt and a pair of jeans he had left behind when he enlisted. Keeping his gaze on Thorne, Sam sat in the chair next to the fireplace.

"Sam, this is Kaiden Thorne." Sky watched her brother's face, searching for some sign of recognition. "He lives across the street."

Sam nodded, his expression blank.

"It's good to see you again, Sam," Thorne said.

"Yeah, thanks." Sam muttered.

"Maybe I should leave you two alone," Thorne suggested. "I'm sure you have a lot of catching up to do."

Sky looked at Kaiden, her gaze searching his.

Thorne reached for her hand. Her fingers tingled at his touch, and then she heard his voice in her mind.

My being here is making him uncomfortable. It'll be better if I go.

Sky nodded. "Thanks for coming by." Rising, she followed Kaiden to the front door. Lowering her voice so Sam wouldn't hear, she asked, "Will you come back later?"

"After he's asleep," Thorne said. Drawing her close, he kissed her, hard and quick, and then he left the house.

Skylynn stared after him a moment; then, with a sigh, she closed the door and went back into the living room.

"So, things look pretty tight with you and that Thorne guy," Sam remarked.

"I like him a lot," Sky admitted, resuming her seat on the sofa.

"Are you gonna marry him?"

"I don't know. He hasn't asked me."

"What if he did?"

"I don't know," Sky said, frowning. Did vampires even get married?

"I'm not married, or anything, am I?" Sam asked.

"No. You dated several girls before you were sent to Iraq, but as far as I know, you weren't serious about any of them."

"Good thing," he muttered. "None of them would want me now."

"Sam . . ."

"You don't know what it's like!" He stood abruptly, his eyes flashing with anger and frustration. "You tell me this is our house, that you're my sister. It's just words. They don't mean anything. It's like I'm nobody."

"Maybe you should go back to the hospital. Maybe they could help you there."

"Even my own sister doesn't want me."

"That's not true! I just don't know how to help you."

"Nobody can help me! Nobody! I'm out of here!"

"Sam, wait! Where are you going?"

"Who the hell cares?" he shouted, and ran out of the house.

"Sam!" She ran after him but he was much faster than she was. She stopped at the end of the block, one hand pressed to her side as she peered down the street. Where would he go?

Telling herself he wouldn't go far, she went back home to wait.

Fighting tears, Sam ran down the street, faster and faster, as if by running swiftly enough, he could leave the past behind and find himself again.

It was impossible, of course, like so many things in life.

After several blocks, he slowed to a walk. Hands shoved in his pockets, head down, he wandered aimlessly up one street and down another until he found himself nearing a strip mall next to the highway.

Music drew him into a small, neighborhood bar. He paused at the entrance; then, muttering, "What the hell," he pushed the door open and went inside.

It was a small place with a western motif. A wagon wheel chandelier hung from the ceiling, there was sawdust on the floor, a brass rail along the bar, a picture of a herd of buffalo stampeding across the plains on one wall, several smaller pictures of cowboys and Indians on another. On the small stage located in one corner of the room, a young woman crooned a ballad while a handful of couples line-danced on the handkerchief-sized dance floor.

Sam found an empty stool at the bar and sat down, only then realizing he didn't have a dime to his name.

He looked up when a bartender wearing a black vest and string tie asked, "What can I get for you?"

"I haven't decided."

"Let me know when you've made up your mind," the bartender said, and quickly moved on.

"Can I buy you a drink?"

Sam looked at the woman sitting on the bar stool beside him. "You talkin' to me?"

"I don't see anybody else sitting there." She smiled, a wide friendly smile. "Are you all right? You look sort of . . . I don't know, lost."

"Yeah," he muttered. "Lost is what I am."

"Maybe I can help you find your way."

Sam looked at her sharply. He might not remember who he was, but he recognized a come-on when he heard it.

"I don't think so," he murmured, and wondered what the hell was wrong with him. She was the most remarkable creature he had ever seen. Her skin was almost translucent. Hair, like brown silk, flowed over her shoulders in luxurious waves. Her eyes, beneath thick dark lashes, were the deepest shade of green he had ever seen.

"Well, my offer of a drink still stands."

"Thanks, but I can't buy you one in return."

"Did I ask?" She signaled for the bartender. "Now, what would you like?"

Chapter 29

Thorne was sitting in front of the fireplace, lost in thoughts of Skylynn, when she knocked on the door.

"Sky," he murmured, "this is a pleasant surprise."

"I need your help."

"What's wrong?"

"Sam's run off." She shook her head. "I'm such an idiot. We were talking. He was feeling bad about not being able to remember anything and I . . . I suggested maybe he should go back to the hospital, and he got upset and ran out of the house."

"How long ago?"

"I don't know. Half an hour maybe. I was hoping he'd come back. I don't think he has any money. He doesn't remember anybody in town. Where would he go?"

"All right, calm down. I'll find him."

"I'll go with you."

"I can search faster on my own."

"But . . . oh, right." She smiled faintly. "Vampire."

"Right," he said with a wink. "Come on, I'll walk you home. It shouldn't take long to hunt him down."

Taking Sky by the hand, he walked her across the street.

He paused on the sidewalk in front of the house. Lifting his head, he closed his eyes and took a deep breath.

It took only moments to sort Sam's scent from all the others.

"Go inside and lock the door," Thorne said.

"What about Sam?"

"I've got his scent. It won't be hard to follow. Don't answer the door for anyone but me."

She looked at him, frowning, and then, remembering Girard, she nodded. "Be careful."

"Don't worry about me."

"I can't help it."

Smiling, he drew her into his arms and kissed her. "And I love you for it. Now go inside so I'll know you're safe."

She gave him a quick kiss on the cheek, then headed for the porch.

Thorne watched her run up the walkway. When she reached the foot of the porch steps, she turned and waved, then hurried up the stairs and into the house.

He waited until he heard the turn of the lock before starting off down the street.

As he followed the boy's scent, Thorne thought about his own past. He could sympathize with Skylynn's brother even though he, himself, had never lost his memory. Still, when he had become a vampire, he had lost everything that was familiar to him. Fear of discovery had kept him away from his favorite gaming halls and the young men of his acquaintance. And it had forever destroyed any hope, however faint it might have been, of repairing the riff with his parents, something he had not realized he wanted until it was beyond his reach.

Once Death had abandoned him, he had wandered across the countryside feeling lost and alone, cut off from everything and everyone he knew. In those days, filled with anger and resentment, he had often killed those he preyed upon. As a young vampire, those deaths had meant nothing to him. Now, older and wiser, denied the pleasures of home and family, he realized how precious mortal life was. And with that knowledge had come an abiding regret for the lives he had so thoughtlessly and callously taken.

He followed Sam's trail into a local tavern. His relief at finding the boy was quickly replaced by alarm when he recognized the woman sitting beside him.

Cassandra. What the devil was she doing here?

She glanced over her shoulder as he walked up behind her. "Kaiden. How nice to see you."

"Cassandra." He glanced from his maker to Sam and back again. "What's going on here?"

She smiled as she brushed a lock of hair from Sam's brow. "I've just been buying this darling boy a drink."

"More than one, I'd say." It was obvious that Sam was far from sober.

Cassandra lifted one shoulder in an elegant shrug. "I may have lost count."

Sam glared at Thorne. "What are you doing here?" he asked, his tone belligerent and thick with whiskey.

"I've come to take you home. Skylynn is worried about you."

"Worried? Hah!" He swayed unsteadily on the bar stool. "She don't give a damn about me. Go way."

"Really, Kaiden, I'm not going to hurt the boy," Cassandra said. "I'm just trying to ease his pain."

"Yeah? Well, I'd say you've done a helluva job. I doubt if he's feeling much of anything right now."

"What does it matter to you?" she demanded, all trace of sweetness gone from her voice.

"He's a friend of mine. Come on, kid, I'm taking you home."

Sam shook his head. "Wanna stay here."

"You see? He wants to stay here. And I want him to stay."

Thorne braced himself as her eyes flashed red. It was a warning he recognized. A moment later, her power enveloped him, stealing his breath, pressing in on him until it felt as if he was being crushed.

It took every ounce of control he possessed to swallow the groan that rose in his throat.

She smiled smugly when she released him. "I want him," she repeated.

Thorne shook his head. "You'll have to fight me for him."

Cassandra uttered a word once only seen scrawled on the walls of the men's room. "Don't be a fool. You're no match for me."

"It doesn't matter. I can't go back and tell his sister I failed."

"Hey," Sam said. "What the hell are you two talkin' about?"

Cassandra patted Sam's shoulder. "Nothing for you to worry about, my pet. Finish your drink."

"No." Thorne plucked the shot glass from the bar and dumped the contents on the floor. "He's had enough."

"Hey!" Sam took a swing at Thorne, his arms flailing as he lost his balance and started to topple off the bar stool.

Swearing with disgust, Thorne caught the kid before he hit the ground, slung him over his shoulder, and held him there with one hand.

"We're leaving, Cassandra. And even though you're older than I am, I want to remind you that the ancient laws still apply."

"Don't talk to me about the laws," she snapped. "I made them."

"Maybe so, but this is still my territory and you're here at my discretion."

And so saying, he turned his back on the vampire who had sired him and stalked out of the tavern.

* * *

Skylynn breathed a sigh of relief when she opened the door and saw Kaiden standing there with Sam cradled in his arms.

"Is he all right?" she asked anxiously.

"He's drunk," Thorne replied. "Where do you want him?"

"Upstairs. His bedroom is down the hall from mine."

With a nod, Thorne followed Sky up to Sam's room, waited while she drew back the covers before lowering her brother onto the bed.

"Do you want me to undress him?" he asked.

"Thank you. I'll wait downstairs."

In the living room, Sky sank down on the sofa, but she was too keyed up to sit still. Rising, she went into the kitchen, thinking a cup of hot chocolate might relax her, only to find that, after she fixed it, she didn't want it. She poured it down the drain, then stood there, staring out the window.

What was she going to do about Sam? He had never been much of a drinker before he left home. What other bad habits had he picked up along the way? Had he turned into an alcoholic, or was that just a one-time bender born out of desperation and despair?

She turned as Kaiden entered the room, bemused that she had sensed his presence before he actually appeared in the doorway.

"He'll be all right," Thorne said, answering her unspoken question. For a moment, he considered telling her about Cassandra's interest in Sam, but then decided against it. Sky had enough on her mind without worrying that a vampire wanted her brother. Besides, he was pretty sure that Cassandra wouldn't bother Sam again. No matter what she said to the contrary, she had always adhered to the laws she had set for their kind.

"Thank you for finding him for me."

"No problem," he replied, taking her into his arms. "You know I'd do anything for you."

She slid her arms up around his neck. "Anything?"

"Just name it and it's yours."

"A kiss?"

"Just one?"

"As many as you can spare." She needed him. Needed to feel loved. Protected. Safe. Needed something to distract her thoughts from a brother who had problems she couldn't fix, who might have deep psychological scars she would never understand.

She looked up at Kaiden, swamped by a sudden rush of guilt because she was using him to escape reality, and because she had prayed and prayed for her brother to come home and now that he was there, she didn't know how to help him. One look into Kaiden's eyes told her he knew exactly what she was doing.

Wordlessly, he swung her into his arms and carried her swiftly up the stairs to her room. A thought closed and locked the door. Still holding Sky, he pressed butterfly kisses to her brow, her cheeks, the hollow of her throat before he carried Skylynn to the bed.

She reached for him, but he gently swatted her hands away.

"Patience, love," he murmured. "We have all night."

She gazed up at him, lost in the dark depths of his eyes as he undressed her ever so slowly, his mouth like fire as he kissed each inch of exposed flesh.

He left her for a moment to remove his own clothing and then he stretched out beside Sky, his arms wrapping around her to draw Skylynn close as his lips claimed hers in a long, searing kiss that burned everything from her mind but her need for this man's touch. The rest of the world seemed to fall away as he rose over her and there were only the two of them locked in each other's arms.

She felt the brush of his mind against hers and the next thing she knew, they were lying on a blanket in a verdant meadow beneath a summer-blue sky. Birds sang in the trees that surrounded the meadow.

She writhed beneath him, his name a cry on her lips as

their bodies moved in perfect rhythm, each one giving pleasure to the other.

She had only to think of what she wanted—a kiss here, a caress there, and it was hers.

She climaxed amid a burst of silver light that seemed to fill her entire being with pleasure almost beyond bearing and then, enveloped in a warmth unlike anything she had ever known, she slowly and deliciously drifted back to reality.

"I feel like I should thank you," she murmured with a smile. "That was incredible."

"You're welcome." He rolled onto his side, carrying her with him.

"How did you do that, make it seem like we were in a meadow?"

"A little vampire magic."

She lay there, cocooned in his arms, spent and content, while the perspiration cooled on her body and her breathing returned to normal.

Thorne nuzzled the side of her neck and she felt the brush of his fangs against her skin.

"You didn't bite me this time," she said. "Why not?"

"I didn't trust myself to stop while we were making love." His tongue slid over her shoulder, making her shiver with delight. "But I wouldn't mind taking a sip now, if you're willing."

"How can I refuse?" she asked with a lazy grin. "You certainly deserve a reward."

He chuckled softly.

Moments later, she felt the faint sting of his fangs and then a rush of sensual heat that rivaled the pleasure she had enjoyed in his arms.

Closing her eyes, she tumbled into a warm red sea.

Thorne sensed the change in her, knew the instant sleep claimed her. He drew back, his gaze moving over her face and then, unable to resist the allure of her sweetness, he bent his head to her neck once again.

Chapter 30

Girard prowled the shadows outside the McNamara house. Why had he waited so long to embrace the dark side of life? The longer he was a vampire, the more he reveled in it. His physical strength and speed were incredible. He might look like an old man, but he had the vitality and staying power of a stud horse. His increased senses were remarkable.

He knew there were two mortals inside the house. He could hear the slow, steady beating of their hearts, the shallow breathing that told him they were sleeping soundly. A third heart—a vampire heart—beat more slowly. Thorne was also in the house.

Girard lifted his head. An indrawn breath carried the scent of musk and fresh blood. So, the vampire had used his whore and then fed on her.

Girard turned away from the house. Melting into the darkness, he reappeared several blocks away. He had never been a patient man, but time was no longer his enemy. No matter how much it galled him to do so, he would abide by Cassandra's decree because he had no other choice, at least for now. He was not fool enough to pit his fledgling strength against that of an ancient vampire, and so he would not harm Kaiden Thorne in the foreseeable future.

Girard smiled into the darkness. There was no need to hurry. He had time to wait for the perfect opportunity to exact his revenge, and when it came, he would savor every delicious moment. He could picture it clearly in his mind, taste it on his tongue, as he imagined killing the woman. He would not make her suffer too long. He was not a monster, after all, and she was only a means to an end. He trembled with the realization that avenging Marie's death was almost in reach. Only then would he find peace.

But there was no rush now. He would wait until Thorne and the woman lowered their guard. Wait until they thought the danger was past. And then, when the woman was alone and vulnerable, her defenses down, he would strike.

Retribution would be swift and final for the woman, but her death would torment Kaiden Thorne for the remainder of his existence.

Ah, vengeance was indeed a dish best served cold.

Whistling softly, Girard left the town in search of prey.

Chapter 31

An hour before dawn, Thorne dressed and left Skylynn's place. Even though she had willingly allowed him to drink from her, the little he had taken had only whet his appetite for more. He was beginning to think that abstaining from his natural instincts for so long had made satisfying the return of his hellish thirst impossible.

As he descended the porch steps, he wondered if there would ever again come a time when he didn't feel the need to hunt every night.

He had almost reached the corner when he caught a scent that made his hackles rise. Desmarais had been there, loitering beneath the tree near Skylynn's bedroom window, and not so long ago.

Swearing softly, Thorne retraced his footsteps. Crossing the street, he walked around Skylynn's house. There was no indication that Desmarais had gone into the backyard or approached any of the doors. Still, his presence so close to Skylynn was unsettling.

Dissolving into mist, Thorne returned to Skylynn's bedroom. She slept on her side, her cheek pillowed on her hand, a faint smile on her lips. A smile he had put there.

Resuming his own form, he went to check on Sam. The

boy was sprawled facedown on the mattress, one leg sticking out of the covers, one arm hanging over the edge of the bed.

Kaiden stood there a moment, then, opening his senses, he moved through Sam's mind. The boy wasn't hiding from anything; his amnesia had been caused by a hard blow to the back of his head. He would let Sky know tomorrow.

Satisfied that neither of the McNamaras were in imminent danger, Thorne walked down the hallway toward the master bedroom. Hunting would have to wait until tonight. No way was he going to leave Skylynn and Sam alone while they were asleep and vulnerable, not when Desmarais had been sniffing around.

The master bedroom was a large square room done in shades of brown and green with lots of ruffles and lace. It was obvious that Paddy hadn't changed a thing since Maureen passed away. Several family photos were scattered across the top of the chest of drawers. A frame on the wall next to the bed held the image of two tiny handprints. A sewing basket sat next to a pair of glasses on one of the bedside tables; a long blue nightgown hung from the back of the door.

It seemed almost indecent to even think of sleeping in the bed Paddy had shared with his wife, but it couldn't be helped. It would be dawn soon. He needed a place to spend the daylight hours, but taking his rest in Sky's bed was out of the question now that Sam was home. And even though the odds were slim that anything would happen during the day, he intended to stay nearby, just in case.

After locking the door, Thorne slipped off his running shoes, stripped down to his briefs, and slid under the covers. He could feel the lethargy stealing over his body, leeching his strength, drawing him down into the thick, velvet blackness that was like death.

* * *

Sky was in the kitchen trying to decide what to have for breakfast when Sam shuffled into the room. His surly expression and the dark shadows under his eyes were ample proof that he'd had a rough night.

"You got any coffee?" he asked, slumping onto a chair.

"Of course. Do you still take it black?"

He snorted. "It ain't coffee any other way."

Ignoring his gruff tone, she poured a cup for Sam and one for herself, then sat at the table across from him. Feeling like a child defying authority, she laced her coffee with two teaspoons of sugar and a healthy dollop of milk.

"What happened last night?" he asked. "How'd I get home?"

"Kaiden brought you back. You were dead drunk."

Sam's gaze slid away from hers. "I don't remember," he said, his tone surly. "But what the hell, I don't remember much of anything else, either."

"Drinking like a fish won't bring your memory back."

"I'm sorry, Skylynn," he muttered. "I know I'm behaving like a jerk, but . . ."

"Hey," she said, smiling. "You can't help it."

"Are you saying I was always a jerk?" he asked with a wry grin.

Sky felt a rush of hope at the familiar banter. "Not always."

"Just most of the time?"

He sounded so much like the old Sam, she wanted to kiss him. Instead, she asked him what he wanted for breakfast.

Later, while loading the dishwasher, Skylynn wondered where Kaiden had gone. After the night they had shared, she had expected to wake up beside him. But then, her vampire rarely did what she expected.

Her vampire. The thought made her stomach curl with pleasure. Last night, after they made love, he had asked if he could drink from her. After what they had shared, there was no way she could have refused. Not that she had wanted to.

She lifted a hand to her neck, thinking how strange it was that something that sounded so hideously repulsive could be so gratifying. Was she being foolish to trust him not to take too much? He had admitted he didn't trust himself to stop while they were making love, though she wasn't sure why that made a difference. She pondered the question for a few minutes. Giving him her blood had been an unexpectedly sensual experience. Was it the same for him? Would she die if he took too much? Or, worse, become what he was? Maybe she would ask him about that later.

In the old movie, *Love at First Bite,* it had taken three bites for George Hamilton's Dracula to turn the girl into a vampire. In *Twilight*, becoming a vampire had been described as a horribly painful process that took days, certainly not something Sky would ever want to experience. In other books she had read, an exchange of blood had been necessary for the transformation.

No matter how it happened, there was always biting and blood involved.

The drone of the lawn mower drew her gaze to the backyard. Looking out the kitchen window, she smiled when Sam waved at her. Once again, she felt a rush of hope that, with time, everything would be all right.

She dried her hands after starting the dishwasher, then went upstairs to change the sheets on her bed. At the top of the stairs, a strange vibration in the air drew her down the hallway to Granda's bedroom. She paused a moment before trying the door, only to discover it was locked.

She frowned a moment, then called, "Kaiden, are you in there?"

There was no answer, of course. If he was in there, he would be asleep. And then, to her surprise, she heard his voice inside her head asking if she was all right.

After assuring him all was well, she went into her own

After lunch, Sam suggested they take in a movie, and Sky agreed. After all, it was hours until dark. Hours until she saw Kaiden again.

On the drive home, they talked about the movie for a few minutes before Sam said, "When I was in the hospital, Boyle said I have a VW. Do I?"

"Yeah. It's in the garage."

"Maybe I'll take it out and see if it still runs."

"Of course it runs."

"How do you know?" he asked, and then his eyes widened in alarm. "You drove my Bug?"

"Geez, don't go ballistic. I only drove it once a week or so, just to keep the battery charged. You should be thanking me."

"Yeah," he said, looking properly contrite. "Thanks."

"You're welcome."

"You should get a new car," he said, breaking for a red light. "This Lincoln is ancient."

"I know, but it belonged to Granda." Skylynn ran her hand lovingly over the dashboard. "Besides, it's in good shape."

"Don't you want a car of your own?"

She shrugged. "I was leasing one in Chicago. I don't know, maybe I'll buy a new one, now that I'm here to stay. If I ever find a job."

Sam pulled into the driveway and cut the engine. "Do you have the keys to the Bug?"

"They're in the yellow jar on the mantel."

With a nod, Sam got out of the car and hurried into the house.

Sky followed him inside, biting down on her lower lip to keep from asking him not to go. She couldn't keep him locked up inside. He was a grown man, after all, but she couldn't help worrying that if he left the house, something would happen to him.

She blew out a breath. On the other hand, driving around town in his own car might help to bring his memory back.

"Don't wait up," he said, twirling the key ring around his finger.

"Sam . . ."

"What?"

"Be careful, okay?"

"Sure."

"If you get lost . . ."

He cocked an eyebrow at her. "I might not know who I am, but I think I can find my way around."

She forced a smile. "Right."

Still, that wasn't going to keep her from worrying about him while he was gone.

She was in the living room, trying to find something to watch on TV, when the doorbell rang. She hurried to answer it, hoping it was Kaiden. A thrill of excitement shot through her from head to foot when she called, "Who's there?" and heard his voice answer, "It's me."

As soon as she opened the door, he wrapped her in his arms. "Hey."

"Hey, yourself. I thought you were upstairs."

"I went home to shower and change clothes."

"Oh. You could have spent the night in my bed, you know."

He explained, quickly, how he had left the house last night, only to return after detecting Desmarais' scent nearby.

"I wish he'd just go away and leave us alone!" Sky exclaimed angrily.

"Hey, enough about him," Thorne said. "I read Sam's mind last night. As near as I can tell, his injury was caused by a blow to the head."

"That's good news, I guess."

Kaiden skimmed his hands up and down her arms. "I missed you."

"I missed you, too."

"Did you?" he asked with a wicked grin. "How much?"

"This much." Throwing her arms around his neck, she stood on her tiptoes and kissed him, amazed anew that such a handsome, sexy man wanted her. Being near him was like having Christmas every day. Each smile, each kiss, was a gift to cherish. He was immortal, powerful, charming, and he loved her. Best of all, he would never die and leave her alone.

"I guess you really did miss me," he murmured as he nuzzled her neck. "How long will Sam be gone?"

"Not long enough."

"Then we'd better not waste any time," he said with mock gravity, and kissed her again.

When they came up for air, he drew her to the sofa, then sat, cradling her on his lap.

"I hate it when we're apart." Skylynn wrapped her arms around his waist, her head resting on his shoulder.

"I'm not too crazy about it, either."

"Do vampires ever get married?"

"What?" Thorne stared at her, astonished by her question.

"You heard me. Or isn't your super-duper hearing working tonight?"

"I heard you. I just . . ." He shook his head. "You took me by surprise, that's all."

"I guess human or vampire, men are all the same. As soon as a girl mentions marriage, they get cold feet."

"Are you seriously asking me to marry you?"

"Of course not. Well . . . I don't know." She bit down on her lower lip, her brow furrowing. "What would you say if I was? Serious? About asking you?"

"I'd probably say you should have your head examined."

"Oh. So, this . . ." Her gaze slid away from his. "What we have, it's just . . . sex? A fling?"

He caught her chin between his thumb and forefinger, forcing her to look at him. "You know that's not true."

"Do I?"

"Skylynn, I'm a vampire, remember? Not exactly prime marriage material."

"It's okay." She wriggled off his lap and onto the sofa. "I understand."

"Like hell!" He scrubbed his hands up and down his thighs. "I love you. If I still had the potion, if we could have some semblance of a normal life . . ."

She lowered her gaze to the floor. "What's so great about being normal?"

He ran a hand over his jaw. She was so young. She had no idea what she was saying. What she was asking. "I'll never be able to share your whole life," he said quietly. "I can't give you a family. I can't share a meal with you, or stay in one place too long . . ."

He sighed as a single, fat tear rolled down her cheek. "Sky Blue . . . Dammit, you mean more to me than anything on this earth. I don't want to hurt you." He raked his fingers through his hair. "I love you more than you'll ever know. I want to be with you always, but without the potion . . ." He shook his head.

"We're together now."

"Darlin', I don't know how long I can trust myself to stay here with you, be close to you, and not . . ." He shook his head. "Dammit, I just don't know."

"I'm not afraid of you. I'm only afraid of living without you."

"I'll stay with you as long as I can."

"Then why can't we get married?"

"What if I start to lose control? What if I have to leave to keep you safe?"

"That could happen now." She took a deep breath. "You could . . . you could make me what you are."

"No!" He sprang to his feet, his expression grim.

"Why not?" Lord, was she out of her mind? What was she

saying? She didn't want to be a vampire. But she didn't want to lose Kaiden, either. "Is it so bad, being what you are?"

He shoved his hands into the pockets of his jeans. "It isn't something I would have chosen."

"Have you ever made another vampire?"

"No."

She took a deep breath. She knew what she wanted, and she wanted Kaiden. "I want to belong to you. Unless you don't want me."

"Didn't I just say I loved you?"

"Actions speak louder than words. I won't ask you again, Kaiden."

He shook his head, charmed by her stubbornness. "All right, Sky Blue, if you're sure that's what you want." Dropping down on one knee in front of her, he took her right hand in his. "Skylynn McNamara, will you do me the honor of becoming my wife?"

Chapter 32

With a joyful "What do you think?" Skylynn threw herself at Kaiden, toppling him over backward. Straddling his hips, she leaned forward to kiss him, then exclaimed, "I can't wait to tell Sam. And Tara."

"Just like a woman," Thorne said with a smile.

She drew back a little so she could see his face. "I've always wanted to get married in a long white dress in a church. . . . That won't be a problem for you, will it? The church, I mean?"

"No."

"Good." She sighed wistfully. "I wish Granda was here to give me away."

He brushed a lock of hair behind her ear. "I doubt if he'd be too thrilled at your choice of a husband."

"Why do you say that?" she exclaimed. "He liked you. A lot."

"Not enough to marry his granddaughter."

She didn't want to talk about that. "It'll be a small wedding. I don't have a lot of people to invite. Just Sam and Tara and maybe a few of my friends from back East, if they want to make the trip." She had a lot of acquaintances in

Chicago but no really close friends other than Tara. "And anyone you want to invite, of course."

"There won't be anyone on my side of the church."

"You won't mind, will you, if we don't have a big, splashy affair?"

"Whatever you want is fine with me." He stroked her cheek. "I won't see anyone but you."

"You really do say the nicest things. Are all vampires as sweet as you are?"

"You think I'm sweet?" He almost choked on the word. He had been called a lot of things in his time, but *sweet* wasn't one of them.

She raised up on her elbows. "Should I get up? Am I hurting you?"

He lifted one brow. "What do you think?"

She stuck her tongue out at him. "Yeah, yeah, I know, you're a big strong vampire."

"Want me to prove it?" he asked with a wicked leer.

"Not right now," she replied primly. "It shouldn't take long to arrange a small wedding."

"What's the hurry? Afraid I'll change my mind?"

"Yes."

"Sky, I've loved you in one way or another your whole life. Married or not, I will always be here to look after you. I'm not going anywhere. So take all the time you need."

"All the time for what?" Sam asked, breezing into the living room.

"We're getting married!" Sky replied. Scrambling to her feet, she smoothed her hair and straightened her sweater.

Thorne sat up, his back braced against the sofa, his arms resting on his bent knees.

"Really?" Sam glanced at Thorne, then back at Skylynn. "That's ah . . . that's great."

"You don't approve?" Skylynn stared at her brother, her hands fisted on her hips.

He shrugged. "Whatever makes you happy works for me. I guess you'll want me to move out."

"Don't be silly. I'll move in with Kaiden and you can stay here. The house is half yours, after all."

"So, when's the big day?" Sam asked.

"We haven't set a date yet. Probably not for a couple of weeks. I need to find a dress and invite a few friends from back East." She worried her lower lip between her teeth. "It might be longer than that. Tara has to be here, and the last time I talked to her, she was in Vermont with her mom."

Sky smacked her forehead with her palm. "Some friend I am! I should have called to see how her dad is doing. I think I'll do that now, before I forget."

"She's something, isn't she?" Sam murmured as he watched his sister leave the room.

"Yeah." Thorne's gaze followed Sam's. Skylynn was something, all right. Part innocent, part temptress and all woman.

Sam dropped into the chair across from the sofa, his long legs stretched out in front of him. "I was driving around tonight, not going anywhere in particular, but things looked familiar, you know? I mean, I don't really remember these places and yet I knew I'd seen them before."

"Sounds like your memory might be coming back," Thorne remarked.

"I hope so. Do you want a beer?"

"No, thanks."

"I don't think she keeps anything stronger in the house."

"It's all right," Thorne said. "I'll get something later."

"You don't drink?"

"Not alcohol."

"Really? Well," Sam remarked, slapping his hands on the arms of the chair, "I think I'm gonna call it a night."

"See you tomorrow."

"No doubt," Sam said, grinning.

Thorne watched Sam go up the stairs and then, unable

to resist, he honed in on Skylynn and opened his vampiric senses.

". . . so glad to hear that," she was saying.

"He's coming home tomorrow," Tara said. "He has to take it easy for a while, of course, but the doctors are optimistic that he'll recover without any ill effects."

"That's wonderful news. So, have you reset the date for your wedding?"

There was a long pause, and then Tara said, "We called it off."

"What? Oh, Tara, I'm so sorry, but . . . what happened?"

"I found out he . . . he . . . he's not to be trusted!"

Sky heard the heartache in Tara's voice, knew her friend was trying not to cry.

"While I've been here, taking care of my mom and trying to keep my dad's spirits up, Lance has been out on the town with another woman."

"Did he tell you that?"

"No. My friend Nancy saw him in a bar with some blonde. When I confronted Lance, he denied it at first, and then he admitted it was true." Tara sniffed loudly. "It's probably just as well. His mother hates me."

"I don't know what to say. Is there anything I can do?"

"No. Men are scum." Tara sighed dramatically. "So, what's new with you? Are you still seeing that guy across the street?"

Sky hesitated, wondering if she should tell Tara about her upcoming wedding now, when her friend's plans were in the toilet.

"Sky? Don't tell me he proposed."

"Not exactly. I asked him to marry me."

"What? Are you kidding?"

"Nope. If you feel up to it, and you can get away, I'd love for you to be my maid of honor."

"I wouldn't miss it, you know that. Now, tell me all about him. What does he do?"

"He doesn't do anything. I guess he must be rich."

"You guess?"

Funny, Sky thought, she had never really wondered about that. Where *did* Kaiden get his money?

"Must be nice," Tara remarked. "That means you won't have to work unless you want to."

"What? Oh, right. Listen, I've got to go."

"Okay. Let me know when you set the date."

"I will. Bye for now." Sky disconnected the call, then sat there, her fingers tapping the side of the phone.

Where did Kaiden get his money? Did he rob his victims of their cash as well as their blood? Of course, he probably didn't need a lot of money. He had lived in that big old house for so long, it was surely paid for by now. Still, there was upkeep on the house and grounds, taxes on the property. Utility bills. He always drove a new car. His clothes were well-made and looked expensive.

It occurred to her that she really didn't know much about the man she wanted to marry, except that he was a vampire, and she loved him.

In the living room, Kaiden frowned as Skylynn hung up the phone. Love really was blind, he thought with a wry grin. He couldn't help wondering if she would change her mind about marrying him now that she realized how little she knew about him. It would be for the best if she did. Oddly enough, now that he had accepted her proposal, he hoped she would never come to her senses.

He looked up as she entered the room. "Everything okay?"

"Yes." She smiled at him, her eyes alight with mischief. "Now that we're engaged, shouldn't you kiss me or something?"

"Or something." Rising to his feet, Thorne drew her slowly into his arms. "What did you have in mind?"

She leaned into him. "What do *you* have in mind?" she asked with a teasing grin.

His gaze moved over her face as he drew her hips against his. "Can't you guess?"

"Is that a gun in your pocket?" she asked, doing her best Mae West impression. "Or are you just happy to see me?"

Thorne shook his head. How had he lived as long as he had without her? She made him feel young, vibrant, more alive than he had in centuries. "What about Sam?"

She looked up at him through the fringe of her lashes, a seductive smile playing over her lips. "We could always go to your place."

"Now, why didn't I think of that?" he mused.

Before she had time to answer, he swept her into his arms. The next thing she knew, she was in his house, in his bed.

"Maybe we should just go to Vegas and be married," Skylynn suggested as she snuggled into Kaiden's arms. As much as she loved making love to him, she knew it wasn't right. From the time she had been old enough to understand, her grandfather had drummed it into her head that intimacy outside of marriage was wrong. She had agreed with him, had been a virgin when she married Nick. But all of her grandfather's good advice had gone right out the window where Kaiden was concerned.

"Whatever makes you happy, Sky Blue."

She snuggled against him. "You make me happy."

His smile warmed her down to her toes.

"If we go to Vegas, I'm sure Tara will understand," Skylynn said, thinking out loud.

"Why the sudden rush?" he asked, even though he already knew the answer.

A faint blush rose in her cheeks. "You'll laugh."

"No, I won't."

"Well, I sort of promised Granda that I wouldn't . . . well, you know, unless I was married. And I was good about keeping that promise, until you came along." She looked up at him, her eyes narrowing. "Did you use your vampire mojo to get me into bed?"

"No," he said, laughing. "But you can bet everything you own that I thought about it more than once."

Chapter 33

Skylynn drove to the bridal shop over in Grover first thing in the morning. She tried on every dress they had in her size, wondering how she would ever make up her mind. They were all gorgeous, and they all made her feel beautiful. Long or short or in-between, the gowns came in a variety of fabrics and rainbow colors. There were dresses in every price range and for every taste. Want to look like Cinderella? They had a gown for that. Want to look like a sexy siren? They had a gown for that, too. Or maybe you wanted to look like a hip rock star? No problem. They had an outfit for that, too, complete with thigh-high boots and a temporary tattoo.

In the end, she chose an off-white floor-length dress with long, fitted sleeves, a square neck, a beaded bodice, and a short, flouncy train. She also bought a matching shoulder-length veil, and a pair of satin heels. Considering that she was out of work, buying an expensive wedding dress for a second wedding was probably an extravagance she couldn't afford, but this time around, she was going to have the best of everything, she thought with a smile. The best husband and the best dress.

Next on her list was new underwear—a lacy white bra

and matching bikini panties, a new nightgown that was little more than a whisper of black silk, along with a matching peignoir and slippers.

It was late afternoon when she got home.

Sam was waiting for her in the living room. "Where'd you run off to so early this morning?" he asked.

"Shopping, of course."

"Good. We're out of peanut butter and jelly."

"Not that kind of shopping, you idiot. I bought a wedding dress. Wait until you see it! We've decided to go to Vegas to be married. You need to rent a tux."

"A tux? For Vegas?"

She glanced pointedly at his jeans, which had the requisite torn knees, and the faded green T-shirt he'd dug out of his closet. "It won't kill you to dress up for one night."

"It might."

"Listen, I skipped breakfast and lunch and I'm starving," Sky said. "What do you say we grab a bite to eat and then see about renting you a tux?"

When he didn't answer right away, she thought he was going to refuse but, in the end, he shoved his hands in his pockets and muttered, "Sure, if that's what you want."

"Great. Let me go hang up my dress and put all this stuff away and then we'll go."

"All right," he said with a sigh of resignation, "but I want to go to the movies when we're done."

"Great movie, wasn't it?" Sky asked as she unlocked the front door. "You can't go wrong with Johnny Depp."

Sam grimaced. "You're just saying that because you think he's hot."

"Well, he is," she said with a grin. "I'm gonna run upstairs and take a quick shower."

"I guess that guy's coming over later." Sam peeled off his jacket and tossed it over the back of the sofa.

"Better get used to 'that guy,' brother dear," Sky called over her shoulder as she headed for the stairs. "I won't be long."

"Yeah, yeah." Sam watched her run up the stairs. If a guy had to have a sister, he could do a lot worse than Skylynn. She was a good cook, easy to get along with, and she made him feel at home even though he didn't remember anything about the place.

He wandered around the living room, perusing the books and the knickknacks on the shelves, pausing to study the framed photographs on the mantel. He picked up a family photo sitting on a side table. He didn't recognize the man or the woman, but he assumed they were his parents. The man, dressed in jeans and a T-shirt, was tall, with dark hair and light eyes. The woman, dressed in white shorts and a polka-dot halter top, had curly brown hair and a wide smile. The little girl with auburn pigtails and missing two front teeth was obviously his sister. The boy wearing the superhero T-shirt could only be him.

"Spiderman," Sam muttered as he set the photo back on the table. "No way."

He was halfway to the kitchen, intent on getting a Coke, when the doorbell rang. Thinking it was probably Thorne, Sam hollered, "It's open. Come on in," and headed for the re-frigerator.

Girard Desmarais knew a rush of excitement when he heard the invitation. He had been inside the house before, of course, but he hadn't been a vampire at the time. Glancing to his left, he released his hypnotic hold on the mortal he had brought with him and sent him on his way. He had intended to use the young man to gain entrance to the house, but that was no longer necessary.

Murmuring, "All too easy," Girard opened the front door and stepped across the threshold.

* * *

Skylynn's heart skipped a beat when she heard the door-bell. At last, Kaiden was here! She took the world's quick-est shower, wondering if Kaiden would have come up and washed her back if they had been alone in the house. She grinned as she stepped out of the shower. Once they were married, she wouldn't have to worry about what Sam or anyone else might think.

She dried off, dressed in a pair of silky black pants and an ice-blue sweater, ran a comb through her hair, and hur-ried down the stairs, wondering, in the back of her mind, what Sam would think if he knew Kaiden was a vampire. She would have to tell her brother the truth sooner or later. Or maybe she would let Kaiden do it.

Sky came to an abrupt halt when she saw Sam standing in the kitchen doorway, a look of astonishment frozen on his face. Soda leaked from a can on the floor, pooling around his feet.

"Sam, what's wrong?"

When he didn't move, didn't answer, she started toward him, felt her own eyes widen in shock when Girard Des-marais stepped into view.

"You!" Sky exclaimed. "What are you doing here? How did you . . . ?"

But the answer was obvious. Sam had unwittingly in-vited a monster into their home.

Kaiden glanced out the window, judging the time. It was still early. Sky and Sam were probably having dinner, which would give him time to satisfy his own hunger before he went to see Skylynn.

He thought briefly of driving across town in search of prey but then, eager to see Skylynn, he decided it would be faster to simply think himself where he wanted to go.

Moments later, he materialized in an alley between the Vista Verde bank and the post office. He didn't have to wait long. The streets were always crowded on a Friday night. He took the first single female who crossed his path. He mesmerized her with a look, grateful that she was young and clean and smelled good. Closing his eyes, he bent his head to her neck, wishing, all the while, that it was Skylynn in his arms, her blood satisfying his thirst.

Ah, Skylynn. Was there ever a creature more lovely, more desirable? He had known many beautiful women in the course of his existence, made love to more than his share, and yet none of them had managed to capture his heart. He had never been one to believe in fate or give credence to the ridiculous theory of love at first sight. Nor had he ever believed in soul mates. Until now. He couldn't deny that it seemed as if Skylynn McNamara had been created heart and soul for him and for no one else. The fact that she knew what he was and loved him in spite of it was nothing short of a miracle as far as he was concerned. He had done nothing to deserve such a rare and wondrous gift. Her love humbled him, made him long more than ever to be worthy of her trust.

If he could find the missing ingredient in Paddy's formula, if he could make and keep a ready supply of the potion on hand, he could give Skylynn the kind of life she deserved. They could travel around the world together. With the potion, he could again walk in the daylight, visit places he had seen only at night. He longed to show Skylynn all the wonders of the world, to watch her eyes widen in awe as they explored distant parts of the globe that were as yet unknown to most of the civilized population. She would have nothing to fear with him. But, more than that, he longed to share the simple things of life with her—mundane things that mortals took for granted, like enjoying a good meal, strolling through the park on a bright summer morning, watching the beauty of a sunrise, listening to the rain on a quiet afternoon.

Thorne glanced at the woman in his arms. She looked up

at him, her eyes blank. He shook his head. Caught up in wishing for an ordinary life, he had momentarily forgotten all about her.

A soft-spoken word released her from his spell and he sent her on her way, none the wiser.

Thorne stared after her. Why was he wasting his time yearning for a life he could never have? Skylynn was here, now. Best to spend as much time with her as he could, because time had become his enemy. Sooner or later, it would steal her away from him.

But for now, she was here and she was his. And with that thought in mind, he willed himself to Skylynn's home, eager to take her in his arms.

He paused a moment on the sidewalk. Lights burned in the front window, as if to welcome him.

He frowned when he noticed the front door was ajar. Even before he reached the porch, he caught the unwelcome scent of Girard Desmarais.

Chapter 34

Skylynn had never known fear such as this before. Sure, she had been scared when her parents died, but Granda and Grams had been there to take care of her, and Sam had been there to comfort her. She had been afraid when Sam went missing. And learning that Kaiden was a vampire had been frightening at first. But even that didn't compare to the soul-deep fear that now held her in its grasp. She didn't know what magic Desmarais had worked on her and Sam, didn't know what kind of preternatural power held them spellbound, but neither of them was able to move or speak. Nor did she know where they were.

She tried to remember what had happened after she'd come downstairs and found Desmarais in the living room, but fear for her life and that of her brother made it hard to think clearly. The only thing she really remembered was trying to revoke Sam's invitation, but before she could say the words, Desmarais had worked some kind of vampire magic that left her incapable of speech. She didn't remember leaving the house.

She glanced at her surroundings. The room was small and rectangular and sparsely appointed. She sat beside Sam on a narrow cot. The only other furniture was a straight-backed wooden chair and a square wooden table. A large crucifix hung on the stone wall behind the cot. Were they in a monastery? She seemed to recall that Desmarais was, or had been, a monk.

The vampire paced the floor in front of the cot. Watching him, she realized he was quite mad. She could see it in the fanatic glow in his eyes. What did he want with her and Sam? It couldn't be the missing ingredient in the formula. He already knew she didn't have it. So, what was he after?

Her whole body went suddenly numb as she realized what he wanted.

It wasn't the missing ingredient.

It was revenge for his wife's death.

She tried to speak, to beg him to spare her brother's life. Sam had no part in this. He didn't deserve to die. He had already been through hell. But, try as she might, she could not force the words past her throat.

Fear twisted inside her belly when Desmarais stopped pacing to stand in front of her. His eyes were cold, unblinking, like those of a snake.

His hand was like ice against her cheek when he touched her. "Don't be afraid. I'm not going to kill you. Yet. But I am terribly thirsty. It's part of being a new vampire, you know, the constant yearning for blood." He smiled, revealing his fangs. "But, all things considered, quite enjoyable."

Had she been able, she would have tried to fight him off but, rendered helpless by his preternatural power, she could only sit there while he grasped her shoulders in his bony hands. She winced as his fingers dug into her flesh.

Had she been able, she would have screamed in protest—even though there was no one to hear her. No one to save her.

As Desmarais bent his head to her neck, she caught a

glimpse of Sam's face. From his expression, she knew he was as horrified at what was about to happen as was she.

Unable to escape the vampire's hold, Sky closed her eyes when she felt the sharp sting of his fangs. There was no pleasure in his bite—as there was in Kaiden's—only pain magnified by gut-wrenching fear and sheer revulsion at what he was doing. The slurping noise he made was disgusting. Blackness clouded her vision. What if he took too much? Oh, Lord, what if he turned her into the same kind of ravening monster that he was?

That terrifying possibility sent her spiraling down, down, into the gray nothingness of oblivion.

Thorne searched every room in Sky's house even though he knew it was a waste of time, and then he walked around the living room a second time. Desmarais' scent was strong here. There were no signs of a struggle, either on the porch, in the doorway, or in the living room.

How had Desmarais gotten inside? Surely Sky wouldn't have invited him in? It had to have been Sam. That was the only answer. Dammit! He should have warned Sam about Desmarais, but who would have thought Girard would come knocking at the door again? Thorne doubted either Skylynn or Sam would have gone peacefully. Desmarais must have used his vampire powers to transport the sister and brother out of the house. For a fledgling, Desmarais was learning to use his powers in record time. Of course, having Cassandra as his sire didn't hurt. The blood of the old ones was extremely powerful. Thorne knew that firsthand.

Closing his eyes, he opened his preternatural senses. He had taken Sky's blood, creating a bond between them, a sort of vampiric GPS. Fear slithered down his spine when he couldn't find her. Either she was dead, which he refused to accept, or she was unconscious.

Either way, Girard Desmarais' days on earth were numbered.

Awareness returned gradually. Feeling. Hearing. Movement. Afraid of what she would see, Skylynn opened her eyes to darkness. She lifted one hand. At least she was no longer paralyzed. Whatever she was lying on was hard and cold. A touch told her it was a floor made of stone.

Rising to her knees and then to her feet, she moved slowly around the room, one hand outstretched to feel her way. Six steps carried her from one wall to the other. She didn't encounter anything in her way. So, was she locked inside some kind of dungeon?

"Sam? Are you here? Sam?"

Pressing her hand against the wall to guide her, she walked around the room. A cry rose in her throat when she kicked something solid. At first, she was afraid it was Sam, but it turned out to be an old-fashioned chamber pot. There was nothing else in the room.

Where was Sam? Was he still alive?

Where was Desmarais?

Most importantly, where was Kaiden? By now, he would know she was gone. Sky took a deep breath. Kaiden would find her. She had to believe that. She just hoped she would still be alive when he did.

Thorne stalked the dark streets, his fear and outrage rising with every step. He was hesitant to feed, afraid that, in his present condition, he would kill whoever crossed his path.

Where was she?

And then, like lightning shimmering across his mind, he felt their link connect.

Kaiden?

Skylynn! Are you all right?

Yes. He heard the underlying note of fear in that single word.

Is Sam with you?

He was, but he isn't now. I don't know where he is. I don't know where I am except that it's dark and cold. I think it's some kind of dungeon.

I'll find you. Even as he sent the thought to her, he was leaving the town behind, the link they shared guiding him unerringly on the path Desmarais had taken. A path that led Thorne to a secluded airport in Atlanta run by the kind of people who worked on a cash-only basis and didn't ask any questions.

It didn't take Kaiden long to discover that Desmarais had booked a nonstop flight to England for himself and two passengers. As soon as he learned Desmarais' destination, he knew where they were going. The Abbey at St. Germaine.

He considered transporting himself to the Abbey but discarded the idea for two reasons. Transporting himself across such a long distance would leave him weak and drained of strength and he couldn't afford that, not with Desmarais waiting at the end of his journey. Not with Sky's life in danger.

Moments later, he had arranged a "no questions asked" flight for himself.

It was an hour before dawn when Thorne's plane landed on a private airstrip outside of London. After paying the pilot an exorbitant fee to stay put until he returned, Thorne willed himself to the Abbey, then located a place in the nearby forest where he could safely go to ground until nightfall.

Rising at sunset, he approached the Abbey's ornately carved double doors. He stared at the entrance for several minutes. His chances of being invited inside were slim to none. The threshold of an ordinary church wouldn't have presented a problem since such places of worship were open to the public. But St. Germaine's Abbey was home to about thirty monks, as well as ten or fifteen slayers-turned-clerics who had taken a vow of silence. They never left the Abbey and rarely had any contact with the outside world, although both slayers and monks were free to leave if they wished.

The monks grew all their own food, made their own wine, and raised cattle and goats for milk and cheese. Strangers were not welcome inside the Abbey. Desmarais had taken refuge with the monks shortly after the death of his wife. If only he had stayed there.

Thorne raked his hands through his hair. All that mattered now was getting Skylynn and her brother out of the Abbey, alive.

Sam paced his narrow prison, a string of curses peppering the fetid air around him. Where the hell was he? It was bad enough that he didn't remember anything about his life before he woke up in the VA hospital, but now he couldn't remember how he had gotten here, either.

He did remember one thing, though. A scary-looking old guy with eyes that burned as red as flame. Red eyes! Nobody human had eyes like that.

Sam shook his head. Maybe he didn't have amnesia. Maybe he was just going insane. That made a lot more sense.

He paused, his brow furrowed. Had he seen that guy before? Something about that long gray cloak . . . Sam massaged his temples. If he could remember one thing, just one lousy little thing, maybe it would all come back to him.

Filled with worry and frustration, he resumed his restless pacing, concern for Skylynn overshadowing fear for his own life. Was she locked up in a cell like this one? He had called her name from time to time, but she didn't answer. Maybe the cell was soundproof. Maybe she wasn't here. His hands curled into tight fists. Maybe she was dead.

What if he wasn't in a cell at all? Maybe he was buried alive in some kind of box. Sweat beaded across his brow. He remembered being locked up, beaten, starved. Shit! Was he back in Iraq? Back in the hands of terrorists?

What if he had never been rescued? Maybe he was still in that sweat box.

He had to get out! Now! Panic spiked his heart rate. Sweat dripped down his face and trickled down his back.

"Help! Somebody, anybody! Let me out!" Pounding on the wall, he screamed, "Let me out of here!"

He had to escape before they came back for him.

"Please," he sobbed. "Please let me out."

As if in answer to his plea, the door creaked open. In the pale light spilling into the cell from a light in the passageway, Sam watched the man in the long gray cloak stroll into the cell.

Sam scrambled backward. "No! Get away from me, you freak. Leave me alone!"

The man walked toward him, eyes red and glowing. "Leave you alone?" His laughter was like dead leaves rustling in a graveyard. "I think not. You have what I need."

Sam shook his head. "I don't have anything!" His gaze darted toward the open door and the freedom that lay beyond. All he had to do was get past the old man. A piece of cake, right?

The thought had barely crossed Sam's mind when the door shut, seemingly of its own accord, and he found himself shoved against the cell's back wall, held in place by one age-spotted hand.

Sam stared at his captor. Who was this guy? He hadn't even seen him move.

"Time for dinner," the man said. His lips peeled back in a savage grin, revealing elongated canines.

Sam went cold all over as he stared at the hellishly red eyes, the sharp fangs.

It couldn't be. There was no such thing. And yet the proof was staring him in the face.

Vampire.

Sam was still trying to grasp the reality of what he was seeing when the man grabbed a handful of his hair, jerked his head to the side, and buried his fangs in Sam's throat.

Chapter 35

Thorne prowled the outskirts of St. Germaine's Abbey, every step adding to his frustration. How the hell was he going to get inside?

When the answer came to him, it was so simple, he cursed himself for not thinking of it immediately. All he had to do was ring the damn bell. His only excuse for not thinking of it sooner was that anger had clouded his reason. Strangers might not be welcome in the Abbey, but St. Germaine's was a religious order, after all, sworn to render aid and comfort to those in need.

Muttering under his breath, Thorne grabbed the bell pull and gave it a jerk. The sonorous peal echoed off the high stone walls.

Several minutes passed before a tall, thin cleric opened the heavy door. He stood in the entryway, blinking up at Thorne, his brows raised in a silent query.

Thorne fixed his gaze on the monk's guileless brown eyes. It took little effort for Thorne to impose his will on the monk's.

"Please," the cleric said, his voice rusty from disuse. "Come in."

Thorne felt a ripple in the air as he stepped over the

threshold. After closing the door behind him, he captured the monk's gaze again. "You did not see me," he said. "You will return to your duties. If anyone asks who was at the door, you will say it was a traveler asking directions. Do you understand?"

The cleric nodded.

Satisfied, Thorne opened his senses. He located Skylynn's heartbeat almost instantly. A moment later, he caught the scent of freshly spilled blood. And with it, the erratic beat of a heart that was about to beat its last.

Moving faster than the eye could see, Thorne followed the scent of blood. It led him down a dark, musty-smelling corridor to a locked iron door. Dissolving into mist, he slipped under the crack along the bottom. A handy talent, he mused as he resumed his own form on the other side of the portal.

His fangs extended as the scent of blood grew stronger, mingling with Girard Desmarais' unmistakable stink.

Swearing softly, Thorne hastened down a narrow, winding staircase to what had been a dungeon in days past, but was now used as a wine cellar. Torches set at intervals along the walls lit the passageway.

He hurried past several wine racks and iron-barred cells until he came to the last two. These cells were enclosed, with only narrow slits in the doors so the former guards could look inside.

Thorne inhaled deeply. Skylynn was in the cell on the right. The scent of freshly spilled blood came from the one on the left. Thorne opened the view port and peered inside, a harsh curse rising in his throat when he spied Desmarais kneeling on the floor, his head bent over Sam's neck.

Desmarais sprang to his feet when Thorne threw open the cell door. "You!" he hissed. Licking Sam's blood from his lips, Desmarais took a step backward, his hands curling into tight fists.

Thorne moved toward the other vampire with murder in

his heart. Desmarais had kidnapped Skylynn, and for that, his life would be forfeit.

"He's dying," Desmarais said, gesturing at Sam. "What's more important? Killing me? Or saving the girl's brother? You can't do both."

And so saying, Desmarais vanished from sight in a swirl of black mist.

Thorne uttered a pithy curse. He had expected Desmarais to stand and fight. The hunter had made no secret of the fact that he wanted Thorne dead. And Skylynn, too.

Skylynn. Dammit. A thought took him into Skylynn's cell. And not a moment too soon. Desmarais had Skylynn backed into a corner.

"You'll never get your hands on her again," Thorne said, his voice little more than an angry growl.

With a howl of frustration, Desmarais again vanished from sight.

"Sky!" Thorne swept her into his arms, his gaze moving over her face, his hands running lightly over her arms and back. "Did he hurt you?"

"No." She stared up at Kaiden, wishing she could see his face. But the inside of the cell was as black as pitch. "Where's Sam? Is he all right?"

"I need to get you out of here." Thorne said.

"Where's Sam?" she asked again, her voice rising. "Where is he?" She pounded on his chest. "Tell me where he is!"

"I'm sorry, Sky. I got here too late. He's dying."

"No! I don't believe you! Where is he?"

"In the next cell."

Wriggling out of his hold, she moved blindly toward the door, her hand tugging on the handle. "It's locked!"

"Move aside," Thorne said. One swift kick, and the door flew off its hinges.

Skylynn hurried to the next cell, her heart pounding as

she reached for the handle. To her relief, the door was unlocked.

"Sam!" Dropping to her knees beside her brother, she cradled his head in her lap. "Sam? Sam! Please, Sam, don't leave me."

When there was no response, she looked up at Thorne. "Do something!"

He gazed down at her. Her brother was more dead than alive. "What do you want me to do?"

For a moment, Skylynn stared up at him, mute. She couldn't say the words. She swallowed hard, blinking back her tears. "Please," she whispered. "He's all the family I have left."

"Are you sure? There's no going back, no changing your mind once it's done."

With tears streaming down her face, she nodded. She had lost so much. She couldn't lose Sam, too.

Thorne glanced at Sam, then back at Skylynn. "You might not want to watch."

Rising, Sky backed toward the far corner of the cell. With her arms wrapped tightly around her waist, she looked at Kaiden. She had asked for this. She would see it through.

With a nod, Thorne knelt beside Sam and gathered him into his arms. Feeling Skylynn's gaze on his back, Thorne hesitated a moment, and then he lowered his head to her brother's throat and drank what little blood he had left. Thorne heard Sky gasp when Sam went limp in his arms.

Hoping she wouldn't regret her decision and that Sam wouldn't hate her for making it, doubting the wisdom of what he was about to do, Thorne bit into his own wrist, then held the bleeding wound to Sam's lips.

"Drink, Sam," he murmured. "Drink, and live."

Girard Desmarais cursed his bad luck as he fled the Abbey. How the hell had Thorne gained entrance to St.

Germaine's? He puzzled over that for several minutes, then muttered, "Of course. Mind control."

Berating himself for not having foreseen such an eventuality, he made his way into the city and the small apartment he kept there.

So, he thought as he removed his cloak and tossed it over a chair, he had blown his chance this time. But there would be others. Cassandra or no Cassandra, he wouldn't rest until Thorne or the girl or both were dead.

Skylynn tugged on Kaiden's arm. "Is he going to be all right?"

"We won't know until he wakes tomorrow night. Right now, we need to get out of here." He couldn't take a chance on Desmarais alerting the rest of the brotherhood, and while the odds of that seemed slim, Thorne thought it best not to take chances. He wasn't afraid of many things, but he didn't want to confront a bunch of former slayers wielding torches and wooden stakes if he could help it.

After draping Sam over one shoulder, Thorne reached for Skylynn's hand. "Do you trust me?"

"You know I do."

"Okay, hold on tight. Don't be afraid."

With an effort of will, he transported the three of them out of the Abbey's basement and deep into the heart of the forest beyond.

Skylynn stared up at him, her eyes wide. "What just happened? How did you do that?"

"Vampire, Sky, remember?"

"Can all vampires do that?"

"As far as I know."

"Wow."

"There's a plane waiting to take us home," he said, and then frowned when he realized how late it was. If they left now, it would be daylight before they reached Vista Verde, and while he might survive a short time in the sun's light, Sam, as a fledgling, would go up in flames.

He considered trying to transport the three of them to California, but quickly dismissed the idea. He had never tried to transport anyone else that far, wasn't sure if he could transport the three of them that far, or what effect it would have on Skylynn.

He explained his reasoning to Sky, then said, "I think we'd better spend what's left of the night in a hotel."

She nodded. "All right."

Thorne squeezed her hand. "You ready? Okay, here we go."

A short time later, they were registered in one of London's best hotels. Sky wasn't sure how Thorne had managed it. Another bit of vampire magic, she supposed, since he had scored a pair of adjoining rooms without so much as a reservation. And such lovely rooms. The furniture looked antique, the drapes were brocade, the paintings on the papered walls depicted scenes of the English countryside.

Wrapped in a warm bathrobe, courtesy of the hotel, Sky stood at one of the windows, staring out at the rain, while Thorne showered.

So much had happened so fast. She glanced over her shoulder to where Sam lay, apparently sleeping, on one of the king-size beds. When he awoke tomorrow night, he would be a vampire. Had she made a mistake in asking Thorne to turn her brother? Would Sam thank her for saving his life, or hate her for what she had done? Would becoming a vampire restore his memories, or erase them forever?

Sky turned back to the window. She had always wanted to visit London, but not like this. Too nervous to stay still, she paced the floor. Where was Desmarais? A hotel wasn't like a house. This threshold wouldn't repel him, but surely he wouldn't come here. Would he?

Now that Sam was a vampire, the odds were two-to-one against Desmarais. Would that fact be enough to make the crazy slayer-turned-monk-turned vampire leave them alone? Somehow, she doubted it.

Her heart skipped a beat when the water in the bathroom stopped running. A moment later, Kaiden entered the room, naked save for the fluffy white towel wrapped around his lean hips.

Stars above, the man was the epitome of male perfection from the top of his head to the bottom of his feet. And he was all hers.

"Are you all right?" he asked, coming to stand beside her.

"I guess so. I'm just so worried, you know, about Sam, about what he'll think when he wakes up." Feeling suddenly chilled, she ran her hands up and down her arms. "Kaiden, did I do the right thing?"

"I guess we won't know that until tomorrow night."

Sky nodded. What if Sam hated her when he woke up and realized what he had become? What if he couldn't control his hunger and he went on a killing spree? Any lives he took would be on her head. Oh, Lord, what had she done?

Needing something to distract her morbid thoughts from what might happen when Sam awoke, she traced the faint white scar on Kaiden's cheek. "How did you get that?"

"Sword fight."

"Really?"

"Yeah. Happened when I was a highwayman. I stopped a carriage to rob the passengers. One of them was a duke. I guess he wanted to impress the ladies because he drew his sword and tried to stop me. He lost."

"Did you . . . kill him?"

"No, just wounded his pride a little."

"What about the scar on your back?"

"Souvenir of a duel over a lovely lady."

"Oh?"

He laughed softly, amused by the jealous note in her voice. "A four-legged lady. Quite the prettiest little filly I'd ever seen. Unfortunately, her owner didn't want to part with her."

"You fought a duel? Over a horse?" She stared at him incredulously. "I don't believe it."

"I was younger then," he said with a rueful grin. "And a lot more foolish."

"I see."

In a voice that was low and softly seductive, he said, "I always get what I want."

Her heartbeat quickened as his gaze moved over her. "Do you?"

His voice dropped to a low growl as he wrapped his arms around her. "I got you, didn't I?"

"Indeed." Rising on her tiptoes, she brushed a kiss across his lips. "You did," she said, and then sagged against him.

It took him a moment to realize she was crying. "Hey, what's this?" he asked. "What's wrong?"

"Nothing, everything."

"Sky?"

"I think we should . . ." She sniffed. "We should postpone the wedding, at least until Sam comes to grips with . . . you know, with his new, ah, lifestyle."

"That's probably a good idea."

"You don't mind?"

"No." He ran his hand up and down her back. "It'll be all right, you'll see."

Hoping to lighten the mood, Thorne chucked her under the chin. "Sam shouldn't be left alone at night for a while, and once you're really mine . . ." He grinned at her. "Well, I'll be wanting all your time, at least for a little while."

Blinking back her tears, she nodded.

Thorne regarded her for a moment, then said, "Something else is bothering you. Do you want to tell me what it is?"

"I love you. You know that."

"But?"

"Well, you're not going to get any older. What happens when I'm not young anymore?" She fought down the fear rising inside her, the fear that he would leave her. "Will you go away?"

"No. The marriage vows say until death do you part, and I'll stay with you, and take care of you, until then."

She shook her head. "I can't ask you to do that."

"You didn't. I love you, Sky Blue. Young or old, in sickness or in health, you'll always be as beautiful to me as you are now."

"Kaiden . . ."

He pressed a finger to her lips. "I'm not immortal, you know. You might outlive me."

She stared up at him. She had never even considered that. Which would be worse, she wondered, growing old while Kaiden stayed forever young and virile, or living without him?

Chapter 36

Sam came awake with a start. Damn, he'd had the most bizarre dream imaginable, worse, even, than the gut-wrenching nightmares that had plagued him when he'd been in Iraq.

Jackknifing into a sitting position, he dragged a hand through his hair as he glanced at his surroundings, annoyed to find that, once again, he had no idea of where he was or how he'd gotten there. He fought off a moment of panic as the thought that he might be going insane rose in his mind once again.

"At least this place beats the last one," he muttered, and then frowned. Something wasn't right. The room was totally dark, yet he could see everything clearly—the dresser across from the bed he occupied, the details of the painting on the wall, a hairline crack in the ceiling. And the noise! He covered his good ear, but it did nothing to shut out the steady thump-thump-thump that sounded like a heartbeat coming from the next room, or the din of traffic in the street below.

He shook his head. He must be hallucinating.

He gasped, his hand clutching at his belly as a sharp pain doubled him over. What the hell was happening to him?

Had he been poisoned? He groaned as the pain grew worse. Maybe he had a hangover. Even his teeth hurt.

Still hunched over, he rocked back and forth on the mattress. He had never hurt like this in his life. Was he dying?

He looked up when the door opened. Thorne stepped into the room, closing the door behind him. He didn't bother to turn on the light. "How are you feeling?"

Sam groaned low in his throat. "I need a doctor."

"No, you don't. You need to feed."

That was an odd way to put it. "I'm not hungry."

"Your stomach hurts, right? Your teeth ache. Your veins feel like they're on fire."

"Yeah, I'm probably coming down with the flu or something."

"Or something. What do you remember about last night?"

Sam stared at Thorne. "What's that got to do with anything? I'm sick, here. I don't want to take a walk down memory lane."

"What do you remember?"

"I had a bad dream."

"Tell me about it."

"That guy in the gray cloak. He was in it. He bit me . . ." Sam jerked upright. "It wasn't a dream, was it? He kept us in some kind of dungeon." Rising, he paced back and forth beside the bed. "He drank my blood! I remember now. He's a. . . ." Sam shook his head. "It had to be a dream."

"No. His name is Desmarais. He's a vampire."

If not for the sober expression on Thorne's face, Sam would have laughed. And then, like a movie unfolding in his mind, he saw everything that had happened last night. Saw it and knew it was true. "Why aren't I dead?"

"Because of your sister."

"Skylynn? What's she got to do with it?"

"It isn't what she did. It's what she asked me to do."

"I don't understand."

"When we got to you, you were dying. Skylynn asked me to save you." Thorne watched Sam's face as he tried to work it out. It didn't take Sam long to connect the dots.

"You'd have to be a vampire . . ." Sam shook his head. Even when he knew the answer, he didn't believe it. "That's impossible. I saw you outside during the day. You ate dinner at our house . . ." He groaned, his arms wrapping around his stomach as a fresh wave of pain knifed through him.

"You need blood." Thorne studied Sam a moment, replaying the boy's last words in his mind, realizing, as he did so, that Sam had remembered something from the past. Thorne smiled inwardly, thinking how pleased Skylynn would be when she found out.

"Blood? Are you crazy?"

"You're a vampire now. It's what you're craving. The pain won't stop until you feed."

"Right. I'll just call room service and order a pint of O Negative." Stumbling to the bed, Sam fell back on the mattress, his hands clutching his stomach.

"Kaiden? Is it okay if I come in?"

"No!" Sam spit the word through clenched teeth. "Go away, Sky. I don't . . . Don't see me like this."

But it was too late. Opening the door, she switched on the light, then moved quickly to her brother's side. "It's all my fault this is happening."

"Your fault?" Squinting against the light, Sam rolled onto his side, his legs drawn up. "Why is it your fault?"

"I asked Kaiden to turn you." She pushed a lock of hair from her brother's forehead, then sat on the edge of the bed. "I'm so sorry, but I couldn't lose you, too."

"Sky." Thorne spoke to her quietly. "Maybe you should go back into the other room."

She shook her head. "I can't leave him."

Sam looked up at her. He could hear the rapid beat of her heart, smell the blood flowing in her veins. His gaze zeroed in on the pulse fluttering in the hollow of her throat, and he didn't see his sister. All he saw was an end to the pain that tormented him.

With a low growl, he reached for her, his only thought to bury his fangs in her throat and ease the agony burning through him.

But Thorne was moving, too. Grasping Sam by the shirt collar, he hurled him across the room, then stood in front of Skylynn, all vampire glamour gone so that when Sam looked at him, he saw a very old, very angry vampire.

"You will not touch her," Thorne said.

"I didn't mean . . . I couldn't stop . . ." Sam looked at his sister, his expression filled with self-loathing. "Skylynn, I'm sorry . . . I don't know what's happening to me."

"I know," Thorne said. "Skylynn, go in the other room. I need to explain a few things to Sam. Then I'm going to take him hunting."

She stared up at Kaiden, a dozen questions running through her mind, but the feral look in his eyes, the harsh tone of his voice, sent her into the other room without an argument.

When she was gone, Thorne closed the bedroom door. "Okay, this is how it is. You're a vampire and there's no turning back. You can accept it and learn to live with it, or I can end your life for you here and now. It's up to you."

"You'd kill me, just like that?"

Thorne nodded. "There's nothing more miserable than an unhappy vampire. Or the people he preys on. I'm going to feel responsible for anybody you might kill, and I've already got enough deaths on my conscience. So, what's it gonna be?"

Sam clutched his stomach again, his face twisting in agony. "I don't want to die." He forced the words through clenched teeth.

"You're already dead."

"Vampire humor. Very funny." But there was nothing

funny about the pain that engulfed him. He had to be dreaming, Sam thought. It was all just too bizarre to be real.

"Trust me," Thorne said, "you're not dreaming."

Sam's head jerked up. "Don't tell me you're a mind reader, too?"

Thorne nodded. "Comes in handy, from time to time. So, back to vampire basics. The three most important things you need to know are these: you don't have to kill to survive. You don't have to be a monster. And if you go on a killing spree, I'll destroy you without a qualm. Got it?"

"Yeah," Sam muttered. "I've got it."

"Okay, let's go. The night's not getting any younger."

Sam followed Thorne out of the hotel. *Staggered* might have been a better description. He couldn't think of anything but the searing pain in his gut. It was worse than the torture his Iraqi captors had inflicted on him.

He listened with as much patience as he could muster while Thorne explained how to call prey to him, how to feed without ripping his victim's throat out, how to tell when it was time to stop, how to wipe the memory of what had happened from his prey's mind.

It all sounded easy until he stood in the shadows with a young woman in his arms. She looked up at him, her eyes glazed, her body limp. Earlier, he had been ready to attack his own sister, but he was thinking a little more rationally now.

He looked at Thorne and shook his head. "I don't think I can do this."

"Sure you can. Just listen to her heartbeat and do what comes naturally."

Sam did as he was told, surprised to find his revulsion waning. He had no way to explain the manner in which her blood called to him, or the way her heartbeat slowed to beat in time with his. He knew the thought of biting into her throat and drinking her blood should have repulsed him. Instead, he licked his lips, willing to do whatever it took to end the searing pain in his gut. Feeling more than a little self-conscious, with Thorne watching his every move, Sam bent her back over his arm, then ran his tongue along the length of her neck.

And did what came naturally.

Chapter 37

Skylynn checked her watch for the tenth time in as many minutes. Kaiden and Sam had been gone for almost an hour. How long did it take vampires to—she swallowed the bile rising in her throat—feed?

She went to the window and peered outside. It was raining. Feeling as though the room were closing in on her, she opened the window and took a deep breath. It hadn't been this hard to accept that Kaiden was a vampire. Why was she having such a hard time where Sam was concerned? Silly question, when it was her fault her brother was no longer human.

She closed the window when a gust of wind carried the rain inside. She turned on the TV, only to switch it off a few minutes later. How could she concentrate on some silly movie when her brother was out there in the storm, looking for someone to eat?

She blew out a deep breath. Where were they? She needed to talk to Sam, find out if he was angry with her, ask his forgiveness for what she had done.

She told herself there was nothing to worry about. Kaiden had been a vampire for hundreds of years. He knew what he was doing. He wouldn't let anything happen to Sam, so why was she so worried?

If anything happened to her brother, she would never forgive herself.

Thorne nodded his approval as Sam licked the wounds in the girl's slender throat to seal them. A few words wiped the memory of the last twenty minutes from her mind, and she left the park, smiling.

"You're a quick study," Thorne remarked.

Sam grinned at him. "That was, I don't know, awesome! So, are all the stories about vampires true? Can I turn into a bat?"

"I don't know. Is that something you want to do?"

Sam frowned as he considered it. "Not really, but in the movies, the vampires always turn into bats and fly away."

"I've never tried it. I'm not sure it's possible to change into anything so small. You know, body mass, and all that."

"What about a wolf? Dracula turned into a wolf. That would be really cool."

"It is . . . cool." In the old days, he had often transformed himself into a wolf to escape his enemies or elude angry villagers brandishing torches and stakes. "It takes practice, but it can be done. You can also dissolve into mist and move faster than human eyes can follow, so you seem to vanish from sight."

"Awesome! What about daylight?"

"The sun is your enemy. It will burn your flesh. If you're exposed to it for more than a few moments, it will destroy you."

"But you used to go out during the day."

Thorne nodded. He had ignored the question the first time Sam mentioned it, but there was no point in denying it any longer.

"Why didn't you burn up?" Sam asked.

"It's a long story."

"So? I've got nothing but time."

"Perhaps."

"What do you mean, perhaps?" Sam asked.

"Not everyone can handle being a vampire. Many don't last a year."

Sam shook his head. "Who wouldn't want this? I feel great, better than I've ever felt in my life."

"But it isn't life," Thorne reminded him. "Some fledglings can't adjust. They long for what they've lost, or, after a century or two, they grow discontented with their existence, or they grow weary of watching the world change while they stay forever the same. Some try to mingle with humanity, to pretend they haven't changed, but after years of watching people they've come to care about die, they seek their own destruction. Some get tired of hiding what they are and have to be destroyed before they become a threat to our existence."

"What kind of threat?"

"We exist on the edge of humanity. If people discover we're real . . ."

"I get it," Sam said, grinning. "I know the drill. Mobs with pitchforks."

"It's no laughing matter. Humans do have the advantage over most of us during the day."

"Most?"

"As vampires age, they grow stronger physically. Their preternatural powers also grow stronger, so that only an extremely talented hunter would be able to take them unaware. It's usually fledglings who fall prey to slayers."

"And that's what I am? A fledgling?"

Thorne nodded. "You're stronger than most, as is Desmarais, because you were both turned by master vampires."

Sam grinned at him, his eyes twinkling. "Gee, thanks, Dad."

Thorne shook his head, bemused by the boy's cocky attitude.

Sam shifted restlessly from one foot to the other. "So, Desmarais? Is he the spooky old guy in the gray cloak? The one who kidnapped us?"

"Yes, and he's a force to be reckoned with. Before he became a vampire, he was one of the best slayers in the world."

"He was a hunter and now he's a vampire? That's a pair to draw to."

"Indeed."

"So, how long have you been a vampire?" Sam asked.

"Over four hundred years."

Sam stared at him, wide-eyed. "Are you kidding me?"

"Do I look like I'm kidding?"

"But . . . nobody lives that long."

"Cassandra has existed longer than any other vampire I know of."

"How much longer?"

"Back to the time of the early Greeks."

"No way!"

"Way." Thorne rocked back on his heels. "Do you need to feed again? If not, we should get back to the hotel. We've left Skylynn alone too long already."

"Sky!" Sam smacked his forehead with his palm. "I forgot all about her. Let's go!"

Skylynn was pacing the floor when Kaiden and Sam materialized in the center of the room. She stared at them for a moment, too startled to speak, and then heaved a sigh of relief. Both of her men were safely home. From hunting. If only they had been stalking game instead of people.

"So," she said, glancing anxiously from one to the other. "How'd it go?"

"Great!" Sam replied, grinning. "Kaiden says I'm a quick study."

"Oh. Well. That's good. I guess."

"Sky, everything I ever thought about vampires is totally wrong. You should try it."

Skylynn blinked at her brother, unable to believe her ears. "Try it? It's not like ordering a new dress. I can't send it back if I don't like it."

"Trust me, sis, you'll like it. I feel great. Better than great." He paced from one end of the room to the other. "The power . . . I can feel it flowing through me. I've never felt this way before. It's . . . it's indescribable."

Skylynn looked at Kaiden. "Are all newly made vampires like this? So . . . so . . . enthusiastic?"

"I really can't say. I've never made one before. But I guess you don't have to worry about him hating you."

"Hating you!" Sam exclaimed. "No way, Sky. No way." He frowned, and then laughed out loud. "Remember that Halloween we went trick-or-treating at Thorne's and I told you he was a vampire?" Sam grinned. "Well, hell, I was right!"

"Sam!" Skylynn pressed a hand to her heart. "Sam, you remember!"

"Of course I remember. Why wouldn't I?" he asked, and then frowned. "What do you know? The doc at the VA was right. It did just come back."

"That's wonderful!" Laughing and crying at the same time, she threw her arms around her brother. "What else do you remember?"

"Everything except what happened right after I got hit." He lifted a hand to his head. "I remember being in a fire-fight. I was trying to protect our rear when a bomb went off. Things are kind of hazy after that. I woke up in a tent. I don't remember how long I was there. Hell, I'm not even sure who captured me. I remember waking up in the VA. The doctor told me my captors had traded me and a couple of other prisoners for one of their guys. . . ." His voice trailed off and then, as if suddenly too weak to stand, he sank down on the sofa and buried his face in his hands.

"Sam, what's wrong?"

"You told me Granda was dead, but it didn't mean anything to me then. I couldn't remember him . . . or how much he meant to me." Sobs shook his shoulders. "How much I loved him."

"Oh, Sam." Sitting beside him, she put her arm around his shoulder. "He loved you, too."

"I didn't even get to say good-bye."

"He went quietly, in his sleep. There was no chance for anyone to say good-bye."

"I want to see him . . . his grave."

"All right. We'll go when we get home." She looked at Kaiden, a question in her eyes.

"We can leave tomorrow," he said. "As soon as the sun goes down."

Chapter 38

The trip home was uneventful. Sam was ready to feed by the time the plane landed. After cautioning Sam to be quick and careful, Thorne transported himself and Skylynn to her house.

When they arrived, Thorne circled the house. Only after assuring himself that no one was lurking in the shadows did he allow Sky to open the front door. Inside, he took her hand and then went from room to room, making sure no one was there and that no one had been there while they were away. It bothered him that Sky wouldn't have anyone to look out for her during the day now that Sam was a vampire. Not that Sam had been much help against Desmarais, but at least Sky had had company during the daylight hours.

"I'm going to take a shower and slip into something more comfortable," Skylynn decided once Kaiden was satisfied that the house was safe. She had been wearing the same clothes since Desmarais whisked them off to England.

"All right."

"Do you want to come up and wash my back?"

"And your front."

Grinning, she started up the stairs, only to pause, one hand on the banister. "What are we going to do about Desmarais? He got in here once without any trouble. What's to stop him from doing it again?"

"I'll be with you at night. During the day, I want you and Sam at my place."

"How's that any safer than here?"

"My house is better fortified than yours. I've warded the windows and the doors against intruders, human and vampire."

"Warded? You mean, like magic?"

"Something like that. Only master vampires are capable of it."

Skylynn looked at him wide-eyed for a long moment; then, with a shake of her head, she continued up the stairs, muttering, "You learn something new every day."

Thorne watched her until she was out of sight; then, opening his preternatural senses, he honed in on his link to Sam. After assuring himself that the boy was safe, Thorne went up the stairs two at a time to see how Skylynn felt about washing his back after he washed hers.

Sam was on his way home when he felt a sudden shift in the atmosphere around him, like the change in the air before a storm. Although he was newly turned, he knew immediately that the woman who appeared beside him, seemingly out of nowhere, was ancient. Preternatural power swept over him and he realized instinctively that she could squish him like a bug with no trouble at all.

"Good evening, Samuel."

He swallowed the fear that rose like bile in the back of his throat. "Hey."

She laughed softly, displaying even white teeth and lethal fangs. "No need to be afraid."

"Who said anything about being afraid?"

Again, a peal of almost girlish laughter, so at odds with the calculating look in her eyes. "I can smell it on you."

"Since you know who I am, how about telling me who you are?"

"Don't you remember?" she asked, pouting.

He shook his head.

"You could say that I'm your grandmother."

Sam stared at her, confused. His grandmother? What the hell was she talking about? And then he laughed as he realized what she meant. This was the vampire who had turned Kaiden.

"Grandma," he drawled. "What big teeth you have."

Her hand shot out, curling around his throat like a garrote. "The better to eat you with, my dear."

Sam stared into her face, into a pair of eyes gone blood-red. Damn, he hadn't even seen her move. Did she mean to kill him?

"Kill you? Of course not," she said, releasing her hold on his throat. "You really don't remember me, do you?"

"Should I?" he asked, and then felt his eyes widen with the shock of recognition. "You!" he exclaimed, wondering how he could have forgotten the first time they met. "You were the woman in the bar. You got me drunk."

She shrugged. "I was bored, and you were so . . . entertaining."

"Are you bored now?"

"No, merely curious. Kaiden has never turned anyone before. Somehow, I thought it would be your sister."

"What do you know about Skylynn?"

"I know everything Kaiden knows, including what he's doing now," she said with a smile. "I would advise you to take your time getting home."

"What's that supposed to mean?"

"Think about it."

Sam frowned at Cassandra, but she was gone before he could ask her anything else.

Sam stared after her and then, realizing what she meant, he chuckled. Had Skylynn been intimately involved with any other man at any other time, he might have hurried home to defend his sister's honor, but he figured it was too late for that. Besides, Skylynn was a big girl, old enough to know what she was doing. Then, too, she was engaged to Kaiden. In some countries of the world, that was as binding as a marriage contract.

He ran a hand over his jaw. So, he had an hour or so to kill—the thought made him laugh. In the last few days, the word *kill* had taken on a whole new meaning.

Hands shoved into his pants pockets, Sam strolled down the street, whistling softly. He didn't know if it was luck or chance or some kind of vampire instinct that led him to the Scarlet Cabaret. He felt a rush of supernatural power as soon as he crossed the threshold. Scattered among the Goths and wannabe vamps, he sensed the real thing. At first he thought it was Cassandra, but she was nowhere to be seen. He ducked behind a pillar as a horrible thought occurred to him. What if it was Desmarais? But even as the thought occurred to him, he knew it wasn't Desmarais. He knew the monk's stink and he wasn't likely to confuse it with anyone else's.

Swearing softly, he moved toward the bar.

The bartender was a petite brunette with big brown eyes and a mouth meant for kissing. "Hey, handsome, what'll you have?"

"I don't know. What have you got?"

She smiled. "Anything you want, honey."

Sam glanced at the glasses neatly lined up on a shelf behind the bar. What did vampires order in a nightclub? He grinned inwardly. A bloody Mary?

"How about the house specialty?" the bartender suggested. "I think you'll like it."

"Sure, bring it on."

Sam watched her sashay to the far end of the bar. She returned moments later carrying a crystal flute filled with red liquid.

"Here you go."

Sam lifted the glass. He held it a moment before sniffing the contents. And then he frowned. Was it blood?

The bartender was watching him carefully.

Sam blew out a breath, then took a sip. It was indeed blood, mixed with a little red wine. "This is the house specialty?"

She nodded. "Like it?"

He hesitated before answering. Was this some kind of trap? How did she know what he was?

"I've worked here a long time," she said, as if that explained everything.

"It's . . . different."

She smiled at him. "I'm Lisa. My father owns the club."

"Pleased to meet you, Lisa. I'm Sam."

"I haven't seen you in here before."

"No." He took another drink. It was smooth going down. "I'm new."

"New in town?" she asked, crossing her arms on the top of the bar. "Or just new?"

"Just new, I guess," he replied. "Funny, I don't remember ever seeing this place before."

"We like it like that."

He drained the glass and handed it back to her. "How about a refill?"

"Sure, honey. I'll be right back."

Sam leaned his elbow on the bar. He was new to all this supernatural stuff, but he had a gut feeling that Lisa wasn't entirely human. Not that he cared. She was a pretty little thing. Her skin-tight black jeans, long-sleeved white silk shirt, and black vest outlined every luscious feminine curve.

He felt a rush of desire as he watched her refill his glass. Whatever she was, he wanted her.

He grinned as he watched her return, her hips swaying provocatively. Unless he missed his guess, she wanted him, too. The night was suddenly ripe with possibilities.

"Like what you see?" she asked as she handed him his drink.

"What's not to like? Would it be too presumptuous of me to ask what time you get off work?"

"In about five minutes. Why? What did you have in mind?"

"Anything you want."

"Would you like to walk me home?"

"Yes, ma'am."

She winked at him. "Just let me get my coat."

She returned a few minutes later wearing a short black leather jacket. "You ready?"

"Always ready."

She laughed softly. "Slow down, tiger. We've got all night."

Sam held the door open for her, then followed her out. "So, tell me about yourself. What do you do when you're not mixing drinks?"

"Lots of things. I paint a little. I work out at the gym. I teach a self-defense class twice a week."

"Guess I'd better watch myself."

"No need," she said with a teasing grin. "I'll be glad to watch you."

When her gaze met his, the attraction between them sizzled like heat lightning.

Lisa slipped her arm through his. "This could prove interesting."

"Interesting?" Sam repeated with a laugh. "Honey, this is gonna be way better than that."

"So, what about you?" Lisa asked. "What do you like to do?"

Sam shrugged. "Work on my car, mostly. Flirt with pretty girls."

"How long have you been a vampire?"

"I'm brand-new."

"Do you like it?"

"Surprisingly, I do."

"You asked for it, then?" she said, frowning. "I could never understand why anyone would want to be a vampire."

"It wasn't a choice I made. My sister made it for me."

"Oh?"

"Well, I was dying and"—he shrugged again—"it beat the alternative."

"Yes, I guess so." She paused in front of a large, two-story house. "This is where I live."

"Nice place." A light burned in one of the downstairs windows. A few palm trees grew alongside the house; rose bushes lined the walkway to the front door.

"Thanks for walking me home."

"You're welcome." He rocked back on his heels, wondering if he dared kiss her good night and then, remembering how Granda had always said nothing ventured, nothing gained, Sam drew her close and covered her mouth with his.

And knew that one kiss wouldn't be enough.

Skylynn and Kaiden were snuggling on the sofa when Sam let himself into the house.

"So," Kaiden asked. "How'd it go?"

"Fine. Why?"

"We expected you home before now. It's almost dawn. Your sister's been worried about you."

"Come on, Sky," Sam said, dropping into a chair. "It's time you stopped playing mother hen. I'm the big brother, remember? Not to mention that I'm the scariest thing on the streets."

Thorne snorted.

Skylynn shook her head.

"Geez, you guys treat me like I'm ten years old."

"I know you feel like you're indestructible," Thorne said. "But you're not. You might want to remember that."

"You're right. I'm sorry if I worried you, Sky. I won't do it again."

"I'm sorry for being such a worrywart."

"You were at the Scarlet Cabaret tonight," Thorne remarked.

"Yeah, how'd you know?"

"I can smell Lisa on you."

Sam's face lit up. "Do you know her? Man, she's something else."

"She is, indeed," Thorne agreed.

"Who's Lisa?" Skylynn asked.

"She tends bar at the club," Thorne said. "Her father owns it. She works there a few nights a week. So, what did you think of her?"

"She's gorgeous," Sam replied. "I've got a date with her tomorrow night."

"If I were you, I'd take it slow," Thorne said.

"I'm not planning to snack on her, if that's what you're thinking, although I have to admit, the thought of tasting her crossed my mind more than once."

Thorne shook his head. "You won't like it if you do."

"What's not to like?" Sam asked, frowning. "She's young, single, beautiful, and she smells good."

"There's just one other little thing you might want to remember," Thorne remarked.

"Yeah? What's that?"

"She's a werewolf."

Chapter 39

Shortly after sundown the next night, Thorne drove Sam and Skylynn out to the cemetery. He waited in the car for several minutes, giving the brother and sister time to be alone with their grief.

In spite of being Undead, graveyards weren't one of Thorne's favorite places. They were grim reminders of how brief mortal life was, how short his time with Skylynn would be. In a few years, she would begin to age. Her youth would fade, her energy and exuberance would diminish, weakened by the passage of years. Not that he would love her less. He would deem it a privilege to care for her for as long as she lived. His only concern—selfish though it might be—was how, having known her, having loved her, he could go on without her. In four centuries, he had never found another woman he needed so badly, or loved so desperately. With each passing day, the thought of facing a future without her grew more and more intolerable.

His only hope was that, as time passed and mortality stared her in the face, she would agree to accept the Dark Gift. He was hoping that the fact that her brother was now a vampire would tip the scales in his favor.

From time to time, when he thought of existing without

her, a little voice in the back of his mind whispered that, as a last resort, he could turn her against her will and hope that, in a century or two, she would find it in her heart to forgive him.

Even as the thought crossed his mind, he knew he would never force his way of life on Skylynn. If she became a vampire, it would be of her own choosing.

With a shake of his head, he got out of the car and joined Sky and her brother at the grave site. Skylynn's cheeks were damp with tears. Sam stood beside her, his arm around her shoulders, doing his best not to cry.

"He was a good man," Thorne said quietly. "A good friend to me. One of the few mortals who knew what I was and didn't try to drive a stake in my heart."

"I still miss him," Sky said, sniffling. "He was always there when I needed him, always there to comfort me when I woke up crying in the middle of the night, or when I had a fight with one of my friends."

Sam nodded his agreement.

The boy was afraid to speak, Thorne thought, afraid that putting his feelings into words would unleash the pain within him and leave him crying like a baby.

Shoving his hands into his pockets, Thorne stared at the headstones. He couldn't remember the last time he had shed a tear.

Skylynn dropped to her knees. Leaning forward, she stroked her hand over the grass that covered her grandfather's grave. "I hope you're with the rest of the family now." She glanced to the left, where her grandmother was buried. "You can take care of each other again."

After clearing his throat, Sam said, "I need to go, Sky."

She glanced up at him. "So soon?"

Sam shifted from one foot to the other. "You can stay if you want. I need to go."

"I'll stay with her," Thorne said. "You be careful. Desmarais is still out there somewhere."

"Yeah, like I'd forget that."

"You and Sky will be staying at my place during the day until he's no longer a threat."

Sam looked belligerent for a moment, and then, with a nod, he disappeared from the cemetery.

"I don't think I'll ever get used to that," Sky said, rising. "The way you can come and go so quickly."

"It's been my experience that you can get used to almost anything," Thorne remarked as they picked their way between the headstones on their way back to the car.

"I suppose," she replied dubiously. "He seems so different. He seems . . . happy to be what he is."

"And that's a bad thing?" Thorne asked, opening the passenger door.

"No, it's just hard for me to understand. I mean, I was afraid he'd hate me for it. Now, it's almost like he wishes he'd done it sooner."

Thorne closed her door and went around to the driver's side. Sliding behind the wheel, he turned to face her, his arm draped over the back of her seat. "Being a vampire is what you make of it. You can brood over what you've lost, or you can appreciate what you've gained. It's all a matter of attitude. Sam decided to look on the bright side."

"Is that what you did?"

"Eventually. I guess you could say Sam's become a well-adjusted vampire in a remarkably short time."

"Well-adjusted," Sky muttered. "Right."

"Is it Sam's easy acceptance of what he is that's bothering you?" Thorne asked quietly. "Or are you having second thoughts about you and me?"

"Could you blame me if I was?"

"Not at all. I'd be surprised if you weren't."

"Were you kidding when you told Sam that that girl, Lisa, is a werewolf?"

"No. She turns fanged and furry when the moon is full." Feeling chilled, Sky wrapped her arms around her

middle. "Can we go home now?" She was in love with a vampire. Sam was enamored of a werewolf. Absorbing that knowledge while parked in a cemetery was suddenly more than she could handle.

With a nod, Thorne started the car and drove toward the exit. He couldn't blame Sky for being spooked. It was never easy for mortals to find out that the monsters were real.

"So, werewolves exist," Sky mused. "Should I be on the lookout for flying monkeys, and giant ants and aliens from outer space?"

Thorne laughed, recalling that she had asked about the possibility of other paranormal creatures when he had told her about saving Desmarais from the succubus.

"I'm pretty sure you're safe from flying monkeys and giant ants," he drawled. "The jury's still out on little green men from outer space."

"What did you mean when you told Sam he wouldn't like the taste of her blood?"

"Werewolf blood burns like acid when we swallow it."

"Really? Why?"

"I don't know, but it does."

"Are you speaking from experience?"

He braked at a stoplight. "Yeah. It's a mistake I never made again." He stepped on the gas when the light turned green.

"Do the werewolves—are there more than one?"

"A few more."

"Do they have to ask your permission to stay here, too?"

"Yep. Vampires are at the top of the food chain, so to speak, followed by demons and werewolves, then fairies and goblins and ogres, then . . ."

"Fairies? Goblins? Ogres? I don't believe you."

He grinned at her. "Okay, I made up the goblins and the ogres."

"And the fairies?"

"No, they exist, or so I'm told. I've never met one."

Sky looked out the window, her mind filling with images of cartoon fairies—the three who looked after Sleeping Beauty, cute little Tinker Bell flitting around Neverland, and the lovely Blue Fairy who turned Pinocchio into a real boy. Did actual fairies look anything like their cartoon counterparts? That they could even be real was inconceivable but she couldn't deny she had a burning desire to see one.

Minutes later, Thorne pulled up in front of her house and cut the engine. "Get whatever you need and then we'll go to my place."

"What? Oh, right. I forgot we're staying with you."

Thorne followed her into the house and up the stairs, stood in the bedroom doorway while she threw a nightgown and a change of clothes into a small bag, along with her hairbrush, toothbrush, and makeup. Going downstairs, she tossed in a magazine and a paperback book.

"I guess I'm ready," she said.

"Are you sure you've got everything? I don't want you coming back here alone tomorrow."

She glanced around the room, her expression thoughtful, and then she went into the kitchen. She found a cardboard box and began filling it with foodstuffs. "I'll need to go to the store tomorrow night. I'm almost out of milk."

"Will you need anything else before then?"

"No, I don't think so." She added a box of hot chocolate and a bag of mini marshmallows. "I've got all the necessities."

Thorne stared at the box of hot chocolate. He could just barely remember what it had tasted like—warm and rich and smooth. But it wasn't cocoa he was thirsty for at the moment. He lifted his gaze to the woman who was rummaging through one of the cupboards. Her blood was also warm and rich and smooth.

She turned to face him, a loaf of bread in her hand. Whatever she had been about to say was forgotten when she saw the look in his eyes.

"Sorry," he said with a shrug. "You have your favorite drink, and I have mine."

"You haven't fed yet, have you?"

"No. I'll wait until Sam gets back."

Sky dropped the bread into the box. "You don't have to go out, Kaiden," she said, and taking him by the hand, she led him into the living room. Sitting on the sofa, she pulled him down beside her, then tilted her head to the side.

"Sky, you don't have to . . ."

She pressed her fingertips to his lips, stilling his words. "Shh, I want to."

"Are you sure?"

"Of course I am. It feels wonderful, you know."

"So they say." He stroked her nape. "It's been a long time since Cassandra fed on me."

"Don't vampires drink from each other?"

"Rarely." Leaning forward, he rained kisses along the length of her neck, ran his tongue over the pulse throbbing in the hollow of her throat before claiming her lips with his.

Her nearness flooded his senses—the floral shampoo she used to wash her hair, the musky scent of her desire, the taste of her toothpaste, the satiny smoothness of her skin beneath his hand, the warmth of her breasts pressed against his chest. And over all, the beating of her heart. His arms tightened around her as his hunger roared to life. His whole being ached for her, ached to possess her completely, to drink her life and her memories, to gorge himself on the crimson elixir that flowed through her veins, to drink and drink until he had taken it all.

With a hoarse cry, he lowered his head to her neck, his need at war with his self-control.

His need won. His fangs pierced the tender skin below her ear and he lost himself in the taste of her life's blood as it flowed ever so sweetly over his tongue. But only for a moment. His concern for Sky was strong, stronger, even, than his thirst. Taking a firm hold on his self-control, he lifted his head and let her go.

She blinked up at him, a faint smile on her lips, her gaze slightly unfocused. "It feels so good. Why did you stop?"

"Because you don't want to be what I am." Standing, he put some distance between them.

Skylynn stared at him, no longer smiling. Had he been that close to taking too much? Could it happen that quickly? What if there came a time when he couldn't stop?

Needing to put more distance between them, Thorne went to the far side of the room and turned his back toward her while his fangs retracted.

"Kaiden?"

"What?"

"Are you all right?"

He snorted softly. "That's a good question, only I'm the one who should be asking it. Are you all right?"

"Yes." She lifted a hand to her neck. The skin beneath her ear felt warm. She could feel the marks his bite had left, but they never lasted very long. By tomorrow morning, they would be completely gone. Odd, that. In the movies, the bites didn't go away. Curious, she asked him about it.

"It's just a movie myth," he replied flatly. "Some vampires feed repeatedly on the same donors. Think how those people would look after a month or so if the bites didn't disappear."

Remembering what she had read on the Internet, she asked, "What about garlic?"

"What about it?"

"Does it repel you?"

He turned to face her, his expression impassive. "It stinks but it won't protect you."

"I'm not looking for protection, Kaiden. I'm just curious. I still have a lot to learn about what's true and what's Hollywood hype."

"Fair enough."

"What about crosses?"

He shrugged. "I like the old-fashioned ones."

"What about holy water? And silver?"

"They burn."

She nodded, her brow furrowing as she tried to recall the other things she had read. "Running water. One of the Web sites said you couldn't cross it."

"That's another fable. I don't have to sleep in a coffin, although it doesn't bother me to do so. I don't need to rest on my native soil. If someone throws a sack of wheat at me, I don't have to stop and count every kernel. Anything else?"

She looked up at him, her eyes wide. "If you had taken too much tonight . . . if I was dying . . . would you have . . . saved me?"

"Would you want me to?"

"I don't know." Life or Undeath? How could anyone be expected to make that choice? And yet, she had made it for Sam. And she would have done it again.

"I won't turn you against your will, if that's what's bothering you."

"Sometimes . . ." She crossed her arms, her brow furrowed as if she couldn't decide whether to finish her sentence.

"Go on."

She looked up at him, her expression thoughtful. "Sometimes, when I'm with you and Sam, I feel like an outsider."

"I can fix that," he said with a rueful grin. "Come on. It's getting late, and you're tired. We should go."

"What about Sam?"

"He'll come home when he's ready. Do you need anything else out of the kitchen?"

"The milk."

"I'll get it." In the kitchen, Thorne pulled a carton from the fridge. He added it to the box of groceries, then carried the carton into the living room.

Sky was waiting for him by the front door, suitcase in hand. "Maybe it would be easier if I just moved in with you."

"Probably."

"But only if . . ." Her gaze slid away from his for a moment. "Are we still getting married?"

"That's up to you. Do you still want to be my wife?"

"Yes."

"Well, then, what do you say we go to Vegas tomorrow night and make an honest woman out of you?"

"I say yes!" she exclaimed happily.

Her smile could have lit up the city, Thorne thought as he opened the door. It certainly lit a fire in his soul.

Chapter 40

Sky woke smiling. It was her wedding day! She glanced at Kaiden, sleeping soundly beside her. Before this day was over, she would be Mrs. Kaiden Thorne for better or worse, for as long as she lived.

Her smile faltered. As long as she lived. How many years did she have left? Forty? Fifty? If she lived to be a hundred, Kaiden would still look thirty. She fought down a rush of resentment. If Kaiden lived another four hundred years, he would still be young. And then there was Sam. He wouldn't age anymore, either. Her brother and the man she loved would both be here long after she was gone.

She tried to ignore the insidious little voice in the back of her mind that whispered it didn't have to be that way. That if she had the nerve, she, too, could be young forever. She could be more than just Kaiden's wife. She could be his equal, a part of his world. She wouldn't have to be on the outside, looking in, always wondering what it would be like to have amazing strength, to never be tired or sick. She would belong. And if, by some miracle, they could find the missing ingredient to Granda's formula, she could have the best of both worlds.

Rising, she went into the bathroom to comb her hair and

brush her teeth. Where was Sam? Only three of the rooms in Kaiden's house were furnished—the master bedroom, where she and Kaiden had spent the night, the kitchen, and the living room. Was Sam spending the day on the sofa?

Curious, she walked down the hallway, peeking into the vacant rooms as she went. She paused, grinning, when she came to the room at the head of the stairs. Inside, Sam was sound asleep in his own bed, one foot hanging outside the covers. Apparently he had carried the bed over sometime last night. Must be nice, she thought, to be strong enough to carry a mattress, box spring, and headboard across the street and up a flight of stairs all by yourself.

Continuing on, she went down to the kitchen, where she made a cup of hot chocolate, then carried it with her as she wandered through the house, imagining how she would decorate the empty bedrooms and the dining room. Of course, there would be no children so they didn't need four bedrooms.

She brushed the thought aside. She wouldn't think about that. They could use the extra bedrooms for other things. One could be a library, one could be a workout room. Or they could just leave them empty. For all she knew, Kaiden might not want to live here after they were married. He had mentioned once that he couldn't stay in one place too long. Maybe it was time to find another place to live. A place by the beach would be nice, or maybe up in the mountains.

She stood in one of the empty bedrooms, sipping her cocoa, as she tried to convince herself that she wasn't bothered by the fact that Kaiden couldn't give her children. Lots of couples were childless, many by choice. She had never really given much thought to having a family. She had just assumed that it would happen eventually.

With a toss of her head, she went down to the kitchen. She wouldn't think about that now. Today was her wedding day. She needed to wash her hair, paint her nails, shave her legs, pack a suitcase. And call Tara.

After putting her cup in the dishwasher, she dropped into one of the chairs. Propping her elbows on the table, she rested her chin on her folded hands. If only she could tell Tara the truth about Kaiden. It would be so nice to have someone to confide in, someone with whom she could discuss the little doubts and fears she couldn't share with the man she loved.

Thorne awoke as the sun began its downward descent. He lay there a moment, his senses expanding. Sam was still at rest. Skylynn was downstairs. He could sense her nervousness, her excitement, and a trace of apprehension. Just getting married was enough to cause a certain amount of anxiety. The fact that she was marrying a vampire was certainly cause for some uneasiness on her part.

If the truth were known, he was a little apprehensive himself. He had never been married before. Never even considered it. He had no idea what kind of husband he would be. But what concerned him the most was the fear that, in a moment of extreme passion or weakness, he would surrender to the ravenous beast that dwelled within him, and Skylynn would pay the ultimate price for his lack of control.

Was he kidding himself, thinking they could have a life together? It would only take one mistake on his part, one error in judgment, to put her life in danger or snuff it out altogether. She was beautiful, desirable, and oh, so fragile. If he hurt her, he would never forgive himself.

And then there was Desmarais. He didn't know where the wily old hunter was, but one thing he knew, Skylynn would never be safe until Desmarais had been destroyed once and for all.

He rose, stretched, and headed for the bathroom. He showered and dressed, then picked up his suitcase and went downstairs in search of his bride.

He found Skylynn in the living room with Sam. Brother and sister both looked up as he entered the room.

Sam frowned.

Skylynn forced a smile. "Hi."

"Hi." Thorne dropped his suitcase by the sofa. He glanced at Sam, then back at Skylynn. "Everything okay?"

"Yes, why?" she asked.

"Well," Thorne said dryly, "it's obvious that something is bothering the two of you."

With a huff of annoyance, Skylynn said, "He invited that werewolf to go to Vegas with us."

"Her name is Lisa," Sam said curtly. "And I asked her to come along as my date so I'd have someone to talk to after the wedding, while you two are . . . you know."

"Seems perfectly reasonable to me," Thorne replied with a grin. "So, are you ready to go?" he asked Skylynn. "Or have you changed your mind?"

"I'm ready," she said, getting to her feet. "Are you coming, Sam?"

"As soon as Lisa gets here."

Thorne glanced at the front door. "She's here now."

"I'll get it." Sam bounded off the sofa and out of the room. He returned a moment later with Lisa in tow. "Lisa, this is my sister, Skylynn. I guess you already know Thorne."

"Yes." Lisa smiled at Thorne. "Nice to see you again."

Thorne nodded. "Good to see you, too. How's your dad?"

"Crazy as ever," Lisa said, her eyes twinkling. She smiled at Skylynn. "Congratulations to the two of you."

"Thank you," Sky replied.

"Okay, now that the introductions are over, I think we should go." Thorne picked up Sky's suitcase and his own. "Is everybody ready?"

"I left my bag on the porch," Lisa said. "I wasn't sure . . ." She looked at Sam.

"We're all set. Let's go."

Kaiden turned off the house lights and locked the door,

then followed the other three outside and down the porch steps.

"Why are we driving?" Sam asked as Thorne unlocked the trunk. "Why don't we just, you know, twitch our noses and think ourselves there?"

"I like to drive," Thorne said, tossing the suitcases into the trunk. "I like that long stretch of open highway."

"Didn't know you were a speed freak," Sam said, grinning.

"Now you do."

Sam and Lisa climbed into the back seat, giggling and laughing like a couple of kids.

After handing Skylynn into the car, Thorne closed her door, then slid behind the wheel.

He turned the key in the ignition and the engine purred to life. "Las Vegas, here we come," he said, and pulled out of the driveway.

Skylynn glanced at the bright lights that lined both sides of the street. She hadn't been in Las Vegas since she was a senior in high school and one of her friends eloped to Vegas to get married. The marriage had ended a week later.

She slid a glance at Kaiden. How long would her marriage last? With luck, she and Kaiden could have fifty or sixty years together. What would it be like when people looked at them and thought she was his mother? His grandmother? What would he think? It was easy for him to promise, now, that he would still love her when she was old and decrepit, but how would he handle it when it actually happened?

Kaiden pulled into the valet parking area of the New York, New York Hotel.

"Do we have reservations?" Sky asked.

He shook his head. "No."

"I should have called ahead. The hotels are bound to be full on a Friday night."

"Not to worry." He got out of the car and came around to open her door. "We'll soon have the best suite the house has to offer."

She frowned at him a moment, and then grinned. "I guess you're going to use a little vampire mojo."

"You guessed right."

Unlocking the trunk, he gathered their bags; Sam took his and Lisa's.

As Sky predicted, the desk clerk advised that all the rooms were reserved.

And as Kaiden had predicted, five minutes later, he and Sky were registered in the penthouse suite. Sam and Lisa had a smaller suite one floor down.

"We'll meet you and Lisa here in the lobby in twenty minutes." Kaiden looked at Sky. "Will that give you enough time to get dressed?"

"Forty-five would be better."

"Okay, forty-five minutes." He kissed the tip of her nose, then pressed the key into her hand. "You go on up and get ready. I'll be there soon."

The penthouse suite was like nothing she had ever seen before, and bigger than her apartment in Chicago. Plush carpets. Cozy corners. A fireplace in the bedroom. A shower big enough for two.

After dropping her suitcase on the king-sized bed, she undressed and changed into the lacy underwear she had bought for the occasion. She brushed out her hair, then pinned the sides up, so that her hair fell in soft waves down her back. Her wedding gown rustled as she stepped into it, then smoothed it over her hips. Standing in front of the full-length mirror, she set her veil in place, then stared at her reflection. Her eyes were bright with excitement, her cheeks flushed. She looked like a fairy tale princess.

She was sitting on the edge of the bed, putting on her

shoes, when Kaiden entered the room. Clad in a tux and a pair of black boots, he looked good enough to model for *GQ*.

He whistled softly when he saw her. "You're beautiful, Sky Blue."

"So are you." The man was born to wear a tux. The thought that he was hers, all hers, sent a quiver of anticipation racing through her.

Taking her hands in his, Thorne drew her to her feet and into his arms. "Are you ready?" he asked, his voice husky with desire. "Because I don't think I can wait much longer."

The wedding chapel was small but lovely. The pews were made of antique oak. The carpet was a deep shade of burgundy. Candles burned in ornate wall sconces and candleholders. The minister was a tall, gray-haired man who smiled a welcome.

Lisa had changed into a long rose pink gown. Sam looked handsome in a tux. And tennis shoes.

The ceremony was short. The minister requested they hold hands while he spoke the words that joined Skylynn and Kaiden as husband and wife "as long as you both shall live." He smiled fondly as he invited Kaiden to kiss the bride.

Kaiden lifted Sky's veil, then cupped her face in his palms. "I will love you all the days of your life," he said quietly. "In sickness and in health. Forever."

"Forever," she murmured.

"Forever," he repeated fervently. And there was no doubt in her mind that he meant it. And then he kissed her, his tongue teasing her lips as his arm slid around her waist to draw her body up against his.

"Get a room," Sam muttered under his breath.

Lisa laughed softly.

Skylynn drew back, her cheeks flushed.

"Sounds like good advice to me." Thorne slapped a hundred-dollar bill into the minister's hand, then took

Skylynn's arm and escorted her out of the chapel without a backward glance.

Sam and Lisa followed, arm-in-arm. "They seem to be in a hurry to get back to the hotel," Sam remarked with a wry grin.

"You can hardly blame them," Lisa replied. "After all, they're on their honeymoon."

"Well," Sam drawled, "it seems we've been abandoned for the night, what would you like to do?"

"Anything you want is fine with me."

"Hmm. We could go to one of the casinos and try our luck at the tables."

"Sounds like fun," Lisa said. "I've never been to Vegas before."

The MGM Grand was booming. Sam held Lisa's hand as they made their way through the crowded casino. "What's your pleasure?" he asked. "Craps? Roulette? The slots?"

Lisa shrugged. "I really don't have a preference. This is all new to me."

Sam decided to shoot craps. It had always been his favorite game, probably because it moved so fast. He threw a twenty on the DON'T PASS line. A skinny blonde woman had the dice. She threw a three.

Sam collected his winnings, but let his original twenty ride.

"I have no idea what's going on," Lisa said.

Sam explained, as best he could, what the rules were, then added, "The easiest bet is the field. If the shooter rolls a two, three, four, nine, ten, eleven, or twelve, you win. The payoff is even. If you bet a dollar, you win a dollar, except for the number two, which pays two-to-one. A twelve pays three-to-one. Your bet's good for one roll of the dice." He handed her a stack of chips. "Go for it."

Lisa placed a five-dollar chip on the field. The shooter rolled a twelve.

"I won!" Lisa exclaimed.

"Beginner's luck!" Sam said. "Try again."

Lisa placed another field bet. And the shooter rolled another twelve.

For the next half hour, the shooter was every field bettor's best friend. And then she rolled a five.

"Can we go try something else?" Lisa asked.

"Sure, whatever you want."

"What do you want?"

"You," Sam replied candidly. "In my arms. In my bed."

Lisa stared at him a moment, then took him by the hand. "I can't wait to try out that big round bed."

Chapter 41

Girard Desmarais scowled as he watched Sam and the girl with him leave the casino hand-in-hand. Laughing and smiling at each other, they were apparently oblivious to everything and everyone else around them.

Girard nodded. He knew if he waited long enough, he would get the two of them alone. Or as alone as anyone could be on the crowded streets of Las Vegas after dark. He smiled as Sam and the young woman turned down a quiet side street, pausing a moment to kiss in the shadows before moving on.

Girard slipped his hands into the pockets of his jacket. The right pocket held a fat wooden stake; the left a snub-nosed revolver loaded with silver bullets and fitted with a silencer.

He would take out the young man and his girlfriend, then wait for an opportunity to exact his revenge on Kaiden Thorne.

Thorne closed the door to the bedroom, and then drew his bride into his arms.

"No regrets?"

"Of course not." Sky looked up at him, her eyes twinkling. "We haven't even been married half an hour. I don't know if you snore," she said with a teasing grin, "or how you'll be about taking out the trash, or . . ."

"You know I don't snore," he said, kissing the tip of her nose. "And I'll be more than happy to take out the trash, as long as I can do it at night."

"Well, no regrets, then."

"You make a beautiful bride, Sky Blue."

"Thank you." Standing on her tiptoes, she slid his jacket over his shoulders. After tossing it on the bench at the foot of the bed, she removed his tie and shirt. He wasn't wearing an undershirt and she ran her hands over his back and chest. His skin was smooth, cool to the touch.

He nuzzled the side of her neck. "What do you think you're doing?"

"Anything I want."

"I think I married a hussy."

"Could be. Do you mind?"

He laughed softly. "What do you think?" Tilting her chin up, he kissed her. "You look so pretty in that dress, I hate to have you take it off, but . . ."

Before she knew how it happened, her veil and dress were on the bench and she was standing there in nothing but her new lace bra, panties, and heels. "How did you do that?" she asked, stepping out of her shoes.

"Magic fingers, babe."

"Well, excuse me if I do it the old-fashioned way," she muttered as she removed his belt and ever so slowly unzipped his trousers.

Thorne obligingly heeled off his boots and stepped out of his slacks. "You've got some magic fingers of your own, Sky Blue." And so saying, he removed the last of her clothing and his own, then drew her down on the bed and wrapped her in his arms.

"I love you, Skylynn," he murmured. "As long as I live, as long as you live, I will love no one but you."

Sam was laughing at something Lisa had said when she suddenly stumbled forward. He caught her before she hit the ground, his nostrils immediately filling with the scent of her blood. And overlaying that, the acrid stink of gunpowder.

"Lisa? Lisa!"

She moaned softly but before Sam could determine the extent of her wounds, a dark shape launched itself out of the shadows and barreled into Sam. He fell backward. His head hit the sidewalk, hard. He lay there, too stunned at first to identify the three muted pops. Too late, he realized they were gunshots.

He sprang to his feet when their attacker turned toward him. Things happened very fast after that, but Sam seemed to see it all in slow motion.

He stared at Lisa, sprawled on the ground, her eyes wide and empty of life, blood streaming from three small holes in her chest, and one in the side of her head.

Girard Desmarais sprang toward him, his face contorted with hatred as he pulled a wooden stake from his jacket pocket and lunged forward.

Sam darted sideways. The stake, meant for his heart, penetrated the right side of his chest. The pain drove the breath from his body and left him momentarily unable to move.

Girard ripped the stake from Sam's chest. He drew back his arm, intending to strike another blow when he suddenly vanished from sight.

Seconds later, Thorne materialized beside Sam, who had dropped to the sidewalk beside Lisa. His blood dripped over her pale face like drops of scarlet rain.

A single indrawn breath told Thorne the girl was dead even before he saw the bullet wounds in her head and chest.

"Sam, we've got to go."

"He killed her," Sam said dully. "For no reason."

Hearing sirens approaching, Thorne said, "We need to get out of here. Now."

"I can't leave her here in the street like so much garbage."

"We won't." Thorne scooped Lisa off the ground. Holding her against his chest with one arm, he took hold of Sam's wrist with his free hand and willed the three of them away from the city to an empty stretch of desert.

"He killed her," Sam murmured. "He wanted to kill me and Skylynn. Why?"

"It's a long story." Thorne lowered the girl's body to the ground. The dirt was hard and cold and rocky, but she was past caring.

Thorne guided Sam a few yards away and eased him down on the ground. The wound left by the stake had closed, leaving an ugly red welt in its place. It would heal completely while he slept, but Sam needed blood.

Biting into his own wrist, Thorne held it in front of Sam. "Drink."

"I'm gonna kill him."

"I'll help you, but first you need to drink."

Sam stared at the blood. And then he lowered his head and took what he needed.

"She's dead?" Skylynn looked at Kaiden in disbelief. "What happened?"

"Desmarais happened. He followed us here."

"How?" Skylynn sank down on the sofa, her arms wrapped around her middle.

"It was easy," Thorne said, lowering his voice. "He has a blood link with Sam." Thorne shook his head. He should have foreseen something like this, should have known

Desmarais wouldn't just give up. He glanced at Sam, who was standing at the window, staring blankly into the darkness.

"Where is Lisa now?" Skylynn asked.

"I buried her out in the desert. I'll take her home later, after Sam goes to sleep."

"I can hear you, you know." Sam shoved his hands into the pockets of his ruined tux. "She never hurt anybody. What am I gonna tell her dad?"

"I'll take care of it," Thorne said.

"No!" Sam whirled around to glare at Thorne. "It's my fault she's dead. I'll . . . I'll do it."

"If anyone's to blame, it's me," Thorne said flatly. "I underestimated Desmarais. I should have known he'd be watching, waiting, that he wouldn't quit until one of us was dead."

"So, how do we kill him?" Sam asked.

"We'll set a trap," Thorne said.

Sam leaned against the wall, his arms folded over his chest. "Is that right? What are we going to use for bait?"

"What he wants the most," Thorne replied.

"No!" Sam declared vehemently. "No way."

"You got a better idea?"

"It's too dangerous," Sam insisted. "I'm not letting him get near Skylynn again." He clenched his hands at his sides. "There's got to be another way."

"Do I have anything to say about this?" Skylynn asked, rising.

"No!" Sam said emphatically.

"Have you got any better ideas, Sky Blue?" Thorne asked. "If so, I'd love to hear them."

"Not really," she admitted, "but we have to do something. We can't go on living like this."

Thorne nodded. Drawing Sky into his arms, he rested his forehead against hers and closed his eyes. This was all Cassandra's fault, he thought bitterly. If she hadn't turned Desmarais, Lisa would still be alive. And getting rid of Girard Desmarais would be a hell of a lot easier.

Frowning, Thorne lifted his head. Maybe Cassandra was the answer.

She met him on the casino floor of the Bellagio. Attired in a slinky red dress sprinkled with sequins and wearing a pair of three-inch silver heels, she rivaled the lights of the casino itself. Her hair flowed over her shoulders like a river of chocolate silk. Ageless and elegant, she looked like a queen among commoners.

"Cassandra."

"Kaiden, I was surprised to hear from you. Is something wrong?"

"You know damn well what's wrong. Your fledgling is running amuck. He killed Lisa Rawlins and came damn close to destroying Skylynn's brother."

"How is young McNamara taking to his new life?"

"Like a duck to water," Thorne retorted. "But I didn't call you here to talk about Sam and you know it. You've got to do something about Desmarais."

Cassandra glided across the floor to one of the dollar slots and placed her hand on the side of the machine. A moment later, lights flashed, declaring her a winner. "He already knows if he destroys you, I'll destroy him."

"He's not after me. He's after Skylynn."

"Ah." She touched the machine again. And won again. "So, what would you have me do?"

"You made him. Get rid of him."

She glanced at him over her shoulder. "You're not serious?"

"Do I look like I'm kidding?"

"I'm rather fond of him."

Thorne stared at her, unable to believe what he was hearing.

She shrugged as she opened her handbag and scooped her winnings inside. "It's true. I find him intriguing."

"Intriguing," Thorne muttered.

"As a matter of fact, we're going hunting together later."

So much for counting on Cassandra for help. It looked like he was on his own.

Feeling vaguely disgruntled with himself, Thorne left her standing there. He had never asked anyone else for help before, had only done so now because of his concern for Skylynn's safety.

So, it was up to him. Determined not to let Sky down, he made two stops before returning to the hotel.

The first was to take Lisa's body to Vista Verde before it was found and savaged by predators.

The second was to visit an old friend who sold illegal firearms.

Skylynn stared at the gun in Thorne's hand. "What am I supposed to do with that?"

"It's loaded with silver bullets," Thorne explained. "It won't kill Desmarais, but if he shows up when you're alone, it'll put him out of commission long enough for you to take his head."

"Take his head?" she asked, horrified.

"Or you can set him on fire. Whichever you decide, you have to do it quick."

Skylynn sat on the edge of the sofa, one hand pressed to her stomach. "I think I'm going to be sick."

"I'm sorry, love," Thorne murmured. "This hasn't been much of a honeymoon, has it?" Sitting beside her, he put his arm around her shoulders, quietly cursing himself for making her a part of his life. If he hadn't been so selfish, he would have left town long before things went this far.

"She won't be alone again," Sam said, his voice gruff.

"I'll be with her every night. If I have to, I'll hire someone to watch out for her during the day."

"We'll both be with her at night," Thorne said, "but you're right, hiring someone to stay with her during the day is a good idea."

"Why do I need someone in the daytime?" Sky asked. "He can't come after me then."

"No, but he can send someone else."

Sky buried her face against Thorne's shoulder. "I hate this."

"It'll be over soon." Thorne glanced at Sam. Damn! Why hadn't he thought of it sooner? The blood link. It had allowed Desmarais to find Sam.

It would also allow Sam to find Desmarais.

Chapter 42

"You want me to find Desmarais?" Sam stared at Thorne. "How the devil am I supposed to do that?"

They had come home from Vegas earlier that night. As soon as they'd arrived in Vista Verde, Sam had changed his clothes and gone to see Lisa's parents. Thorne had spent the early part of the evening moving some of his things into Skylynn's bedroom. His original plan had been for her to move in with him, but at the moment, it seemed easier for everyone concerned if he stayed with Sky and her brother.

It wasn't until Sky went upstairs to get ready for bed that Thorne had a chance to talk to Sam, alone.

"How'd Lisa's folks take the bad news?" Thorne asked.

"About how you'd expect." Sam shook his head. "I thought her old man might take my head off, but he didn't blame me. The only good thing to come out of all this is that two more people want Desmarais dead."

"Speaking of Desmarais," Thorne said. "There's a link between the two of you."

"What kind of link?"

"A blood link. It's how he followed us to Vegas. If we're lucky, it's how we'll find him." Since Sam hadn't ingested

Desmarais' blood, it was a slim hope, at best, Thorne mused. But it was all they had. "Close your eyes and concentrate on Desmarais, on his whereabouts."

Sam shook his head. "I don't think I can do that."

"You can and you will. We can't keep waiting for Desmarais to strike us. We need to carry the fight to him, catch him with his guard down."

Sam nodded. Closing his eyes, he tried to picture Desmarais in his mind—an old man with gray hair and cold, calculating brown eyes, his body shrouded in a gray cloak— but all he could see, all he could think about, was Lisa lying dead on the street, blood dribbling from the wounds in her chest.

Sam shook her image away and tried again. *Desmarais, you bastard, where are you?* But, again, images of Lisa flooded his memory. How was he supposed to concentrate on Desmarais when he was overwhelmed with guilt? If he hadn't asked Lisa to go to Vegas with him, she would still be alive, smiling, and happy.

Feeling a hand on his shoulder, Sam opened his eyes to find Thorne standing beside him.

"Let it go for tonight," Thorne said.

"No! You're right. We need to find him. I need to find him!"

"Tomorrow night will be soon enough," Thorne said quietly. "Is there anything I can do?"

"No." Sam ducked his head and surreptitiously wiped the tears from his eyes. When he spoke again, his voice was filled with remorse, his expression haunted. "I can't even go to the damn funeral in the morning."

"I feel so bad for him," Skylynn said when Thorne told her about his discussion with Sam. "He's lost so much. Our parents. Grams. Granda. And now this. I know he just met Lisa but they really seemed to hit it off. . . ."

"It would never have worked out." Thorne undressed and slipped into bed beside Skylynn. Propping a pillow behind his head, he slipped his arm around her shoulders.

"Why not?"

"Werewolves and vampires don't mix. Sooner or later, one of them would get angry and the fur would fly."

Sky snuggled closer to Thorne. So much had happened in such a short time, it was hard to think straight. They had been kidnapped by Desmarais. She had begged Kaiden to turn Sam into a vampire. Sam had regained his memory. She and Kaiden had been married. Before they had even made love as husband and wife, Kaiden had left her alone in their marriage bed. *I've got to go,* he had said. *Sam's in trouble.* She could hardly have objected.

And now Lisa was dead, and Sam was in mourning for a girl he hardly knew.

"Our marriage didn't get off to a very good start, did it?" Kaiden stroked his knuckles over her cheek. "But I'll make it up to you when this is all over. I promise."

He just hoped it was a promise he could keep.

Chapter 43

Because Thorne didn't trust Sam to protect Skylynn on his own, he decided they would both stay with her after the sun went down. Knowing that Sam needed to feed at least once a night, Thorne considered teaching the boy how to call prey to him. But after thinking it over, he decided against it, at least for the time being. It wasn't an easy thing for a young vampire to master. For one thing, it took a great deal of concentration to control another's mind, something most fledglings had a difficult time doing in the beginning. Not that you could blame them. New vampires had a lot to deal with—incessant hunger, a constant barrage of sounds and smells, learning how to control one's increased strength and preternatural senses, the loss of old friends, family, and lifestyle. In the beginning, it was easier, and much more satisfying, to hunt for prey than call it to you.

Shortly before midnight, Thorne went out in the front yard. Standing there, cloaked in the drifting shadows of the night, he opened his senses, searching for prey in the neighborhood.

After twenty minutes, he gave it up as a lost cause. There weren't many young people in the area and it seemed as though all the old folks had gone to bed.

Pulling his cell phone from his pants' pocket, Thorne punched in the number for the Scarlet Cabaret.

Sam paced the living room floor, his hunger growing with every step. He needed to feed, badly. It was probably a good thing Sky had gone to bed, he thought darkly. He wouldn't want to be responsible for what might happen if she was in the same room with him now. Dammit, where was Thorne?

Sam clenched his fists. He needed to go out, but he couldn't leave Sky home alone. His steps grew shorter, quicker. His veins felt like they were constricting. His fangs ached. He had known hunger as a mortal, but this was a hundred times, a thousand times, worse. Where the hell was Thorne?

Sam went to the window and peered outside. It would only take him a few minutes to go into town and locate some unwary mortal.

He couldn't wait any longer. With his mind made up, he turned away from the window. He had taken only a few steps when Thorne appeared in the living room, accompanied by a tall brunette wearing a long black cloak over a black dress. She appeared to be about fifty years old.

"Sam, I'd like you to meet my friend, Olivia. Olivia, this is my brother-in-law, Sam."

"Uh, I'm pleased to meet you, ma'am."

"Thank you."

Sam looked at Thorne, wondering who the woman was and why he had brought her home.

"She's agreed to let you feed off her."

"What? I . . ." Sam shoved his hands in the back pockets of his jeans. He was hungry, sure, but this woman was old enough to be his mother.

"You can take care of it in here," Thorne said, "or take her up to your room if you'd rather feed in private."

Olivia removed her cloak and laid it over the back of the sofa, then held out her hand. "Sam, is it? Don't be shy."

Feeling like a teenager sneaking a girl up to his room for the first time, Sam took the woman's hand and led her up the stairs.

Thorne grinned as he watched Sam and Olivia leave the room. For a moment, he stood there, thinking Sam was in for a treat. Olivia's blood was clean and sweet, almost as tasty as Skylynn's.

Her name had no sooner crossed his mind than she came down the stairs, her slippered feet making a soft shushing sound.

"Who was that woman?" Skylynn asked, her voice low.

"A friend of mine."

"Oh?" There was a wealth of accusation in that one, simple word.

"She frequents one of the clubs I visit from time to time."

"I see." Sky pulled the bathrobe tighter, as if it could protect her from a truth she didn't want to hear. "And what kind of club would that be?"

"Calm down, Sky Blue. She's a vampire groupie. Sam needs to feed and I don't want him going out alone as long as Desmarais is prowling around."

"Oh. You're right, of course." She looked at him a moment. "You're not going to"—she cleared her throat— "to drink from her after Sam's done, are you?"

"No."

"Good. Because if you're thirsty . . ."

"I appreciate the offer, darlin', but that's not why I married you."

"I know, but I'd rather you drank from me than from some other woman."

"Don't be jealous, Sky Blue. It doesn't mean anything."

"It means you're with another woman."

"I'm not 'with' them." He knew where she was coming

from; he understood her jealousy. After all, few things were more intimate than a vampire feeding, which was why, in all his long life, he had rarely fed on men unless there was no other choice. Women tasted sweeter. They smelled better. And it was just more appealing, more natural, to take a woman in his arms.

"I'm sorry," Sky said. "It's just that this is still so new to me. If you're thirsty or . . . or hungry . . ."

"Oh, I'm hungry, all right." He pulled her up against him, his hand stroking her back. "Hungry for you."

"I think I can fix that." She took his hand, a seductive smile on her lips as she headed for the stairs. "Dinner for one in the Sky Blue room. No waiting."

Chapter 44

"What are you doing?" Cassandra fired the words at him like bullets. "I've warned you time and again to leave Kaiden Thorne alone."

"I haven't touched him," Girard retorted hotly.

"You're splitting hairs. You kidnapped his girlfriend, or wife, or whatever she is now, and her brother. You killed Lisa Rawlins for no reason. Are you trying to make me destroy you?" She tossed her head. "Assuming that neither Kaiden nor Lisa's father beats me to it."

"Kaiden Thorne killed my wife! Am I supposed to just forget that?"

"If you want to go on existing, I suggest that you do."

For a moment, they stood only inches apart, glaring at each other.

"It's not that easy," Girard said, his gaze sliding away from hers. "I loved Marie. She was my whole life."

"You're not a slayer anymore, Girard," Cassandra said flatly. "You're a vampire now. Whatever happened in your mortal life has no bearing on the present. The sooner you put your old life behind you, the happier you'll be."

"That's easy for you to say," he said, his anger returning.

"You've been a vampire for so long you've forgotten what it was like to be human!"

She regarded him for a moment, her eyes cold and hard. "Perhaps I made a mistake in bringing you across."

"No. I like being what I am. And I'm good at it. You said so yourself."

"This is my last warning, Girard. This isn't my territory, but I will defend it, and Kaiden, if necessary." She fixed him with a hard stare, her eyes glowing red, her power burning into him like sparks from a wildfire. "You would do well to remember that."

Chapter 45

The next few days passed peacefully enough, although the strain of worrying, of being unable to go out during the day, was beginning to wear on Skylynn's nerves. Kaiden had assured her that there was little to worry about from Desmarais when the sun was up, but if that was true, why had Kaiden insisted she remain inside during the day? The only time she'd been permitted to leave the house had been to go grocery shopping, and that had been at night, with Sam and Kaiden accompanying her.

Kaiden hired a professional bodyguard to stay with her during the day. His name was Jasper Curran, but everyone called him Tank, probably because he was built like one. For all that he was the biggest man she had ever seen, she rarely knew he was in the house. He stayed out of her way, checked the grounds regularly, and drank an enormous amount of black coffee. He showed up at sunrise, and left at sundown. Even though she had objected at first, she found his presence comforting.

Tank wasn't the only one who came and went on schedule. Olivia stopped by to visit with Sam every night at midnight, like clockwork.

Skylynn wasn't sure how she felt about that. It seemed

so decadent somehow, her vampire brother being nourished by an older woman. But she kept her thoughts to herself. It was her fault that Sam was a vampire, after all, and apparently new vampires needed to feed every night.

Sky didn't mind letting Kaiden drink from her now and then. It was, in fact, quite pleasurable. But she was in love with Kaiden. She couldn't help thinking that letting a stranger feed from you would be like making love to someone you didn't know. Of course, some women got a thrill from that. She couldn't help wondering about Olivia. Did the woman let strangers feed from her, or only vampires she knew?

To pass the hours of daylight, Skylynn went on a cleaning spree. She washed all the dishes in the kitchen cupboards, wiped down the refrigerator, inside and out, arranged all her CDs and DVDs in alphabetical order, and sorted the books on the shelf by the author's last name.

She watched TV until the screen went blurry.

She mopped and vacuumed and dusted until there wasn't a speck of dirt anywhere.

She reread a dozen of her favorite books.

At the end of a week, she took Kaiden aside and told him, as patiently as she could, that if she didn't get outside soon, she was going to go insane.

"All right, Sky Blue," he said. "Where do you want to go?"

"I'm sick of cooking. I want to go out to dinner. And then to the mall. And then to the movies."

So it was, on a Friday night, that the three of them piled into Kaiden's car and drove downtown.

Sky was in the mood for Italian, so they went to Luigi's, where she ordered chicken alfredo. Kaiden ordered a bottle of wine for the three of them.

"We can drink wine?" Sam asked when Kaiden filled his glass.

"A little, from time to time."

With a small grunt of surprise, Sam lifted his glass, took a sip, and smiled.

"Too bad you two can't have a bite of this," Sky said. "It's delicious."

Sam looked at Kaiden, who shook his head. "I don't advise it."

"What happens if we eat mortal food?"

"Try some and see."

Head cocked to one side, Sam looked at Kaiden for several moments, then shook his head. "I think I'll stick to the wine."

"It's a smart man who can learn from the mistakes of others," Thorne said, grinning.

Sam and Kaiden finished the last of the Chardonnay while Sky lingered over a large bowl of spumoni.

Kaiden smiled as he watched her savor the rich dessert, which consisted of layers of ice cream, whipped cream, candied fruit, and nuts, deciding there and then that if he ever had the opportunity to indulge in mortal food again, spumoni would be the first thing on the menu.

After leaving the restaurant, they went to the mall.

Inside, Skylynn took a deep breath. "I didn't realize how much I missed shopping!" she exclaimed.

Sam groaned. "She's gonna want to visit every store in the place," he muttered.

And he was right.

She tried on clothes and shoes, sampled perfume and powder, stopped in the candy shop to buy a pound of honeycomb. Moving on, she bought several bars of scented bath soap and a bottle of lavender bubble bath.

"You'd better wind this up if you still want to catch a movie," Sam said as they came out of yet another store.

"One more stop," Skylynn said, and made a beeline for the fast food court where she ordered a hot dog and a Coke.

Sam shook his head. "How can you be hungry again so soon?"

"I don't know, but I am."

She carried her order to a small table, grinned at Sam and Kaiden as she took a bite of the hot dog. "Bet you wish you could have some," she teased as she took another bite.

"Think again," Sam said, grimacing. "The smell is making me sick."

Muttering, "Sorry," she took another bite of the hot dog, and then frowned.

"What's wrong?" Kaiden asked. "Isn't it any good?"

She shrugged. "Yes, but . . ." She pushed the plate away. "It's making me nauseous."

"You probably just ate it too fast," Kaiden said.

"Yeah, I guess so. Are you two ready to leave?"

"Ready?" Sam exclaimed irritably. "Ready? I've been ready for over two hours."

"Just let me stop in here for a minute," she said as they approached the bookstore.

Sam looked at Kaiden for help. "If we let her go in there, we'll never get her out."

"Well, this is her night," Thorne said with a shrug. "Whatever she wants to do is fine with me."

With a resigned shake of his head, Sam followed the two of them into the bookstore.

Skylynn smiled at Kaiden as he slid under the covers beside her. "Thank you for tonight. It was great to get out of the house."

"No problem."

"Of course, this is nice, too," she murmured, snuggling up against him.

"Nice, huh? Maybe I can do better than nice."

She laughed softly as his hand slid over her thigh. "Very nice?"

He rose up on one elbow, his eyes hot.

A thrill of excitement raced through Skylynn. She knew

that look. It made her heart beat faster, caused her whole body to tingle with anticipation. She closed her eyes as his hand curled around her nape to draw her head toward his. He claimed her lips in a searing kiss, his hand sliding seductively over her thigh, the curve of her breast. She surrendered readily to his touch, her own hands busily exploring her husband's hard, muscular body.

She moaned low in her throat when he rose over her, his tongue sliding along the length of her throat. "Now, Kaiden," she murmured. "Now, now, now!"

The sweet sting of his fangs at her throat made their joining all the more satisfying, magnifying every touch, enhancing every caress. Floating in a sensual sea of pleasure, she writhed beneath him, wanting to be closer, closer, murmuring for him to take more, to take it all.

She was breathless, sated, when he rolled onto his side, carrying her with him, his arms wrapped around her waist, his face only inches from hers.

Kaiden put his mouth to her ear. "Still nice?"

Sky placed her arms over his and squeezed. "Beyond nice. Beyond seismic." She sighed when he nuzzled her shoulder. "It was phenomenal, positively cataclysmic." She grinned. "Have I stroked your ego enough, or should I go on?"

"You can stroke me anytime you want, for as long as you want." He caught her earlobe in his mouth and bit down lightly, and then rose over her, his dark eyes alight. "As long as I'm afforded the same privilege."

Chapter 46

Thorne stood with his arms folded across his chest, trying to rein in his impatience as Sam endeavored to locate Desmarais' whereabouts.

"Concentrate, Sam. Desmarais drank from you. Your blood is in his veins. Put everything from your mind but the link that stretches between you. Picture it as a wire that connects the two of you. Listen to the blood flowing in your veins. Now open your senses and follow that link back to him."

With a wordless cry of frustration, Sam closed his eyes. Hands clenched tightly at his sides, he stood there for several minutes, then shook his head. "The only connection I feel is the one that leads to you."

"Damn!" He had been afraid of that. "Don't worry about it. I was afraid it wouldn't work, but it was worth a try."

"Now what do we do?"

"Go back to my original plan."

"And use Skylynn as bait? No way!"

"It's the only way."

"Can't you just hunt him down?"

"I'd have to leave the two of you alone to do that."

"But you're willing to leave Skylynn alone?"

"That's different. We'll both be nearby."

"Won't Desmarais know that? And won't he suspect a trap, if we leave Skylynn alone?"

Thorne shrugged. "There's always that chance."

"I don't like it."

"Right now, it's all we've got. I have a blood link with Sky and one with you. That gives us an advantage. So, this is what we're going to do . . ."

Sam listened as Thorne outlined his plan, and prayed that it would work.

Skylynn sat in her car on the side of the road. The hood was up; the emergency lights were flashing. She had a sharp stake tucked under her left thigh, a bottle of holy water in the pocket of her sweatshirt. The gun Kaiden had given her was hidden under a blanket on the floor. A bag of groceries on the back seat was her supposed reason for being out alone after dark.

Sam and Kaiden were hiding somewhere outside. She didn't know exactly where they were, but every few minutes, Kaiden spoke to her mind, assuring her that he was nearby, telling her not to be afraid.

It was amazing, the way he could plant words and images in her mind, the way he could read her thoughts. She felt herself blushing when she suddenly had an image of the two of them locked in each other's arms the way they had been last night. She knew he was doing it to distract her, to take her mind off the fact that she was bait.

She glanced out the window. There was a wooded vacant lot on one side of the road, an abandoned gas station on the other. She tapped her fingers on the steering wheel. What was she doing here? Desmarais would never believe she was stupid enough to go out at night by herself. What if Desmarais showed up and Sam and Kaiden didn't? There was no way she could hope to fight off the vampire alone, no matter how many weapons she had. He was twenty times stronger than she was. Faster. Able to materialize or vanish at will. A wooden stake, holy water, and a gun were puny weapons against such an adversary.

Stop worrying. Kaiden's voice sounded in her mind, instantly putting her at ease. *I won't let anything happen to you.*

You'd better not. If he . . . if he kills me, I'll haunt you for as long as you live.

Kaiden's laughter rang in her mind, sounding so real, so close, she almost expected him to be in the car beside her.

Sky's hands gripped the steering wheel. What was that? Leaning forward, she peered out the windshield. Had she seen something? Or was it just her imagination? No. There it was again! A shadow without shape or substance gliding along the edge of the road.

She reached under her thigh to make sure the stake was still there, then wrapped her other hand around the bottle of holy water.

Fear clogged her throat, making it impossible to scream when Desmarais suddenly appeared in the passenger seat, the hood of his long gray cloak partially covering his face.

"Having car trouble?" he asked, his voice low and deceptively mild.

Skylynn nodded, her heart pounding wildly.

"It was nice of Thorne to use you for bait," Desmarais said. One bony hand circled her throat.

She had known vampires were strong, but it took only one squeeze of his hand and the world started to go dark. She clutched his arm with both hands, trying to break his hold, but he had a grip like iron.

"Perhaps he didn't realize it would work to my advantage. I've been forbidden to kill him outright, but now, when he comes to save you and I kill him, it will be self-defense."

She knew a momentary sense of relief when he relaxed his grip on her throat, followed by a renewed sense of panic when he leaned toward her, his fangs lightly brushing the skin of her throat.

Knowing she had only one chance, Skylynn let her arms fall limply to her sides and then, ever so slowly, she reached for the stake under her thigh.

Murmuring, "Please," she began to struggle again, hoping it would prevent him from realizing what she was doing.

"Go ahead, beg," Girard said. His fangs gleamed whitely in the darkness.

"Please," Sky repeated, hoping to buy some time. "I've never done anything to you."

"You're whoring for Kaiden Thorne," Girard said, his hand tightening around her throat again. "That's crime enough. I'll have you and him and that brother of yours."

Adrenaline exploded through Skylynn's veins as she yanked the stake out from under her thigh and drove it into Girard's side. She was surprised by how easily the wood pierced his flesh.

With a savage cry, Desmarais reared backward.

Before she could withdraw the stake and strike again, he disappeared.

It took Skylynn a moment to realize that someone had opened the door and yanked the vampire out of the car. Gasping for breath, one hand at her throat, she stared out the passenger side door.

Two dark shapes struggled in the moonlight.

To her horror, she realized the man fighting Desmarais was Sam. Something was wrong. Kaiden was older, stronger. He was supposed to confront Desmarais. Sam was only supposed to be Kaiden's backup.

Feeling as if her blood had turned to ice, Skylynn glanced frantically from one side of the road to the other. Where was Kaiden?

A sharp cry drew her attention back to the fight. She screamed, "No!" when Desmarais hurled Sam into a tree, gasped when her brother slammed into the trunk then sprawled facedown on the ground and lay still.

Skylynn stared at him in shock. Sam was a vampire. He couldn't be dead.

Heedless of the danger, she retrieved the gun from the floor and got out of the car, her only thought to protect her brother if he still lived, or to avenge his death.

She was halfway across the street when Desmarais sprang toward her.

With a shriek, she fired the gun, hoping it would slow him down enough for her to get away. And it might have, if she hadn't missed. Pivoting on her heel, she sprinted for the car, but she was too slow. She screamed when Desmarais' fingers dug into her arm, causing her to drop the gun, which went skittering off into the shadows. She stumbled and fell when he suddenly released her.

Glancing over her shoulder, she saw a blur of movement launch itself at Desmarais.

"Kaiden!" Her relief at seeing him was short-lived. The fight between Desmarais and Kaiden was far more vicious than the one between Desmarais and Sam had been. This battle was like a full-blown nightmare come to life, the flash of fangs, the hellishly red glow of their eyes as they engaged in a brutal, silent struggle that was like nothing she had ever seen before.

Kaiden moved with a quickness and grace that seemed to defy gravity. Desmarais fought like a demon, but he was no match for Kaiden's ancient strength.

Skylynn held her breath as Kaiden shoved Desmarais against the crumbling wall of the gas station. At this distance, with his back toward her, she couldn't see what Kaiden was doing, but Desmarais' shriek sounded as if it was being torn from the bottom of his very soul. The anguished sound hung in the air, then died away, followed by an eerie stillness.

Skylynn's gaze was fixed on Kaiden's back. He stood

there a moment and then, to her horror, he produced a long, wicked-looking knife from inside his jacket.

Skylynn pressed a hand to her mouth to keep from crying out when Kaiden lifted the blade. Afraid she was going to be sick, she turned away, her arms wrapped tightly around her middle. She felt numb inside, cold all over. She knew it was just nerves, the aftermath of everything that had happened, but she couldn't stop shaking.

"Skylynn?"

She opened her eyes at the sound of Kaiden's voice.

He stood in front of her, his brow furrowed. "Are you all right?"

"Y . . . yes. Are you?"

He nodded. "It's all over now. He'll never bother you again."

She glanced across the road but there was no sign of her brother. How could that be? He'd been there only minutes ago. What had happened to him?

She tugged on Kaiden's arms. "Where's Sam?"

"He's taken Desmarais' remains into the woods. The sun will take care of what's left."

She nodded, her mind filling with grotesque images of Desmarais' body going up in flames. And then it hit her. It was over, really over. She didn't have to be afraid any more. Desmarais was dead.

She looked at Kaiden askance when there was a sudden tremor in the air.

"Go get in the car," he said. "I'll be right back." He took a deep breath, then turned to face the vampire. "Cassandra."

"You killed him." It wasn't a question but a statement of fact.

Thorne nodded. "He didn't give me much choice."

"Such a waste," Cassandra murmured, her voice tinged with regret.

"If you say so."

"He was born to be a vampire."

"I'm surprised you didn't come rushing to his defense."

"Kaiden, you know I would never have chosen him over you." She made a vague gesture of dismissal. "I warned him several times to leave you alone. He should have listened. Ah, well." Rising on tiptoe, she pressed her lips to his.

Cassandra kissed him far longer and deeper than usual. Thorne knew her well enough to know she was doing it not only to prove that, in some ways, he still belonged to her, but because Skylynn was there. He could see her staring at them, wide-eyed, through the car window.

"You're such a tease," Thorne muttered irritably when Cassandra broke the kiss.

"You'd better go," she replied with an impish grin. "Your woman is watching us, and she's jealous."

"Yeah, thanks a lot."

"See you soon, love," Cassandra said cheerfully, and with a wave of her hand, she disappeared into the shadows.

"Wow, she's something else, isn't she?" Sam remarked as he came up beside Thorne.

"You have no idea. Come on, let's go home."

Skylynn sat on the sofa wrapped in a blanket while Kaiden lit a fire in the hearth.

Try as she might, she couldn't erase the memory of Kaiden and Girard Desmarais locked in combat. Even though she hadn't watched Kaiden take Girard's head, her imagination had no trouble painting the grisly image in her mind.

"Are you warm enough?" Kaiden asked, coming to sit beside her.

She nodded, though she couldn't stop shaking. She told herself there was nothing to worry about anymore, no reason to be afraid. Desmarais was dead. Sam and Kaiden were home, safe, and all was well, but that knowledge did nothing to ease the queasiness in the pit of her stomach. She frowned, wondering if it was the events of the night that had her feeling like she needed to vomit, or if she was catching the flu. Now that she thought about it, she had been feeling queasy for several days.

Kaiden put his finger beneath her chin, his gaze meeting hers. "Are you okay? You look a little pale."

"I'm fine."

"So, all's well that ends well," Sam remarked, dropping into the chair beside the sofa.

Skylynn looked at Kaiden. "You could have been killed."

He shook his head. "No way. I'm older. Faster. Stronger. He never had a chance. I knew he wouldn't be able to resist coming after you, even though he knew I'd be waiting."

"I don't want to talk about it anymore." Desmarais was dead. Tomorrow, she would move her things into Kaiden's house and they would start their life together as man and wife. There would be adjustments to make and problems to work out, but she would worry about all that later. For now, she just wanted to enjoy being with Kaiden.

"Well, I'm going out for a little midnight snack," Sam said. "See you guys tomorrow night."

Kaiden nodded.

"Be careful," Sky said, but Sam was already gone.

She stared at the flames a moment before asking, "Who was that woman, Kaiden? And why was she kissing you?"

Chapter 47

Skylynn spent the next morning packing her grand-mother's dishes, silverware, and pots and pans. She would have left a few place settings and a pot or two for Sam, she thought with a grin, but really, what was the point? Her vampire brother wouldn't be doing any cooking, and he certainly wouldn't be hosting any dinner parties.

Of course, neither would she. The thought sobered her.

Sky glanced at the cardboard boxes spread out on the counter. She really didn't need all the cookware her grand-mother had collected over the years. Kaiden didn't eat and she didn't see herself doing a lot of fancy cooking for one. Still, she couldn't bring herself to get rid of her grand-mother's things. Some of them, like the Mickey Mouse cookie jar, held special memories. Others, like the Meissen Crossed Swords coffeepot, were antiques. Her grand-mother had cherished the glossy white pot with its delicate blue design, partly because it was beautiful, but mostly because it had been a gift from Granda on their first wedding anniversary.

After packing the last of the kitchen goods, Sky went into the living room and began sorting through the books in the bookcase. She would leave Granda's for Sam.

She was placing the last of her books in the box when her stomach began to churn. She made it to the bathroom just in time.

Later, after wiping her face with a cold cloth, she took her temperature. It was normal. She took a couple of aspirin, washed them down with orange juice, and went back to work.

"Looks like you've been busy," Thorne remarked, glancing around the McNamaras' living room.

Skylynn nodded. "I left all the furniture for Sam, along with Granda's books and all the stuff in the lab. I haven't discussed it with Sam yet, but I think we should donate all of Granda's medical records and journals to a hospital or a library or something."

Thorne nodded. "That's probably a good idea."

"What's a good idea?" Sam asked, bounding down the stairs.

"Donating Granda's medical records and equipment to a hospital or a library," Skylynn explained. "They are no good to any of us."

"S'okay with me." Sam glanced at all the cardboard boxes scattered around the living room. "It's gonna be lonely in this old house, all by myself."

"I'll be right across the street," Skylynn said. "It's not like I'm moving across the country."

"Yeah. Well, come on," he said briskly, "let's get started."

It took less than an hour for Kaiden and Sam to move all of Skylynn's belongings into Thorne's house.

"Wow!" Skylynn remarked when they were finished. "That was fast. Maybe we could start a new business. After Dark Movers."

"Yeah, right," Sam muttered.

"So, where do you want all this stuff?" Thorne asked.

"I'm not sure," she said, glancing at the boxes stacked in

the living room. "I'll put it all away tomorrow. That'll give me something to do while you're sleeping."

"Great!" Sam slapped his hands against his thighs. "Let's eat."

Thorne looked at Sam, one brow arched in wry amusement.

Skylynn shook her head as if he had made a faux pas at the dinner table.

Sam glanced from Thorne to his sister. "Too blunt?"

"Just a little," Skylynn said.

"You go on," Thorne told him. "I'm fine."

"I can take a hint," Sam said with a grin. "The newlyweds want to be alone."

"Good call," Thorne said. "Now get lost."

"Don't need to ask me twice," Sam retorted good-naturedly, and strolled out of the house.

"So, Mrs. Thorne," Kaiden said, drawing her into his arms. "Welcome to your new home."

"Thank you, Mr. Thorne."

"I want you to be happy here, Sky, so feel free to redecorate the place any way you like. Paint, paper, whatever. And don't worry about the cost. I can afford anything you want."

"I would like some new carpet. Do you have a preference for color?"

"Anything you like is fine with me."

"What about your furniture?"

Thorne glanced around the room. "Get rid of it all." Taking her by the hand, he led her up the stairs and into the master bedroom. "Any ideas for this room?"

"I have a few."

"Such as?"

"Well, for one thing," she said, removing his shirt, "this has to go." She moved her hands over his chest, leaned forward to kiss his bare shoulder while she unfastened his belt. "This, too, I think."

"Indeed? Going for a major renovation, are you?"

She nodded as she reached for the zipper of his jeans. "I think these will have to go, too."

He obligingly removed his boots and socks so she could strip him of his jeans, murmured, "Careful now," as she began to tug them over his hips.

She grinned at him. "Don't worry, I promise not to damage anything you might need later."

When he stepped out of his jeans, she tossed them aside.

"Are you through?" he asked, his lips twitching.

"Almost." She ran her fingers along the waistband of his silky black briefs. "I really like these. They're very sexy."

"I'm glad I have one thing you like," he said with a laugh.

She glanced at the bulge in his briefs and murmured, "Make that two things."

"My turn," he said. "A body as shapely as yours should never be covered."

She stared up at him, wide-eyed. "Never?"

"Never when we're alone," he amended as he lifted her sweater over her head. The rest of her clothing quickly followed. "I think we should give the bed a try," he suggested.

"I think you're right." Taking him by the hand, she climbed onto the mattress, pulling him after her. "We'd best give it a good workout so I can decide whether to keep it or not."

He drew her into his arms, loving the feel of her bare skin against his own, the way she melted against him. "I absolutely agree," he said, his voice husky with longing.

She draped her leg over his, wanting to be closer, wanting to be part of him. Whispering, "Kiss me," she twined her arms around his neck, her mouth seeking his, her hands moving over him, hot and restless with need.

He groaned softly as her tongue sought his. She was fire and honey in his arms, an impossible wish fulfilled, a nighttime fantasy magically brought to vibrant life. He wanted all of her, every thought, every caress, every breath. He wanted to please her in every way possible, to make every hope and dream she'd ever had come true.

His mind and body merged with hers, their joining like summer lightning streaking across the sky. When he nuzzled her neck, she tilted her head to the side, giving him easy access to her throat.

She moaned softly, her hands clutching his shoulders as his bite brought them both to fulfillment.

"I've been thinking," Skylynn remarked later, when their bodies had cooled.

"Oh? About what?" Although he wasn't cold, Thorne pulled the covers over the two of them, then wrapped his arms around her again, her back to his front. She fit him so perfectly, satisfied him so completely. How had he lived so long without her?

"Well, not right away, you understand, but in a year or two or three, I think I'd like to be what you are."

Thorne sat up, then drew Skylynn up beside him so he could see her face. "Are you serious?"

"I thought you'd be pleased."

"That doesn't begin to describe it, but what changed your mind?"

"Well, you're a vampire. Sam's a vampire and he seems to love it." She shrugged. "I just want to fit in with the rest of the family."

Thorne stared at her, then pulled her into his arms. "I love you, Sky Blue. Vampire or human, I'll always love you."

She smiled against his chest. "Will it hurt?"

"No, love."

"And the blood? Will I learn to like it?"

"I guarantee it."

"It's settled then."

"There's no hurry. Whenever you're ready, I'll . . ." He frowned as she bolted off the bed and ran into the bathroom. What the hell? "Sky?" He followed her into the bathroom and found her bent over the toilet. Kneeling beside her, he draped one arm around her shoulders. "What's wrong?"

"I don't know."

Rising, he wet a cloth and wiped her face, then drew her to her feet. Wrapping his arms around her, he closed his eyes and opened his senses. Was she ill? Sometimes, he could smell sickness or disease on those he had fed upon.

But Skylynn wasn't sick.

Feeling as though he had been punched in the gut, he gazed down at her, his jaw rigid.

"What's wrong?" she asked.

He put her away from him, his answer curt and filled with accusation. "You're pregnant."

Skylynn stared at Kaiden, too stunned to think, too startled to speak. Pregnant? That was impossible. He had told her so himself. Vampires couldn't create life.

"Say something!" he demanded, and even as his anger rose, and with it the urge to kill whoever had dared touch her, he knew she hadn't been with another man. And yet, she carried the proof in her womb.

"You can't think . . . I've never . . . it's impossible."

"I know." He drew her gently into his arms, and just like that, his anger dissolved.

"You must be mistaken," she said. "And even if it was true, which it can't be, how could you tell?"

"I can hear the heartbeat, quick and quiet."

She blinked up at him. "You can hear it?" She placed one hand on her stomach. She couldn't be pregnant, so what could it be?

Swinging her into his arms, he carried her back to bed and cradled her to his chest. He frowned as a new thought inched its way into his mind. Could it be? Was it possible?

All those months when he had taken McNamara's formula, when he had been able to consume mortal food and drink, when he had been able to abide the sun's light and be awake during the day . . . when his vampire nature had, for want of a better word, gone into hibernation . . . He shook his head. Vampires couldn't create life, and yet he could hear two heartbeats.

Thorne placed his hand over Skylynn's womb and blinked back the sting of tears in his eyes as he sensed the barely discernable movement of new life beneath his palm.

"I guess it's a good thing we got married." He cupped her face in his hands and kissed her lightly, tenderly. "Because we're going to be parents."

Chapter 48

"You're what?" Standing in the middle of the living room, Sam stared at Skylynn. "I thought . . . vampires couldn't . . ." He looked at Thorne for an explanation. "How the devil did this happen?"

Thorne shrugged. "The usual way." He hugged Skylynn, who was sitting on the sofa beside him. They had come downstairs after taking a shower. Sky had been too excited to sleep, too anxious to call Tara and share the news, in spite of the late hour. Too eager to tell her brother he was going to be an uncle.

"You know what I mean," Sam said.

As succinctly as possible, Thorne told Sam about Paddy's formula.

Sam frowned. "That was for you? And that's how you were able to be out in the sun, and eat regular food?"

"Yeah."

Sam dropped into his usual place in the chair beside the sofa. "I thought you liked being a vampire."

"I did. I do. But it was nice being able to go outside during the day again, to eat mortal food." He looked at Skylynn. "To dream about a future with the woman I love."

"Then why did you stop taking the potion?" Sam asked.

"I ran out. I tried recreating it, but . . ." Thorne shrugged. "I couldn't make it work. There was an ingredient in it that I couldn't duplicate and no one could figure out what it was."

Sam looked at Thorne and started laughing.

"What's so funny?" Thorne asked irritably.

Sam held up one hand while he continued to laugh.

Skylynn looked at Thorne, her brows raised.

"Sorry," Sam said, blowing out a breath and wiping his eyes. "It's just that, years ago, Granda made me memorize the ingredients to a formula. He wouldn't tell me who it was for, he just insisted that I remember it, and that I never write it down. When I asked him why, he just said somebody we knew might need it someday." He looked at Thorne. "That someone is you, isn't it?"

"I sure as hell hope so," Thorne said, a sense of anticipation building inside him.

"Sam, are you telling us that you know what it is?" Skylynn exclaimed in disbelief. "That you know what the potion's made of?"

"Well, I've got some kind of formula up here," Sam said, tapping the side of his head. "I don't know for sure if it's the one you're looking for. To tell you the truth, I forgot all about it until now."

Thorne scrubbed one hand up and down his thigh. Could it be true? Could Sam have had the answer all along?

"I think the ingredient you've been looking for is blood," Sam said, grinning at Thorne. "Your blood. Of course, I didn't know the formula was for you. Or that you were a vampire when Granda made me memorize it. Or that your blood wasn't normal."

Thorne stared at him, then shook his head. "That can't be it. I had the potion analyzed in a lab by some of the top scientists in the world. They would have been able to detect something as common as blood."

"You idiot," Sam said mildly. "Vampire blood isn't common."

Of course, Kaiden thought. Even though Paddy hadn't given him the formula, the old man had given him a short lesson in how it was produced, though it had made little sense to Thorne at the time.

I dump all the ingredients in a beaker, Paddy had said, *and then I let the whole mess simmer for a wee bit until it's cooked just right.*

Thorne nodded as hope soared within him. His vampire blood would bind all the ingredients together, and then, somehow, his blood evaporated, all but the part that made him a vampire. That explained why the potion had given Desmarais the strength and vitality of a vampire, although it didn't explain how it had allowed Thorne to endure the sun's light. But what the hell. The whys and wherefores didn't matter, as long as the formula worked.

"Do you know what this means?" he asked, glancing from Skylynn to Sam.

"Yeah," Sam said, laughing. "It means we can all go to the beach next summer."

Thorne leaned forward and slapped Sam on the shoulder. "I guess it's a good thing Sky asked me to save your life."

Thorne pulled Skylynn close and kissed her soundly. Then, swinging her up into his arms, he twirled her around the room until she cried, "Kaiden, stop! I'm getting dizzy."

"Sorry, love." He set her lightly on her feet, then took her hands in his. "Do you know what this means, Sky Blue. It means we can have a normal life."

She nodded, too happy to speak past the lump in her throat. Thanks to Granda's wisdom and the return of Sam's memory, she and Kaiden and Sam could be a real family, after all.

Epilogue

Tonight was the night.

Skylynn stood in front of the mirror in the bathroom, carefully plucking her eyebrows. She had washed her hair, painted her nails, shaved her legs, and put on her prettiest, sexiest nightgown. It was long and black, a mere whisper of gossamer silk.

Moving into the bedroom, she stood in front of the full-length mirror in the corner. She looked good for her age, she thought. Not that thirty-four was old, exactly. But it wasn't young, either.

Their son, Josh, a very grown up nine and their daughter, Janae, a sweet and spoiled seven, both had their father's dark hair and their mother's blue eyes. From time to time, Sky wondered if her children would become vampires even though Kaiden assured her that such a thing was next to impossible. But she wasn't so sure. He had also told her that vampires couldn't create life, yet they had two beautiful children, children that were so healthy they had never had so much as a cold or a cavity.

A lot had happened in the last ten years. Kaiden and Sam had managed to recreate Granda's formula so that they rarely needed blood, and then only a little. They were still vampires, after all.

Eight years ago, Tara had decided to move to California. It had been love at first sight when Sam and Tara met. Sky-lynn had worried that Sam's being a vampire might pose a problem, but Tara had only laughed and said she didn't care what Sam was, as long as he was hers. They had married six months later. Sky loved having her best friend for a sister-in-law.

Three years ago, they had all moved up to Northern California. It had taken some getting used to, living in a small town, having to drive the kids to school, not having a mall nearby. But, on the plus side, Sam and Tara lived in the house behind them. Kaiden had put a gate in the fence so the kids could run back and forth.

Sky glanced over her shoulder as Kaiden strolled into the bedroom. He whistled softly when he saw her.

Sky smiled at her husband. He was still as wickedly handsome and sexy as ever, still had the power to make her insides curl with pleasure with just one look. He wore a pair of jeans low on his hips and nothing else.

"Are you ready, love?" Coming up behind her, he slipped his arms around her waist and nuzzled her neck.

"Yes."

"You're sure? There's no going back, once it's done."

"We've been over this a hundred times." Sky leaned against him. She was thirty-four years old. Kaiden had been thirty-nine when he was turned. She didn't want to wait any longer, or get any older. "I'm beginning to think you don't want me to do it."

"I just want you to be happy."

"I am happy." She smiled at him in the mirror. "Happier than I ever dreamed possible," she said, and then frowned. "Are you sure it will work? I mean, now that you're taking the potion again . . ."

He placed his fingers over her lips. "I'm still a vampire,

Sky. Besides, I've been drinking a little blood every day. Stolen from a blood bank," he added when he saw the expression on her face. "If it doesn't work this time, then I'll stop taking the potion for a while."

"Let's do it, then. The kids are spending the night over at Sam's."

With a nod, Kaiden took Skylynn by the hand and led her to the bed. Sitting down on the edge of the mattress, he tugged her down beside him. "Have I told you lately how much I love you?"

"Not since last night."

"Never doubt that I love you. Whatever the future holds, you'll always be the sunshine in my world."

His words sank deep into Sky's heart as she wrapped her arms around him. He kissed her, slowly at first, his tongue teasing her lips before delving inside to tangle with hers.

He kissed her again, and yet again before he eased her down on the mattress, his hands moving over Sky, readying her for what was to come.

When she was breathless with anticipation, he removed his jeans, slid her nightgown over her head, and then rose above her. For a moment, he gazed into her eyes, humbled by the depths of her love, her unconditional trust.

Murmuring that he adored her, he kissed her again, ever so tenderly, and then he gathered her into his arms. Her hair was like fine silk against his hand as he brushed it over her shoulder, baring the smooth line of her throat to his gaze. He could hear the rapid beat of her heart, smell the blood flowing sweetly through her veins.

Murmuring, "This time forever, Sky Blue," he bent his head to her neck.

After tonight, she would be his as never before.

Always and eternally his.

If you're a lover of vampire romance,
read on for a taste of
Amanda Ashley's *Desire the Night*,
coming in September.

Gideon Marquet stared into the darkness, his limbs aching from the weight of the heavy silver chains that shackled his ankles to the thick cement wall behind him. His body felt like it was burning from the inside out, causing his veins to shrink, while his skin grew painfully tight with the need for sustenance.

So long since he had fed.

So long since his thirst had been satisfied.

His eyes narrowed as a tall woman entered the basement. Clad in a shimmering white robe trimmed in white fur, she looked like an angel when, in truth, she was anything but.

The hem of her velvet robe made a soft, swishing noise as she drew closer, then knelt outside the cell.

Gideon groaned inwardly as she picked up the slender, silver-bladed dagger that rested beside a golden jewel-encrusted goblet on a low wooden table. His body tensed as she began to chant, her voice soft, almost hypnotic. He winced as she reached between the bars and dragged the blade across his right thigh. Lifting the goblet, she held it under the wound to collect the dark red blood that leaked from the long, shallow gash. When the goblet was half-full, she made a similar cut in his left thigh, chanting all the while. When the cup was full, she left the basement.

She returned a short time later.

Gideon sat up a little straighter, his fangs extending as the cell door opened and a young blond girl clad in a wrinkled brown dress was pushed inside. She fell to the floor, crying out as she scraped her knees on the cold cement. His hands clenched as the warm, sweet coppery scent of her blood filled his nostrils.

Blind with panic, the girl, who couldn't have been more than nineteen or twenty, scrambled to her feet and ran to the iron-barred door.

"Please!" she cried, her hands fisting around the bars. "Let me out! Please, oh, please, let me out of here!"

But her frantic plea fell on deaf ears.

The girl sobbed hysterically as the woman turned and left the basement.

With her only hope gone, the girl darted to a far corner of the cell, her back pressed against the bars, her arms wrapped tightly around her waist. Tears flooded her cheeks as she murmured, "Please, don't."

But all he heard was the frantic beating of her heart, the whisper-soft sound of the blood flowing through her veins.

"Please." She fell to her knees, hands raised in supplication.

But that wouldn't save her.

Nothing could save her now.

It was feeding time.

Books by Bestselling Author
Fern Michaels

___The Jury	0-8217-7878-1	$6.99US/$9.99CAN
___Sweet Revenge	0-8217-7879-X	$6.99US/$9.99CAN
___Lethal Justice	0-8217-7880-3	$6.99US/$9.99CAN
___Free Fall	0-8217-7881-1	$6.99US/$9.99CAN
___Fool Me Once	0-8217-8071-9	$7.99US/$10.99CAN
___Vegas Rich	0-8217-8112-X	$7.99US/$10.99CAN
___Hide and Seek	1-4201-0184-6	$6.99US/$9.99CAN
___Hokus Pokus	1-4201-0185-4	$6.99US/$9.99CAN
___Fast Track	1-4201-0186-2	$6.99US/$9.99CAN
___Collateral Damage	1-4201-0187-0	$6.99US/$9.99CAN
___Final Justice	1-4201-0188-9	$6.99US/$9.99CAN
___Up Close and Personal	0-8217-7956-7	$7.99US/$9.99CAN
___Under the Radar	1-4201-0683-X	$6.99US/$9.99CAN
___Razor Sharp	1-4201-0684-8	$7.99US/$10.99CAN
___Yesterday	1-4201-1494-8	$5.99US/$6.99CAN
___Vanishing Act	1-4201-0685-6	$7.99US/$10.99CAN
___Sara's Song	1-4201-1493-X	$5.99US/$6.99CAN
___Deadly Deals	1-4201-0686-4	$7.99US/$10.99CAN
___Game Over	1-4201-0687-2	$7.99US/$10.99CAN
___Sins of Omission	1-4201-1153-1	$7.99US/$10.99CAN
___Sins of the Flesh	1-4201-1154-X	$7.99US/$10.99CAN
___Cross Roads	1-4201-1192-2	$7.99US/$10.99CAN

Available Wherever Books Are Sold!
Check out our website at www.kensingtonbooks.com